Praise for the Camaro Espinoza series

'Hard-boiled action . . . Camaro Espinoza, who did tours in the Middle East, is tougher than an army boot . . . it's deeply satisfying to watch her take out an animal like Lukas.'

New York Times Book Review on *Walk Away*

'A trifecta of triumph . . . A complex and compelling protagonist (coupled with richly defined secondary characters), authenticity of voice and vista, and resonant timeliness . . . Camaro Espinoza is a name to remember, and readers will find themselves rooting for her despite the many liberties she takes with conventional law and order. Justice is in the eye of the beholder, after all.'   *Strand Magazine* on *Walk Away*

'Sam Hawken has created a deep and dangerous female lead in *The Night Charter*. If you're ever in trouble and need a kickass heroine to get you out of it, look no further than army veteran Camaro Espinoza.'
Mari Hannah, author of the Kate Daniels series, on *The Night Charter*

'Camaro Espinoza, the intense and capable heroine of a series of novellas from Hawken, makes her full-length debut in this hard-boiled thriller . . . Camaro has an ironclad sense of justice . . . Hawken delivers a potent climax that winds its way through an unremitting firefight to a satisfying conclusion.'   *Publishers Weekly* on *The Night Charter*

Also by Sam Hawken

The Dead Women of Juárez
Tequila Sunset
Missing
The Night Charter

WALK AWAY

SAM HAWKEN

MULHOLLAND
BOOKS
HODDER

First published in Great Britain in 2017 by Mulholland Books
An imprint of Hodder & Stoughton
An Hachette UK company

1

First published in paperback in 2017

A CIP catalogue record for this title is available from the British Library

Paperback ISBN 978 1 473 60999 0
eBook ISBN 978 1 473 60998 3

Printed and bound by Clays Ltd, St Ives plc

Hodder & Stoughton policy is to use papers that are natural, renewable
and recyclable products and made from wood grown in sustainable forests.
The logging and manufacturing processes are expected to conform to the
environmental regulations of the country of origin.

Hodder & Stoughton Ltd
Carmelite House
50 Victoria Embankment
London EC4Y 0DZ

www.hodder.co.uk

*For Mariann, because there's nothing she won't do
for family.*

WALK AWAY

CHAPTER ONE

CAMARO ESPINOZA DRIPPED with sweat. There was no time, no place but the moment, and she thought of nothing but fighting. The bag dangled to the floor in a line of others, all undisturbed. She alone forged ahead with the war.

She'd gone thirty minutes on the heavy bag and had ten minutes still ahead. She shifted from a jab-cross-and-takedown combination to a jab, jab, and cross as she circled the bag clockwise. Her hands were swathed in wraps, and the leather bag popped as she laid into it punch by punch.

A punch started at the floor and worked itself up through the rising heel, the turn of the hips, the torsion of the shoulders, and then the final explosion. Camaro's fists ached in time with her muscles, every heartbeat pushing fresh pain through her in a steady, rapid pulse. She breathed in through the nose and out through the mouth, exhaling on the follow-through, emptying her tired lungs completely.

The timer sounded again. Thirty seconds down. She caught the bag between her hands and drove her knee into it, alternating leg to leg. When the timer marked off another half minute, she released her grip and fell back, leaving smears of perspiration behind.

Camaro went down on the mat, back flat against it, and forced herself into a series of spring-ups that felt like torture. She did as many as she could squeeze into the time and then labored onto her feet again to begin a fresh set of jab-cross combinations.

She heard Miguel clapping his hands as the timer wound down. It went off. Camaro stepped back from the bag, panting heavily, her shoulders rising and falling. Her arms were as heavy as lead.

Miguel crossed the empty gym, passing the sparring cage, and stepped onto the mat. "Sixty seconds!" he called. "Get some water in you. Go!"

A liter-and-a-half bottle of room-temperature water sat near the wall in the pool of a ratty white towel. Camaro bent, feeling the strain in her back, and picked it up. She was careful to only sip and not to guzzle.

"Thirty seconds," Miguel reminded her. He was a sturdy man, built low to the ground. His dark hair was shot through with gray. "That's enough water."

Camaro tossed the bottle away. Miguel came close, and they bumped fists. "One more round," she managed.

"You can do it. Focus and power. Focus and power. You don't feel no pain."

The timer sounded, sharp and clear. Camaro turned back to the bag.

She did another five minutes. Jabs, crosses, knees, and takedowns. The last two sets of spring-ups were nightmarish. After the second set she made it to her feet only with effort. Thirty seconds remained, and she bulled through it. When the timer sounded its last alarm, she fell against the heavy bag and hugged it.

Miguel cheered her. *"¡Lo hiciste!"*

He picked up her towel for her and offered it. Camaro mopped her face and then her arms. She had stitches in the brow over her left eye. The gym felt stifling, but it was only her body heat and the remnants of the workout.

"Feeling that, huh?" Miguel asked.

"Yeah."

"You don't pace yourself. It's full throttle all the time."

Camaro fetched up her water bottle. This time she took a mouthful, swirled it around, and then swallowed. "You don't get to call time-out because you're tired."

"True that."

The gym was clean, swept, and quiet. The whir of the fans overhead was the only other sound. Even the interval timer was silenced now. Camaro glanced around. "Where is everybody?"

"Gone. You're the last one."

"What time is it?"

"After nine."

"You could have stopped me."

Miguel shrugged. "I figured you had to get something out. None of my business. As long as I'm home by midnight."

"Let me get cleaned up."

"Take your time."

Like the rest of the gym, the showers were deserted. Camaro rinsed her body until it was free of every trace of the workout she'd done. The hot spray pounded her muscles. She stood a long time with her head bowed under the flow, her honey-brown hair turned dark by the water and falling around her face.

When she was finished, she looked at herself in the mirror for a long moment. The stitches in her brow were marked with a single butterfly bandage. She let it be, shouldered her bag, and went out.

She found Miguel near the front of the gym. His office was a raised cubicle built of wood painted white and red, a desk, and a chair where he sat and looked down on the people coming in. His cash register was a simple metal box. He didn't take credit cards or checks. Those who trained here paid cash on the first of the month. It got them a locker and guaranteed one-on-one time with Miguel or his son, Rey.

"All done?" Miguel asked.

"Yeah. I'm sorry."

"Don't be. It's not like I never went to a New Year's Eve party before. They're getting along fine without me."

"I'll drop something extra in the box when I come back."

Miguel made a face. "I can't be bought."

"All right, then. I'll take a discount."

"I can't be ripped off, either."

"Okay," Camaro said. She turned toward the door.

"Hey, where you headed off to tonight?" Miguel asked.

"Nowhere in particular."

"You want to swing by the house? Have a few beers, watch the ball drop?"

Camaro considered. "Thanks, but I think I'll probably just go home."

"Nobody at home, though, right?"

"Not this time."

"You change your mind, you got my number. We're gonna party till dawn, so…"

"I'll think about it. Happy New Year, Miguel."

"Happy New Year, Camaro."

She went out through the front door and onto the street. Out there the palm trees on Washington Avenue were still ringed with Christmas lights, and the liquor and tattoo shops across the street were open for business. All around South Beach, the holidays lingered in the final hours of the year.

Camaro's bike was at the curb. She strapped her bag to the pillion seat and swung a leg over the saddle. The engine started with thunder, and then she was gone.

CHAPTER TWO

IT WAS IN the low seventies on the ride home. In the north it was cold, very cold, and the news was full of reports about how much snow they were getting, how much school the children were missing, and how the airports were jammed with weather delays. Florida escaped all that. There was a time when Camaro welcomed the kind of isolation only a blizzard could bring, but she was far away from it now.

She paid the toll and took the Causeway to get out of Miami Beach, cut through Overtown, and skirted the northern edge of Little Havana before turning toward home. Off the freeway the Harley glided through well-lit stretches where revelers partied in the streets, and delved into the shadows between the streetlights before coming out the other side unscathed. The sky was stained orange by the sodium vapor of the lights, and she was one woman alone on a bike, moving through the city without being caught up in it. There was the solitude of being free of people altogether, and there was the aloneness of being among more people than could easily be counted. Camaro was overlooked completely, and there was a comfort in her anonymity.

Ahead of her a limousine cruised in the right lane with the sunroof open. Two young women in party dresses and costume-jeweled tiaras drank from bottles of wine and took turns tooting on a plastic horn. The other windows were wide open to the night. Music and laughter spilled out, and as Camaro caught up with them a man leaned out and flicked his tongue at her before cackling drunkenly and blowing her a kiss. "I love you, baby!" he called to her. She accelerated past.

Camaro headed into the heart of her own neighborhood of Allapattah. Here there were no clubs and no limos, and the lights and bustle tourists called Miami were far away. All the whitewashed architecture

7

and pastels were left behind in favor of little houses with one or two bedrooms and bars on the windows, duly kept lawns, and no questions. But she didn't live far from a park, and on New Year's Eve they played live music all night long.

Only the sidelight in the carport was on when Camaro arrived home. Her truck waited silently, abandoned for the evening. Camaro sidled past it and put the bike under the carport roof. She killed the engine, pulled off her helmet, and let her ears adjust to the sudden quiet. She listened. A surge of loud voices from a nearby house carried to her, followed by a few light pops of fireworks set off too early. A dazzle of sparks erupted in the sky, flaring red and dying in green. Her neighbor, old Mrs. Cristiano, was already in bed with hours left to go before midnight, the windows of her house black.

Camaro dismounted and unstrapped her gym bag from the pillion seat. She let herself in through the side door, made sure it was locked behind her, and stepped into the utility room off the kitchen. Her workout clothes were damp with sweat. Camaro fed them to the washing machine and dropped in a detergent pod before switching it on. With the sound of water rushing in the utility room, she went to the kitchen and fetched dinner from the refrigerator. The fluorescent bulbs in the light fixture overhead gently buzzed, an insect noise that only barely registered on the ear.

The rib eye was thick-cut and weighed almost a pound and a half. Camaro set it aside while she steamed carrots and green beans for one. As the vegetables worked, she seasoned the steak with kosher salt and ground pepper, then seared it off in a cast-iron skillet with butter. It went into the oven to finish.

She found a bottle of Jack Daniel's in a bottom cabinet and took it to the kitchen table with a clean tumbler. While she waited on the meat she broke the seal, poured herself a single, and downed it. For a moment the heat in her belly pulsed with the ache of her muscles.

The steak came out extra rare, and she ate it alone at the table with two more fingers of whiskey. When the food was all gone, she put the plate in the sink and carried the bottle to the living room. She turned on the television and switched to *Dick Clark's New Year's Rockin' Eve* to watch Ryan Seacrest and some idiot blonde emcee the musical entertainment all the way up till the midnight hour. Now and again Camaro tilted the glass to her lips before pouring out another measure.

Finally the ball dropped in Times Square, and the new year was begun. Camaro powered the TV off and heard the sizzle and shriek of rockets soaring and exploding all around Allapattah, plus the rattle of firecrackers set off by the string in the streets. Somewhere not so far away, men's voices shouted, punctuated by the higher-pitched noise of excited women. Camaro missed the coffee table with her tumbler, and it fell on the floor. She picked it up and set it right. Threading the cap onto the empty bottle was a challenge for awkward fingers.

She weaved her way to the bedroom and undressed in the dark. She slept in her underwear and woke only once before dawn to pull the covers over her body.

CHAPTER THREE

Morning came slowly, with pain. The blinds were shut, but slivers of light escaped the slats and arrowed across the bedroom to strike where they could cause the most damage. Camaro put a pillow over her face and attempted sleep again. Finally she rose and tried to brush the taste out of her mouth. What toothpaste could not destroy, she attacked with coffee and sausage and eggs. The food helped.

She washed the remains of the previous night's meal away, careful to grease the inside of her skillet before hanging it up by the sink. A liter bottle of water from the refrigerator was cold and bit into her headache while she sat in front of her computer.

Camaro browsed the news, but there was nothing she cared to read. She navigated to Craigslist. She selected the list of U.S. cities and saw them arranged alphabetically from Atlanta to Washington, D.C. Choosing Atlanta first, she found the Missed Connections listings in the personals and scanned the ads there. When nothing caught her eye, she moved on to Austin and from there to Boston.

There was nothing until she reached Detroit. The message was simple:

C THIS IS A. I NEED TO TALK TO YOU. URGENT.

Camaro paused, her finger poised over the mouse button. She read the message again, then clicked Reply.

A THIS IS C. WHAT DO YOU NEED TO ASK ME FIRST?

There was no immediate response. She used a dummy e-mail account

10

for Craigslist and for nothing else. Every fifteen minutes for three hours she checked it, until she couldn't stay in her seat anymore and had to move.

Pacing was good for a while, and then she brought out a yoga mat and placed it in the center of the room. She worked her way through poses, straining muscles and tendons until her limbs felt hot and ached dully. Only when she was done did she allow herself to check again. There was a single e-mail in her box.

WHAT WAS THE NAME OF OUR FIRST DOG?

Camaro typed.

ALPHIE.

The next reply came within minutes of Camaro's message. It was a phone number.

In the drawer of her nightstand there was a simple flip phone capable of little more than calls and texts. Camaro turned it on and checked the charge. It was nearly full. She dialed the number. It rang on the other end three times, then picked up.

"Camaro?"

"Is this your regular phone?" Camaro asked.

"No, I bought it from a 7-Eleven."

"Good."

The woman on the other end of the phone sighed. "I'm glad you called."

"You're my sister. I'll always call."

"It's been a couple of years."

"You're still my sister, Bel."

"And I'm still glad."

"Is there a problem?" Camaro asked.

Annabel fell silent.

"Bel? Tell me."

"Things were going really good here," Annabel said. "I got a job

11

and a place to live. Becca's in pre-K now. I have friends. We have playdates."

"Bel, you wanted me to call you. We can't talk about playdates. If it's not important, I have to go. You won't be able to call this number again."

"No, wait! It's Jacob. Jake. He's my boyfriend. We met about a year and a half ago. He was real nice. Becca likes him. He has a job and everything. He's not like Corey was. We went out a lot. It was good."

"What are you telling me?" Camaro asked.

"It's not so good anymore."

"What can I do about it?"

"You don't understand," Annabel said. "He's in my life. We go out, we stay in...he's always around. Or most of the time, anyway. It's hard to get rid of someone when they're so close to you."

"Why do you want to get rid of him?"

Annabel sounded small. "I'm afraid of him."

Camaro sat forward. "Did he hurt you? Did he hurt Becca?"

"No, he didn't hurt Becca. I don't think he would ever hurt a kid. He likes her. They get along real well."

"Did he hurt you?" Camaro asked Annabel again.

"It was my fault," Annabel said.

"Jesus Christ, Bel."

"We were getting along great, but I can't make him happy. He tells me what he wants and I do it, but it's never good enough. And he drinks. Camaro, I can't deal with this. I need your help. It can't go on."

Camaro reached up to rub her brow and touched her stitches instead. She sighed into the phone. "I don't understand how this happens. Everything you've been through and you can't...I don't understand."

"I know. I *know*."

A sob carried over the line. Camaro frowned at the sound. "Don't cry," she said.

"I'm an idiot."

"You're not an idiot."

"I am. And I need you."

"What exactly do you want me to do?" Camaro asked.

"You have to make him go away. I can't leave this place. It's too good for me and for Becca. We have to stay. He has to go."

Camaro was silent.

"Camaro, I need your help."

"Tell me where you are. I'll come."

CHAPTER FOUR

THE CURTAINS WERE drawn in the motel room's window, but Lukas Collier knew it was snowing outside. It had been snowing all day, and the day before and the day before that, too. Snow lay six feet deep in places, with drifts twice as high, but somehow the city of Denver went on functioning.

Three days before, Lukas had skidded on some ice in his stolen Buick and crushed the right side of the front bumper. The headlight still worked, but it was pointed in the wrong direction. Rather than draw attention with a wonky headlight, Lukas used one of the credit cards he'd taken from the Buick's owner and bought himself a room to rest and drink and see in the new year.

The room was festooned with beer bottles and a couple of empty fifths. It reeked of cigarette smoke, and the ashtray by the bed overflowed. When one credit card was declined, Lukas switched to another. He had a third for when this one died. They were all lasting a while because the man Lukas took them from was laid up in a hospital somewhere with his head broken open. A man in his condition did not call his bank to cancel cards.

He had the television on. It was a rerun of *Who Wants to Be a Millionaire?*, and he paid no attention to it, nor had he to anything that had come on before it. He lay nude atop the sheets with a beer to hand. He hadn't shaved in a week, and his hair was messy.

The toilet flushed, and the bathroom door opened. A naked girl emerged, her skin looking pinched and tight from the chill in the room. She hurried to the bed and threw the covers over herself. Orange hair spilled on the pillow. Her makeup needed redoing. "You should turn up the heat, baby," she said.

14

"Cold's good for you."

"I think you just like seeing my nipples get hard."

"That, too."

He pushed himself up against the headboard and fished a cigarette out of the pack by the bed. He sparked his lighter to it and inhaled deeply before exhaling through his nose.

The girl touched his arm and traced one of his tattoos. His right arm was completely sleeved, the left partly done. His chest and stomach were inked, and he had a grizzly bear on his shoulder blade. He wore his hair long.

"You got any money left?" she asked.

Lukas eyed her. He tucked the cigarette into the corner of his mouth and used his free hand to pull the covers from the girl's body. She might have been twenty-one, but she had a teenager's looks. A pink heart inked her right hip. She lay back to let him look at her.

"So...you got any money left?"

"Some."

"How much?"

"What does it matter?"

"You don't need to be rude. I'm just asking."

He smoked and watched the television. She started to cover herself again. He stopped her. "Keep 'em off."

"I'm *cold*."

"You know how to warm up."

Lukas saw her smile out of the corner of his eye. "Yes, sir," she said.

When they were done again, she left the bed to throw away the condom. Lukas sat up and gathered his jeans off the floor. His wallet was fat with cash. He counted out a hundred and put it on the bed beside him. She snatched it up and spirited it away in the little pink-and-yellow-striped purse she brought with her.

Lukas lay down again. He wanted beer, but there was no more.

The girl sat on the edge of the bed with her purse on her lap. She rummaged inside until she came up with a small glass pipe and a baggie the size of a postage stamp. "You want to smoke with me?" she asked.

"That shit? Hell, no. My body is a temple."

"If you let me smoke a little, I'll do you once for free."

"Whatever," Lukas said. He searched for the television remote.

The first blow to the motel room door did not burst the lock, but it bent the cheap metal inward. The second blasted the door open, and a flurry of wind and snowflakes chased into the room. Blazing headlights framed a tall figure made burly by a tactical vest and winter gear.

The girl screamed and dropped her pipe on the carpet.

Lukas saw a heavy pepper-spray canister in the figure's hand as the man surged forward into the room. Lukas's hand went beneath the pillows.

Orange spray erupted, painting the wall where Lukas had been. Lukas rolled off the bed and crabbed sideways, putting the girl between him and the newcomer. The Colt in Lukas's grip was hard and cool. He brought it up and fired, three shots at a range of less than ten feet. The report was thunderous in the small room. The man with the pepper spray buckled and collapsed to the thin carpeting. He didn't move.

"Oh, Jesus!" the girl screamed. She clawed for the bedsheets to cover herself. "Oh, Jesus!"

Lukas shoved her out of the way and jumped into his jeans. He put his boots on without bothering with socks and grabbed a T-shirt and jacket off the back of a chair.

The room was still bathed in light from the vehicle outside, and despite the ringing in his ears Lukas heard the engine rumbling. He paused over the motionless corpse on the floor. "Sorry, Stanley," he said.

Lukas stepped out into the freezing twilight and found a Ford Super Duty idling with the driver's door left open. The dome light was on, and the vehicle pinged a steady warning. He climbed into the truck and slammed the door. He put the transmission in reverse and peeled backward out of the parking space, wrenching the wheel around and skidding the tires on the sloppy, icy asphalt. One glance back, and he saw the girl in the room, still naked and wailing. He put the truck in drive and stomped the accelerator. He was gone before the first siren sounded.

CHAPTER FIVE

IT WAS RAINING, a cold rain that alternated between sleet and droplets. Annabel Espinoza sat in the living room on the couch with all the lights off but one. Her daughter, Rebecca, was asleep.

The house was small and welcoming, with big front windows to let in the sunlight when there was any. Annabel had flower beds on both sides of the front walk and in the shadow of the picket fence enclosing the lawn. All were barren now, fallow for the winter months, though the lawn still held a fresh emerald under a mantle of water and ice.

She got up from the couch and went to the kitchen. She set a kettle on the stove to boil and selected a bag of chamomile tea to go with her teacup. After a time the kettle steamed, and the sound of Jake's engine carried from the street. She heard his footfalls on the doorstep before his key in the lock. Automatically she got a second cup and saucer for him and put them on the kitchen table with sugar and milk.

"Michelle?" Jake called.

"I'm in here."

He entered through the dining room, still wearing his wet jacket. When he swept the knit cap off his head, his blond hair stood up crazily. There had been a time when she found his perpetual look of untidiness boyish, even handsome, but that time had passed in bits and pieces until now there was nothing except a pit in the bottom of her stomach. She faked a smile, but it was weak.

"I didn't think you'd be awake," Jake said.

"I wasn't feeling good. Why are you here so late?"

"You don't want me around?"

"No, it's...I didn't expect you now."

Jake drew her close and kissed her on the forehead. Annabel put her arms around him reluctantly. "I'm going to have some tea," she told him. "Do you want some?"

"I don't have tea on my mind." He reached around to grope her behind.

"Jake, I'm really not feeling good."

"Oh, come on. Everybody says sex makes your immune system stronger."

"Jake, I don't—"

He caught her by the hair and gripped it tightly. A muscle in his jaw twitched. "Aren't I asking nicely?"

"Jake, please don't hurt me."

"Don't make me."

Annabel did what he wanted right there in the kitchen. She gripped the edge of the table and closed her eyes to everything until it was over. Afterward he did not seem to notice her brush the moisture from her eye.

"*Now* let's have some tea," he said.

They sat down opposite each other. Annabel poured hot water into their cups. She steeped her tea bag in silence, aware of Jake doing the same on his side of the table. Her lip trembled, but her hands did not shake.

"Quit acting like I kicked your dog," Jake said finally.

"I'm not doing anything."

"Exactly. You're not doing anything. You don't say anything. You just sit there with your tea."

"I told you I feel sick."

Jake put his teacup down too hard. "Then go to bed. I'm not keeping you up."

"I don't want to fight."

"What else is new?"

Annabel held her cup in both hands when she drank. The heat fortified her, and her insides stopped quaking. She thought of Camaro. "Are you staying over tonight?"

"Why? Now you don't want me to? All the time you used to ask me

18

if I'd stay, and then you'd act all hurt when I didn't. Now look at you. It makes me want to pop you one right in the mouth. Help you get that stupid look off your face."

"I only asked."

"You have a lot of questions tonight. Do you have something going on?" Jake asked.

Annabel kept her face still. "No. Why?"

"You put any more thought into what I told you?"

"Yes."

"I really need another loan. Me and Derrick, we're just about to close a deal on a real sweet place out by the water. People can walk right down to the beach and surf. It's gonna be nice. Everything we want."

"I need more time."

Jake checked his watch and tapped the face. "I've already given you three weeks. How much more time do you need?"

"Not much longer."

Jake grunted. "Okay, but you better hurry it up. The landlord's not going to hold the place for us forever, and we have to sign a lease agreement soon. So scrape up whatever cash you got or cut me a check. If you can afford to keep this place, you can spare some for our future."

"Jake, I told you before that all my money's tied up in the house."

"But you always have enough for new clothes. How many pairs of shoes do you have? Huh? How many purses? I've never seen anybody with so many purses in my life. Those all cost money. You've got it all squirreled away, but you have it. I just want what's mine."

Annabel looked into her cup. "I'll try."

He pointed his finger at her, and she flinched. "No, you're not gonna try. You're gonna *do*. It's bad enough I have to practically beg you to do me, but now you're going to hold out when my business is at stake? I don't think so. So get with the program, Chelle."

"Okay," Annabel whispered.

"What?"

"I said okay."

"Good girl."

"So…are you?"

"Am I what?"

"Staying."

"Nah. I just wanted to stop by and let you know what you've been missing."

CHAPTER SIX

DETECTIVE TERENCE LITTLE stood in the steadily falling snow outside the Sunrise Motel and brushed a flake from the notebook on which he scribbled. It was so cold, the ink in his pen was sluggish. From time to time he rolled the pen vigorously between his hands to get things flowing again. The freeze was polar.

The parking lot was full of lights, flickering and solid. A trio of Denver Police Department vehicles stood in the main traffic lane, blocking off one exit and forming a natural barrier to the news trucks gathered in the street beyond. Light bars cast red and blue across the face of the motel while members of the Crime Scene Investigations Section shuttled in and out of the room where the body lay. Bright camera flashes still popped inside the room, but it wouldn't be long before the corpse was cleared.

Terence saw the girl dressed and bundled up and sent away in an ambulance, and his initial notes were complete. Now he marked his thoughts in the margins.

"Excuse me," a man said. "Detective Little?"

Terence looked up, his concentration broken. He saw a man and woman in long, dark coats approaching across the fresh layer of snow. They wore matching black scarves, and they had expensive haircuts, the man with a neat beard. The man was not tall, but he stood rigidly upright.

"It's Detective Little, isn't it?" the man asked when he came close.

"Yes," Terence said carefully. "Who are you? You shouldn't be here. This is a crime scene."

The man produced an identification wallet and displayed his credentials. "I'm Keith Way of the United States Marshals Service. This is Deputy Marshal Piper Hannon. I understand you're the man in charge."

"That's right. What brings you out tonight, Marshal?"

"Deputy Marshal. We just got into town from Wichita," Way said. "We have a fugitive investigation under way, and we think our cases are linked. Can you show us around the scene?"

Terence regarded the marshals. Way had a hard, tan face that was not unhandsome, though his nose had clearly been broken more than once. Hannon was younger than Way by seven or eight years, a small and slender figure in her coat, her expression solemn and her eyes unreadable. When Terence looked at her, she simply looked back.

"Yeah, sure," he said. "Follow me."

They went to the room. Terence stepped aside to let Way and Hannon through the broken door. The two stepped over the corpse with no sign of distaste. Hannon produced a tiny digital camera from the pocket of her coat and proceeded to snap pictures of the room. Way stared at the dead man. "Any witnesses?"

"One. A prostitute who spent the day with our shooter. Problem is, she never got a name, and she's so freaked-out by what happened, her description of the man is almost useless."

"His name is Lukas Collier," Way said.

Terence glanced around the room. "Did you just pull that out of thin air, or did I miss something here?"

Hannon took shots of the dead man.

"Have you identified your victim?" Way asked.

"Yeah, Stanley Yates from Norfolk, Virginia. He's a bounty hunter."

"That's how I know who did the shooting," Way said. "Stanley Yates was pursuing a skip out of Virginia. Felony bail jump on a charge of carrying a concealed weapon. The skip's name is Lukas Collier."

"He's a long way from Virginia now. What's your interest?"

"A little over a year ago, Collier gunned down a marshal in New Jersey. He was already a fugitive on that charge when the court in Norfolk let him make bail on the weapons beef. It's a whole mix-up, and you don't need to know all the details. The thing is, Collier belongs to us."

"How does Yates figure into the picture?"

"The bail was pretty steep. Yates figured he had to make good on the bond. We tried to warn him off, but he didn't listen. Now we see what happens."

"I guess that explains the pepper spray," Terence said.

"He was a professional," Hannon said suddenly. "No license to carry firearms in the state. Pepper spray is something anyone can have."

Terence crouched over the body. It was rigid and bluish from settling blood and the frigid temperature. He used his pen to prod an empty loop on Stanley Yates's tactical vest. "Pepper-spray cowboy," he said. "Makes sense now."

"Where's Yates's truck?" Way asked.

"What?"

"Yates's truck. He drove a Ford Super Duty. Dark blue. It would have Virginia plates."

"There was no truck on the scene."

"Did you check other vehicles in the lot and match them to guests?"

"We did. There was a stolen Buick in the lot we guess our shooter came in with."

"And it's still here."

"Right."

"So, what, did you figure Collier just walked away? What did your witness say?"

"She said he left, but she didn't specify. The woman was in shock and suffering from hypothermia when we got to her. I figured we'd get more once she had a chance to come down in the hospital."

Way fixed Terence with a glare. He had heavy brows that settled down over his eyes. "You listen to me, Detective. You have a cop killer running around in a stolen vehicle *right now*. He might even be close enough to catch on one of the main highways if we're quick enough. I'm going to have my partner write down Yates's license plate number, and you're going to put it through every channel you have. It's a big truck, and it's easy to spot on the road. I don't want Lukas Collier getting out of this state."

Terence straightened up. "I'll get right on it."

"If Collier gets away because you were too busy waiting for your witness to get her head together, I'm going to be very disappointed."

CHAPTER SEVEN

AT MIDDAY IN Northern California there was a steady, bleak rain. Clouds obscured the sun. Camaro got into a cab at the airport and told the driver where to go. She watched the city of Monterey slip away after they joined the highway and thought ahead to the next thing, a moment long delayed, when she'd see her sister again.

Monterey was a small city, and Carmel-by-the-Sea barely qualified as a city at all, with fewer than four thousand people to its name. Camaro had looked the place up online when Annabel told her about it, and it seemed more like a town that happened to grow a little larger than intended, tucked against Monterey Bay.

As they passed the threshold into Carmel itself, her impression didn't change. It was generously wooded here. The houses fit into the landscape, and in the afternoon streets there was peace. Not a single home had bars on the windows or doors. The asphalt was even and dark, without a pothole anywhere. When they drove down a street lined with businesses, she saw no franchises, no big-box stores.

They drove a little while longer and went down a crooked lane to a cul-de-sac among more trees. The driver stopped broadside to a small house with a picket fence and friendly windows in front. Neat curtains tied up with bows framed the glass. A sign with the street name and house number hung from a flawless white upright, and the path from the gate to the door was lined with tiny, solar-powered lamps.

The driver shut down his meter. "Thirty-eight dollars even."

"This is it?" Camaro asked him.

"Yeah, this is the place."

She paid the driver cash and stepped out into the rain. The taxi slipped away and left her on the sidewalk. The homes on either side of her sister's were likewise quiet. Through the picture window in the front of one, Camaro saw an older woman sitting with a mug of something in front of a large plasma television.

The gate made no noise when she pushed it open. There was only the sound of the falling droplets on grass. A tree without leaves stood in the yard. Its branches were the right height for climbing.

Camaro stepped onto the porch. She paused a long moment before pressing the doorbell. The sound of chimes carried from inside.

Footfalls sounded on the far side of the door. It opened, and Camaro was suffused with warmth and the smell of cinnamon. Annabel was there.

Camaro put down her bag, and they embraced on the doorstep. Annabel was shorter than her by inches, and slight. She clung to Camaro and squeezed her, and when her body trembled, Camaro knew she was crying.

"You came," Annabel said into her shoulder.

"I said I'd come."

Annabel pushed away from Camaro and held her at arm's length. Camaro saw her notice the stitches on her brow. Annabel's eyes glistened with tears. "I know," she said, "but you're here. You're here."

"I wouldn't stay away," Camaro said.

"Thank you." She hugged Camaro again fiercely. "Thank you so much. You're soaked. Get in here."

Camaro stepped across the threshold into the house. The air was scented, and the Christmas tree was still up. The living room had a fireplace, and three stockings were hung. The floors were hardwood.

Annabel pressed the door closed and locked it. "I didn't know when you'd be here. I don't have any lunch for you."

"It's all right," Camaro said.

"Mommy, who is it?"

The little girl Camaro saw was nearly three years older than the one Camaro remembered. She was small, almost five, and had light hair from her father but the soft coloring of her mother. A woolen sweater made her look pudgy. Pigtails sprouted from her head, clipped with pink barrettes. Camaro held her breath.

Annabel rushed to Rebecca's side and put an arm around her. She urged Rebecca forward. "Becca, this is your auntie. Auntie Camaro. You remember her, right?"

Rebecca regarded Camaro with dark eyes. "No."

Camaro knelt. She looked her niece in the face. She extended a hand. "It's okay if you don't. I remember you. Shake hello?"

Rebecca stood motionless for a long moment before reaching out. They touched fingers, and then Rebecca withdrew hers definitively.

"Let's go to the kitchen. We were coloring," Annabel said.

The kitchen was neat, the countertops made of rich wood, the appliances stainless steel. There was room enough for a large table with a view of the backyard. A climber and swings stood lonely and wet in the rain.

Camaro put her bag in the corner and stripped off her wet jacket. She hung it on a peg by the back door beside a child's raincoat. When she sat at the table, she sat opposite her sister. They looked at each other across a scattering of crayon drawings.

For a while they said nothing. Camaro spoke first. "Nice place."

"Thank you."

"Pricey?"

"Kind of. But I fixed it up."

"How much do you have put away?"

"Not a lot. Some."

"Same here," Camaro said.

"What did you buy?"

"A boat."

Annabel smiled. "Like Dad always wanted."

"What do they call you here?" Camaro asked.

"Michelle Amado."

"Michelle. You took Mom's name."

"Yeah," Annabel said. She looked sad. "Who should I tell people you are? What name should I give them?"

"Tell them I'm your sister. And they can call me Camaro."

Annabel nodded. "No lies."

"No lies are the best lies," Camaro said. "I'm your sister, and I came to visit. No one needs to know from where or anything about me at all."

"Right. You're right."

"What do you do?"

"Me? I work in a clothing shop. It's a little place. I know the owner, Wilson, really well. He hired me without any references, and he's been a great boss. He never asks me anything about my past."

"That's good. If he ever does, just tell him it's complicated."

"I think he knows." Annabel took a deep breath. "What do you do with your boat?"

"Charters."

"That's awesome. You're a fishing boat captain. You still ride?"

"Yeah."

"That's good."

Camaro watched Rebecca color. The girl was in the middle of a detailed drawing of a house not unlike her own, except the colors were wild and garish where this home was warm and welcoming. The grass was electric blue.

"You've been fighting," Annabel said.

Unconsciously, Camaro raised fingers to her brow. "Sometimes."

"Are you okay?"

"I'm okay."

"I worry sometimes."

"Don't. Tell me about your problem," Camaro said.

Annabel swallowed. "I don't think we should talk about this in front of Becca."

"Okay."

Annabel gathered up Rebecca's drawings and crayons. "Hey, baby, why don't we take all of this into your room for a little while. Auntie Camaro and I have to talk a little bit about grown-up stuff. That's okay, right?"

"This one is almost finished."

"Well, you get it all done, and then we'll put it on the refrigerator." Annabel hustled her daughter out of the room.

Camaro waited. She heard them talking in muffled voices elsewhere in the house. The walls were thick here, the house old.

Annabel returned. "Do you want something to drink? Coffee? I have tea."

"I don't need anything."

Her sister sat down. "Okay. Okay, I'm ready."

"Tell me," Camaro said.

"His name is Jake. I told you that."

"Who is he? What does he do?"

"He's a surfer. That's how we met. I always wanted to learn, you know? He was teaching part-time for this surfing school. He was always a real gentleman. He treated me right."

"What does he do besides surf?"

"He works at a lumberyard in Pacific Grove."

"Where's that?"

"It's another town. It's not far."

Camaro found a rough spot on the tabletop and picked at it with her thumb. "And he's a bum."

"He's not a bum. He has a job."

"I don't care that he's got a job. He's just another bum," Camaro said. "One more bum on top of every other bum you ever picked up."

Annabel looked as if she might bolt from her chair. "It's not the same. He was good to Becca, and he was good to me, and he never asked me for anything except money once in a while when he was short. It's expensive to live here, Camaro. He did the best he could."

"But he hurt you. He's hurting you."

Annabel's face wrinkled, but she didn't speak.

"If he hurt you, he's not a good guy. He's a dirtbag. I want to hear you say it," Camaro said.

Annabel wrung her hands. "Please fix it, Camaro. Just fix it for me."

CHAPTER EIGHT

A REPLAY OF a college football game played silently on a television in the corner of Jeremy Yates's office as he snoozed. He had his boots on the desk and his ragged office chair tilted to capture his long, rangy form at rest. A cup of coffee sat on the blotter, gone completely cold. Outside the windows, soft snowfall flickered green and red from the brilliant neon signs that announced YATES ALL-NITE BAIL BONDS.

The telephone on the desk rang. Yates stirred. It rang twice more before he woke completely. He was seventy-one, and wakefulness came slowly. He coughed and dropped his feet to the floor and stretched his long arms over his head until his back popped. Only then did he answer. "Bail bondsman."

The connection popped, and Yates heard the murmur of voices in the background. He looked at the clock. It was after nine.

"Is this Jeremy Yates?" asked a man.

"Yeah, this is Jeremy Yates. Who is this?" He scrubbed his scalp with his fingertips and stirred up his slightly too-long hair. He was sharper now. He smoothed down his mustache, then ran his hand over his scratchy cheeks and chin. It had been a few days since he shaved last.

"This is Keith Way of the U.S. Marshals Service. You'll remember me?"

"I remember. I don't have any word about Lukas Collier."

"I do."

Yates grabbed a pen from a mug on the desk and found a scrap of paper for writing. "Is he caught? Where's he at?"

"We have people searching for him right now."

"Where?"

"Salt Lake City. A little out of your area."

"Collier's in Utah?" Yates wrote "UTAH?" on his paper, then circled it. To one side he started listing the states adjoining Utah: Nevada, Idaho, Wyoming, Arizona, Colorado. "I'll tell my son. Last I heard, he was headed toward Denver. He could be out where you are by now."

"Yeah, that's the thing. Mr. Yates, your son is dead."

The room shrank. His body buzzed with electricity, and he heard the hum of blood rushing through his ears. "What?" he said at last.

"He's dead. He was killed by Lukas Collier last night in a Denver motel room."

Yates's grip loosened on the phone, but then he clutched it again more tightly. He sat upright in his seat, blinking away a sudden blurriness in his vision. "When exactly?"

"About midnight, local time."

"And you're telling me about this *now?*"

"We've been busy."

"It's been a day! You couldn't spare one goddamned minute to tell me my son was murdered? What the hell happened?"

Way continued. "From what we can tell, Stanley died instantly."

"Stanley? I didn't know you two were on a first-name basis."

"I met with him once after Collier skipped. I *told* him not to pursue the man. It's the same thing I told you on the phone, but neither of you wanted to listen to reason. And this is what happens when people don't listen to reason."

Yates swallowed something bitter. "Where is Collier going?"

"We're working on that."

"How?"

"We have leads."

"What leads?"

Way paused. "Collier fled the scene of the crime with your son's truck. But that's not your concern."

"What is my concern?"

"I'll give you the number of the Denver Police Department so you can make arrangements for the transfer of your son's remains."

There was a vibration at the center of Yates's body that slowly built in intensity as he held the phone to his ear. It was warm and growing warmer, crawling up his spine and through his bones until it put his teeth on edge. He still gripped the pen. The plastic snapped. "It was mighty kind of you to call, Mr. Way. Thank you."

"You're obviously out of the picture, so I won't bother to update you on the Collier situation until it's done."

"You do that. Good-bye."

Yates put the phone in its cradle. He slumped forward in his chair and caught his head in his hands. He cradled his skull for a long time, listening to his heartbeat. The tears he feared might come did not erupt.

A footstep scuffed in the back of the office. Tricia Yates appeared in her coat and boots. His wife had been in and out of the office all day in between shoveling the walks. She never let him do it. "Did I hear the phone ring?"

"Yes."

"Do I need to put some coffee on for you?"

"No. Why don't you go on to bed? I'll lie down on the cot after a while. I'll talk to you in the morning."

"Love you," she said.

"I love you, too."

She went. Yates collected the broken pieces of the pen. He put them in the wastebasket. The desktop computer was sleeping. He woke it and entered his password. On the sheet of scratch paper there were his brief notes. He clicked on the Dropbox icon and entered his son's account information. A folder of text files opened. He clicked the first one.

CHAPTER NINE

CAMARO SPENT THE day at Annabel's house as rain drummed on the roof. For lunch Annabel made toasted cheese sandwiches with four different kinds of cheese and a slice of ripe tomato. Annabel put a couple of logs in the fireplace to warm the room. They sat together on the couch, watching the flames flicker and listening to the pop of the wood as it burned.

Rebecca brought a dollhouse out of her room and set it up in the radius of the fire, playing with cloth dolls and doing the voices of mother and father and baby, too. Camaro listened to the little girl and smiled.

"What is it?" Annabel asked her.

"What?"

"You're smiling."

"She reminds me of you," Camaro said. "When you were her age. She's exactly like you."

"Is she?"

"Yes. Exactly."

Camaro observed Rebecca as she walked her mother and father dolls hand in hand out into the pretend yard, where the baby sat on the ground next to a hairy dog. She spread out a checkered kerchief as a picnic blanket, and the whole family sat around to eat imaginary sandwiches. Everyone laughed, and the mother kissed the father on the cheek.

"She'll ask someday," Camaro said. "About her father. And when she does, tell her the truth. Whatever she does then, it'll be on her and not you."

"Everything is on me. I'm her mother."

"That's the kind of thinking that drove Dad crazy. Kids have to screw up on their own. You can't save them."

32

"You always tried to save me."

"That's my choice. I do it because I want to, not because I have to."

Annabel put her hand on Camaro's and threaded their fingers together. She said nothing for a while, and Camaro did the same. At the make-believe picnic, the mother was telling her baby the story of the Three Bears.

"I'm glad you came. I'm grateful."

"I haven't done anything yet," Camaro said.

"But you will."

Camaro looked at Annabel. "How bad did he hurt you, Bel?"

Annabel turned away.

Camaro closed her grip on Annabel's hand. "How bad?"

Annabel pulled her hand free.

"Bad enough. Let go."

Camaro watched her sister closely. "Whatever he did to you, it wasn't your fault."

Annabel sniffed and touched the corner of her eye. "I know."

"And he's never going to do it again. Ever. He'll have to come through me first."

"I know."

Annabel patted Camaro on the arm. Camaro felt a surge of heat, and she clenched her teeth until the moment passed. The muscles in her jaw unwound slowly. She looked back to Rebecca. The little girl whispered now, the heads of her dolls pressed together in secret conference. Camaro heard nothing but the breathy susurrus of her tiny voice.

"I could use a drink," Camaro announced.

"I have beer. It's Jake's brand."

They retreated to the kitchen, and Annabel pulled a six-pack of Bud Light bottles from the bottom shelf of the refrigerator.

"You're kidding me," Camaro said.

"He likes light beer."

"I'd rather drink water."

"I'm sorry."

"Don't be. Throw them away. He's never coming back to drink them."

Annabel took them to the sink and twisted off the tops one by one, pouring the beer into the drain. She had a recycling bin next to the trash. They sat down at the kitchen table. Annabel directed her gaze out the window. Her eyes were puffy and rimmed with red. "I'm tired of crying," she said at last.

"He's not worth it."

"You never cry," Annabel said.

"No."

"You know, sometimes I used to wish I were you. When I was little. I remember when you had your thirteenth birthday and I was nine, and you seemed like you were all grown up already. And Dad took you riding around on that ratty old Harley he was always getting you to help him with. I wanted to be grown up, too. I wanted to be on the back of the bike."

"It was never a competition," Camaro said. "He loved us both the same."

"I know that now. But it took me a while. When you were gone and he got sick, I was so mad at you for going, because maybe he wouldn't have fallen apart. You know? Like maybe he would have kept it together if he wasn't worried about you getting shot in some desert somewhere. Because he'd never say so. He'd just watch the news and get drunk and start yelling at me and everybody else. I couldn't wait to get out of there."

Camaro watched the rain. "I never meant to hurt him. Or you. It's just when the towers came down…I had to do something. I couldn't do nothing."

"That's you," Annabel said, then smiled weakly. "Trying to save everybody."

"It's not a good habit to get into. Somebody always needs something."

"Like me."

"Don't start that again."

"I'm sorry."

"And stop being sorry."

"I'm…okay."

Camaro looked around at the kitchen and the neat counters, the cabinets with frosted-glass fronts, and the hanging rack of copper-bottomed pans. She encompassed all of it with a wave of her hand. "You have all of this. And a daughter who loves you. That's the kind of thing people wait a whole lifetime for. Dad never had it. I don't have it. This is what you fight for. So I don't want to hear you say 'I'm sorry' again. You understand me?"

Annabel straightened up. "I do."

"Tomorrow I'll go deal with this," Camaro said. "And then it'll be over. It'll be over."

CHAPTER TEN

THE RAIN CLEARED overnight. Camaro slept in the guest bedroom and woke with the sun through her window and the smell of cooking bacon. She found Annabel in the kitchen, making eggs to match. A stack of pancakes stayed warm beneath a towel.

"I figured you'd be hungry," Annabel said.

"I am."

"Then let's eat. After that I have someone to watch Becca, and I can take you to see Jake."

"What do you mean, you're going to take me?"

"I'm going to be there."

"No, you're not," Camaro said. She sat at the table. "You're going to lend me your car, and I'm going to go see him on my own. You're not going to be a part of this at all."

"But you said I should fight."

"Not this kind of fighting. I need to know you're here safe with Becca. That lets me do whatever I need to do."

Annabel turned out two fried eggs onto a plate, then added two strips of bacon. She laid on pancakes and put it all in front of Camaro. "You're not going to..."

"No, I'm not. We're going to talk. He's going to listen. Then we walk away."

"He's hard to scare, Camaro. He's tough."

"We'll see." She shook pepper over her eggs and cut into them with a fork. The yolks ran. She ate the whites and soaked the bacon in what was left. Afterward she drizzled her pancakes lightly with maple syrup. They smelled of nutmeg, and when cut they smelled even more intensely.

36

Annabel set places for herself and Rebecca. "Good?"

"Good. Now tell me where I can find Jake."

Annabel gave Camaro Jake's address and explained how to link her phone to the little Subaru Crosstrek parked on the street. She hugged Camaro one last time at the door.

Jake's house was in Salinas. The drive would take half an hour. The Crosstrek had satellite radio, and Camaro played with the channels until she found one playing Black Sabbath's "Paranoid." She left it there as she drove the quiet Sunday streets of Carmel-by-the-Sea before hooking up with the Salinas Highway for the rest of the drive.

Salinas was not Carmel. There were no picturesque houses on its streets, and the stores were in strip malls or planted in the asphalt acreage of parking lots. Camaro found Jake's small, burnt-orange house on a street across from a small apartment building, the concrete of its driveway separated from the concrete of the neighboring house's driveway by a teetering wooden barrier. A CENTURY 21 sign was posted just inside the chain-link fence in a yard consisting mainly of mud.

Camaro parked by the apartments and got out. The air was crisp from the morning, and her jacket was still damp from the day before. She cracked her knuckles and crossed the street.

She stopped at the gate and listened, but there was no dog. She found the latch unsecured and stepped through. The short walk was uneven and cracked, and the porch was simply a poured slab of cement raised no more than an inch or two off the ground. It was awash in bits of dirt flooded over by the rains.

The curtains were open in the front window. Camaro looked at a room mostly empty except for a couch and a television. Bud Light bottles sat collected at one end of the couch. An Xbox was connected to the TV, the wires strung out on the floor.

Camaro turned to the front door and knocked. A minute passed, and no one answered. She heard nothing on the other side.

Another gate led off the porch onto the driveway. Camaro let herself out and looked down along the house. Three windows were visible along the side, the last a part of some disorganized extension at the rear of the house. She went to the first and put her hands up to peer inside. There was a hallway with a bathroom visible at the end of it. At the second she found herself looking into a bedroom messy with clothes thrown wherever there was a spot.

The window farthest back was blocked by a set of wooden shelves. She rounded the house's back end and found a better angle. A sunroom had been transformed into storage space piled with boxes and disused exercise equipment, a wheelbarrow, and even a pinball machine. Camaro backtracked and headed up the driveway.

"He's not there," someone said.

Camaro spotted the man over the wooden divider between the driveways. He stood under his carport. He smiled at her as she came closer.

"Where is he?" Camaro asked.

"I don't know," the man said. He was dark-skinned and had a broad slab of mustache that looked pasted on. "He hasn't been home for a couple of days. Could be working, could be at one of his girlfriends' places."

"Girlfriends?"

"Oh, yeah. He's got a couple."

"How well do you know him?" Camaro asked.

The man shrugged. "What's to know? He likes to party, and he likes the ladies. I know he gets plenty of tail when he goes out teaching surfing in the summers. Is that where you met him?"

"I've never even seen him," Camaro said.

"You're not one of his girls?"

"Do I look like I am?"

The man considered her. "No. I guess not. You don't look like the rich-bitch type."

"I'm not."

"Actually you look like you want to twist somebody's nuts in a knot."

"Listen, where can I find him? Where does he work?"

"Carlson Lumber. It's over in Pacific Grove."

"You know the address?"

"No, but I have the Internet. You got the Internet?"

"Yeah, I do," Camaro said. "Thanks."

"No problem. You gonna kill him?"

Camaro stepped away. "No. But people keep asking me that."

"I'll look for you on the news."

Camaro went back to the SUV and used her phone to look up the lumberyard. She twisted the key in the ignition, and the engine thrummed to life. The GPS said thirty-five minutes.

CHAPTER ELEVEN

THE YARD WAS an unremarkable place: high walls with great towers of fresh-cut wood stacked against them. A warehouse-sized building dominated the center of the lot, its rolling doors thrown wide open to show the cavernous interior where lumber was measured and sheared to order. A forklift was busy on the sales floor, carrying a heavy load of two-by-fours.

Camaro parked the Subaru among the scattering of trucks in the plain gravel lot. As she approached the warehouse, she saw the manager's office and a sales counter and angled toward them. A man in overalls worked the register.

"Morning, miss," he said when she came close. "What can I do you for?"

"Jacob Collier."

"Jake's around out back. Want me to call him up?"

"No, I'll find him."

Outside she rounded the warehouse and walked in the space between the stacks and the corrugated aluminum wall of the building. Wisps of music carried from ahead, along with men's laughter and voices. Camaro's pace quickened.

The area behind the warehouse was an echo of the front. Large sliding doors allowed the whole rear end of the structure to be opened to the outside, though they were halfway closed now. Another forklift stood idle in a puddle of mud, a portable CD player on the back of its seat playing Kid Rock. Four men in work shirts and jeans loaded planks onto the lift. They stopped when they saw Camaro.

One whistled. Camaro ignored him and came closer.

"Hey, honey," said another. "You lost?"

"Which one of you assholes is Jake?"

Everything stopped. Kid Rock boasted and crowed while the drums bashed and the electric guitars crunched. Camaro looked from one man to the next, and each one stared back at her. The last man on the left stepped forward. "I'm Jake."

He was lean, his flannel shirt worn open over a white cotton T-shirt. His boots were caked in mud, and his pants carried a fuzz of sawdust. Jake removed the work gloves he wore. He tossed them to one of the other men. Camaro stood waiting.

"Who are you?" Jake asked.

"My name's Camaro."

Jake laughed. "The sister! The famous sister. Finally came out from whatever rock you were hiding under, huh? And just to see me?"

He came toward her, and Camaro advanced to meet him. They stopped an arm's length apart. Jake had five inches on Camaro. She figured him for a hundred and sixty pounds or somewhere close. He glared down at her. She stared back.

"What?" Jake asked. "What do you want?"

"My sister's off-limits. You don't come around, you don't call. She never sees you again. That's it. That's all I have to say."

Jake studied her. "You some kind of badass?"

"I'm telling you how it is."

"You came all the way from wherever you were to tell me to get lost? What, Chelle can't do that for herself? Me and her, we're gonna have words."

"No," Camaro said.

"Nobody tells me no. Especially not some bitch."

He pushed her. She hit him in the throat.

The punch was hard and fast. Jake gagged and his face turned a brilliant red. He grabbed for his neck with one hand and reached for her with the other. Camaro gripped his forearm like a baseball bat and cranked it hard at the same moment she pivoted her hips into his.

Jake's elbow went into her armpit, and Camaro applied pressure and leverage to lock the joint. Jake made an incoherent sound, like he was seizing up from the inside. Camaro drove her shoulder down into his arm until the ligaments popped noisily. Jake screamed then.

The other men rushed them. Camaro wheeled around and pulled Jake with her. "Back the hell off or I'll break his arm."

They stopped sharply as Jake keened with pain.

Camaro released him, and Jake fell into the mud. She kicked him in the side of the head, snapping his skull around violently. He collapsed, his eyes rolling, and she kicked him again and again as the other men watched but didn't move.

She stopped. Her heart thumped, and she breathed heavily through the mouth. "She's off-limits. If I catch you within a mile of her, you will die. Do you understand me?"

Jake lolled in the wet, sticking mud. He made burbling sounds.

"Do you understand me?"

"Yeah. Yes. I understand," Jake managed.

One of the other men moved. Camaro fixed him with a glare. "You want some of this?"

The man shook his head. "No, ma'am."

"This is between him and me. He knows why," Camaro said. "Now I'm leaving."

She backed away with her eye on the men. Jake vomited spectacularly, painting the ground and the front of his shirt. The men near him recoiled. Kid Rock played on.

Camaro made it all the way to the Subaru before she heard someone yelling for the police. She got in the SUV and started it up, backing out fast but not spinning her tires in the gravel. At the road she accelerated away. When she had gone a quarter mile she heard the distant wail of a police siren.

CHAPTER TWELVE

CARLY RUSSO CAME through the front doors of the Carmel Police Department's small station at three-thirty in the afternoon and waved to Chris Miller at the desk. She had her civilian clothes on, her uniform tucked away in a bag. Miller buzzed her through to the back. There she entered the locker room and made her way to the last locker on the right. The lock on it was brilliant pink.

She was alone, and everything was silent, including the single shower. Carmel had three women on its tiny police force, though sometimes it seemed like it was only her among the boys.

She stripped off her clothes, and her tattoos were exposed. On the inside of her right arm she had inked in decorative script "And though she be but little, she is fierce." On her side was a branch of cherry blossoms. A pair of wings spread out across her collarbones from a crowned diamond. None were visible when she wore her uniform. At five foot five and 106 pounds, with short hair and light makeup, in uniform she seemed as conservative as any citizen might desire.

Once changed, she went out.

"Anything amazing?" Russo asked Miller when she reached the desk.

"Not unless a visit from Mrs. Salazar is amazing."

"She was in today?"

"Of course. She said some homeless folks were rooting around in her garbage cans all night. I told her it was probably raccoons, but she's not listening to anybody. She wants an officer to stop by later. You can give it to whoever."

"Great," Russo said. "I'm sorry I missed her."

"You'll get your chance. Anyway, I have to split. I promised my wife we'd get on the road early."

43

"Where are you headed again?"

"Spokane, to see her folks."

"Have a good time."

"Always," Miller said.

Russo straightened up the front-desk area and made certain all the flyers and pamphlets were orderly. After that she spritzed down the countertops with cleanser and wiped them until they shone. The phone did not ring, and traffic was whatever passed in front of the station. The scattered desks remained empty. The only sound was the faint buzz of the fluorescent lights.

The phone call came a little over two hours after her shift began. "This is Travis Caldwell over in Pacific Grove," said the man on the other end. "Is this the officer on duty?"

"I can get you the sergeant, but I'm manning the phones. Carly Russo."

"Russo? You're not Shawn Russo's kid, are you?"

Russo smiled into the phone. "That's right."

"I'll be damned. How is Shawn?"

"Good. He's down in La Jolla now with my stepmom."

"Retirement is nice," Caldwell said.

"Yes, sir."

"Well, tell him I said hello the next time you talk to him, will you? It's been too long."

"I will. Was there something I could help you with, sir?"

"Oh, right. I almost forgot. Listen, we had an assault-and-battery case come in this morning we could use a little help on."

Russo grabbed a pad and a pen. "What can we do?"

"Fella name of Jake Collier got himself busted up pretty good at his job today by a woman with a serious chip on her shoulder. He's still at Community Hospital last I heard. Concussion, lost some teeth, cracked a rib. She came damned close to breaking his arm off at the elbow."

Russo tucked the phone between her ear and shoulder and used the terminal at the counter. She typed in "Jake Collier" and was rewarded with an electronic jacket. She saw a string of arrests for disorderly conduct, public drunkenness, and other misdemeanor violations. "Jacob Collier? I'm looking at his record right now."

"That's right. Lives in Salinas."

"Do you need me to e-mail his sheet to you?" Russo asked.

"You can do that if you want. Couldn't hurt to take a look. I imagine it's a lot like the one we have for him. Man likes to party. But that's not why I called. Do you have any record of a woman named Camaro Amado?"

"Camaro? Like the car?"

"That's right."

Russo submitted the request. "I don't have anything here."

"How about Michelle Amado?"

She checked. "Nothing. Who are they?"

"Collier and the witnesses say a woman named Camaro was the one who did all the damage. She has a sister who lives in Carmel, Michelle Amado, which is why I'm calling you. As far as we can see she's clean, but apparently this Camaro put a hurt on Collier at her sister's request. I was thinking about taking a drive over there to look into it myself, but I was wondering if you could have a unit knock on Michelle Amado's door. Where one sister is, the other one can't be too far away. Maybe you could see if either one of them is willing to come in voluntarily?"

Russo scribbled down all the names. "Give me the address, and we'll have someone go right over."

Caldwell recited it for her, and she wrote it down. "Tell your officer to be careful. I don't know anything about this Camaro woman, but I saw firsthand what she did to Jake Collier."

"Yes, sir. I'm on it."

"Good talking to you, Carly. Stop by our shop sometime and say hi."

"I will. Good-bye."

Russo hung up the phone. Immediately it rang again. "Carmel Police Department, Officer Russo speaking."

The line crackled. A man spoke. "Officer Russo, this is Deputy United States Marshal Keith Way."

Russo straightened unconsciously. "Yes, sir. How can I direct your call?"

"I'll make it quick, and you can pass this up the chain. I'm on the road to your area right now. I just got off the line with the Salinas PD. It's about a man named Jacob Collier."

Russo blinked. "Jacob Collier?"

"That's right. I understand from talking to Salinas that he gets around the Monterey Bay area. Jobs in different towns. Party type."

"Yes, sir. I know the name. I just—"

"Good," Way said, cutting her off. "I need to get a line on him. We have a fugitive situation, and Jacob Collier may be involved. Give me an e-mail address over there in Carmel so I can send you the fugitive's jacket. His name is Lukas Collier, Jacob Collier's brother. We have reason to believe he's headed for the coast. He's wanted for murder."

"Oh, wow," Russo said.

"Yeah. Wow. E-mail address?"

Russo gave it to him. "Do you want me to—"

"This is how we're going to work it. If Jacob Collier has known hangouts in your town, we need you to do a sweep for our fugitive. If you spot him, *do not attempt to apprehend him*. That's our job."

"You really should talk to my sergeant."

"I'll talk to him soon. Get that e-mail and start distributing copies of the attached sheet. How many officers do you have?"

"Twenty-one, but they're not all on duty."

"Tell your sergeant we need all hands on deck. I'm going to give you my cell phone number, and if there's anything not in that e-mail you people need clarification on, call me."

"Yes, sir. I'll take care of it, sir. But you ought to know—"

"Get working on that, Officer Russo. I'll be in touch."

Way ended the call. Russo stood dumbly for a moment with the receiver in her hand. It clicked and a dial tone sounded. She put it in the cradle.

The e-mail was already in the department's in-box when she checked. She clicked on a PDF, and a wanted flyer for Lukas Collier came onscreen. He was dark-haired with a half-grown beard and eyes like hard glass. He glared out of the screen at her. Russo forwarded the e-mail to all senior officers, including the chief.

She found Sergeant Mullins in his office. "Sergeant," she said, "we have kind of a situation."

"Mrs. Salazar again?"

"No, sir."

Russo told him the story. He checked his e-mail. She stood by while he scanned the other documents attached to the message. He stood up sharply and adjusted his uniform. "This needs to go to the chief," he said.

"I already sent it ahead."

"He's off today. He's not going to check work e-mails. I'll drive out and talk to him directly. In the meantime, do exactly as this marshal says and get Lukas Collier's particulars out to everyone on patrol. Put a copy on everybody's desk. You say his brother's in the hospital?"

"Yes, sir. That's the other thing. Pacific Grove PD wants us to—"

"Never mind what they want. We have a federal fugitive headed our way. Everything else goes on hold. Why are you still standing here? Get moving!"

"But the brother's in the hospital because he got assaulted, sir! Pacific Grove says the assailant's in Carmel right now."

"Didn't I say I don't have time for that? You can type it all up in a memo or something and then put it on my desk for whenever. I promise I'll look at it."

Russo left the office reluctantly.

CHAPTER THIRTEEN

LUKAS COLLIER USED a plastic comb on his wet hair and dragged it into something presentable. There was a spot of shaving cream behind the point of his jaw, and he used a hand towel to wipe it away. His face was a little pink from the hot water. He ran his fingers over his cheeks and felt nothing but skin. Being shaved closely reminded him of being in the Marines, a memory that was partly welcome and partly disagreeable.

He had new clothes laid out on the bed. He used deodorant under each arm before pulling on an undershirt still scratchy from the package. A loose blue work shirt went over that, and he put on a pair of boot-cut jeans. He'd bought a bundle of thick socks with blue soles. He donned a fresh set of steel-toed boots. His other pair had Stanley Yates's blood staining them.

The curtains on the hotel room's window were open, and the Las Vegas Strip glowed in the dark. Lukas had chosen the place at random, paid cash at the front desk, and put in a call to Konnor Spencer from the courtesy phone. They made plans to meet at nine. It was a quarter of now.

The room came with a phone, but he didn't use it. Lukas went down to the gift shop in the lobby and bought a prepaid phone off the rack, then paused just outside the casino to unwrap it. Once it was activated, he dialed and waited for an answer.

Jacob sounded as though he had the stuffiest of colds. "Hello?" he asked. "Who is it?"

"Jake, it's me."

"Oh, shit, Luke."

"What's the matter with you? You sound sick."

"I'm a little busted up."

Lukas glanced around. No one was watching. "What are you talking about?"

"Chelle."

"What about her?"

"Chelle got me, bro."

Across the lobby, Konnor appeared. He was a big man in a denim-and-leather motorcycle jacket, his head shaved bald. A thick chin beard fell into a braid that nearly touched his chest. Konnor waved. Lukas raised a hand, then turned his back. "What do you mean, she got you?"

"She wants me gone. She didn't say anything to me, and the next thing I know, she called her sister. She came to town and got right up on me. They say I have a fracture in my jaw, man. Some of my teeth are out."

Lukas spoke quietly into the phone. "Are you telling me some chick jacked you up?"

"She's like a ninja or something, Luke. One minute she was telling me off, the next minute I was pickin' my head up off the ground. She's not afraid of anything. She would have taken us all on. She calls herself Camaro. It's crazy."

"Where are you now?"

"I'm at home. Where are you?"

"Never you mind where I am. Do you have cops on you?"

"No. They want Chelle's sister. I told them everything I know. They took me home and left me here."

"So they didn't ask anything about the money?"

"No, I don't think they talked to her, and she won't say anything. She thinks I'm trying to set up that surf shop. She doesn't know where the money's going."

"You better hope not, because I'm not having this thing screwed up because of you. I let you in on it because you're my brother and you said you were ready to take it to the next level. Are you ready to take it to the next level, Jake?"

"Absolutely."

"Good."

Konnor held back at a respectful distance. People flowed in and out of the casino and paid neither man any mind.

Lukas exhaled. "This isn't what I need right now, Jake. Low-profile. Remember when I said low-profile? The people in LA aren't going to understand, you end up on the news."

"I know, I know. I'm sorry. I screwed up. I never knew Chelle was gonna blow up on me like that. And her sister. She tried to break my arm. I have it in a sling, and it still hurts. They wanted to give me a cast so I wouldn't move it."

Lukas motioned for Konnor to wait a little longer. "I don't have time to listen to your problems right now."

"I got to get some payback, Luke."

"You will. We won't go anywhere until you get yours. And then it's all LA. You and me."

"Okay. Just hurry, okay?"

"I'll call again when I'm close." Lukas disconnected before Jacob could say any more. He put the phone in his pocket and turned to Konnor. The two men clasped wrists and bumped shoulders.

"Long time, my brother," Konnor said.

"Yeah, long time. You put on a few pounds since I saw you last."

Konnor patted his belly. "My old lady keeps me fed. Hey, was that Jake on the phone?"

Lukas scowled. "Yeah."

"Trouble?"

Lukas waved it away. "Nothing you need to worry about. Let's drink some booze and play cards."

They wound their way into the casino and sought out the blackjack tables. Their dealer was dressed like Alice Cooper in a white top hat and directed them toward their seats with a flourish. "Welcome to my nightmare, gentlemen," he said.

Lukas threw down some cash. Alice made it disappear, then gifted him with chips. He repeated the same trick with Konnor. A waitress swung by the table, and Lukas ordered beers for the both of them. "I need to make some bank tonight," Lukas told Konnor.

"Runnin' low?"

"Cross-country travel ain't as cheap as it used to be."

"You still going to come through in LA? They're gonna expect you to deliver, and that takes cash."

Cards were dealt. Bets were made. Lukas signaled for a hit. Konnor held. "Jake has a line on some money. He's been stepping it up for a while now, and we have a big score coming. Everything we need."

"All right, 'cause I have to tell them you're going to make good on our order. I can't cover the expense with what I have to spend."

Lukas asked for another card. "It'll be done. Jake's not good for much, but he's good at wheedling cash out of his old ladies. I heard he has some legal assistant he's been getting a bankroll from for a while now. Not enough to take us over the top, but good money."

The cards were turned. Lukas had twenty. The dealer had nineteen. "Winner," Alice said, and pushed the chips to Lukas.

"You've always been lucky, Luke," Konnor said. "That's what I always said."

"It's like the man says: the harder I work, the luckier I get. And I'm working hard on this one."

"You know I'm in it with you all the way. I got people lined up in LA who'll turn your straw into gold."

Lukas smiled thinly. "That's what I like to hear."

The beers came. Lukas tipped Alice a ten-dollar chip, and then they played another hand.

CHAPTER FOURTEEN

HIS SON WAS dead.

It was evening of the second day after Stanley died. Trish made them dinner and manned the desk as calls came in after afternoon court set the bond amounts. Yates hadn't told her yet and wasn't sure how he was going to. Every passing hour made the task more difficult. She would want to know why he hadn't said something as soon as he heard. She would be brokenhearted in a way Yates could only partly understand. Stanley was his son, but there was something between a boy and his mother that ran deeper than that.

He didn't cry. He felt, but he did not let it go. There were other things to do. Crying now would only keep him from moving forward. That was not all right with him.

The first thing he'd done was go through the paperwork for Lukas Collier's bond. Trish had made the decision to extend Collier the bond, even though it was a massive $150,000. Collier had ties to the community through friends and a few distant relatives, but more important, his girl put up her house as collateral. It wasn't a palace, but real estate values in Norfolk were good.

Everything was in order. All the documents were signed and filed with the court, and Stanley had made certain to catalog the names and addresses of everyone even remotely connected to Collier who lived in the area. But Collier vanished three days after bonding out of jail, and no one in Norfolk seemed to have a clue where he might have gone.

Yates got this story from Stanley's files. His son kept detailed notes on his phone and tablet and uploaded them regularly to an online backup. Each day of the hunt was given its own folder, and calls and visits were marked with the time they happened and detailed with everything that occurred.

It became clear right away that Collier was headed west. He had old ties to California, from when he was stationed at Camp Pendleton as part of I Marine Expeditionary Force. Yates did not like the idea that he and Collier had anything in common, but they were brother Marines, though a generation apart and worlds different in every other way. Collier served in Iraq for a year and a half, and the First Marine Division saw serious action. If nothing else, Collier had bravery.

But this had only mattered a little bit in the overall picture. Stanley drew on law enforcement and simple legwork to trace Collier along his route. By the time Stanley followed him to Kansas, he had a solid idea of where the man was headed: California. Collier had connections in Los Angeles and San Diego. Camp Pendleton was just a part of it. But he was trending northerly, away from the sunny coasts of the south. That was where the brother came in.

A separate folder held all the information Stanley had on Lukas Collier's brother, Jacob. There was an image lifted directly from the California Department of Motor Vehicles, plus a few mug shots from misdemeanor arrests. From what Yates could tell, Jacob was the more harmless of the brothers. Lukas Collier was a killer at least twice over in civilian life, the number he might have laid to rest in Iraq a closely held secret.

Yates found the number to the Salinas Police Department and dialed. A man answered, identifying himself as Officer Powers. "My name is Jeremy Yates, and I'm a bail bondsman in Norfolk, Virginia," Yates told him. "How are you today?"

"I'm fine, sir. You're calling from a long way away. What can I do for you?"

"I'm doing some background on a potential client. He's given us the name of a brother who supposedly lives out your direction. Jacob Collier. I was wondering if you'd run him through your system to see if he's really there."

"That's a real popular name around here."

"How's that?"

"I can't really go into it. Let's just say you're not the first person to call about him."

"Can you still look him up for me?"

"Of course. I can do that. We should have something for you. Just a second. Wait…yes. Jacob Collier has a Salinas address. The one we have on file is current with the address on his license. Sometimes that doesn't match up."

"Could you confirm the address for me?"

"Sure," Powers said, and he recited the information.

Yates hung up the phone. He tore the sheet of paper off the legal pad and folded it in half with the address above the fold, then sent Jacob Collier's picture to the printer. He already had a wanted flyer for Lukas Collier. Stanley had made that one.

Yates went to his bedroom and spun the dial on his gun safe. Inside he had nearly thirty guns, all secured behind eight locking bolts. It opened with a heavy clank. He ignored the long arms and selected a pistol from among several. It was a stainless steel AMT Hardballer in .45 caliber, kept unloaded. He topped off the magazine with hollow-point ammunition and slid the magazine home but didn't work the slide. In the closet he found a holster for the weapon. The gun would sit on his hip, hidden by the edge of a jacket.

He stepped out of the closet, and Tricia was there. She saw the gun slipped into its leather. "Jeremy, what's going on?"

"I need to get some gear together."

"Why?"

Yates looked at her. When he took a breath, it hitched. He slid the holster into place on his right side. "There's something I have to tell you, Trish."

He watched her expression crumble, and she sagged in the doorway, held up only by the frame. A high-pitched keening sound started in her chest and rose rapidly, chased by torrential sobs that clotted her throat. Yates stood with his hands at his sides for a long moment, and then he went to her. He folded his wife up in his arms and held her close as she cried. Something warm ran down his cheek. He did not have to touch it to know what it was.

"Let it go," he said at last. "Let it all out."

She cried for a long time, and after that she became quiet. She listened to what Yates had to say, and together they packed his things.

CHAPTER FIFTEEN

ANNABEL MADE DINNER for them, a Parmesan-basil tomato soup served with crusty bread. There was a different blend of herbal tea, this one with a perky aroma about it, which complemented the soup in a natural, tonal way. Camaro ate quickly, as did Rebecca.

"It's good?" Annabel asked.

"Yes. When did you get so domestic?"

"I don't know. It seemed like something to do. I mean, I have this great kitchen. I have to do something with it, otherwise it's a waste, right? I couldn't keep on heating up chicken tenders and french fries for dinner. Wilson turned me on to the tea shop here in town. They have all kinds of amazing stuff there. When Becca got a cold last year, they fixed me up with a special blend that cleared her sinuses and helped her sore throat. It was terrific."

"Can I play on the computer?" Rebecca asked.

"Sure, baby. Go play some games."

Rebecca got down from her chair and fled the room. Camaro shook her head.

"What?"

"I don't know. Her. You."

"You're making fun of us."

"No, I'm not," Camaro said. "I'm not. I think it's great."

Annabel reached for Camaro's hand, and Camaro allowed her sister to take it. Annabel squeezed lightly. "Everything I've done here is important to me. I'm different. I'm better."

"I know you are."

"But you're still Camaro. Thank God."

"What's that supposed to mean?"

Annabel smiled. "It means I never want you to change. You're perfect the way you are."

"That's not what you used to think."

"I grew up."

Camaro didn't reply.

"Let me clear the table," Annabel said.

Camaro sat while Annabel cleaned up. Her eyes drifted toward a large plastic case and a small folding table in the corner. "What's that?"

"Oh, that? That's my beading stuff. I'm really into beading now."

Camaro finished her tea. The sensation of it faded at the back of her throat and disappeared. Outside it was clear and cold, but bad weather was coming again. It was an invitation to a fire and a blanket and having nowhere to go.

Annabel sat again and waited a while before speaking. It was a good silence between them. "Do you want to tell me what you did to him?" she asked.

"No."

"Did you hurt him bad?"

"Not enough."

"But he's not dead."

"No. I could have killed him," Camaro said.

"I know."

There was more quiet.

"When do you want to leave?" Annabel asked finally.

"Soon."

"I can't convince you to stay?"

"There's no way that would work," Camaro said.

"I understand. But I'd like another chance to be sisters again. These last couple of years and then all the time you were in the service…it's like you were on another planet. Getting pictures of you in Italy and Kuwait and Afghanistan wasn't the same as having you around. You went and disappeared. I think Dad would want us to try."

Camaro looked outside. In the autumn it would be absolutely beautiful under trees whose branches were bare now but would be a riot of color at the change of seasons. It was not the same in Florida. There were no real seasons there, only times when it was hot and times when it was less hot.

She thought of her father, of a twelve-hour flight from Japan and the quiet, oppressive stillness of the funeral home. He had not looked like himself. He was too thin, and his color was all wrong. She and Annabel barely spoke before the funeral, or after, and then Camaro was gone again. Another flight, and then the lights of Tokyo.

"I love you, Camaro," Annabel said.

Camaro found it difficult to look at her. "You know I love you."

"Stay."

"I can't."

"Can we come visit you at least? The door's open now that everyone's seen us together, so it's not like it's a secret anymore. Becca and I can come, and we'll all go to Disney World together."

"Disney World is in Orlando."

"Then we'll take the bus. Whatever. Don't you understand that we're a family, and families belong together? I've seen you three times in fifteen years. I don't want us getting old like this."

Camaro shook her head. "You don't want what I'd bring into your world."

"I've survived so far."

"I know."

Annabel placed her hands flat on the table. "Then that's it. We're going to see each other more, and we're going to change things. And whenever you start to run away from me, I'm gonna run after you. Because it's not just me anymore. It's Becca, too. She deserves to have her aunt in her life."

Camaro let the slightest of smiles crease her face. "You didn't just get domestic. You got crazy, too."

"We're both crazy, Camaro. You and me. That's why we need each other."

"You have to do something for me," Camaro said.

"What? Anything."

"Work out your man issues. You're no good at picking them, and you never have been. I can't keep coming back to fix your troubles. If you want into my life, you keep your complications out of it. I have things the way I want them. I don't need another Jake."

The corners of Annabel's mouth turned down. "Do you think he'll come for me?"

"I won't be here if he does."

"Wait," Annabel said. She got up from the table and left the room. Camaro toyed with her teacup.

Annabel returned with a plastic case and a paper bag. She put both of them on the table. They were heavy and thumped solidly. The side of the case was emblazoned with the name GLOCK.

"What are you doing?" Camaro asked.

"It's…my gun."

Camaro looked in the bag. Two boxes of .45-caliber ammunition lay inside. She shoved them away and popped open the case. Inside, laid out in foam rubber, was a Glock automatic pistol and two empty magazines. The trigger was equipped with a lock.

She lifted the gun out of the case. "Where did you get this?"

"I bought it online. It's new."

"You know how to use it?"

Annabel shook her head.

"Where's the key?"

"I keep it with my others."

"Bring it."

Annabel went and brought them back. Camaro unlocked the gun and set the lock aside. "Tomorrow I want you to get a chain or a thong to hang the key on. Keep it around your neck all the time. You don't ever put the gun away without making sure it's secure first. You understand?"

"I understand."

Camaro opened one of the boxes of ammunition. They were fully jacketed, their heads perfect brass circles buttoned with a primer, arranged in neat rows in their plastic case. She gave a magazine to Annabel. "Load it."

"I don't know how."

"That's why you're going to load it now."

Annabel accepted the magazine and took the first bullet from the case. She tried to put it in backward. Camaro corrected her. The next bullet loaded faster and the one after that. By the time she reached the tenth, she had it down. "What about the other one?"

"We're going to use that one for practice."

Camaro's sister picked up the Glock with nervous fingers. She held it awkwardly. Camaro reached over and steadied her grip. She nodded toward the empty magazine. Annabel fed it into the well. It snapped together with a loud, metallic click. "Okay, now we pretend it's loaded?"

"Yes, but you can't make it fire just by putting in the magazine. You need to work the slide. Grab it with your other hand at the top and pull. Good. Now let it go."

"It's stuck."

"That's because the magazine is empty. When the slide locks back, you're out of ammo. There's a lever on the side called a slide stop. Push it with your thumb."

Annabel jumped when the slide ratcheted forward. "Should I put on the safety?"

"There's no safety on a Glock. The gun won't fire unless you pull the trigger all the way through. It's a good gun. Now stand up and I'll show you how to hold it."

They got up together, and Camaro molded Annabel's form to her own. Annabel aimed out the window, hands together around the weapon, body braced. She put her finger on the trigger. Camaro told her to stop. The only time to touch the trigger was when it was time to fire.

"When it's loaded it's going to be heavier than you expect. And it's going to kick when you pull through," Camaro said. "You hold it steady like that and keep a firm grip. Aim for the center of the body. Don't try to hit an arm or a leg. Center of the body."

"I don't want to kill anyone."

"If it's down to this, you don't have any choice. Do you want to die?"

"No."

"What about Becca?"

"No!"

"Then put the shot right in the middle. Don't hesitate."

Annabel lowered the gun. "This is crazy. What am I trying to prove?"

"Is there a range around here?"

"In Carmel? Are you kidding?"

"Then we'll find one. Somewhere you can get practice. Before I go, I want you to be able to draw and fire. You don't own a gun to show off to people or to make noise. It's for killing. You have to know how to kill with it."

Annabel pushed the Glock into Camaro's hands. "I feel sick."

Her sister sank into her chair. Camaro sat down with the gun between them, its muzzle pointed in a neutral direction. "I need to know you're safe when I go."

Annabel covered her eyes with her hand and nodded. "I know."

"I wish it didn't have to be this way."

"I know."

"Just promise me you'll do what it takes. Now and when I'm gone."

"I promise."

Camaro put her hand on the gun. "Okay."

CHAPTER SIXTEEN

JEREMY YATES DROVE the rented Hyundai Santa Fe from Monterey to Salinas in less than half an hour. The onboard GPS guided him expertly through the little streets of Jacob Collier's neighborhood until he found the burnt-orange house. Weather that began as a drizzle when he left the airport turned into a full downpour by the time he reached the place. He drove by without slowing, noting the porch light burning but none in the windows.

Yates proceeded to the end of the block and pulled up to the curb. He killed the engine and drew the AMT from its holster to chamber a round. He laid the pistol on his thigh for a moment, breathing deeply and watching Collier's little house in the side mirror.

The rain didn't slow, and no one moved around the property. Most of the neighboring driveways were empty, the owners away at work. Once he was certain no one was headed in or out, Yates turned up the collar of his fleece-lined jacket and stepped out into the rain. Instantly his hair was plastered to his skull. His boots splashed in the little rivers streaming along the asphalt, the curb washed in a swirling current.

Yates walked down to the house and stopped at the driveway to survey the property. It was obvious no one was home, his initial impression confirmed. He let himself in through the front gate and braved the pools of rainwater to stand on the flooded porch and look inside.

He skirted the entire house, peeking through windows. Finally, he returned to the front door. He unbuttoned his jacket and produced a slim leather case from an interior pocket and flipped it open. The collection of picks was matte black.

Kneeling at the door, Yates engaged the lock with his picks. The lock itself was as old as the house and very loose. He tried the knob, and the door fell open in silence.

Yates took one last glance toward the street and went inside.

The front room was carpeted thinly, the furniture ramshackle and cheap. The television was the nicest thing in sight, along with the video game console.

He left soaking prints on the carpet as he closed the door. His jacket was sodden. Water dripped from the tips of his fingers and ran down the back of his neck from his scalp. Anyone who paid attention would know someone had been there.

In the kitchen he found a plate with the remains of a burrito stuck to it. The beans were still moist, though the burrito itself was cold. It had not been there more than a day. On impulse, Yates checked inside the refrigerator and found it empty of almost everything except bottle after bottle of Bud Light. The freezer was packed with microwavable meals. The microwave itself was filthy.

Yates went into the hallway that bisected the house and found a small table with a telephone on it and three different books of Yellow Pages. There was no answering machine. He moved on.

The bedroom was a mess and almost seemed as though it had been ransacked by searchers. Yates checked the drawers in the dresser for a gun or a knife, but there was nothing. His gaze alighted on the bed and a yellow piece of paper mostly covered by the sheet.

He pulled the sheet aside and found three pages of carbon copies. It was a police report, scrawled in an uneven hand that was difficult to read. A drop of water fell from Yates's nose and landed on the topmost page. He brushed it off and kept reading. He made a mental note of two names: Camaro and Michelle Amado. There was an address given. After a moment's hesitation, Yates folded up the carbon copies and stuffed them inside his jacket.

The bathroom smelled of mildew and body spray. On the closed toilet lid there were discharge papers from a local hospital. Yates flipped through them but found nothing as interesting as the two names in the police report. The report said Collier had been beaten. The hospital documents revealed how badly.

Yates abandoned the discharge papers and made his way deeper into the house. He found the cluttered back room and the laundry nook where Collier's combination washer and dryer stood empty and quiet. There was nothing to find.

A car horn sounded outside. Yates froze. He put his hand on the .45 at his hip and waited thirty seconds. The horn did not sound again, and no one appeared at the front door. Noiselessly Yates retraced his steps to the front room. He stepped up to the living room window and stood to one side, peering out around the curtains. A car was parked in the street, its hazard lights blinking. As he watched, a woman came down from the apartment building directly across from Collier's house, a sweater pulled out to shield her head. She dashed to the car and got inside. A moment later it pulled away.

Yates locked the front door behind him and splashed back out to the sidewalk. He ran the rest of the way to the Hyundai and got in. His breath was short, and he coughed forcefully until he produced phlegm. He opened the driver's door and spat into the street.

The police report was still dry as he unfolded it onto the steering wheel. The address for Michelle Amado was in Carmel, which the GPS said was thirty minutes away.

The house sat bereft of life in the side mirror, promising someone's eventual return. The police report indicated Michelle Amado was Collier's girlfriend. Yates looked from the paper to the mirror and back again. He chewed the corner of his mustache.

Yates tossed the police report onto the passenger seat and started the SUV. He twisted the knobs on the dash, and warm air spilled out of the lower vents over his wet legs. He looked at the house again, then put the vehicle into drive and pulled away from the curb.

CHAPTER SEVENTEEN

HANNON DROVE THE U.S. Marshals Service's Suburban while Way balanced a laptop on his knees. His phone was between them, sending out a middling Wi-Fi signal the computer could use while they were still in motion. They passed a sign declaring Salinas ten miles away. They had been on the road for thirteen hours without breaks, save to get gas or use the restroom. Way hadn't slept for forty-eight hours, though Hannon had done better in that time.

"What do you have?" Hannon asked him.

"I have all the information on Jacob Collier, plus the latest off the line from the California Highway Patrol."

"Any luck with the Ford?"

"No. Lukas has to have switched cars by now, otherwise we would have picked him up for sure. So until he pokes his head up on a camera where we can pull facial recognition, we're stuck. He could be driving anything at this point. Car, truck, bike. Anything."

Hannon peered out the windshield at the dark clouds gathering overhead. "This isn't bike weather. We're driving into something nasty."

"I thought California was supposed to be dry."

"Someone tell the weatherman," Hannon said, turning on the headlights.

"Right now the only thing we have is the Jacob Collier lead. He was in the hospital yesterday, he checks out, and then he disappears off the face of the earth. Salinas PD says they're doing drive-bys of Jacob's place, but there's nothing so far. He's not at home, and he's not at work. His car is exactly nowhere."

"You think Lukas is already there?"

"I don't know. He could be. God*damn* it. All I want is ten seconds. In ten seconds it's all taken care of."

"You'll get it."

Way chewed his thumbnail and watched the speedometer. "We have to pick it up."

"We're almost there, Keith."

"We need to be there now!"

"We're ten minutes out. There's no reason to get crazy about it."

"I'm not crazy about it. I'm thinking we don't have time."

"There's time."

Way's knee jiggled as he sat, jostling the laptop like an earthquake. His flesh crawled with the urge to get up and move around.

"Deep breaths," Hannon said.

"Funny," Way returned.

A droplet hit the windshield. A second fell, but the real rain was still ahead of them. Way's leg still jiggled. He put his hand on it to keep it still, but that only worked for a moment.

"Do you want to skip the cop shop completely?" Hannon asked him.

"What do you mean?"

"If you're so hot to track down Lukas's brother, we could go straight to the source. Sit on Jacob's house and see where that leads us. We don't need to check in with the locals first. There's time to bring them up to speed."

Way shook his head. "No. It'd be a waste of time. Lukas will never go to Jacob's place. He may not know for sure we're coming, but he has to know somebody's going to keep an eye on Jacob just in case. No, they're going to be somewhere else together. A friend's house. A girlfriend's place. Somewhere like that."

"Did Salinas PD give a list of KAs?"

"Got it here. As soon as we're on the scene, we need to draft some of the locals to hit the list, and while they're at it they can canvas the whole neighborhood. No stone unturned. Someone has to know his habits, who his people are. We'll dig it up and throw a net over the whole thing."

The SUV's GPS indicated that their exit was coming up. They passed into a sheeting rain, the gloomy skies finally giving up the deluge. Hannon put on the windshield wipers. Way stared out at the rain a moment, then grabbed his phone.

"Who are you calling?"

"I'm going to let them know we're almost there. I want them on their toes."

Way dialed the chief of the Salinas Police Department, his private line. It rang a handful of times and then went to voice mail. Way cursed and cut the call without leaving a message.

"Local bullshit," Way spat.

"What's going on?"

"I tell the chief to be on his line and the asshole doesn't even pick up," Way said, his voice rising in the confines of the Suburban. "Does he not get it? Did I not explain it was important? I swear, this is the kind of shit that gets me every goddamned time. Every time!"

"It could be nothing," Hannon offered, her tone even. "He might be in the bathroom. Call the main switchboard."

"I shouldn't have to call the main switchboard."

"I'm only giving you options. I'm on your side, remember? All the way. That's what I promised."

Way rubbed his eyes with thumb and forefinger. They felt gritty and dry, and the sensation had only gotten worse over the course of the drive from Salt Lake City. "You're right," he said. "You're right. You're right."

"It'll all work out," Hannon soothed. "Lukas just ran out of country to cross. We're at the coast. He's done."

Way looked out the window and felt suddenly mournful. "It'll be done when he's dead," he said.

CHAPTER EIGHTEEN

CAMARO SAT ON the couch with Rebecca, watching a Disney DVD. It was one of the new movies, and Camaro wasn't sure what it was called. Rebecca referred to it as "the princess movie," and that seemed to be good enough for her. Camaro listened to the songs and smiled at the jokes and didn't care.

"The snowman is funny," Rebecca observed.

"He is," Camaro replied.

She heard Annabel bustling in the kitchen. Dinner had been a cherry-and-onion-stuffed pork tenderloin served with steamed baby carrots. Camaro did not know where these recipes were coming from. Annabel worked without cards or a cookbook, slicing and rolling and tying and roasting as if it were something she did every day.

That afternoon they'd gone to a local shop and picked up six bottles of Corona Extra that Camaro let chill in the refrigerator for two hours before opening the first one. She had her third in hand and drew from it occasionally, tasting the cold more than anything else. Outside the winter rainstorm refused to let up. It came down all day long with only a few respites, and even then the sun never shone. Camaro found it harder and harder to imagine Carmel in the warmer months.

They had just reached the final credits when Annabel slipped into the living room. Rebecca clapped her hands for the end of the movie. "Let's watch it again!"

"In a minute, babe," Annabel said. "First I have something for your auntie."

Camaro saw a cupcake on a small dish in Annabel's hands. It had pink frosting and a white wrapper meant to look like lace. A single candle flickered atop the cupcake. "What's this?" Camaro asked.

Annabel sat on the couch and offered the plate. "It's for you."

"What for?"

"Don't you know what day it is?"

Camaro glanced at her watch. The date showed 5.

"January fifth," Annabel said. "It's your birthday. Happy birthday."

Camaro took the plate and held it with both hands in front of her. The candle wept a single waxy tear. Rebecca clapped her hands again. "Happy birthday!" she said. "Make a wish!"

Camaro closed her eyes. When she opened them again, she blew the candle out. The flame vanished and left a curling tendril of smoke. She was thirty-three years old.

"It's a chocolate cupcake," Annabel said. "I know you like chocolate."

"You didn't have to do this," Camaro told her.

"It's just a cupcake. I didn't buy you a new car."

"Can I have some?" Rebecca asked.

"I'll give you half," Camaro replied.

She carefully removed the wrapper and peeled away the paper. The cake glistened with moisture. Annabel plucked out the candle. Camaro tore the cupcake in half and gave Rebecca the portion with more frosting. Her niece attacked it like a wild animal, getting pink all over her face and on the tip of her nose. Annabel laughed, and Camaro felt lightness inside.

"She likes hers," Annabel said. "You eat yours."

Camaro obeyed. The chocolate cake was rich, the icing creamy. Camaro wanted milk.

"Good?" Annabel asked.

"Great."

"There's a bakery down on Ocean Avenue. They do the most amazing pastries."

"Thank you."

"Let me hug you," Annabel said, and she leaned over to put her arms around Camaro and squeezed tightly. When they broke, Annabel wiped her eyes and sniffed. "I'm just glad we could be together on your birthday. Now give me that plate. I'm loading the dishwasher. Becca, go wash your face."

Annabel left the living room, and Becca trudged off to the bathroom. Camaro was alone when the first blow struck the front door.

A splinter from the frame spun away under the initial impact, and on the second kick the wood began to give way completely. Camaro leaped up from the couch. She took one step, and the door exploded inward, letting in a rush of cold air and the noise of the rain. Jake spilled in behind it, soaked from head to toe. "Chelle!" he bellowed.

Camaro came at him straight on and laid a hard right into his nose. She felt cartilage give, and there was blood. Jake took a wild swing at her, and she let it go by, countering with an overhand left into his temple. He was rocked and fell against the wall.

She heard Annabel scream and the echoing cry of Rebecca as Jake came off the wall with full force. Camaro pivoted and tripped him up with her foot. He spilled face-first onto the floor.

"Camaro!" Annabel cried.

Camaro latched on to him and dropped two hammer fists into the back of his skull. His forehead struck the floor, and he struggled to rise against her weight. She snaked an arm around his throat, grabbed her wrist with her free hand, and cinched the choke in hard.

Jake rolled, and Camaro rolled with him. They crashed against the TV stand, and the Disney movie started playing again. Jake kicked Camaro's shins with his boots and scrabbled at the lock around his neck.

He hit her with his elbow, right on the lowest ribs. Camaro let a short bark of pain pass her lips but held on. Jake hit her again, and she felt her hold slip. He made it to his hands and knees and tucked under, rolling forward and carrying her with him. Camaro hit the coffee table with the small of her back. A shock of hurt passed up her spine, and she lost her grip on her wrist. They fell apart.

Camaro found her feet quickly. Jake was already standing. Annabel and Rebecca were gone. Jake's hand dropped to his waist and came up with the click of a lock blade snapping into place. He brandished the weapon between them, four inches of blackened steel jutting from his fist.

"You want some of this?" Jake asked. "Come on and try it."

"Jake!" Annabel stood at the mouth of the hallway that led to the rest of the house. She held the Glock in both hands awkwardly, extended full length at the elbows, her stance shaky. The muzzle trembled.

"Annabel, wait," Camaro said.

"No. You get away from her, Jake!"

Jake looked from Camaro to Annabel and back again. He smiled, his face battered, scraped, and bruised. He was missing an incisor. "Annabel?"

"Michelle," Camaro said.

"Okay, *Annabel*. You going to shoot me now? Is that it? You gonna kill me?"

Annabel shook visibly. "Don't make me do it, Jake. Go away. Go away and never come back."

He didn't lower the knife. "Your sister already tried that one. I'm not going away. You're mine. You belong to me. No matter what your name is. Nobody is gonna come between us. Nobody."

"Jake, don't!"

"I can take him," Camaro said.

"I'll cut you wide open."

Camaro looked at him steadily. "You'll try."

Jake shook his head. "Crazy bitches."

He moved. The Glock in Annabel's hands spoke, an angry bark. Jake lurched to one side and caught his shin on the coffee table. He flopped and fell, the knife flinging from his grasp to land in the corner, then lay still.

"Oh, my God," Annabel said.

Camaro went to him. The entry wound was wet, directly over the heart. Jake stared at the ceiling. She checked his pulse at his wrist, then his throat.

"Is he dead?" Annabel asked.

"He's dead," Camaro said. Rebecca cried out and stepped into the living room. Annabel knelt to cover her face, but her hand was still filled with the pistol. She dropped the weapon on the floor as if it were hot, then folded Rebecca in her arms.

Camaro left Jake and took up the gun. "Take her to her room. I'll call the cops."

Annabel looked up. Her face was streaked with tears, and she trembled violently. "They'll take me away, Camaro. They'll take Becca away."

"No," Camaro said. She lowered herself to Annabel's level. "That's not how it's going to happen."

"Why not?"

"Because you didn't kill him."

"He's dead, Camaro!"

"Yes. But you didn't kill him," Camaro repeated. "*I* killed him."

CHAPTER NINETEEN

CARLY RUSSO STIRRED when her phone vibrated on the nightstand. When it buzzed again, she came barely awake and fumbled in the dark to find the switch for the bedside lamp. Blinking back the glare, she took up her phone and checked the number. "Carly Russo," she answered.

"Officer Russo, this is Detective Adkins. Do you remember me?"

"Of course, sir."

"Listen, I need you right now over on Raymond Court. Can you remember an address, or do you need to write it down?"

"I can remember."

"Okay," Adkins said, and he told Russo where to go. "I need you here an hour ago, okay, Russo?"

"I'm already getting dressed, sir."

"See you soon."

Russo threw back the sheets and hustled into the bathroom to wash her face and get the sleep from her eyes. Her uniform had come back from the cleaners that afternoon and was still in its plastic bag, hanging from a hook on the door of her bedroom closet. Russo dressed as quickly as she was able. She hopped on one foot as she put on her socks, and she took her polished shoes from their place by the end of the bed. Her service weapon and belt were on a chair.

With no time for makeup or even coffee, she was out the door of her apartment and down to the parking lot in thirty seconds. Her patrol unit was parked in a reserved space. She got behind the wheel and started up. She was already on the move by the time she clipped her safety belt on.

It was a matter of five minutes' drive to reach Raymond Court, and before she got there she saw the telltale flashing of red and blue lights in the darkness. It was a little past ten, and she saw three other Carmel police units parked in the small cul-de-sac, plus an unmarked vehicle with a light on the dash. A van from the Monterey County Sheriff's Department waited beneath a streetlight.

She parked. The rain had finally slowed, and it was only misting down. Iris Cooper, one of the other women on the force, stood on the front lawn of a perfect house with warm yellow light in its windows. She waved Russo over when she came near. "Russo," she said. "Hold up."

"What's going on?"

"Homicide," Iris said. Where Russo was slight, Iris was stout, and the woman stood taller as well. She had been a uniformed cop in San Francisco.

"Seriously? Who? How?"

"Remember that guy we were supposed to keep an eye out for? Jacob Collier? He's the DB."

"DB," Russo said. "Dead body."

"That's right. Shot right in the chest."

"Detective Adkins said he wanted me here."

"Yeah. He said he thinks you're a people person. Whatever the hell that means."

"I'd better go in."

Russo went to the open front door and saw it was broken. She reached to her duty belt and extracted a pair of latex gloves. She put them on before proceeding into the house. In the middle of the front room, Jacob Collier lay dead, his body awkwardly splayed, one elbow cocked in a position that would have caused pain if he'd been able to feel pain at all. She felt ill.

Adkins stood with his back to her. He turned when Russo cleared her throat. "Oh, great," he said. "Russo. Just who I wanted to see."

Adkins was the Carmel Police Department's only detective. He was an older man, close to retirement age, his face pleasantly like that of a grandfather. Other people were at work in the house, crime-scene investigators from the county. They had tripods set up but were no longer taking pictures. One took note of spatters of blood on a wall. Another was busy putting plastic bags over the dead man's hands.

"What can I do?"

"There are some U.S. marshals coming. As soon as they show up, this is going to turn into a circus. The chief put them off as long as he could. I still haven't had an opportunity to interview the shooter and the witnesses in detail. I want to put you beside one of them and see if you can get her talking. The shooter."

"About the homicide?"

"About whatever. I got nothing from her. We don't have a lot of time. The things people say before they end up at the station can mean a lot. You know that, right?"

"Yes, sir."

"She's in the kitchen. Camaro Espinoza is her name. Sit down, introduce yourself, and see what you can come up with."

"I'll do whatever I can."

"She's through there. Good luck."

Russo found her heart beating rapidly. She passed down a short jog of a hallway into a well-appointed kitchen. Bobby Hill, another Carmel police officer, stood near the stove, watching a woman at a table by the window. The woman's back was to her, hair falling free to her shoulders. She wore a denim-blue Henley, and Russo saw she had no shoes on.

"Carly," Hill said.

"Hey, Bobby. Here to help out."

"She's all yours."

Hill left the kitchen, and Russo was alone with the woman. She waited a moment to see if Camaro would do anything. She didn't. Russo went to the table. She cleared her throat. "Hello. I'm Officer Russo. I'm with the Carmel Police Department."

Camaro looked at her briefly, then returned to staring out the window. Russo found the quick, cold assessment daunting. Up close she saw Camaro was an attractive woman with a strong nose and even features. She wore no makeup, but she was not diminished by that.

"May I sit down?" Russo asked.

"Sure."

Russo took a seat at the end of the table and sat turned toward Camaro. "They want me to talk to you."

"About what?"

"About the man you shot."

Camaro looked away from the window and put her full attention on Russo. "You ever shot anybody?"

"Me? No way. This is Carmel-by-the-Sea. This kind of thing doesn't happen here."

"That explains why your detective doesn't know what he's doing."

"He's not so bad."

"If you say so."

Camaro started to turn away from her again, and Russo spoke quickly. "I pulled my weapon at a traffic stop once. The guy behind the wheel reached between the seats, and I was sure I'd have to shoot him. He was just going for his insurance papers. It could have been bad."

"It is bad."

"Why did you kill him? That man, Jacob Collier?"

"He brought it on himself. He threatened my sister with a knife. I had no choice."

"If that's the case, then there's no reason not to talk about it. Self-defense makes sense. You didn't try to kill him on purpose…did you?"

Camaro regarded her a moment, and the merest smile passed over her lips. "You know it was me who busted him up yesterday."

"Yeah," Russo said. "You really worked him over."

"Like I said, he brought it on himself. If he was able to keep his hands off my sister, he wouldn't have been in that situation. Now he's dead. For what? She was never going to go back to him. That was over. But some men—they can't figure out when no means no."

"He's not a little guy. How did you…how did you beat him down like that?"

"I've had some experience," Camaro said, and then she did look away. Russo felt her closing up.

"You have stitches," Russo said. She touched her own brow.

"It's nothing."

"You get in fights a lot?"

"Not when I don't want to."

"Were you a cop? No, not a cop. Military? Something like that?"

"I've said everything I'm going to say," Camaro told her. "You can find out all about me when you put me in the system. I'm not going anywhere."

"I can help you," Russo said.

"I don't need any help. Go tell the detective what you got out of me."

CHAPTER TWENTY

WAY APPROACHED THE house with Hannon hurrying in his wake. He proceeded up the walk with his identification out, then burst into the front room, where two men were putting the body in a rubberized canvas bag. A man in plain clothes watched them. A shield hung from the breast pocket of his jacket. He looked up when Way came in. "Whoa. Crime scene here, sir."

"I know," Way said. He thrust his badge and ID at the man. "I've been trying to get here for two hours while your people gave me the runaround. What the hell is this, some kind of game to you? Smallville politicking?"

"I don't know what they said," the detective told him, "but we're just following the procedure. This isn't the sort of thing we're used to dealing with."

"Well, first things first: cut the bullshit. I'm Deputy U.S. Marshal Way, and this is Deputy Hannon. We are your first, last, and everything when it comes to the Collier brothers. Everything you learn, everything you say, everything you do will pass through one of us. I have a double murderer on the loose, and now his brother's dead on someone's carpet. I need answers, and I need them right now."

"I understand, but there are ways to ask, Marshal. Maybe they do things differently where you come from, but around here we still say *please* and *thank you*."

Way said nothing at first. When he spoke, his voice was careful. "I'd like to know everything you do about what's going on here, *please,* sir. *Thank you.*"

"I appreciate that. We'll be as cooperative as we can. I'm Detective Eric Adkins, Carmel Police Department. This is Officer Iris Cooper, and I have Officers Hill and Russo watching the witnesses."

"These are the sisters? The Amado sisters?"

"Well, there's Michelle Amado, but the other one is named Espinoza. Camaro Espinoza."

"Do we have full workups on them yet?"

"No, but—"

"See that it's done. Give everything you have to Deputy Hannon. Tell whoever you have to tell that I want the autopsy of Jacob Collier expedited and the results in my e-mail by tomorrow morning. Wake up everybody. We are on the lookout for Lukas Collier. I know you have his name and face spread around, but now you really need to be on your toes, because as soon as he hears what's happened to his brother, all bets are going to be off."

Hannon stepped forward. "Have you taken statements from the witnesses?"

"Nothing official. We're just trying to get them talking," Adkins said. "One sister is in shock, and the other sister shut down like a robot as soon as I started asking questions. I asked Officer Russo to take a run at her to see what she could figure out."

"Who did the shooting? Amado or Espinoza?" Way asked.

"Espinoza."

Way turned to Hannon and shut Adkins out completely. The men from the Coroner Unit were carrying out Jacob Collier's corpse. "Okay, obviously the situation on the ground is a joke, which we figured. Our first priority is getting everything we can squeeze out of these women, so I want you to talk to Michelle Amado and drive her until she's given us something we can use or she breaks. I'm happy either way."

"What about the other one?"

"I'll handle the other one. If I feel like she's not responding to me we'll see about switching out, but I want to put myself in front of the woman who pulled the trigger. This did not happen by accident. First a severe beating, then a bullet. This was cold stuff. Premeditated."

Hannon nodded. "I've got it."

"Good. Let's move."

Way pointed at Adkins. "Who's where?"

"The Espinoza woman's in the kitchen. The Amado sister and her daughter are back there."

"Show my colleague where to go. I'll be in the kitchen, but don't come to me unless you have something good to tell me."

"Yes, sir."

Way went to the kitchen. He made a note of the hanging pots and the immaculately clean cooking area. The counters gleamed. Everything was in place. Hardwood flooring clicked under his heels. The sound caught the attention of the cop at the table. Russo.

"Deputy U.S. Marshal Way," he told her. "Are you finished questioning the subject?"

"I wasn't . . . Yes. I'm all done."

"Wait out there with your detective. I'll call you if I need you."

Russo nodded and left swiftly.

Camaro Espinoza sat perfectly still. He could barely tell she was breathing.

"I'm Keith Way, with the United States Marshals Service," Way announced.

"I heard."

He approached the table and stood over her. "I am here pursuant to a federal fugitive warrant, and I want some answers."

"Send Russo back in," Espinoza said.

"You're all done dealing with the locals for now. This is between you and federal law enforcement. Now, I'd like to know exactly what went down here tonight, and I want you to tell me in detail. Nothing gets left out."

"Did you see the body?"

"I did."

"Then that's all the detail you get."

Way grabbed the back of the Espinoza woman's chair and kicked it around to face him. He leaned in closely. "Let's cut the shit. You tell me what I want to know right now, or I will be the worst thing that happens to you all week."

Espinoza studied his face. Way saw only composure in hers.

"Gosh. Why didn't you say so?" she asked.

He stepped back but didn't sit down. "The woman who owns this house is your sister?"

"That's right."

"Her name's Amado. Yours is Espinoza. Which one of you is married?"

"Neither. We're half sisters."

"Where do you come from? Carmel? Salinas?"

"No."

"My understanding is yesterday you beat the living shit out of Jacob Collier and put him in the hospital. Today he's dead from a bullet you put in him."

"Jake Collier was an asshole. Someone was going to kill him sooner or later."

"You got to be the lucky one."

"I guess so."

"Where'd you get the gun?"

"It belongs to my sister."

"You know your way around guns?"

Espinoza shrugged.

"I'm going to find out everything about you," Way said. "I'll know your shoe size."

Espinoza looked at him and was quiet. Then she said, "I'm a seven."

Way barked a laugh. "You don't even know how much trouble you're in."

"How much trouble am I in?"

"You just killed my best chance at stopping a cop killer. You do the math."

CHAPTER TWENTY-ONE

LUKAS DROVE A dark green Honda Accord he'd stolen from a parking lot in Las Vegas. The ignition was wired together, the steering column stripped, but he kept to the speed limit on the whole eight-hour drive to Salinas, passing through sleepy Bakersfield along the way. He considered stealing another car there.

The skies were dark and portentous as he made the last few miles to Jake's Pearl Street address. The signs of rain were everywhere, and when Lukas cracked the window to let cigarette smoke out, he smelled water in the air.

He parked two blocks away from Jake's house, the car partially backed into an alleyway, providing him a quick start in almost every direction. A gusty wind picked at him as he walked the rest of the way. He stopped at the corner by a telephone pole riddled with staples and scraps of wet paper. He looked down the street.

The police cruiser made no attempt to conceal itself. It was parked directly in front of Jake's house. Lukas saw the officer behind the wheel. It was impossible to know if he'd been spotted. He walked forward instead of back, crossing the street as if he belonged there, then stopped as soon as the house on the corner obscured him from view.

Lukas stepped up to the corner again and peered around to get a second look at the car. It had not moved, nor had the cop inside. Lukas pulled back.

There was no sign of Jake's truck. Jake was gone, and Lukas's calls went directly to voice mail.

Instead of crossing the street a second time, Lukas looped around to the next block and crossed there, coming back to his car the long way around. He got behind the wheel and thought. After a long while he called up a memory of the place Jake said he worked during the off-season. He remembered it was a lumberyard, but the specifics escaped him. With the phone he searched for lumberyards in the area and came up with three. One caught his eye. He dialed its number.

"Carlson Lumber, this is Spencer speaking, how can I help you today?"

"Yeah," Lukas said, "I was trying to get ahold of Jake Collier."

"Jake?" the man said. There was something in his voice.

"Yeah, that's right. Doesn't he work there?"

"Sure. Jake's been here for years. Listen, can I put you on hold? I think somebody else can help you better."

"What's going on?"

"Just hang on."

The line went quiet. Lukas thought the man had hung up, but the timer on the call continued to count. He waited until finally someone new picked up. The voice was younger, but his tone was somber. "You're calling about Jake?"

"Yeah, who is this?"

"My name's Derrick. I work with Jake. Who's calling?"

Lukas considered his answer. There was no reason the cops would be listening here. "I'm his brother."

"You're Lukas?"

"That's right. Where's Jake?"

"He's not here."

"So where can I find him?"

"I don't know how else to tell you except to tell you, but...Jake's dead."

Lukas was suddenly breathless. He sucked air. "How?"

"He got shot last night," Derrick said. "It's crazy, man."

Lukas licked his lips. "Who?"

"Do you know Michelle?"

"Michelle? His girlfriend? His girlfriend shot him?"

"No, no, no. I heard about it from some guys I know in Carmel. He broke into his girlfriend's place and started swinging a knife around. The next thing you know, Chelle's sister shoots him right in the chest. Kills him. Just like that."

Lukas felt a twinge of pain in his skull. He rubbed his temple with his thumb. Thoughts of his last conversation with Jake swirled around and emptied into his forebrain. Michelle. Rebecca. "Camaro," he said.

"You know her?"

"Jake told me about her. He said she came out to where he worked and laid a hurt on him. Messed up his arm. Messed up his face."

"I've never seen anything like it," Derrick agreed. "She was all over him in a second. Me and the boys, we were going to get involved, but Jake told us to back off so he could handle it. But she wrecked him, man. She totally wrecked him. Now she killed him. Jake should have let us deal with the situation."

Lukas nodded stiffly. The pain in his head increased. He had to pry his teeth apart to speak. "Where is the chick staying? Does she have a hotel or something? What can you tell me?"

"I don't know anything about that. I'm sorry. But I know where Chelle lives. I can give you her address in Carmel."

"Give it to me."

Derrick obeyed. "You probably don't want to go over there, man. The cops are going to be worked up for a while. Nobody gets shot in Carmel. This is like DEFCON One stuff. Like the president got killed."

"You've been a big help," Lukas said.

"Whatever I can do. Me or any of the guys...you need something, all you have to do is ask. I'd be proud to carry his casket at the funeral."

Lukas almost laughed. "What's a number I can use if I need to get in touch with you again?"

"Yeah, let me give it to you."

Lukas wrote the number on the back of a gas station receipt and crushed it into his pocket. It was easier to breathe now, but only just. He wanted to smash the phone into pieces against the steering wheel to have something to break. He kept his voice even. "I'm going to look into this, and then I'll get back to you. And listen, don't mention you talked to me. Not to anybody. I have some trouble I'm dealing with, and I don't need the cops breathing down my neck, you understand me?"

"Yeah, I understand. No one will hear anything from me."

"Good job. I'll talk to you soon."

"Okay. I want to say sorry about—"

Lukas hung up the phone and dropped it on the passenger seat. He started the car by twisting two wires together and drove away.

CHAPTER TWENTY-TWO

ANNABEL WOKE FROM a dark dream that began to fade the moment she opened her eyes. She felt heavy-limbed and tired, but it was eight-thirty in the morning and it was time to move. On the bed beside her, Rebecca slept with a stuffed hippopotamus clutched to her chest.

She paused a moment to brush Rebecca's hair from her face, then slipped out of bed and into the adjoining bathroom. With the door only half closed, she ran the shower and scrubbed herself thoroughly. She toweled off and blow-dried her hair, and when she looked out again Rebecca was still sleeping.

The house was still. She walked silently down the hallway and emerged into the living room. Before this moment it might have been possible to forget. Now it came to her like a hammer blow. The bloody stain marking the floor was still there. Spatters of red flecked the curtains and the wall.

Annabel stood rooted to the spot. She saw bright spots and realized she was hyperventilating. She slowed her breathing. Careful to skirt the empty space where Jake's body had lain, she went to the kitchen.

"Good morning," Camaro said.

Annabel jumped at the sound of Camaro's voice. Her sister was at the kitchen table, outlined by the light falling through the window. It didn't look like she had changed. It didn't look like she had moved at all.

"You scared the hell out of me," Annabel told her.

"Sorry."

She switched on the lights, and the kitchen became a friendly place again. "Do you want coffee or tea? I was thinking coffee."

"Coffee's fine."

"You want French roast? Hazelnut? Hawaiian blend?"

"Coffee."

She selected a K-Cup marked EIGHT O'CLOCK COFFEE and put it in the machine. She used a pitcher to fill the reservoir and started the process. "It's just a minute," she said. "The water has to heat up."

"That's fine."

Camaro sat with her hands folded in front of her, as quiet as the house itself. Annabel approached her slowly. When she pulled out the chair, it scuffed slightly, the sound incredibly loud in the hush. Only the buzzing of the machine as it warmed the water cut the silence. She sat down. "Did you sleep?"

"For a while."

"Are you okay?"

"I'm fine."

"They talked to me, and I said everything you told me to say. They never pushed me. You were right."

"Cops like easy answers," Camaro said.

"So what happens now?"

"Now we wait to see if they charge me for killing Jake."

"What will you do if they...if you have to go to court?"

Camaro glanced at her. "I'll go."

"They'll ask you questions under oath. Me, too. It's against the law to lie."

"Do you think Jake would give a shit about something like that?" Camaro asked. "They can ask all the questions they want. Never change your story. If you change your story, then they have you. I can't leave here worrying about whether you can handle it."

"I can handle it."

Camaro looked more closely at her. She put out a hand to cover Annabel's. She squeezed it. "I know you can. *You* have to know you can."

Annabel let Camaro hold her hand. She didn't want to pull away. "I have to get Becca's things together for school. Then I have to drop her off and go to work. You can come with me if you want."

"I think I'll stay here for now."

They had coffee together, and then Annabel went to Rebecca to wake her up. She laid out her daughter's clothes, and while Rebecca dressed,

Annabel cooked a warm breakfast for all of them. Rebecca colored at the table between taking bites of oatmeal, drinking orange juice, and talking to Camaro. The scene was so basic and ordinary that Annabel was almost able to forget the night before.

In the end, Annabel dressed for work and left the house with Rebecca in tow. They went up the walk toward the parked Subaru. She noticed the police cruiser only when the woman officer got out of her car and approached them.

"Good morning," the officer said.

The woman was young and slight and unthreatening, and she smiled easily. Annabel put herself between Rebecca and the policewoman anyway. She glanced back toward the house, hopeful Camaro might emerge, but Camaro was somewhere inside and out of sight. She breathed deeply. "What can I do for you, Officer?"

"I've been assigned to watch over you for a couple of days. I'll take the mornings, and Officer Hill will take the afternoons. It's for your safety."

"Safety? I don't understand. We're not being threatened."

The young officer came close. "Why don't you go ahead and put your daughter in the car, then I'll explain."

Annabel's hands shook as she buckled Rebecca into the booster seat in the back of the SUV. She kissed Rebecca lightly on the forehead and said, "I'll be right back," before closing the door.

The policewoman was waiting. "I'm sorry," she said. "I don't want to scare you. You seem like a real nice lady, and your daughter's nice, too."

"Tell me what's going on, Officer...?"

"Russo."

"Officer Russo. Is there something else to worry about?"

"Did anyone talk to you last night about someone named Lukas Collier?"

"Lukas? That's Jake's brother, right?"

"Yes."

"The lady with the marshals mentioned his name. She wanted to know if Lukas had called Jake lately, or if Jake ever mentioned his name."

Russo took this in. "There's a chance—just a chance—that Lukas

Collier might be in the area. We have the police in Salinas and Pacific Grove and the County Sheriff's Department looking into it. The U.S. Marshals have a warrant for Lukas's arrest. And they're worried, you know, that he might do something when he finds out his brother was killed."

Annabel closed her arms around herself. "Do something? Like come after us?"

"Probably nothing," Russo said. "I mean, this is *Carmel*. And there are way too many cops looking for him if he tries something stupid. But to be on the safe side, we're going to do like I said and make sure everything is okay. All right?"

"All right. So do you follow me, or how does this work?"

"I'll follow you. It's time for your daughter's school? She goes to Carmel River?"

"Yes."

"I'll tail you there."

They parted. Annabel walked toward the driver's side and then stopped with her keys in her hand. "Excuse me, Officer Russo?"

"Yes?"

"What about my sister? Who watches my sister?"

Russo looked at the house. "They didn't tell me, but I think your sister can probably look out for herself, don't you think?"

Annabel was slow to nod. "Okay. But don't forget about her."

"Nobody will. Let's hurry. You don't want to be late for school."

CHAPTER TWENTY-THREE

YATES WATCHED THE home of Michelle Amado for hours without seeing any evidence of Jacob or Lukas Collier. With his energy dwindling, he drove away to a small Italian restaurant, where he fortified himself with a porterhouse steak with sautéed spinach the server assured him was organic, plus potatoes and cannellini beans. It was all very expensive, but everywhere in Carmel seemed expensive, and the restaurant was the closest to a family-style place as he'd been able to find on short notice.

When he returned to Michelle Amado's home, the street was alive with flashing police lights, and over the next couple of hours more and more police arrived. He stayed as far back from the end of the cul-de-sac as he could without moving out of sight and watched the cops do their work. They brought out a body in a bag, and his heart leaped, but somehow he knew it was not Lukas Collier. A locksmith came for a while but left by midnight.

Eventually all but one police vehicle left the scene, and the one that remained showed no inclination to depart. Yates saw a young woman behind the wheel, reading something with the small overhead light on. It rained off and on.

He was still in place when he saw a mother and child go to their vehicle. The cop conferred with the mother for a few moments, and then all of them drove away. Yates waited ten minutes to see if the policewoman would return, but the street stayed empty. He got out of the rented SUV.

The gate to the front walk was slightly ajar. Yates cast a look around to see if there was movement in any of the other three houses near this one, but he'd watched all of those people leave in the early morning hours, off to jobs that didn't include all-night vigils and police. Yates was alone. Almost.

At the front door he depressed the lighted button for the doorbell. He examined the door and saw it had been kicked hard. When the door came open, he saw where the frame had been refreshed with new, unpainted wood. And then he saw the woman.

She looked at him frankly, standing in her sock feet just inside. Her body was relaxed, but Yates saw the coiled spring under the surface. He found himself automatically checking her hands for weapons. She had none.

"Who are you?" she asked.

"Ma'am, my name is Jeremy Yates. Are you Michelle Amado?"

"No," the woman said, and offered nothing else.

"May I ask your name, then?"

"You're not a cop," she said.

"No, ma'am." He produced a badge wallet and showed it to her. "I'm a bail fugitive recovery agent."

"What's that?"

"We pick up people who fail to appear in court."

"A bounty hunter."

Yates winced. "That's one way to put it."

The woman's eyes narrowed. "My name's Camaro."

Yates thought of the police report. "Camaro. Michelle Amado's sister?"

"That's right. What do you want?"

"I wondered if I might have a few minutes of your time."

He saw the decision ticking over behind her eyes until finally she stepped back to let him in. Yates closed the door behind him. His gaze strayed to the middle of the living room floor and the broad patch of crimson that indicated a dead body.

"My sister just left. How did you know there was anyone here?"

"I took a shot in the dark," Yates said. "May I sit?"

Camaro motioned toward the couch. She took a chair near the cold fireplace and watched him while he sat down. He was a tall man, and his legs were too long to fit behind the coffee table. He nudged it slightly out of place, at the same time noticing where something heavy had struck the far edge with enough force to crush a mark in the wood. A picture of what happened in this room began to form.

"Someone got themselves killed here last night," Yates said.

"Yes."

"Would that someone be Jacob Collier?"

Camaro didn't answer right away. He saw the calculation again. "Yes."

"Unfortunate, especially given that you put him in the hospital in pieces not too long before."

"You know a lot. Where are you from?"

"Norfolk, Virginia. It's not really Jacob I'm after but his brother, Lukas. He skipped bail and disappeared on his way out west to see Jacob. Along the way he killed my son."

A deep silence descended between them. He kept his face studiously neutral. "I'm sorry," Camaro said at last. "But if you're looking for him, I don't know where he is."

Yates tweaked the corner of his mustache and nodded slowly. He selected his words carefully. "Ma'am, it's my belief that Lukas Collier isn't far away from here. He might even be in town. And it's also my belief that as soon as he finds out what happened here, he's going to be very interested in talking to the person who killed his brother. The question is, who that might be. Now, it could have been your sister, but I had a look at her not twenty minutes ago, and she doesn't look the type."

"But I do."

"Yes, ma'am. You do. Where'd you serve?"

"Overseas, mostly. Iraq. Afghanistan."

"Army?"

"Yes."

"I was in the Marine Corps myself. Vietnam. A little bit before your time, I'd guess."

Camaro acknowledged this with a nod. "So I killed Jake. Lukas will want me."

"That's right. And I expect the police are thinking along the same lines, because they had a car out there all night and an officer trailing your sister when she left this morning. Though I notice they left you here all by your lonesome."

"If you want Lukas, you're going to have to get in line. There were a couple of U.S. marshals here last night. They were pretty hot to find out all about Lukas."

"I suspect that would be Deputy U.S. Marshal Keith Way."

"You know him?"

"I've had occasion to speak with him on the phone. He was on the scene where my son died. He told the both of us to step back and let the Marshals Service handle bringing in Lukas. I've never been one to sit on my hands. My son, Stanley, wasn't either."

"I don't really know how I can help you," Camaro said.

"The marshals want to bring Lukas in because he killed one of their own. I don't know the whole story, but you have to know that killing a cop anywhere in the world is a real bad idea. Lukas, though, he's meaner than hell, and he doesn't give a good goddamn about what anybody else wants or does so long as he gets the thing he's after. And as of last night, the thing he'll want most in this world is to kill you."

"He can try," Camaro said.

"He can. And he has the background for it. He served some time in the Corps, did some shooting in Iraq. Maybe he's not what I'd call an expert killer, but he would have been trained well enough. He's not the kind you'd want to turn your back on. I'd like to find him."

"You and everybody else in this town."

"I'd also like to float a little offer your way. You give me the high sign before you tell the marshals or the local cops or anyone else, and I will resolve your Lukas problem."

"You want to be the one to kill him."

"Yes, ma'am."

She looked at him directly. "Don't call me ma'am. Call me Camaro."

CHAPTER TWENTY-FOUR

AFTER YATES LEFT, Camaro went in the bathroom and lifted up her shirt to look at her back. There was a livid bruise where she'd crashed into the coffee table, spreading under the skin like a purple oil slick.

She lingered in the front room for a while, staring out the window, before heading out the front door to walk the streets of Annabel's neighborhood. She felt the day stretching out emptily before her, wanting to be filled.

Her impression of the town on foot was much the same as it had been from the comfort of a car. Carmel was very quiet, with every block seeming isolated from the next thanks to wooded lots and houses like perfect little cameos.

She sensed the police cruiser coming up behind her before she heard the engine. When the car pulled even with her, the passenger-side window went down, and Officer Russo peered out from behind the wheel. "Good morning, Ms. Espinoza."

"Good morning."

"Seeing the sights?"

Camaro stopped and the cruiser idled beside her. "Something like that."

"Why don't you get in and I'll give you a tour?"

Camaro thought and looked both ways down the street. No one appeared. She let herself into the car. They sat with a mounted shotgun and a new-looking computer terminal between them. Russo had the heater going.

After Camaro buckled up, Russo rolled. They kept a slow pace. Russo scanned the street. "Where are you from?"

"Florida."

"Oh, yeah? Where?"

"Miami."

"Nice. I'd like to go there."

"I'm guessing you already knew where I come from," Camaro said.

"What makes you say that?"

"Because as soon as your people finished talking with me last night, they put me in the system."

Russo smiled. She had a pretty and delicate appearance belied by the policewoman's gear she wore. "My bosses wanted to know all about you."

"What do they know now?"

"Nothing major. Name, address, outstanding charges."

"I have outstanding charges?"

"Not any they mentioned. But I was sitting in front of your sister's place most of the night. I get stuff through the computer. Lots of interesting reading about you."

They turned a corner. An old woman waved from the sidewalk, and Russo waved back.

Camaro watched Russo drive. The young woman was careful behind the wheel, almost formal. "How long have you been a cop?"

"Three years."

"That's not a long time."

"No, not really. And it's not like anything happens here, anyway. Not like in Afghanistan. You're amazing."

"I'm not."

"I saw your record. You got medals and the whole thing. How many women ever got the Silver Star?"

"Not a lot."

"No kidding. You have to tell me your story."

"I'd rather not."

Russo looked disappointed. "Is it because I'm a cop?"

"It's because I don't talk about it," Camaro said. "With anyone."

"Okay," Russo said, though it clearly wasn't.

"You can tell me something," Camaro said.

"What?"

"How tight were Jake Collier and his brother?"

"So you know about Lukas."

"I heard he killed a cop. And I heard he might be headed this way."

"Who told you all of that?"

"Am I wrong?" Camaro asked.

"No. We're keeping watch over your sister and her daughter until we know more."

"How about me?"

"I guess they figure you can take care of yourself."

"Or they're hoping Lukas pokes his head out and tries to kill me for shooting Jake."

Russo shook her head. "Nobody's expendable."

"Someone's always expendable."

Russo drove on. Camaro looked in the side mirror at the road behind them. She saw a green car make the turn with them. It had made the last turn with them, too. "How much do you know about Lukas Collier?"

"We have a picture and a sheet, and that's it. Some trouble in Los Angeles, but that might as well be on the other side of the world when it comes to Carmel. We don't really do city things here."

"I noticed."

"It's nice, though. We don't get any real trouble here. Not like in Salinas. In Salinas they have gangs."

"Comes with the territory," Camaro said.

"I'm not saying we can't handle things," Russo added quickly.

"Tell me about Jake. What was his story? Was he the kind to do what he did last night?"

"Him? I don't think so. There's nothing in his jacket that would make me think he'd ever break into someone's house with a knife. He was always one of those surfer dudes who's out in the water when he's not getting drunk and disorderly. Seems like every month in the summer we're arresting one of those guys for something."

"My sister knows how to pick 'em," Camaro said.

"She's not the only one. I've seen Jake and his crew with all kinds of girls. In the summertime it's the worst, because they're always taking up with tourists and getting them to give up all their money to buy beer and surf wax. I heard one time this lady up from LA bought Jake a brand-new convertible. For *cash*. Some guys have the gift."

They were away from the residential neighborhoods and in the shopping district of Carmel. One tiny boutique after another slipped past Camaro's window. They passed a simple white church with a red sign that declared it THE CHURCH OF THE WAYFARER. The green car was still with them.

"What do you think?" Russo asked her.

"It's a pretty town," Camaro replied.

"But boring."

"Maybe a little."

"Maybe a lot."

"Okay, maybe a lot," Camaro said, letting the slightest smile show.

"My name's Carly," Russo said. "You can call me that if you want."

"Okay."

"But you won't, will you?"

"I don't get personal with people who want to arrest me."

"I'm not here for any of that. We're keeping an eye on things for a while. This is just the two of us talking."

Camaro nodded and looked out the window. She knew when she glanced in the mirror again, the green car would be there.

"Of course," Russo said, "if it's too formal in the car, we can talk somewhere else. You like coffee?"

"Sure."

"Still want the rest of the tour?"

"I've seen enough, but I'll take the coffee. Are you buying?"

"I think this counts as official business," Russo said, and smiled. She touched the accelerator, and the cruiser picked up speed. "Yes, ma'am. A cup of coffee coming right up."

Camaro let her drive and paid no attention to where they were. She watched only the green car as it trailed them turn by turn.

CHAPTER TWENTY-FIVE

WAY AND HANNON commandeered a meeting room at the Carmel Police Department for their use. It had an eight-foot-long table, a speakerphone, and chairs for seven. At one end were a whiteboard and a screen in the ceiling that could be lowered at the touch of a button. At the other end, a small coffee station was assembled.

Way spread out his things as he wanted and linked into the department's Wi-Fi connection. He used the locals' printer to spit out color ink-jet pages, many of which were posted and piled around his workstation. He had photographs and printouts from the previous night's crime scene, and he reviewed the Coroner Unit's report.

It had been another twelve hours without sleep. Way drank an entire pot of coffee and directed Hannon to brew more. He knew she was waiting for an opportunity to say something about rest, but he kept her busy enough that there was no time. For now, she was deep into the records of three towns in Monterey County, digging up known associates and piecing together the life Jacob Collier had.

She was out of the room now. The machine burbled, and Way's eyelids fluttered. "No, it's okay," he said out loud. "I just need some more coffee."

He put his head down and the words echoed around his mind. *More coffee... more coffee.* He was vaguely aware of slipping into sleep and tried to raise his head, but it was too late. He slept despite himself, and the memory came with it.

"More coffee," Way said.

"The thermos is empty, man," Jerry told him.

"What?" Way said. "That's a two-liter container."

It was a chilly autumn night in Newark, the city settling down into midnight in fits and starts. It would never truly sleep, but it might doze awhile, half awake and ready to pounce on the unwary. Between twelve and three a.m. there would be a handful of shootings, a goodly number of stabbings, and at least one death. Maybe it would be murder or maybe it would be misadventure, but that person would still be dead. A citizen had a one-in-eighty-five chance of being a victim of a violent crime in Newark. It was a wonder the place did not disintegrate into open anarchy in the streets.

Way was bundled up against the gathering cold. The winter promised to be a savage one, and already the temperatures regularly dropped below freezing at night. They were talking snow, and it was only November.

Beside him, Jerry Washington was dressed in a puffy Jets jacket and a black watch cap. His face was dark, his cheeks scrubbed with the beginnings of a winter beard. When he smiled, he flashed sharp teeth. He shook the empty thermos vigorously, but it was silent. "Drained it dry. You're gonna be pissing all night."

"I've got an iron bladder," Way told him.

"That's you. Iron Man."

"What's it like being Iron Man's sidekick?" Way asked.

"What sidekick? I'm Batman, dude. Everybody's Batman's sidekick."

They laughed in the car, their breath visible.

Way looked out the window. They were in the Central Ward, on a street full of potholes and heavily tagged by the locals. A corner store had a painted sign that said HAPPY LIQUOR. Its windows were gridded over with metal, the front door equipped with a steel shutter that was already pulled down a little in preparation for the end of the night. Shadows moved around inside, visible through the advertisements that papered the glass. After a while a young couple came out with a grocery sack and crossed behind the car, huddled close against the cold.

The building they wanted was a hundred feet away, made of dark brick with white lintels. A single yellow bulb burned above the street-level door, and those windows that weren't boarded over were half lit and half not. The address was spray-painted on the bricks in bright yellow.

Headlights appeared down the block, and Jerry nudged him. "Hey," he said, "that look like a Caprice to you?"

"How can I tell from just the lights?"

"That's a Caprice," Jerry said.

The car approached slowly through splashes of streetlights until it was near enough to see clearly. It was a Chevy Caprice, burgundy, from the mid-'00s. The pulse quickened in Way's temples. "It's the one."

"You want to call it in?"

"Let's see how it goes."

The Caprice slowed until it came to a gentle stop in front of the old, broken building. A loud rattle broke Way's concentration, and he saw the owner of Happy Liquor closing the shutter on the entrance. The interior had gone black.

It was absolutely dark inside the Chevy, but there were some hints of movement. After a moment the dome light came on, and Way saw a black man behind the wheel, a white man in the passenger seat. The two of them leaned close to say something, then bumped fists. The white man got out. Lukas Collier.

Way waited until the Caprice started to pull away. He drew the Glock from inside his jacket and retracted the slide just enough to see the gleam of brass. He let it go. Beside him, Jerry drew his own weapon.

Lukas stayed on the street for only a few seconds. He pushed open the door into the building. As soon as it swung shut behind him, Way and Jerry were out of the car and moving. They crossed the street at a jog.

"We should call in the car," Jerry said.

"I'll do it," Way told him. "You go on ahead. I'll be right behind you."

Jerry touched him on the arm as he passed, and then he slipped inside.

Way pulled a phone from his pocket and dialed 911. When the operator answered, he was quick. "This is Deputy U.S. Marshal Keith Way. I'm serving a fugitive warrant in the Central Ward and have a vehicle and driver that need to be stopped."

"I'll take that information from you, sir," the operator said.

"It's a burgundy Chevrolet Caprice with New York plates. The driver is Marcus Murray. I'm going to give you the plate number now. Please notify Detective Frank Armisen of the stop."

The operator took the information. "Do you need backup at your location?"

"I think we're okay. I'll call if there's a change."

Gunshots sounded abruptly, popping off inside the building in rapid succession. Way fumbled with his phone and dropped it. The face shattered on the sidewalk. He grabbed for it, but the display was dead. He threw it down and went for the door as he heard the first shouts.

A baby was crying somewhere when he hit the lobby. A staircase climbed upward, the steps worn and wooden. "Jerry, call out!" Way yelled. "Jerry, call out!"

"Third floor!"

Way thundered up the steps with his weapon in his grip. He rounded the first landing and made the second floor before he heard another gunshot. People peeked out of their doors, but he did not have time or breath to warn them back inside. He kept climbing.

The crying baby was louder than ever when he reached the third floor. A light fixture hung loosely from the wall, the bulb and glass shade shattered. He passed a garbage chute with a hatch hanging from a single hinge. A man was shouting and Jerry was shouting and mixed into it was the desperate wail of a woman.

He charged down the hallway and found one door open. Way fell in beside the door and looked in. He saw a messy front room with a playpen and a television and a broken-down couch. Papers and magazines were everywhere, scattered among discarded mail and empty bottles of beer. A few fuzzy toys poked up through the mess.

"Jerry, where are you?" Way called.

"Right here!"

Way looked again, and he saw Jerry backing out of a hallway inside, his weapon up. Jerry didn't look in his direction as Way slipped into the apartment. He had opened his mouth to say something when Lukas Collier bellowed, "I will shoot this bitch right in the head!"

The woman was visible down the hallway in one of the bedrooms, partially obscured by the half-closed door. Lukas had her around the neck, the four-inch barrel of a heavy Smith & Wesson pressed to her temple. The woman was flushed and crying, and so was the baby she held.

"Jesus," Way said.

"I got this," Jerry said. He kept his weapon level.

"My phone is busted," Way told him. "There's no one coming."

"I got this," Jerry said again.

"You back the hell off or she's dead, you understand me?" Lukas said.

Way raised his Glock. "There's no way out, Lukas," he said. "Let the woman and her kid go. This doesn't have to go bad for anybody."

"Fuck you," Lukas spat. "You back out of the apartment. You close the door, and you stay in the hall."

"We're not going anywhere," Way said. He looked to the woman. "Ma'am, we're going to keep you safe."

"Don't talk to her, talk to me!"

"Lukas," Jerry said, "listen to me. There's nothing we can do for you if you hurt that woman or her baby. Or is it your baby?"

"It's not my goddamned baby."

"Okay, man, it's cool. But you have to let them go. You don't have to throw down your gun, but you have to let them out of there."

Lukas pushed the barrel of the gun harder against the woman's temple until she screamed again. The whites showed around both of his eyes. "No deal," he said.

"I got the shot," Way whispered to Jerry.

"Don't do it, dude," Jerry whispered back. "The hammer's cocked on that thing."

"He's gonna kill her no matter what."

"What the hell are you saying? Stop talking to each other!"

Jerry pointed his weapon at the ceiling and put his free hand up. "Lukas, it's cool. It's totally cool. I'm going to make you a deal, all right? It's a good deal."

"I don't want any deals. Get out of here!"

"You know I can't do that. But this is what I can do: I can come in there and you can hold me hostage."

Way blanked for a second, and then the words crashed down on him. "Jerry, what the hell?"

Jerry ignored him. "I'm gonna put my gun down now. And then I'm gonna come in the room. You let the lady and her kid go, and you take me instead."

Lukas's face purpled. The veins in his neck stood out. "If you are screwing with me..."

"No way. This is for real."

"Jerry, you are not going in there," Way said.

Jerry put his pistol on the floor. "It's handled, Keith," he said. "Get ready to get that woman out of here."

"Jerry..."

"Are you ready, Lukas?" Jerry asked.

Lukas hesitated. He gripped the woman tightly. The baby squalled, and its mother wept. "No tricks."

"No tricks. I'm coming in."

Way's feet felt leaden as Jerry stepped into the hallway. For a moment Lukas was obscured completely, but then Jerry was into the room and Way could see again. He was conscious of sweat on his face and on his palms. A rapid tremor passed through his body, and his teeth chattered. He stilled them.

"I'm here," Jerry said. "Let the lady go."

Lukas released his grip on the woman and shoved her forward. She stumbled and then rushed past Jerry into the hallway. Way caught a glimpse of Lukas surging toward Jerry before the bedroom door slammed shut.

Way yelled Jerry's name and rushed the door, kicking it open to see the two men. Lukas held his pistol to Jerry's skull. "Outside!" Lukas ordered. "Outside!"

"Keith, it's okay," Jerry said. "I've got this. Close the door and wait outside. We don't want anything to happen here."

"You've got nowhere to go," Way told Lukas. His gaze strayed past the man to an open window. Cold air spilled in through it.

"Keith, step away, man. It's all right."

Way aimed at Lukas's face. "Game's over, Lukas. It's time."

"You son of a bitch," Lukas said. He moved the gun from Jerry's head. Way pulled his trigger without thinking. Both men toppled backward. Jerry slid from Lukas's grasp with a wound in his head. Lukas's gun tumbled away, lost under a couch.

Way was frozen. He held his weapon but could not feel it. He was rooted. Jerry filled his vision.

Lukas clambered to his feet. "Nice shot, asshole."

Way tried to shift his aim. His arms would not obey. His mouth worked soundlessly. Lukas fled through the window. Way watched him go.

A long moment passed. Jerry was motionless on the floor.

Way moved. He ran back into the hall, retracing his steps until he found the broken-down garbage chute. The hatch still opened. He dropped his weapon in, thinking that later he could claim Lukas had taken it with him. He heard the gun descend, thudding and banging. Only then did he return to the apartment. He fell to the ground by Jerry's side. He touched the back of his head and felt nothing but pulp and bone fragments. Jerry's right cheekbone was shattered by the .40-caliber round.

Way took a deep breath. "Somebody help! Somebody help now! Call nine-one-one! Call nine-one-one!"

In the depths of the memory, he felt it. Something seized him by the shoulder and shook him. Way's head snapped up, and he was far from Newark, ensconced in the meeting room of the Carmel Police Department's headquarters.

Hannon shook him again. "Keith?" she asked. "Keith, are you all right?"

Way blinked rapidly. He had not felt asleep, but he did not feel awake either. "What?"

"Where'd you go? I said your name like five times."

"It's...it's nothing. I'm just tired."

Hannon put a fresh cup of coffee on the table by his laptop. "You need to sleep. Even fifteen minutes is better than nothing."

"When I get him," Way said.

"Keith, we don't even know if he's coming."

"When I get him," Way said firmly.

Hannon didn't answer. Way swallowed a mouthful of hot coffee and turned to his computer again.

CHAPTER TWENTY-SIX

LUKAS FOLLOWED THE police unit as it passed through Carmel, but when it made a U-turn at an intersection and slotted into a no-parking zone near a coffeehouse, he elected to drive on. In the last few moments of the tail he'd managed to get another good look at the woman he assumed was Camaro.

The police had closed their net over Carmel. Michelle Amado's house was under surveillance, or at least while she was home, and they had their hooks into the sister, too. But they couldn't cover everything all the time. They would go where they felt the links were weakest and leave the rest of the chain alone.

He brought out his phone and put it to his ear as he drove. It rang a few times before Derrick answered. "When do you get off work?" Lukas asked him.

"At four. What's up?"

"I want to get together with you and anybody else who saw this Camaro chick in action. Is there somewhere we can meet?"

"Where are you now?"

"What difference does it make? Can we meet or not?"

"Yeah, sure, sure. There's a place called Flickers on Lincoln Street in Carmel. We used to go there with Jake all the time."

Lukas kept driving. He checked his mirrors. He saw no police. "I don't need anywhere high-profile."

"This place is as low-profile as it gets, man."

"All right. Five o'clock. Don't let anyone follow you."

"Got it. I'll be there."

Lukas ended the call with a grunt. He made two lefts as soon as he was able and headed toward the sea. He spent the next few hours

105

watching the breakers roll in, sitting on the damp sand as the sun gleamed in the clear, cold sky. A few intrepid surfers were out on the waves, clad in black and blue wet suits, ignoring the chill of the water. It put Lukas in mind of years long past when he whiled away the days and weeks of summer in the company of his brother and his friends. They'd surf all day, then light a fire on the beach to make burgers. Jake always knew the best places to buy weed, and they would smoke it with the surfer girls and afterward get laid.

That was all over when Lukas caught a case and the judge told him jail or service. Lukas chose the Marines, and they took him away from beaches and surfing and put a gun in his hand. Later they put people in front of that gun, and he did what they trained him to do. Maybe it was reflex at that point. Maybe he liked it a little. When it was all over with, he couldn't imagine going back to the life he had before. Those were the years before he was born. He was himself now. But still he had the memories.

When it was close to five, Lukas reluctantly abandoned his place on the beach and made his way back to the car. He navigated his way to the bar and parked on the street.

The bar reeked of old cigarette butts and stale beer. It was barely lit, the better to hide the sticky floor, and it was already mostly full of patrons. This was a bar for locals and serious drinkers. The old man behind the bar mixed drinks with long-practiced mastery, ignoring the patrons violating California's strict indoor-smoking laws and hollering out orders as they came done.

Lukas had no idea who to look for, but when he saw the little brown-haired man in the work shirt approaching him, he knew it was Derrick.

The man offered him his hand. "Lukas?"

"Yeah."

"Glad to meet you. I just wish it wasn't like this. Come on over and meet the guys."

Derrick brought him back into the corner, where two other men sat in a cramped booth with barely enough room for two more, beer bottles in front of them. They looked at Lukas, and he looked at them. He knew at first glance they would be no good at all.

"This is Loren, and this crazy guy is Nic."

Lukas nodded to them.

"Let's sit down and have some beers. You want a beer, Lukas? I'm buying."

"I'll drink."

"Loren, why don't you run up and get four longnecks from Frank?"

"I'm still finishing this one."

"Loren," Derrick said warningly. "Come on."

The man named Loren got up from the booth and left his beer behind. Derrick scooted in, and Lukas took the side that would let him watch the front.

"Were you with Jake when this Camaro chick beat him up?" Lukas asked Nic.

"Yeah. Crazy, man. I've never seen anything like it. She knows kung fu or some shit."

"And he just let her beat his ass?"

"No, it wasn't like that," Derrick said. "He was fighting all the time. She sucker-punched him, and then he was trying real hard to get into her, but she was mean, man, real mean. Like I said, we would have helped him, but Jake said no."

"He said no," Lukas said.

"Yeah."

Loren returned with the beers. Lukas did not volunteer to move, so the other two were forced to scoot to make room for a fourth man. Lukas took a draw from his bottle and felt the refreshment go down. He sighed heavily. "What did he do? Did he try to screw her, or what?"

Derrick shook his head emphatically. "She was there because of her sister, Michelle. Chelle must have found out Jake had another girl on the side, and this was her way of kicking him to the curb. I mean, *really* kicking him. Jake said this sister has been away somewhere and the two of them never talk. But then she shows up like this?"

"Something was always up with Chelle," Loren said.

"How so?"

Derrick cut in. "Jake said she never actually came out and said it, but he was pretty sure Michelle was stashing money away somewhere. He came to her for loans a few times, and she helped him out. He figured there was more where that came from. That's when he started talking about you and LA and how we could get into some serious cash."

"He wasn't wrong about that. What's your interest?"

"Well...we thought maybe we'd be able to buy in. As partners, you know? He said you had the LA connections and it was just a matter of putting the money together. He had a real stash coming together. We were just waiting for you."

"But then his girl calls her sister."

"It's bullshit," Nic said. "Jake always treated Michelle like she was a princess. I mean, he had something going on the side, but that doesn't mean she wasn't his number one."

"Who's this other chick he's got?"

"Vicki," Derrick said. "She lives in Pacific Grove. She's a legal secretary or something. They met when Jake got done up for public urination about a year ago. She was working in the lawyer's office. They were pretty hot and heavy for a while, but it's true Chelle was always Jake's girl. He loved her. That's what makes it so nuts. Him dead."

"Where was Jake keeping his money?"

Derrick looked to the others. There were blank expressions. "I'm not real sure. Got to be at his place. I mean, you can't put that kind of money in a bank where the IRS can find it."

"So I need to get into his house."

"Yeah, it has to be somewhere. You know, under the mattress."

"I can't go near his place," Lukas said. "If I do, the cops are gonna be all over me. I need someone to take care of it for me."

No answers came. Lukas ground his back teeth.

"We were kind of hoping we'd be *silent* partners," Derrick said at last.

Lukas leaned in, and the others shrank back. "You want to make the kind of money we're talking about, there are no silent partners. Everybody puts in their share, everybody takes a risk. And if that means you have to bust into Jake's place to find his stash, then that's what you do. I need that seed money to put things together in LA. After that, the rest of you can pick up your end and start making back your investment."

"But what about the sister? You gonna kill her for what she did to Jake?" Loren asked.

"What if I do?"

"I'd want to help, that's all."

"How are you gonna help me?" Lukas asked. "You couldn't even help Jake when he was gettin' his ass beat by a girl."

"It doesn't make any difference, anyway," Derrick said. "The police are going to be all over this. She'll be untouchable."

Lukas took another drink. They watched him. He took his time speaking again. "Nobody's untouchable."

CHAPTER TWENTY-SEVEN

IT WAS EVENING, and the streetlights were on before Annabel's Subaru returned. She smiled when she saw Camaro. "You're still here."

"Where else would I be?"

"I had this idea that I would show up after work and you'd be gone. Maybe a note on the refrigerator, but that's it."

"I'm not going anywhere," Camaro said.

Annabel kissed her on the cheek. "Good. Are you hungry? I'll make dinner."

"Nothing fancy."

"Is chicken breast too fancy?"

"Chicken breast is fine."

Camaro felt a tug on her finger, and she looked down. Rebecca was there. "Will you play dollhouse with me, Camaro?"

Camaro knelt down. "Sure, I'll play dollhouse with you."

"Good. You can be the daddy and I'll be the mommy."

"Typecasting," Annabel said.

"Shut up."

Camaro sat down with Rebecca by the dollhouse, and the little cloth dolls were solemnly distributed. Rebecca then took Camaro on a room-by-room tour of the house itself. Careful attention was paid to decor, and Rebecca was careful to mention that Mommy and Daddy slept in separate rooms.

"Why is that?" Camaro asked.

"Because they fight too much."

Camaro frowned. "My Daddy doesn't want to fight with Mommy."

"Good, because if Daddy tries to hurt Mommy, he'll get shot."

Rebecca began to set a tiny dining room table with plastic plates and put the baby in its high chair. Camaro watched with her doll held loosely in her hands. She felt something she was not quick to identify, and she was slow to speak. "You know," she said quietly, "Jake wasn't your daddy."

The little girl didn't look at her. She loaded a plastic turkey into an oven. "I know. But he still got shot. Have Daddy come home from work."

Camaro obeyed, and they played out dinnertime. There was no fighting.

After forty-five minutes, Annabel called them to the kitchen. Camaro smelled olive oil and the enticing scent of frying. The table was already set, and each plate was presented with a fried chicken breast topped with diced tomatoes, parsley, feta cheese, and some sort of sauce. "I thought I said nothing fancy," Camaro said.

"It's not. It's just chicken fried in a falafel mix with tahini and a salad. You want beer or wine?"

"Beer."

They sat and ate. Each bite of the chicken was a burst of spice. Camaro tasted garlic and jalapeño. The salad was delicate and fresh, the tahini light. She thought of her own meals, taken alone at a plain table in her kitchen.

Rebecca excused herself at the end of the meal, and Camaro was left alone with Annabel. Annabel drank from a glass of Chardonnay. "I guess you know," she said.

"I heard."

Annabel put her hands over her eyes. "I've never even *met* Jake's brother."

"That doesn't matter. When he hears Jake was shot, he's going to go on the warpath. That puts me in danger, but it means trouble for you, too."

"So what do I do?"

Camaro regarded the empty bottle of beer beside her plate. She picked it up and rolled it between her hands before putting it down again. "You should think about getting out."

Annabel looked at her. "Out? Like *out* out?"

"You started over before. You can start over again."

"No. No way. I'm not going through all of that. I won't put Becca through it. This is our home. Everything we have is here. All my friends, my job, my house. I can't walk away."

Camaro took Annabel by the wrist, but gently. She spoke softly. "You may not have a choice."

Annabel shook herself free. "I won't go. I'm not going to go. Nobody's going to run me out of my life. I don't care who they are, I don't care what they do."

"This man, Lukas, he's not like Jake. He's bad. He's really bad. Jake came at you with a knife, but Lukas will come at you with a gun. He's trained. A vet. He killed a cop in New Jersey, and he killed a bounty hunter in Colorado. He may have killed more people than that."

"More people than you?"

Camaro fell silent.

"You've always told me to make the right decisions," Annabel said. Her voice quavered. "Ever since we were kids, you told me that. This is the decision I've made: we stand up for ourselves and we fight. Just like you said we should."

"That was before I knew about Lukas Collier."

"It doesn't make any difference. And if he tries anything, I'll kill him, too."

CHAPTER TWENTY-EIGHT

LUKAS WAITED IN the dark.

The apartment was neat and small, very much a woman's space, with soft colors and clean lines visible even among the shadows. It smelled nice, a scent of lavender hanging in the air. No one smoked in this place. The kitchen was tidy and organized, without so much as a single dirty plate in the sink.

He heard her footsteps outside before her keys in the lock. The door came open, and a little boy entered. He was no more than nine, with auburn hair. His mother was right behind him. Lukas waited until they were completely inside and the lights came on before he spoke. "Hello, Vicki."

The woman called Vicki froze with the door almost closed. She snatched at her son. Lukas saw the sudden flash of terror in her eyes, her body poised for flight, but she didn't scream. "Who are you?" she asked in a quiet voice. She had control.

"I'm Lukas. Close the door and lock it."

Vicki was short and redheaded. Her coat was open, and he caught a glimpse of swelling breasts contained by a pale red blouse. She set her purse and keys down on the dining table not far from the door. "What are you doing here?"

"Why don't you take off your coat?" Lukas said, and he smiled.

"If you're looking for money, I have about a thousand dollars hidden in the bedroom. It's all yours."

"That's good to know. Sit down. Take a load off. You must have had a long day."

She came to the couch with her hand on her son's shoulder. The boy had said not a word, nor had he made a single sound. Their coats were

113

wet from the spitting rain. Vicki gathered her son's and then took off her own. She laid them over the arm of the couch despite the damp. Outside the weather had come and gone in waves, and now it was turning drizzly all over again. It made a gentle sound. Vicki looked at him with careful eyes. Lukas wondered if her red hair was real. Judging from the boy's, he guessed so. Without the coat, Lukas was better able to see her curves, and he understood Jake's interest. She had a plain gold chain around her neck with a golden heart dangling from it just even with the top button of her blouse. Her fair skin looked soft and smooth. Lukas thought she was about thirty. The boy was as thin as a stick figure.

"Jake mentioned you were a fine woman," Lukas lied. "I've been looking forward to meeting you for a long time."

"H-how did you get in?"

"Through the front door."

"No, I mean..."

"Relax," Lukas said. "I'm not here to hurt anybody. It just so happens I need a place to stay, and Jake said if I was ever in town."

Vicki looked at the floor before she looked at him. "I guess that's okay. But Jake."

"Yeah, it's bad news about Jake. I know you have to be feeling it, too. Jake wasn't the brightest, but he had a good heart."

"I loved him. Brendan—my son—loved him."

Lukas glanced at the boy, who still hadn't made a sound. "I'm glad. A man needs love in his life. I don't suppose that kid is his."

"No."

"That's all right."

"Can Brendan go to his room?"

"Why couldn't he? I'm not a bad guy, and this is your house. Go have fun, Brendan."

Vicki whispered in her boy's ear, and the child slipped off the couch. He paused only a second, and then he dashed from the room. A moment later a door closed deeper in the apartment.

They stared at each other for a while. Lukas never let his smile fall. Vicki spoke first. "What can I do for you?"

"I'm hungry, for a start."

"Oh. Do you want something to eat? I have some lasagna I can heat up. It's what we were going to have for dinner anyway."

"Lasagna's good."

She went to the kitchen, and he watched her go. He kept his eye on her as she moved around the little prep area, cutting pieces from a tray of lasagna and heating them in the microwave. She got down glasses and took a bottle of Perrier and a bottle of Bud Light from the refrigerator. These she put on the table in the small eating space. She set places for three. She called for her son.

The little boy emerged from his room. He'd changed shirts, but it did nothing to hide his frail form. He sat opposite Lukas and watched with owlish eyes.

"How old's your boy?"

"Eight."

"Good age."

Vicki sat at the table, and Lukas cut into his food. He put a forkful into his mouth and chewed. The taste made him screw up his face. "What is that?"

"It's eggplant lasagna."

"Who makes lasagna with *eggplant?*"

Lukas saw a shot of fear pass through her. "Jake liked it."

"I'm pretty sure he didn't," Lukas said. He twisted the top off the beer and drank directly from the bottle to wash out his mouth. He pushed his plate away. "I'm not eating that."

"Do you want me to make you something else? I can make something else."

"You do that," Lukas said, and he had more beer.

She abandoned her food and retreated to the kitchen. He listened to her awhile. Across from him, Brendan ate delicately from his plate. Lukas scowled at every bite the boy took. He left the table.

He found Vicki putting together a meatball sandwich on a crusty long roll. She glanced at him and smiled weakly. Her hands shook.

Lukas stopped her with a touch on the arm. "You got nothing to worry about. Didn't I say so?"

"I'm sorry. It's just finding you here...it's not what I expected. Brendan—"

"I told you not to worry about him," Lukas said, his voice rising. "Go with it. The sandwich looks good. You look good."

"I just want to put it under the broiler to melt the cheese."

She stiffened for a moment, then kept on with the sandwich. Lukas grinned to himself and went back to the dining area. He waited at the table for her to return. Brendan finished his food. The sandwich was hot and spicy and filled Lukas's mouth with enough good taste to make the disgusting eggplant lasagna go away. Vicki picked at her plate while he devoured it. He hadn't realized how hungry he'd been.

"So you're staying here?" Vicki asked.

"If you don't mind. Everywhere else is too public. I told you, I have people watching out for me. Lots of trouble following me around these days. I was counting on Jake to help me deal with it, but Jake's gone. His friends are no goddamned help."

"Yeah," Vicki said, and she attempted a smile. "Those guys..."

"That's why I need a place where no one knows to look for me," Lukas said. "All of Jake's friends are gonna be watched, but you're a little secret. His girl on the side."

"It's a small place," Vicki said. "Brendan has the only other bedroom. I mean, there's the couch, but..."

Lukas reached across the table and touched her face. "Are you worried about something?"

She closed her eyes, and a visible tremor passed through her.

He got up from his seat and stepped around behind her. He laid his hands on her shoulders and felt the micro-shivers still shaking her. Lukas pulled the hair away from her ear and stooped low to speak quietly to her. "I don't have to sleep on the couch."

"Brendan, go to your room," Vicki said shakily.

"That's a good idea," Lukas said. "Your mother and I have something to talk about."

Brendan hesitated. Lukas glared at him. The boy fled the table.

"Smart kid," Lukas said. He touched the topmost button on Vicki's blouse. "Does he have a smart mama?"

"Please, don't."

Lukas closed the back of his hand at the nape of Vicki's neck. "If I have to get specific about what I need, I might get frustrated. And if I get frustrated, I'll need somebody to take it out on. You get what I'm saying."

"All right," Vicki breathed.

"I thought so," Lukas said. He pulled the Colt from its place and put it down in front of her. He felt her brace herself at the sight of it. "Now, why don't you show me where the bedroom is? And make sure the sheets are clean."

CHAPTER TWENTY-NINE

CAMARO LAY AWAKE in the spare bedroom. She was still dressed from the day. Her phone vibrated on the nightstand, and she answered it. "I don't recognize this number," she said by way of greeting.

"It's Jeremy Yates calling. You gave me your cell."

She sat up on the bed. "Why are you calling, Mr. Yates?"

"Forget the mister. I'm just Yates to my friends."

"Why are you calling me? It's late."

"That it is. I've found it's better to burn the midnight oil when a trail is hot. I spent a few hours talking my way around Carmel and Pacific Grove, trying to scare up some names. And now I have one: Derrick Perkins. Ring any bells?"

"No. Should it?"

"From what I gather, Derrick and your best friend Jacob Collier were good buddies. I missed Derrick pretty much everywhere I tried to find him tonight, but I have an address for him in Salinas. I could use some backup."

"I'm not armed."

"If things go well, you won't need to be. Now, did I make a mistake in calling, or are you interested in helping me track down Lukas Collier before he can cause trouble for your family?"

Camaro slipped off the bed and went for her boots by the door. She keyed on the speaker and set her phone down on the dresser. "I'm interested. You just need to tell me when and where. I have to figure out how to get to you. The police are sitting on the house."

"There's a church not far off from where you're at," Yates said. "If you cut through the woods behind your sister's place, you can probably make it to the road. I can meet you there whenever you're ready."

"Give me fifteen minutes."

"See you soon."

Camaro switched off the bedside lamp before opening the bedroom door. In the hallway she heard the sleeping sounds of Annabel and Rebecca in the master bedroom. Her niece did not want anything to do with her own bed. Camaro crept down the hall and into the living room. Through the front windows she saw the Carmel Police Department vehicle standing in the rain. It was dark in the car, and she couldn't see the driver.

Her jacket was on a hook by the front door. She put it on and stole her way back through the kitchen to the rear door. Light rain pelted against the glass as she slowly turned the knob and exited into the night.

The swing set was silent and unmoving in the dark. Camaro jogged past it to the fence at the back of the yard. She grabbed the top and scrambled up the wet wood until she could throw herself over. On the far side she dropped into a cushion of dead, sodden leaves. The woods stood all around, black bark glistening in the half-light reflected from a neighbor's backyard floodlight.

She set off across the broken ground, counting off the distance in her head. She heard the road before she reached it, a car passing in the night. Emerging from the woods onto the gravel shoulder, she looked both ways. Only a couple of houses occupied this stretch of road, set back behind gates of wood or iron. Camaro spotted the church. It was lit on the outside, though parts were shrouded in darkness. A playground nestled in one of the shadowy pockets, and she cut down the drive until she was out of the light and completely concealed.

An SUV came along. It entered by the same drive and cut its headlights as soon as it was off the road. It slowed and then stopped, the engine idling. Camaro saw Yates behind the wheel, illuminated by the dash lights. She came up on the vehicle and rapped on the window. He popped the locks.

Camaro felt a blast of heat as she got into the SUV. She wiped water from her face. "Right on time," she said.

They exited onto the road, and Yates gave the SUV gas. Camaro noted the manila folder on the armrest between them. It was stuffed with papers. "You mind?"

"Help yourself."

She found Jake's information on top, along with a series of booking photos and what looked like the picture from his driver's license. Underneath were pages of handwritten notes torn from a pad of yellow paper. Underneath those was a flyer with a photo of Lukas Collier. He glowered out at her, long-haired and bearded. "So this is him?"

"The man himself."

Backing up, she looked through Yates's notes. They were detailed, filled with arrows and circles and underlining. She saw the list of names that included Derrick Perkins, along with the addresses of each man, or at least most of them. "Where do you get all of this stuff?"

"Part of my business is knowing how to get information on anyone," Yates replied. "You start by making phone calls, and then you knock on doors. Depending on who you call and who you see, your search won't take too long."

"Derrick slipped you?"

"Not because he's smart. Something's going on with him. People I talked to say he seemed worked up. They thought it might have something to do with Jacob getting killed, seeing as how they were friends and all. But one bartender I talked to said he met up with a man matching Lukas Collier's description."

"Lukas has a lot of balls."

"Like I said before, the man is pissed. You killed his only brother. I expect he'll run just about any risk to make sure you're dead before he moves on."

They were moving fast. "You don't think he's hiding out with Derrick Perkins, do you?" Camaro asked.

"If he is, then I'm the luckiest man alive."

"So, no," Camaro said.

"No. But if they've talked, Lukas might have let something slip. And he might be around again to get Derrick's help. This hasn't been Lukas's place in a while, so he'll need people to keep him safe and secure. It doesn't look like Jacob's crew amounts to much, but they're better than nothing."

Camaro sat back. "I need a gun."

"With the eye of the law on you? Not too smart."

"Neither is being out here with you."

"Fair enough. But you've already done plenty. If there's shooting to be done, best to let me take care of it."

They rode in silence the rest of the way, cruising through sleeping town and country until they were in Salinas. Yates followed the GPS all the way to Derrick's address and parked the SUV out front. He drew his weapon and checked it. Camaro looked at the stainless steel gun and wanted to put her hand around it. Yates stashed it away. They got out of the vehicle together.

It was a quiet street, and the hour was close to midnight. Small homes lined the street, some single-family and some duplexes. Derrick lived in one of the duplexes, and his lights were still on. Camaro approached the house with Yates close behind. "Hold up," he said. "You don't know what you're walking into."

"You said yourself Lukas probably isn't here."

"Even so, I'd feel better if you'd let an old man put in the work."

Camaro allowed him ahead of her, and they passed into the shelter of the carport. A flimsy screen door covered a lime-green inner door. Yates pulled the screen door open and knocked. He had his badge wallet in his hand.

"Who's there?" a woman asked through the door.

There was a small peephole, and Yates brandished his badge in front of it. "Bail enforcement, ma'am. Please open the door."

The locks rattled. A Latina woman opened the door a few inches. A security chain spanned the gap. "Bail what?"

"Bail enforcement. I'm here to see Derrick Perkins."

"Derrick isn't here."

"When will he be back?"

The woman looked past Yates to Camaro. Camaro stared back at her. She saw hesitation in the woman's eyes. "I don't know. He's out drinking. Maybe two or three o'clock."

"Mind if we wait inside?"

"Yes, I mind. I told you he's not here."

"He's here," Camaro said.

The woman looked stricken. "Look, he's drunk. Leave him alone."

"Open the door," Yates said.

She tried to push it shut, but Yates had his boot in the gap.

"Go away! Go away!"

"Fuck this," Camaro said. She pushed her way past Yates and put her shoulder to the door, and the security chain tore free of its moorings. The woman screamed.

Yates drew his gun. The sight of it silenced the woman. Camaro was in a short, darkened hallway leading to a kitchen. Light came from beyond. She passed through quickly and looked left and right at the next corridor. A man poked his head out of one of the bedrooms. He gawked at her for an instant and then vanished, the door slamming shut.

"I got him!"

"Watch yourself, goddamn it," Yates called after her.

Camaro rushed the door. It was flimsy, made of thin wood with just a cheap metal push-button lock in the knob. She kicked it, and the splintery fragments caved in instantly. She lost five seconds pushing the ruins aside, and then she was in the bedroom. Derrick was nearly out the window.

Derrick shouted as Camaro seized him by the belt and the back of his shirt and hauled him back in. He stumbled drunkenly and fell on his ass. The stink of beer came up from him like a cloud. Camaro dropped a knee on his leg, pinning it to the floor, and punched him once. He fell backward, his hands over his face. "Don't kill me! Don't kill me!"

She dragged him to his feet and pushed him down the hall. Yates was at the end of it, his gun held openly to keep the woman silent. The four of them passed into the living room, where the TV played. Yates pointed to the couch. "Sit down."

Camaro kicked Derrick in the backside, and he fell down beside the woman. A trickle of blood ran from a split in his lip. The two of them were pale with fear.

"Remember me?" Camaro asked Derrick.

"This is not how I would have played it," Yates said under his breath.

"We got him," Camaro said. She kicked Derrick sharply in the shin and made him yelp. "Right, Derrick? That's your name, isn't it?"

"Please don't kill us," Derrick said.

The woman began to weep. She threw her arms around Derrick, and the two of them shivered together.

"Nobody's going to get killed," Yates said. "I'm in pursuit of a bail fugitive, and I think you know him. Lukas Collier."

Derrick looked up at the name. "He's not here."

"You mind if I look around?" Yates asked.

"Go ahead."

Yates left the room, and Camaro heard him opening and closing doors. After a few moments he returned. "How long has it been since he was here?"

"Leave Rosalinda out of this."

"Just talk, asshole," Camaro said. She ignored Yates's look.

"He's never been here. He doesn't even know where I live."

"Derrick, Rosalinda, I'm a reasonable man. I know the two of you don't want to be charged with aiding a felony fugitive, so I'm going to ask you once where I can find Lukas."

"I'm telling you, he's not here."

"Where is he?"

"I don't know."

"But you were with him earlier tonight," Yates said.

Rosalinda clung to Derrick tightly. He pried himself loose of her grasp and addressed them. "Yeah. Yeah, I was."

"What did he want? What did you tell him?"

"He wanted to know about Jake's girl. And her sister. Anything at all I could tell him about them. But I don't know anything. I don't know *anything*. I never even saw Chelle's sister before she showed up at the yard the other day." He shot a look toward Camaro, his face dark.

"Where did he go?" Camaro asked.

"He didn't tell me where he was going."

"That's bullshit," Camaro said, and she stepped toward Derrick. He shrank back, and Rosalinda whimpered. "Tell us where he is."

Yates touched her arm. "Camaro? Take a minute. I think he's telling the truth."

"Yeah," Derrick said. "I am telling the truth. Why would he tell me

123

anything? I'm not anybody to him. I was friends with Jake. I don't know Lukas at all. You have to believe me."

"I will beat you until you are dead if you're lying to us," Camaro said.

"I'm not. I swear."

Yates holstered his weapon. "I think it'd be better for all of us if you didn't report this to the police. You lie to us, that's one thing, but there are federal marshals looking for Lukas, and if you lie to them, it's a felony."

"I'm telling you the God's honest truth," Derrick swore.

Camaro moved before Yates could catch hold of her. She grabbed a fistful of Derrick's shirt and pulled him toward her. They were face-to-face, and she smelled him even more strongly now. "If he gets in touch with you, I want you to tell him something. You tell him I will go up against him anywhere, anytime. If he wants me, all he has to do is ask. I'll even leave you my number."

"Camaro," Yates said.

Camaro told Derrick her number. "Repeat it back to me."

Derrick failed, and Camaro reeled it off again. He failed and began to shake afresh. Camaro tightened her grasp on his shirt.

"Camaro," Yates said again.

"Repeat it back to me," Camaro said. Derrick squeezed his eyes shut.

"I know it," Rosalinda said. "I have it."

Camaro waited until Rosalinda repeated it correctly before she let Derrick go. He fell back limply against the couch, and Rosalinda threw her arms around him protectively. Camaro scowled at them both. "You tell him," she said. "You tell him what I said."

"Let's go," Yates said.

Camaro waited a beat longer until Rosalinda could not look her in the eye, and then she followed Yates out into the night.

CHAPTER THIRTY

In the end, Way could not resist. He went to a small room with two bunks inside and fell asleep for hours. When he woke he was confused about where he was and what he was doing. He felt himself, and everything was there, his clothes rumpled and smelling vaguely stale.

He sat on the edge of the bunk for a while, gathering his thoughts. A soft knock sounded on the door. "Come in," he said.

Hannon entered with a small green folder. She looked fresh, and he wondered if there was somewhere else she might have slept. Her clothes were neater than his. He felt like a pile of discarded laundry.

"Good, you're awake," she said.

"How long were you going to let me sleep? It's almost midnight."

"You needed it."

"I need to find Lukas."

"We will. But you wanted this first." She brandished the folder.

"What's that?"

"It's Camaro Espinoza. A complete package of records, including her military service, tax returns, the whole thing."

"Let me see."

"Why don't you get a cup of coffee first?"

Way nodded and got up. They went into the hallway. The police station was eerily still. "Talk to me, at least. What's her story?"

"She's thirty-three and originally comes from Los Angeles but lives near Miami now. She joined the army in 2001, three days after 9/11, and trained as a 68W Health Care Specialist."

"So she's a nurse?"

"A combat medic. She's served all over the place, in the United States

125

and overseas. Been deployed to Iraq and Afghanistan. She saw frontline action in both places."

"You told me before she had the Silver Star."

"Yes. That's a fun story. In 2009 she was assigned to a combat outpost in Nuristan Province in Afghanistan. The army was going to shut the place down because it couldn't be secured, but before they could get everyone out, the Taliban hit them. They mortared the hell out of the troops there, then overran them and set the whole outpost on fire. Our guys fought for fourteen hours, and Camaro Espinoza was right in the middle of it."

"How'd she get the medal?"

"She repeatedly exposed herself to enemy fire to retrieve injured soldiers or to provide covering fire while they withdrew. She kept on doing it even after she took three wounds, and she dragged one guy a hundred yards under heavy fire to save his life. Two soldiers on the ground that day got the Medal of Honor."

"Sounds like a real shitstorm."

"I wouldn't have wanted to be there."

"So why did she get out?"

"It doesn't say. She did another deployment to Afghanistan after that, and then she was in the U.S. for a while before she resigned in the summer three years back."

"Honorable discharge?"

"What do you think?"

Way found the coffee machine waiting for him. The carafe was full. He poured out a measure, then dosed it heavily with sugar and creamer. "What then? She's out of the army. What does she do?"

Hannon gave him the folder. "You can read all about it."

Way sat down with the file and read. He turned the pages slowly, absorbing details. There were many. "Is all this true?" he asked.

"Yes, as far as I can tell. I'm going to make more calls in the morning. Eventually she turns up in Florida. Owner of Coral Sea Sport Charters, a fishing outfit. And that's where she's been until she came here."

"Does the Marshals Service have a reason to step in?"

"She has an outstanding warrant in New York City for bail jumping. We could leverage that."

"Uh-huh. Is this woman even Michelle Amado's sister?"

"Military records indicate she has a sister, but the sister's name isn't Michelle Amado. It's Annabel Watts. Maiden name Espinoza."

"Wait, the sister is married?"

"Widowed. Her husband was shot to death outside their house in New Orleans under suspicious circumstances. Unsolved homicide. And then the sister vanished, too. You want to know when?"

"When?"

"Three years ago this summer."

"What the hell?" Way asked. "Are we sure this Annabel Espinoza, or Watts, or whatever her name is, are we sure she's Michelle Amado?"

"Keep looking."

Way searched the folder until he found it: a printout of a Louisiana driver's license. "We need to go see the Espinoza sisters. Right now."

"Keith, it's the middle of the night."

"Right now."

CHAPTER THIRTY-ONE

THEY CRUISED NOWHERE in particular. Yates said nothing. Camaro listened to the rush of warm air from the vents and the comforting bass of the engine. Finally she spoke. "What is it?"

"We don't know each other too well," Yates said, "so I'm not sure exactly how frank I can be with you."

"You can tell me anything."

"All right, then. I don't much care for cowboys and Indians. It's not the way I operate, and it's not the way I like my partners to operate."

"We're partners?"

"For the moment. I agreed to let you in on the search for Lukas Collier, and you agreed that when the time comes I kill him. I find it to be a mutually beneficial relationship, given that Lukas won't rest until he puts a bullet in you."

They slowed for a yellow light and stopped for a red. "So what's the problem?" Camaro asked.

"What exactly did you do in the service, if you don't mind me asking?"

"I was a 68 Whiskey."

"Run that by me again?"

"The old MOS code was 91 Whiskey."

"You said you'd been in Iraq and Afghanistan. I'm gonna guess you didn't spend a whole lot of time in the rear."

"No," Camaro said. "I was out there."

"You have it all over you. Back in the Civil War days they called it seeing the elephant. No man's the same after he's seen the elephant. I can attest to that personally. And I suppose now no woman's the same, either."

"If you have something to say, just say it," Camaro told him.

"All right, I will. You are way too eager to bump up against Lukas Collier."

"And you aren't?"

"It's different for me. I lost someone precious to me."

"My sister and my niece are precious to me," Camaro said. "As long as Lukas is running around out there, they'll never be safe."

"And you think calling him out is the best way to keep them safe?"

"You wouldn't get it," she said.

Yates chuckled to himself. They drove some more. He seemed to make turns at random. They went down residential streets and then out onto thoroughfares bright with lights. From time to time they saw a police cruiser, but they were never pulled over. They were an invisible ship in the night.

"Ms. Espinoza, I went to Vietnam in 1965 and I was there two and a half years, until the goddamned VC shot me in the leg and broke my femur. If you want to talk about seeing the elephant, lady, I've seen it, touched it, and even rode on it. There's not a thing you can tell me about your wars that I couldn't tell you about mine. So don't think I don't understand where you're coming from. I'm old, but I didn't turn stupid."

Camaro looked out the window as a 7-Eleven slid by. She frowned at her reflection. "I'm sorry."

"It's just a reminder that we're in this together. So you want to poke at this particular anthill and see all the ants come running out. I get it. That's how they fought my war; we'd go out into the boonies and walk around, trying to get the VC to shoot at us. Most times they didn't, but sometimes they did. It was a relief sometimes when the bullets started flying, because at least then we weren't waiting for something to happen. It was *happening*. That's why I stayed longer than I should have."

A McDonald's sign drew into view. It advertised twenty-four-hour service. Yates put on his blinker and slid into the parking lot. It was deserted at this hour, and the inside of the restaurant was half dark. A double drive-through waited for them. "I'm going to get myself a Quarter Pounder," Yates said. "And lots of fries. How about yourself?"

"I'll take the same," Camaro said. "No onions. No pickles."

He ordered and drove through and paid, and soon they were back on the road with a bag of hot food between them. Camaro ate the salty fries and drank some of the Coke that came with the meal. She thought of Derrick Perkins and his girl. She saw their faces filled with terror. The memory brought nothing with it.

"That hits the spot," Yates said. "Rule Number One when it comes to doing my kind of work: never go out with an empty stomach. Hunger can do strange things to your head."

"I'm not in your line of work," Camaro said.

"How does Camaro Espinoza make a living?" Yates asked.

"I run a fishing charter."

Yates looked at her sidelong. "All by yourself?"

"What's that supposed to mean? Yes, all by myself."

"No offense meant. Can't be too many lady captains around. Especially not ones with good looks and a hard punch."

"My father liked to fish. He took me out whenever he could afford it. When I was younger, he said he only wanted two things: a cherry 1967 Camaro and a fishing boat."

"Did he ever get them?"

"No."

Yates drained the last of his soda noisily. He shook the cup, and the ice rattled. "I love fishing. I go whenever I can. Get out there looking for cobia, drum, sea trout, maybe some croaker."

"You have a boat?"

"Me? No, ma'am. Maybe someday when I retire."

Camaro looked at him. "You retiring sometime soon?"

"I suppose that's one way of saying you think I'm old."

"That's not what I meant."

"It's all right. I am old. I turned seventy-one last August."

"I would have guessed lower than that."

"Clean living. I don't drink but once in a while, I haven't smoked in thirty years, and I only eat red meat once a week. How about you?"

Camaro shrugged. "I don't smoke."

"Well, you're young yet."

Yates got them on the highway back toward Carmel. They were the only vehicle on the road. The streetlights flashed past one at a time in a silent rhythm, playing shadows across the interior of the SUV. Camaro let him drive for nearly twenty minutes without interruption. "Lukas is going to come at me."

"Absolutely."

"But you wish I hadn't done it anyway."

"It's not my preference, that's true, but I'll take what I can get. Now, let me get you home so you can get a good night's rest. I get the feeling it's going to be the last chance you get for a while."

CHAPTER THIRTY-TWO

LUKAS WAS ASLEEP when the call came. He stirred at the sound of the phone trilling in the dark and opened his eyes to see Vicki's bedroom take shape around him. Images of somewhere warm and faraway faded instantly.

He felt Vicki lying next to him in bed, her naked buttocks pressed against his hip. She made a disturbed noise at the sound of the phone. Lukas took the call. "Derrick," he said, "it's the middle of the night."

"I have to talk to you," Derrick said.

"What the hell about?"

"Her."

Lukas sat up. The covers dragged from Vicki's shoulders, and she fumbled for them, pulling them back up over herself. He got out of bed. His skin prickled in the cold room, and he snared his boxer shorts from the floor. "Are you screwing with me right now? Because if you're screwing with me I will tear out your lungs."

"No, no, no," Derrick said. "I swear it's the truth. She was here. She was just here. Her and some guy. They came busting in and scared the shit out of Rosalinda. I thought they were going to shoot both of us."

He went into the next room. It was dark there, too. He paced in the middle of the living area. "What did you tell them, Derrick?"

"Nothing! They wanted to know where you were staying or where you'd be, and I told them I had no idea. I didn't say anything about Vicki or any of that. I would never give you up, man. I owe it to Jake."

"You owe it to me," Lukas said. "Jake's dead. I'm alive. What did they want to know? Where to find me? Who I'm hanging with? That kind of thing?"

Derrick made an affirmative sound. "The guy had a gun. Rosalinda said he showed her a badge, but he wasn't a cop. He was bail...bail—"

"Bail enforcement," Lukas said. He chuckled. "Those sons of bitches aren't gonna give up, are they? Was this guy old? White hair? Real lanky?"

"That's right. He didn't tell me his name."

"It's Yates," Lukas told Derrick. "Jeremy Yates, I think. The old fart has to be a hundred and one years old. His son thought he could take me down with a can of pepper spray and some big talk."

"Where is he now?"

"Dead. That's where he is now. I shot his dumb ass back in Colorado. He had a nice truck."

Derrick cleared his throat. "So, uh, this Yates guy wants to take you down? Like back to jail?"

"Something like that. I think he's got other things on his mind now, especially if he's hooked up with that woman. He knows when he's got a good piece of live bait, and he wants to reel me in. He thinks I'm stupid enough to go for it when he's standing around waiting to blow my head off."

"That's the thing," Derrick said.

"What is?"

"Well, he's not the one calling you out. Chelle's sister, Camaro? She told me to tell you something."

"Spit it out, then."

"She says she'll go up against you anywhere you want. Anytime, anywhere, she said. And she gave me her phone number to give to you. I mean, maybe this Yates guy wants to kill you, but I looked in her eyes, man, and she wants you just as dead. She killed Jake. She'll kill you, too."

Lukas shouted down the line. "You think I'm scared of some dumb cunt? I'll tear that whore apart piece by piece if she tries to take me on."

Derrick fell silent. Lukas cast around himself for something to throw, but the apartment was too orderly for that. He made a fist and punched the air.

"What do you want me to do?"

"You need to get that money from Jake's house. All of it. Just because Jake's gone doesn't mean the deal is dead. I got a date in LA that I'm gonna make, no matter what I got to deal with first."

"Do you need help with the woman?"

"Maybe. I'm going to handle this all myself from now on. I might need you, but I might not. You just wait for my call. When things happen, they're gonna happen fast. That woman is gonna know what it means to wave a cape in front of a bull. You understand what I'm saying, Derrick?"

"Yeah, I understand. She's asking for it."

"If she comes back, you let me know. But don't you forget about that money. The money. That's what's important. You get that?"

"I get it."

"Thanks for calling."

"Anytime, man. Anytime."

Lukas ended the call. He stood silently in the middle of the room for a long moment, centering himself. Disordered thoughts fell into line, and an idea began to form.

CHAPTER THIRTY-THREE

ANNABEL WOKE TO the sound of furious pounding on the front door, followed by multiple rings of the bell. A jolt of fear and energy shot through her, and she put her hand over Rebecca's sleeping form. The girl was deeply asleep and heard nothing. She breathed steadily even as the pounding resumed.

A robe hung from a hook on the closet door. Annabel slipped out of bed and put it on. She wished for the gun she'd used to kill Jake.

She stopped at the spare bedroom. "Camaro?" she asked. She pushed the door open. The bed was empty, the covers only wrinkled but not pulled back. "Camaro?"

There was no answer. The doorbell jangled repeatedly as she went to the front of the house, turning on lights along the way. She saw the police cruiser parked where it had been when she went to bed. There was another car parked behind her Subaru, unmarked. She recognized the faces through the peephole.

"Marshals," Annabel said when she opened the door, "it's late."

Way pushed into the room past her. Hannon paused before entering, her face slightly pained. She touched Annabel on the arm. "We know it's late."

Annabel closed the door behind them. "You could have woken up my daughter."

"Where's your sister?" Way asked.

"She's not in her room."

"That doesn't answer my question. Where is she?"

"I don't know. Can you please keep your voice down? My daughter—"

"Maybe your daughter can shed some light on this situation," Way said.

"How? She's only five."

Way brandished a green folder. "I'll bet she knows more than she ever would have admitted. Like the fact that she was born Rebecca *Watts* and not Amado."

Annabel froze. She felt the muscles in her chest seize together, then slowly unwind to allow oxygen into her lungs. A hand on the wall steadied her. Hannon watched her carefully. Way's eyes were fire.

"And your name is Annabel," Way continued.

Tears welled up. Annabel was blinded. She wiped at them and they stung. "Yes, my name was Annabel Watts."

"Was? If I go looking, will I find a legal name change? What about your Social Security number? Will that match? Who was Michelle Amado?"

Annabel sniffed. "She's me."

Way pointed at the couch. "You'd better sit down."

She took one end of the couch while Hannon took the other. Way blazed with energy, slapping the green folder against his leg. Hannon was quiet, still watching. "This isn't what you think," Annabel said.

"What is it, then?"

"I had to get out of my old life. I couldn't stay in New Orleans."

"Was it your husband? The husband who conveniently turned up dead?"

"It wasn't convenient," Annabel said. "It was horrible."

"What happened to him, Annabel?" Hannon asked.

Annabel wiped her eyes again and took a deep breath that hitched beneath her breastbone. "I loved my husband very much. His name was Corey. He gave me Becca, and I was always grateful for that. I still am. But he…he wasn't a good person. He did things that got him into trouble. A lot. And one day that caught up to him."

"And your sister? How did she figure into it?" Way asked.

"She helped me escape."

"What then?"

"Look, she has nothing to do with this," Annabel protested. "After my husband died I never looked back, not even for her. I kept going until I got to the coast, and I settled somewhere no one would ever find me. We didn't even talk about it."

"But she still found you," Hannon said. "You kept in touch."

"We set up a way to talk without anyone making a connection between us. A code if I ever needed help again. I didn't use it all this time, until...until Jake."

"You brought your sister here to kill Jacob Collier," Way said.

"No! He was no good for me, but I couldn't get rid of him on my own. Camaro, she knows how to make people do what she wants. She's always been stronger than me."

Way laughed shortly. "So she comes all this way to beat the shit out of your boyfriend because you don't know how to change the locks and get a restraining order? Is that what you're telling me?"

"It's the truth."

"Oh, man," Way said. He rubbed his forehead. He giggled crazily for a moment, turning his back to her, as giggles turned into laughter, and laughter into a fit of coughing.

Hannon moved closer to Annabel on the couch and reached to take her hand. She frowned at Way's laughter. "You're not the first woman to start a new life away from a bad situation," Hannon said. "You won't be the last. We're not here to ruin everything for you."

Way turned to face Annabel again. "Unless it turns out that your sister killed your husband, too. If *that's* true, then you are in for a world of pain."

"Did she kill your husband?" Hannon asked quietly.

"No, no, never," Annabel said. "Camaro wouldn't do that."

"But she is a killer," Way said. He showed Annabel the green folder again. "I have the paperwork to prove it. What would I find if I decided to go digging down in Miami?"

"Camaro is a good person," Annabel said.

"Where is she?" Hannon asked.

Annabel pulled her hand free of Hannon's. "I said I don't know."

"Okay," Way said. "Okay. If that's how you want to play it, then that's what we'll do. We didn't have to turn your life upside down, but I guess now we have to. We'll check your financials and everything else all the way down the line until we bump up against something illegal, and you'll go to jail. Your daughter will end up with the state."

Annabel felt more tears coming. "I swear to God I don't know where she is."

"All right. It's done. We'll take you both down."

"I'm here."

Camaro's voice brought Annabel's head around sharply. She saw Camaro in the entryway to the kitchen, her jacket saturated by the rain. Her hair was just as wet and hung around her face in dark tendrils.

Way pointed a finger at her. "Freeze right there. Don't move a muscle."

"I'm not going anywhere," Camaro said.

"Hannon, cuff her."

CHAPTER THIRTY-FOUR

WAY DIRECTED CAMARO to sit in the chair near the fireplace, her hands cuffed behind her back. Annabel gave Camaro one last look before Hannon hustled her out of the room. "Don't say anything, Michelle," Camaro called after Annabel, but Annabel did not reply.

Way stood opposite her for a long time in silence, swatting his leg with the green folder. Camaro stared back at him.

"You called your sister Michelle," Way said at last.

"That's her name."

"It wasn't always."

"So you know."

"I know. What I don't know is why she went through all the trouble to set up a phony identity with a new name and the whole thing, while you went on being Camaro Espinoza."

"I'm not in hiding," Camaro said.

"Aren't you? Maybe you just don't care. I get the feeling that's the real answer. You just don't care."

Camaro waited and breathed and said nothing.

"I've been looking at your life," Way said. "It's all here in this folder."

Camaro didn't answer.

"Who do you think you are?"

"I don't look for trouble."

Way smiled tightly. "But you're always in it, aren't you? Like now. You're in a whole lot of trouble now. You're linked to the deaths of two men involved with your sister."

"What are you talking about?" Camaro said.

"Your sister's in hiding. Her husband is dead. And I'm going to see to it that charges are filed in the death of Jacob Collier."

139

"Why? What's he to you?" Camaro asked.

"He was my link. He was how I was going to nail Lukas Collier, and you had to go and shoot him. And all because he was doing your sister wrong. What was it? Did he get too rough with her? Because that's the kind of thing little sisters call big sisters to help sort out.

"Good old Jake," Way continued. "He had no idea what he was walking into. Your sister looks like she's the type to get pushed around, and if what I heard about her husband is true, she doesn't have the best taste in the world. But you—coming at you is like diving face-first into a chainsaw."

"Uncuff me," Camaro said.

"Why? You going to make a try for me next?"

"I'm not stupid."

"No, you're not. But you are unlucky, because this mess you got yourself into involves me. I do not like being lied to. I do not like people stepping on my toes. I do not put up with interference in an operation. And most of all, I do not like you. I haven't liked you since we first met, and I like you less now. Where were you tonight?"

"Out. With a friend."

"You have friends in the area? I thought your sister came out here alone. I thought you set up shop in Miami. That's three thousand miles of country. Hard to make friends over that kind of distance. Or did you meet on Facebook?"

Camaro stared at Way. She tested the cuffs. She did not know how to slip out of them the way a magician would. "Are you going to take me in?"

"I could."

"Then if you're gonna do it, just do it," Camaro said. "I'm not answering any more questions. I'll hire a lawyer if I have to, but we're done. Let me out of these cuffs now. I want to see my sister."

Way stood over her. "You don't give the orders around here."

"Even you have to follow the rules. So charge me or uncuff me."

He regarded her. "Stand up."

Camaro stood and turned her back on Way. He used his key on the cuffs, and her wrists were free. She turned back to him. "You still going to have them book me for murder in the morning?"

"Are you going to tell me where you went tonight and who you were with?"

"No."

"Then I am. The Carmel Police Department will be in touch. Or maybe you'll want to just head on over there and turn yourself in. Because if I have to come looking for you, I will. You won't like it if I do."

"Does it make you feel tough to push a woman around?" Camaro asked him.

"Why do you ask?"

"Jake Collier liked that."

"Are you threatening me?" Way asked.

He glowered at her, and she returned his black look. "You take it however you want. Just get out of my sister's house."

CHAPTER THIRTY-FIVE

ANNABEL CRIED IN her arms for an hour. Camaro made her drink a cup of tea and take a sleeping pill and then saw her off to bed. In her own room she stripped down to a T-shirt and underwear and got between the covers for the first time that night.

Consciousness dropped away from her like a yawning chasm bereft of floating dreams, and she awoke at the first sign of light through the curtains of her bedroom window. She checked the time and then her phone to see if she had slept through a call, but there were no calls recorded.

She tried again to sleep. Instead she lulled into a half doze that carried her a couple of hours further before she heard Rebecca's high voice ringing in the hall and the murmur of Annabel's replies.

The guest bathroom was well ordered, a small bowl by the sink piled with fragrant soaps that looked like seashells. Good towels were on the racks, but there were no others to use. Camaro washed herself under the hot spray and got the night out of her hair before toweling off and using the blow-dryer and a borrowed brush.

By the time she made it to the kitchen Annabel was cleaning up the remains of breakfast. Her eyes were still puffy from the night before, but she wasn't crying anymore. She rinsed plates and bowls in the sink and set them on a rack to dry. "Do you want something?" Annabel asked. "I can make you anything."

"I'll just have some oatmeal and some juice."

"Coffee?"

"Okay."

Camaro sat at the table while Annabel busied herself preparing a simple meal. Soon there was a piping-hot bowl of oatmeal in front of her, along with a glass of orange juice and a steaming cup of coffee. The oatmeal had been mixed with raisins and had a dusting of cinnamon over the top. "Voilà," Annabel said.

"Thanks."

Annabel sat down with her. Her hands were aflutter, on the table or in her lap. She was alive with skittish energy. They didn't talk.

Camaro finished her oatmeal and drained the glass of juice. Now that her coffee had cooled a little, she drank. Annabel still stared at her.

"Say it," Camaro told her.

"Are you going to turn yourself in?"

"No."

"Why not?"

"Because I didn't do anything wrong. And neither did you. That marshal can talk all he wants, but he's got nothing. If he had, he would have taken me in last night. He's bluffing."

"Where did you go? When the marshals came, you were gone."

Camaro waited before she answered. She drank more coffee. "I went to find out about Lukas Collier."

"He really is here?"

Camaro nodded. She finished her cup. "He's somewhere. I have to find out where."

"I'm not saying this is exactly right, but it could be that this is something the police should handle. If the marshal gets what he's after, he'll leave us alone. He won't turn up the money and then he'll go back wherever he came from and things can get back to normal. It's the best thing for everybody."

"You want to take a chance on that guy?" Camaro asked.

Annabel crossed her hands. They trembled. She squeezed one in the other. "I'm afraid, Camaro."

"You were the one who was ready to shoot Lukas yourself," Camaro said.

"That was when I thought the police would help. But now they know where I come from and they know my real name. Everything I've built here is going to fall apart the minute the secret gets out. No one will ever believe anything I say. I couldn't make it."

"What do you want me to do?" Camaro asked.

Annabel shook her head helplessly, then dragged nervous fingers through her hair. "Stay with us until this blows over. Just...stay close and be my sister. Don't go looking for trouble. Be here."

Camaro listened and watched Annabel struggle with a tangle of emotions. She could feel them coming from Annabel, and they came into her, too. They sat at the bottom of her stomach and lay there, promising turmoil but weighed down by a sense of calm. She reached for Annabel, and they clasped hands tightly across the table. "Okay," Camaro said. "I won't go looking for trouble. I'll be here with you. As long as it takes. I promise."

"That means a lot to me, Camaro. It means a lot to both of us."

Camaro let Annabel hang on for a long minute, then slipped her hand away. "I have to make a phone call. I'll clean this up when I'm done."

"No, no, I'll get it," Annabel said. "You make your call."

"I'll be back."

She heard the clink of dishes in the sink as she left the kitchen. Rebecca was in her school clothes already, playing with the dollhouse near the fireplace, though now the dolls had been joined by a stuffed hippopotamus and a cat with a star over its eye. Compared to the little family they were enormous, but none of the imaginary people seemed to mind.

"We're having a garage sale," Rebecca told Camaro when she came close.

"Oh, yeah? Anything good?"

"Lots of baby clothes that don't fit."

"I'll have to check it out. Be right back."

Camaro retreated to the guest bedroom and closed the door. There she sat on the edge of the bed and brought out her phone. She dialed Yates. He answered on the first ring.

CHAPTER THIRTY-SIX

YATES PUT HIS phone down and adjusted the visor to better block the morning sun from his eyes. His body was sore from sitting behind the wheel for hours.

After leaving Camaro at the church for her trek back home, he circled around and headed out to Salinas again. There he navigated to Derrick Perkins's street and killed the lights and the engine on a stretch of curb that allowed him a good view of the carport and the front and side of the duplex.

He made note of the same two cars that were present when he first visited the location, and he assumed they belonged to Derrick and his girl. Yates scribbled down the makes, models, and colors of the cars, as well as their license plates. Given an opportunity, he might make a call and see what he could learn about them, but for now he was more interested in what he would see at the house.

The watch went on until morning. For a while all the lights in Derrick's place were out, and then in the early hours they came on again. Right around dawn Yates saw Rosalinda flee the house through the drizzle, dashing to her car in a long coat. She started up without looking around and drove past Yates without seeing him.

It was brighter out when Derrick emerged in his work clothes and a denim jacket. He went to his car and started it but let the engine run a while before backing out from beneath the carport. He turned the opposite direction from Yates, and it was easy for Yates to fall in behind him as he headed out.

The call from Camaro had changed things. She had to take a step back and stick close to home. Blood was responsible for blood, and that was something they both understood.

Jacob Collier's house waited silently with its yard of mud. No cop watched the place. They'd given up on that.

He parked and watched Derrick sneak around the side of the house and vanish in the back. Yates's phone rang again. He answered. "This is Yates."

"Yates, it's Anita."

"Good morning, ma'am. How are you today?"

"Busy," Anita Matthews said. "Night court was working overtime, so I had a pile of bonds to post before I could get a look at that information for you. I have it all now. When can you pick it up?"

"Well, I'm in the middle of something at the moment. I'm pretty sure I'm watching Derrick Perkins break and enter at Jake Collier's place."

"Do the cops know?"

"Doesn't seem like it, and I'm not much in the mood to call them."

"You don't expect Collier to show up there, do you?"

"No, but that doesn't mean he won't turn up later. Maybe Derrick and Collier will take a lunch break together. I like my chances. Thanks for putting me onto him."

"Bondspersons have to stick together. So I should hang on to this stuff?"

"Can you give me the highlights?" Yates asked.

"There's not a whole lot here that you didn't know already. Jacob Collier got around, collecting fines and a few days' worth of jail time here and there. Nothing serious, like pulling a knife on someone or home invasion. And sure as hell nothing like what his brother's into. In fact, the worst thing Jacob ever did was get busted for domestic battery against some woman named Vicki Nelson. I tried running her name, but she's clean. The case didn't even go to court."

Yates sighed. "A man who mistreats a woman isn't any kind of man at all."

"Amen to that."

"Is there anything I can work with? Any associates I don't know about? Maybe some more family somewhere?"

"I'm afraid not. Jacob and Lukas are all alone in the world. No mother or father, no aunts or uncles, and no cousins. It's just the two of them. Or I guess now it's just Lukas. If I were in his shoes, I'd be hot for payback."

"That's where my mind is, too." Yates shifted in his seat to relieve the soreness in his back. "I figure Lukas is holed up somewhere in the area, trying to figure out the best way to get at the woman who shot his brother."

"You have me to fall back on if you get any thoughts. I'll make whatever calls I need to make. I meant what I said; we stick together out this way."

"I am much obliged to you. I'll try to come by your office just as soon as I can and get those records from you. And whatever it cost you, I'll reimburse."

"It's on the house. Just be careful, Yates. There's been too much bloodshed already."

"I will do my best. Thank you, Anita."

They said their good-byes, and then Yates was alone again with his thoughts. He stayed that way for ten minutes, until Derrick reappeared with a worn gym bag slung over his shoulder. It seemed loose, not fully packed, but there was something inside.

Yates started the SUV.

CHAPTER THIRTY-SEVEN

HANNON WOKE EARLY. She had a cup of coffee from the machine in her room, showered and did her hair and put on the day's makeup. Using the room's small ironing board, she pressed her blouse and ran the iron over her jacket for good measure. She dressed and put on her gun, flush against her right hip in a leather holster.

A plastic bag on the handle of her room's door had a wrapped muffin and a banana in it, courtesy of the hotel. She ate the muffin though it was entirely too sweet and put the banana in her bag. Afterward she left her room and went next door to Way's. The continental breakfast was still hanging there, untouched. Hannon considered knocking, then stepped away. She retrieved her bag from her room and left the hotel.

The rental car waited in the lot, spotted with overnight rain. Only a little still fell, hazing down over her until she got behind the wheel, stoked the engine, and headed to Carmel.

She greeted the officer behind the desk and was buzzed into the back area. Way still had the folder of information on Camaro Espinoza, but more had come in overnight about Annabel Watts. Hannon called the New Orleans Police Department.

She drilled down through a layer of push-button menus to find a human being and identified herself as a deputy U.S. marshal. She asked for a detective named Alberta Vaughn. The conversation lasted five minutes. When they were finished, Hannon thanked the detective and hung up. "Shit," she said aloud to the empty room.

She had the paperwork cleared up by the time she heard Way's voice in the bullpen. She slipped the printouts into a marbled folder and faced the door.

Way gave her a black look as he entered. "Surprised to see me?" he asked.

"You needed a break."

"I need coffee."

"It's ready."

She waited until he had caffeinated. They considered each other over his steaming cup. "What are you sitting on?" he asked.

"Nothing. Except the fact Camaro Espinoza didn't kill her sister's husband. Annabel Watts is hiding for exactly the reason she said she was: to steer clear of her husband's past. Whatever happened to him could have happened to her. We've seen it a hundred times."

"I still don't like it," Way said.

"There's nothing there, Keith. This is just a woman looking for a new life."

Way partook deeply of his cup, then topped it off. He thrummed his fingers on the edge of the table as he leaned against it. A thoughtful nod won through. "Okay."

"Do you still want to have Camaro Espinoza charged?"

"I'm thinking about it."

"What else are you thinking?"

Way shrugged. "I'm thinking if Annabel Watts was so serious about protecting her new life, she might have had a good reason to see her boyfriend dead. Especially if he threatened to rat her out to her friends or her boss. Whoever could cause the most trouble for her. She doesn't pull the trigger herself, of course. She gets her sister to do it because she knows her sister has the experience. And now there's a new threat: Lukas. She'll want him out of the picture, too, so she can go on living as Michelle Amado."

"Camaro Espinoza isn't going to hunt down Lukas Collier."

"Do we know that? I mean, what do we really know about her besides what's in the paperwork? Where was she last night in the middle of the night? Talking to her is like talking to a wall. You don't know what's behind it."

"So what do we do?"

Way considered that. "We give her a gun and see what she does."

"You want to arm her again?"

"Yes. And if she knows something about Lukas we don't, we use her to get to him. But she doesn't get to kill him. Nobody kills him but me. Nobody."

Hannon kept her thoughts to herself. She watched Way finish his coffee.

"Let's get this ball rolling," he said.

CHAPTER THIRTY-EIGHT

ANNABEL GATHERED HER things for work. She had Rebecca's backpack by the door, already stuffed with school supplies and a set of snacks in an insulated bag. Camaro sat on the couch. "Are you sure you don't want to come along and say hi to Wilson?" Annabel asked. "I'm sure he'd love to meet you."

"I'll do fine here."

"Okay. Becca, come on. We have to leave."

"Coming!"

She paused by the door. "There's stuff in the fridge for sandwiches if you get hungry. I'll be back around five. I thought we could go out somewhere tonight. Carmel has great restaurants."

"Okay," Camaro said.

"Do you have anything dressy?"

"No."

"Maybe I'll see what I can get you at the store."

"You don't know my size."

Annabel smiled. "I'm a professional, Camaro. I can guess anybody's size."

"What's my size?" Camaro asked.

"Wait and see. If I get it right, you pay for dinner."

"Okay."

"Becca, let's *go!*"

Rebecca hurried into the front room with a Barbie doll dressed to ski. "Sorry, Mommy."

Annabel left the house and didn't lock the door behind her. She took Rebecca's hand. They went down the walk together. On the street, a police cruiser sat waiting. Officer Russo was behind the wheel. When

151

Annabel held the gate for her daughter, Russo got out. She had a black plastic case in her hands.

"Good morning," Russo said.

"Good morning."

"You remember me, right? Carly Russo?"

"Of course. Is that my gun?"

Russo hefted the case. "Yes. It's being returned to you. The city isn't pressing any charges against your sister for what happened since it was self-defense. I don't know if you want to take it with you, or..."

Annabel spared a look back toward the house. She saw Camaro through the front window and waved. Camaro came out onto the porch, then advanced up the walk. Russo turned to her as she came, and Annabel thought she colored slightly at the sight of her.

"Good morning," Russo told Camaro. "I was just telling your sister that there aren't going to be any charges filed in the matter of Jacob Collier."

Camaro glanced at Annabel and then at Russo. "No one's afraid I'm going to shoot someone else?"

Russo smiled awkwardly, and this time Annabel was certain she blushed. "No, no, nothing like that. We'd rather you didn't, but that doesn't mean your sister can't have her gun back."

"Take it, Camaro," Annabel said. "I have to go. Becca's going to be late."

Camaro accepted the Glock case. "I'll make sure it's put away," she said.

"Good thinking," Russo said. "Thank you."

"Have a good one," Camaro told her, and she turned away.

"You, too. It was nice seeing you."

"Is there anything else you needed?" Annabel asked Russo.

"I was asked to talk to you again about Lukas Collier."

"I have to get Becca to school, and then I have to go to work. Maybe we can talk at the school?"

"I'll follow you."

Annabel led Rebecca to the Subaru and made sure she was secure in her car seat. As she pulled out of the cul-de-sac, the police cruiser stayed in her rearview mirror.

She hoped Russo would stay in her car when she reached the school, but Russo got out when she did. Rebecca was already unbuckling herself by the time Annabel got to her. Russo waited quietly while Annabel made sure her daughter put on her backpack for the short walk to the entrance.

"Let's hurry. We only have a couple of minutes."

They walked.

"You work at Garment, right?" Russo asked.

"Yes," Annabel said.

"I love the clothes in there. One time, I—"

They were a dozen feet from the entrance when Russo stopped. Automatically Annabel stopped with her, and she saw Russo's face pale and her eyes widen. Russo's hand went for her gun.

Annabel turned at the instant of the first shot. The man approaching them on the sidewalk had his pistol out, and he squeezed off three rounds, one after the other in rapid succession. The bullets crashed into Russo, and Annabel felt a hot spray fall on her cheek as the young woman went down. Near the front of the school, children screamed shrilly and teachers rushed to gather up as many as they could.

Russo was on the ground. Her legs flexed weakly. The man put his sights on Annabel. "Say good-bye," the man said.

She saw Jake in his face. The hardness around the eyes that Jake sometimes got and the cast of his jaw. Annabel stepped between him and Rebecca. He pulled the trigger, and she felt hot wetness burst inside her. Her world tipped over. She staggered against Rebecca, heard her screaming, then collapsed onto her knees.

The man came closer. The gun was still up. Annabel opened her mouth, and there was blood. She tried to call out to Rebecca to run and keep running, but there was nothing from between her lips. She sagged onto her hands.

He shot her again, the bullet spearing through her shoulder. Annabel couldn't keep herself from the pavement. She crumpled completely, her legs kicking feebly as if she might still make her feet. Her head rushed with her pulse, a coursing river that sounded against her ears. Black spots floated everywhere.

Rebecca wasn't near her. The man stepped back, shooting again. Children were still wailing. Annabel couldn't pick out her daughter's voice.

The sidewalk was covered in slick red, more and more as her heart beat. She fell into the pool. One grasping hand found Russo's pant leg. The policewoman didn't move at all. Annabel gagged on the liquid in her throat.

Her head was so heavy she couldn't turn it. Sounds faded, and then there was darkness.

CHAPTER THIRTY-NINE

LUKAS RETURNED TO the car. Vicki was in the backseat with her son, and both were drawn and pale. At a distance they were only figures, but up close it was possible to see where their hands and feet had been bound up with duct tape. He had considered gags but at the last moment decided against them.

He slipped behind the wheel. "Nice and smooth," he said. "Comfortable back there?"

Vicki's voice was unsteady. "Who did you kill?"

"What does it matter to you? So long as it's not you I'm killing, you don't have to worry."

She didn't reply. Lukas ground his back teeth together for a long moment, surveying their faces, before finally turning back toward the front. He started the engine and put the car in gear. They drove. Sirens were audible not far away.

He hummed to himself as he drove. In the theater of his mind, the cop went down over and over, and then Jake's girlfriend. It had been done cleanly, which was more than he could say for some. The message was sent.

"You know what I'd like?" he asked Vicki. He saw her in the rearview mirror. "I'd like to get some ribs. Tender ribs with a good rub, mopped down with sauce. I could eat a whole rack of 'em right now. You any good at making ribs?"

She didn't answer him. Lukas drove a little farther as his thoughts darkened. He was about to shout when she cleared her throat and spoke. Her voice was rougher than before. "I can make you ribs if you want them. But we have to stop at the store."

Lukas considered. He watched her carefully in the mirror. Her eyes

155

were puffy, verging on tears. The sight of them made him angrier. "You want me to pull up in the parking lot so you can make a scene with people around?"

"No! No, it's nothing like that. We'll be quiet. I promise you we'll be quiet."

He grunted. "I'll think about it."

A Carmel PD cruiser came roaring at them in the opposite lane, lights flashing and siren alive with noise. Lukas kept on, his hands on the wheel, and didn't glance over as the car passed. It was gone within seconds. He breathed no harder. His heart didn't speed.

"I'm gonna take you home," Lukas said after they'd driven awhile longer. "And then I'm going out with the kid. I think anything's hinky while I'm out, you're gonna need a closed casket. That's all I'm saying."

He heard her crying. It made him wring the steering wheel in his hands. He didn't look at her, because he knew the sight would make him angry all over again.

Lukas shook his head as the crying went on. He tasted something bitter. "You bitches just don't get it, do you?" he asked. "You and that other one—you don't know a man does what he has to do. Gettin' teary, talking about your *feelings*. You think I don't have feelings? Is that what you think? *You think I don't have feelings!?*"

"No, I don't think that!" Vicki cried out. "I don't think that."

Now the boy cried. Lukas fumed. "You tell that kid to shut his mouth, or I'll shut it for him."

He listened to Vicki shush Brendan. The sound of it was maddening. He pounded the steering wheel with the heel of his hand. They were close to Vicki's apartment now.

"You got until I park this car to shut that kid up."

"No," Vicki managed. "Brendan, it's okay. Just calm down. Mommy's here. You're all right."

"That's how boys come out weak," Lukas said. "You get a boy raised by his mama, he doesn't know what being a man is. Now me and Jake, we had our old man to look up to."

He murmured the last to himself a few times, listening to the boy grow quieter and quieter, until finally they pulled into the parking lot outside Vicki's building. Lukas parked and killed the engine. He sat for a long moment, listening to the hot metal of the engine tick, and mother and son breathing raggedly. Unconsciously he rubbed an old scar on the back of his hand. That day the skin had been laid open enough to expose the bone.

"You two ready to stop wasting my time?" Lukas asked.

"Let him come in with me. I promise we won't go anywhere. We won't call anyone."

"Can't take the chance."

"I've been *good!*" Vicki exclaimed.

Lukas laughed. "Yeah, I guess you have. But I'm still taking the kid. You get things ready, and I'll bring home the meat."

"Please... don't hurt him. He's little."

"Don't give me a reason to," Lukas said, and he turned in his seat again. He fixed them both with his gaze. "Don't ever give me a reason."

Vicki looked as though she might cry again. "I won't," she whispered.

Lukas pulled a knife. "Then you don't have anything to worry about."

CHAPTER FORTY

COMMUNITY HOSPITAL OF the Monterey Peninsula was in a wooded area west of Carmel. Camaro reached it in the backseat of a Carmel police officer's cruiser. When he released her from the rear, she sprang past him, pushing through the doors into the lobby.

A security guard saw her coming and took an involuntary step backward. He put his hand on his belt, where a canister of pepper spray sat just ahead of a walkie-talkie. "Is there something I can help you with, miss?"

Camaro stopped just short of him. "Where's the emergency room?"

"Right down that way and on the left," he said. She moved, and he called after her. "But you're not allowed in there. Miss, you're not allowed in there!"

She kept going until she saw the signs. Automated doors swung open ahead of her. Soon she registered the sounds of medicine and the scent of antiseptic. Nurses in scrubs walked here and there among curtained bays. Two doctors sat side by side at computer workstations, reviewing files. Camaro went to the central hub, the nurses' station. A black woman in a white coat looked up as she approached. "Ma'am, this is not a public area."

"My name is Camaro Espinoza. My sister is Michelle Amado. She was brought in with a gunshot wound. I need to see her."

"Amado? She's—"

"I'll take it from here, ma'am," a man interrupted. Camaro turned toward his voice. Way was there.

"Where is my sister?" Camaro demanded. "Where is my niece?"

"Your niece is fine. Your sister is in intensive care. She had a round of emergency surgery. They're going to take her back in again in a couple of hours."

"The cops said—"

"They don't have the latest. I have the latest. She's in a room not far from here. I'll take you there."

Camaro made a fist reflexively, then pried her fingers apart with will. "Okay."

"Follow me."

They walked, but not fast enough to suit Camaro. "How badly is she hurt?" she asked.

"Four bullet wounds. From all accounts she was shot with a .45, so it's not pretty. The shooter put one into her at close range, but thankfully it wasn't one to the head; otherwise we wouldn't be talking. She was lucky. Unlike Officer Russo, who wasn't."

"Carly Russo?"

"You know her?"

"I met her. Is she alive?"

"No."

Camaro's arms prickled. "It was Lukas Collier, wasn't it?"

"Yeah, it was. According to witnesses, he came out of nowhere with a gun, shot Officer Russo and your sister, then took off after your niece. But she was quick and slipped him. I know Lukas Collier, and I know if he'd gotten to her she'd be dead right now."

"Where did they take her?"

"She's being looked after by Children and Family Services. When it's time, you can see her. Right now is not the time."

He led her to a new area. It was different here, quieter, and the rooms were kept half lighted. Camaro smelled the nameless odor of the grievously injured, the sick, and the dying. "Don't keep me from her."

"I won't. Believe it or not, I'm not an asshole. I just need certain things."

"What do you want?"

"What do you have to give me?" Way asked.

"Nothing."

"So you had no idea this might happen."

"How could I possibly know something like that? You were the people who had the cops following us around. I've never even seen Lukas

SAM HAWKEN

Collier. If I'd known he was going to shoot Bel, I would have been with her every minute of the day."

The elevator ascended. "You may not know much about Lukas, but he clearly knows about you and your family. He knew where to go and when to go, and he knew exactly how to get what he wanted. This is him calling you out. When we hear from him, and I guarantee you we'll hear from him, he's going to want you on the hook somehow. Anything to get you close enough that he can do to you what you did to his brother."

"He's crazy."

"Yes. He is. And the thing is, I've got no leverage. We have no idea where he's laying his head, what he might want you to do. Nothing. And before the end of the day we're going to have the FBI crawling all over this town, your family, and you with a microscope, looking for something they can use. You think I'm difficult to deal with? Try your stonewall routine with a special agent."

They reached an area near a nurses' station. Way stepped through a set of automatic doors and waved Camaro to the left. "I can't give them anything I don't have," she said.

"Then there's not a whole lot left for us to talk about. I'll tell the FBI everything I know about you and your sister, and the secret you're trying to keep will be all over before you know it."

Camaro stopped. "Fuck you."

Way smiled broadly. He pointed at the closed door of a nearby room. "She's in there. Think about what I've said. I'm guessing something's going to pop into your head. I'll be waiting."

She went in. The fluorescents overhead were switched off, but light came through the vertical blinds in the window. It was a private room with only a single bed. Annabel lay on crisp white sheets with a blanket across her body. A saline drip fed into the back of her left hand. A ventilator made her chest rise and fall with regularity. Wires sprouted from beneath the neck of her gown, trailing toward the monitors nearby. Heart rate, blood pressure, blood oxygen, and respiration were tracked. Her eyes were closed. Hannon sat on the chair beside her.

"Hello, Camaro," Hannon said quietly.

"I want to see my sister alone."

160

"I know you do."

"So leave."

"I have something to talk to you about."

"I already talked to your partner."

Hannon shook her head. "This is something even Keith doesn't know about. And I think you'd like to keep it that way."

Camaro looked at Annabel. She looked at Hannon. "Okay, talk."

CHAPTER FORTY-ONE

HANNON PRODUCED A thin folder from underneath her jacket. She didn't rise but held the folder out to Camaro. Camaro took it. Inside were papers full of numbers and years, a neatly gridded layout under Annabel's name, and Camaro's.

Camaro looked at the columns of numbers. She closed the folder. "So?"

"Part of what we do when we run deep background checks on people is analyze their financial information," Hannon said. "Credit ratings, debt burden, income, taxes paid, taxes owed. It's pretty thorough. We can know everything in a day, from the first car you bought all the way to what's in your retirement account. Nobody can hide from the Internal Revenue Service. The Social Security Administration is a big help, too."

Annabel slept. Her breathing was mechanical. Camaro held the folder in both hands. "Okay," she said.

"Why don't you sit down?"

The room had one more chair. Camaro sat in it and watched Hannon watching her. The marshal seemed barely into her thirties, and the shape of her eyes revealed Asian heritage somewhere, though they were light even in the semidarkness of the room.

"You spent twelve years in the army," Hannon said.

"You know I did."

"Most people when they go in, if they don't leave after the minimum hitch, they stick around for a full twenty. So they can get a pension. You were on a steady promotion track, and you had all the commendations, but you quit. Why?"

"Does it matter?"

Hannon was steady. "How much did your sister steal from her husband before he died?"

162

"I don't know what you mean."

Hannon smiled thinly. "I mean that your sister lives in a house worth hundreds of thousands of dollars and drives a new car, even though she only works part-time at a clothing store. Before she left New Orleans, she was making nineteen thousand a year working at a McDonald's. And that's more money than she ever made in her life. Her husband was getting disability because of a bad back, but that wasn't much. Then she drops out of sight and comes back again as Michelle Amado with plenty of cash to spare."

"What difference does it make? She's the victim."

"I don't think so. I think she conspired to rip her husband off. And I think whatever she got from him she shared with you."

Camaro glanced toward the door. "Is this where Way comes in?"

"I told you, I haven't shown him any of this. Which is good, because the first question he'd ask after he figured out your sister was living on stolen money was how you managed to swing the purchase of a halfmillion dollars of Custom Carolina for your sportfishing business when the most you ever made in the army was around forty-one thousand a year."

Camaro said nothing.

"You can tell me the truth, or I can give that information to Keith and he'll tear you and your sister to pieces. He won't care if she's hurt or what it'll do to you."

"So what do you want me to do?" Camaro asked.

"I want you to tell me the death of Jake Collier has nothing to do with this money."

"He hurt my sister. That's all."

"Are you sure that's all it was? The two of you go through all the trouble of splitting up, working out a code to get in contact, and she calls you out to California to do something she could have asked the police to do? I've seen your record. I know where you've been and the things you've done. She has to know all the things I do, maybe more, and I think she wanted you to come out here and kill him."

"No," Camaro said. "No."

"I'm not saying she lied about what Jake did to her. I'm saying she let you believe what you wanted to believe."

Camaro fell silent. She thought back to what was said, and then further back to times she'd put behind her. What she'd tried to bury.

"She used you, Camaro. She pointed you at Jake Collier like a loaded weapon to protect the things she has. Did he ever ask her for money?"

"Yes," Camaro said slowly.

"Did he know where it came from?"

"No. No one knows."

"But he still asked for it. She had to protect herself. He was abusing her, and then he wanted to take away the only thing she had going for her and her daughter. That money is keeping her afloat. When it's gone, she's going to have a hard time making it in a place like Carmel. So if Jake Collier tried to take it, he had to go."

"My sister is a lot of things, but she's not like that. She's…she isn't what you think. And I'm not what you think. I wouldn't kill someone for money. Anyone I ever killed had a reason to die."

"You have a lot of faith in her."

"She's my *sister*," Camaro said. "You think you know her? You don't know anything about her. All of these numbers you have, that's not who she is. It's not who I am, either. It's just more bullshit. She had no one who could help her, and she came to me. Because that's how it works. You never turn your back on family."

"I want to believe you," Hannon said.

"Then believe it. Because my sister is not a monster. The man who did this to her, *he's* a monster." Camaro turned the folder over on her lap. She put her hand flat on the marbled paper surface. "You let me find him, I'll finish it."

"I can't be a party to that."

"Then what's the point of all this?" Camaro snapped. "You want me to stand aside while she dies, and do nothing? Because that doesn't work for me."

"Camaro, don't do something you'll regret. Whatever happened in your past, it doesn't have to be like that now. Help your sister. Help yourself."

"I'm done talking about this. Just go."

"Camaro," Hannon said.

Camaro rose and held out the folder. "Take it."

Hannon accepted the folder. "You're making a mistake."

"My sister did not use me."

"Are you sure about that?" Hannon asked.

Camaro didn't answer, and Hannon left.

She was alone with Annabel. She put her hands on the foot of the bed and looked out across Annabel's still form. The cycle of the respirator grated on her. "I'm here," she said. "I'm not going away."

CHAPTER FORTY-TWO

WHEN LUKAS RETURNED to the apartment with Brendan, he let the boy go in first. He secured the door behind him. Brendan ran to his room. Vicki stood with her hands hanging loosely by her sides, as pallid as she had been all morning.

"What are you waiting for?" Lukas asked her.

"I don't...I'm not sure what to do."

"You do like I said. Put those ribs in the cooker and get 'em started. I need to make a call."

"What happens then?"

"Whatever I want. So do it!"

He went to the bedroom and closed the door before he brought out his phone. He listened awhile to be certain Vicki was busy in the kitchen and not fleeing the apartment with Brendan. Only then did he dial the number. Camaro answered. "Did you get my message?" Lukas asked without introducing himself.

"You are dead," Camaro said.

The flat anger in her voice made Lukas laugh. "You're a real hard case, huh? I bet you got Jake real scared before you knocked his teeth out of his head. But I don't scare like that."

"What do you want?"

"What do I want? I want you. I want you sucking blood through a hole in your chest, and I want to see you die. I want you to die like Jake died. And I'm going to piss on your corpse when it's over."

"The cops are all over me. I can't get away from them."

"You better figure out a way, *and* you better figure it out soon. I heard on the radio that your sister ain't quite dead, so I'm gonna give you some time to watch her number come up. Then we'll settle it. You're gonna jump how and where I say you jump. And don't even think about screwing with me. You started this."

Camaro was quiet.

"You still with me?" Lukas asked.

"I'm here."

"You were wrong to prod me like you did. I don't take to that."

Again Camaro didn't answer.

"I spent a goodly amount of time down in Mexico," Lukas told her. "I learned a few things from the boys down there. They take revenge real serious. When there's a problem, arms and legs come off. They like to show off the heads."

There was silence.

"You think about what I've said. You have anything you need to say?"

"I'll tell you when I see you," Camaro said.

"When you see me, you'll be dead."

CHAPTER FORTY-THREE

AN HOUR LATER a cab dropped Camaro at the Holiday Inn. Yates met her in the lobby. They went upstairs to his room. Camaro beat her fist against her leg as he worked his card key in the lock. He held the door for her, and she went in first. Yates put on the lights.

The room had one king bed, perfectly made, and a desk area where Yates had set up a laptop and a portable printer and a scanner. Post-it notes were tagged to the wall in neat lines above the spot where he worked, each one with marker scribbling on it. There was one other chair, but Camaro didn't take it. She walked to the far end of the room and stopped by the window. It was full dark outside, but it had stopped raining.

"How long ago did he call?" Yates asked.

"A little over an hour."

"You called me right away."

"I did."

"Not the police."

"The police aren't going to be able to help me with this."

Yates sat in the chair by his computer and stretched his long legs out in front of him. He folded his hands over his stomach. His expression was dark. "This son of a bitch doesn't give a goddamn who he hurts."

"We've got to find him."

"This is my fault," Yates said.

"What? How?"

"There was something about his bond that I didn't like. It wasn't just the money, it was the man. You should have seen his girl come in to put her house up for his bail. She was shaking like a leaf. My

168

wife made the call. I could have said no. If I had, he'd still be in jail."

"He would have found some other bail bondsman."

"My son would still be alive."

Camaro stepped toward him. She thought of something to say and then reconsidered it. "Your son's gone," she said when the silence had grown too long between them.

"I know," Yates said.

"My sister is still alive. My niece is still alive. If the two of us work together, we can fix this. You can still get him for what he did."

"Why do I get the feeling I'd have to get in line behind you?"

"He's yours," Camaro said. "I'll help however I can. Whatever it takes. I'm in."

Yates considered this for a long while. Camaro let him think.

"When is he set to get in touch with you again?" Yates asked.

"He didn't say exactly. However long it takes Bel to die."

"How is she?"

"They say she might make it."

"But there's no guarantee."

"No."

Yates turned to his computer and called up a file on the screen. He had a list of names and addresses and phone numbers displayed alongside driver's-license photos of several men. He tapped the screen. "You and I already had a talk with Derrick Perkins, but there are two other bums who've gotten arrested with Jake Collier in the past. Both of them work at Carlson Lumber in Pacific Grove, all of them have Salinas addresses."

Camaro came closer. She looked at the men. They gave dead eyes to the camera. "What are their names?"

"Loren Masters and Nic Thompson. Now I'm wondering if one of the two might throw in with Lukas on something like this. I followed Derrick all day today. He went to Jake's place and came out with something he took to a shipping store and left there. I talked with the nice lady behind the desk, and she was kind enough to tell me the package is headed to LA."

169

"What's in it?"

"I have no idea. Neither did she."

"What address was it sent to?"

"Central Avenue. Right near downtown, or so the map tells me."

"So what do you figure? Do we talk to him again?"

"You'd think that, but if he's running errands for Lukas, he's probably scared as hell of something happening to him or his girl. You know now Lukas will kill anybody he can get his hands on if his first choice isn't available. I'm not sure we can break through that threat without knowing a lot more about what he's up to."

"So we get on these other two and squeeze them," Camaro said.

"Spoken like a true professional. Now, I happen to know Loren Masters came to work in the afternoon, so he's probably there until closing. I'd suggest we pay him a visit and put some pressure on him. Either he comes clean right away, or we crush him and then find out what he knows. I'd rather come at Derrick with the truth in hand already, so he knows lying will do no good."

"If the guys at the lumberyard see me coming again, they'll call the cops," Camaro said. "The Pacific Grove police already have me on their radar because of what I did to Jake."

"I'll run interference. You find Loren and make him pop. Make it quick, though. I'm an old man and I get tired easily."

"Okay," Camaro said.

Yates got up and drew his pistol. He checked it over, then returned it to its holster. "You got yourself a gun?"

"There's my sister's gun. The one I used to shoot Jake. It's back at her house."

"Best to leave it there. You already killed one Collier brother, and I suspect it'll look bad if you kill the other one, too. This isn't self-defense anymore. This is search and destroy."

"Make sure you shoot straight. Lukas isn't going to give you a second chance."

"I'll shoot plenty straight when the time comes."

Yates clicked the mouse attached to his laptop, and the little printer whirred. A single color printout ran out of the machine. Yates handed it over. Camaro looked at it. The faces of Derrick, Loren, and Nic stared up at her. She memorized Loren's face, then folded up the sheet and put it in her back pocket.

"You ready?" Yates asked.

"You don't even have to ask," Camaro said.

"Then let's do this thing."

CHAPTER FORTY-FOUR

WAY SKIPPED LUNCH and dinner and kept working. Hannon moved in and out, running interference with the local police and the representatives of the County Sheriff's Department. Way had no time for them. When they brought something useful to the table, Hannon relayed it to him. When he had an order to give, she brought it to the right person. It was best this way. He had a headache aspirin couldn't cure.

The door to the meeting room opened and then closed softly. Way felt Hannon at his back. "What is it now?"

"You need to take a break."

"I'll take a break when this is done."

"No, you need to take a break now. You've been at this for eight hours solid. Whatever you're looking for isn't there. At least take a minute to put something in your stomach."

"Leave me alone," Way said.

"Keith—"

"Leave me alone!"

Hannon said nothing. She left the room, and it was quiet. When he heard the door open again, he felt his headache spike, and he growled a sigh. "I'm not taking a break and I'm not hungry."

"I'm not delivering food," a man said.

Way started and swung around in his chair. The man wore a suit jacket, tie, and slacks and held a coat folded over one arm. FBI credentials dangled from his breast pocket. He tapped them and smiled.

"Jesus Christ," Way said.

"Not exactly. Special Agent Lewis Brock. I'm from the resident agency in Watsonville. I've been trading phone calls with your partner all day."

"I hadn't heard."

"Somehow I doubt that," Brock said, though he smiled. "She's really good, your partner. She makes it sound like you're helping out, but what she's really doing is keeping you out of things. It took all day for me to figure out what she was doing. I should have come right away and saved her all that energy."

A tic flickered at the corner of Way's eye. "If you've been talking to Hannon, you know we have the situation under control. We don't need direct FBI support."

Brock put his coat over the back of one of the chairs. "That's not really the sort of thing the U.S. Marshals Service gets to decide. Your bailiwick is fugitives. But this isn't just a fugitive case anymore, is it? Your man is running around killing people. Killing cops. Mind if I sit?"

Way gestured toward a chair. Brock sat in it. "We're hours away from getting our fugitive," Way said. "As soon as we have him, it's over. If you want to help out, that's fine, but—"

"Help out?" Brock interrupted. "You misunderstand me. This is an FBI case, and we're going to take it from here. I have four agents in Carmel right now interviewing witnesses and reviewing the scene. I'm going to personally go over everything you have to see what's useful. The minute your fugitive decided to bump it up to the murder of law enforcement, he became our problem, not yours."

"It's too bad the FBI doesn't give as much of a shit when a deputy U.S. marshal gets killed," Way said.

"How's that?"

Way snatched Lukas's updated wanted sheet from the tabletop and brandished it at Brock. "Lukas Collier killed one of my brother marshals right in front of me. With *my gun*. As far as I know, the FBI didn't send so much as a condolence memo to our offices. But now, just as soon as I have this son of a bitch in my sights, you're all over it and making sure you get yours. That's convenient. Real convenient."

A notch appeared between Brock's brows, and he leaned forward to put his hands on the table. "I think we're getting off on the wrong foot."

"You think so?"

"I'm not the bad guy here. This is a simple jurisdictional matter. You don't have the authority to conduct this kind of operation. I do. But that doesn't mean we're going to freeze you out. No, I *want* you and Deputy Hannon to work this thing with us. You know Lukas Collier better than anyone, and I wouldn't dream for a second of taking away your chance to put away the guy you've been after all this time. So let's not fight. Let's do this together."

Way stood up. "I'm not interested."

"Deputy Way, don't be an idiot."

"You know what? Screw you and screw the FBI. And screw everybody else who sat on their asses and let Lukas Collier run around the country doing whatever the hell he wanted. Because what's happened here is on you people. If he'd been picked up after Newark, this would never have happened. He should have been in a prison cell waiting for a needle by now, but nobody listened to me. So take this whole thing and stick it up your ass because this is my operation and my bust, and that's the end of it. Are you reading me?"

Brock's face was calm. "I'm reading you loud and clear."

"Now, if you'll excuse me, I'm going to go out and do some real police work. By the time you FBI guys are finished stroking yourselves, I'll have my guy. Period. End of story."

Way grabbed his coat and stormed out of the meeting room, slamming the door behind him. A small group of uniformed cops looked up at him, their conversation stopped in midsentence, but none stepped in his way or said a word. He passed them in a hurry, barely aware of Hannon rushing to catch up with him. "Keith, what's going on?" she asked.

"You have that list of Jake Collier's KAs that I asked for?"

"Sure, but the FBI—"

Way turned on her. He was burning. "They can do whatever the hell they want. You and I are going to run down these guys and see if they know anything about Lukas. Maybe they saw him, maybe they talked to him on the phone. Anything at all that might give us a clue about where he's laying his head. So if you're coming, grab your shit and meet me at the car. I'll give you two minutes."

Hannon paused. "Okay. I'll be right there."

CHAPTER FORTY-FIVE

Yates drove the Santa Fe to Pacific Grove with Camaro in the passenger seat beside him. They didn't play the radio or talk and instead let the hum of the tires on wet pavement do the speaking for them. Camaro looked over at Yates from time to time, but his face was blank.

When they finally drew within sight of Carlson Lumber, Yates released a breath that sounded like pressure venting.

"Loren better still be here," Camaro said.

"That's his truck over there in the corner. The white Tundra."

They rolled into the parking lot. Inside the broad open doors at the front of the main building there was bright illumination from lamps in aluminum shades. No one moved among the giant racks of lumber.

When they got out of the SUV, they met at the back bumper. Camaro saw Yates tug the edge of his jacket down to cover his gun. "Once we hit the entrance, I'll peel off to distract anyone working at the front," Yates said. "You keep on walking like you've got business somewhere. I'll keep talking until I see you coming out, and then we'll leave together. Sound like a plan?"

"Let's do it," Camaro said, and they went.

At the counter was a man in a bright yellow safety vest. Camaro didn't recognize him from before, and she didn't keep her eyes on him long. They passed under a blast of heat from an overhead fan. Yates split from her, arrowing toward the man and calling for his attention. No eyes were on Camaro. She went on.

She hadn't spent any time in the interior of the building, but now that she was in it she realized the full scale of the place. There were rows upon rows of lumber, the whole place smelling of the sawdust that lay in drifts and sprays on the concrete floor. The racks went all the way up to the ceiling.

The first two men she saw weren't Loren Masters. One smiled and lifted his chin in greeting, but Camaro waved him off. "Just looking," she said, and she kept going.

Loren was at the far end of the building, scribbling on a stack of lumber loaded onto a forklift. The moment he saw her, his face changed, falling slack and turning pale in the instant of recognition. He dropped the black marker in his hand and ran. Camaro went after him.

She caught up to him in the building's rearmost corner and put her foot in the back of his trailing leg. He stumbled hard and crashed to the floor with a cry. Camaro pounced onto his back, trapping his waist with her legs and snaring a free arm in the same moment. She caught the cuff of his pant leg with one hand and rolled, levering off the back of his head with her knee. They tumbled together until Loren was on his back and his arm was caught between her legs, the elbow joint locked open. Camaro dropped a calf over his face and cranked the limb. He yelped in pain.

"Shut up," Camaro snapped at him. "Shut up."

"Oh, shit, my arm, my arm," Loren wailed against the back of her leg.

Camaro put pressure on his elbow until he ground out another sound of pain. "I will break it right now," she promised him. "Just keep yapping."

"Okay," he said. "All right. I'm not saying anything."

"If I let you go, are you gonna run again?"

Loren shook his head violently.

Camaro released the arm bar and back-rolled onto her knees. She rose before Loren did, careful to block him into the corner. She glanced back once, but no one seemed to hear them. They were alone. "I swear, if you run—"

"I won't," Loren said. "I promise. Don't do me like you did Jake."

"I want to know where Lukas is."

"Lukas?"

Camaro punched him low and hard. Loren folded over, gagging. She grabbed him by the back of the collar and threw him against the wall. He put his hands up weakly, still coughing. She cocked her fist to punch him again.

"Don't do it," Loren managed.

"Where's Lukas?"

"I don't know." Camaro moved for him, and he threw his hands up again. "Wait! Wait! I've seen him. I just don't know where he is right this minute."

"This morning he shot a cop and my sister," Camaro said. "The cop is dead. If you don't want to deal with me, you can explain to the cops how you were just helping Lukas out a little bit. I'll only hurt you. They'll take your life apart."

"I saw him a couple of days ago at Flickers. But I haven't seen him since then. I swear to Christ that's the truth."

"What's Flickers?"

"It's a bar in Carmel. We like it there."

"You talk to Lukas on the phone?"

"No."

"Did he say where he's keeping himself?"

"No, nothing like that," Loren said, panting with pain. "He wasn't interested in talking to me. He was all Derrick, Derrick, Derrick. The two of them were all hugs and kisses. You should talk to Derrick."

"I already talked to Derrick. Now I'm talking to you. What's Derrick moving for Lukas?"

"What do you mean?"

Camaro hit him again. He bled from a broken lip. "I'm not going to warn you again."

Loren wiped his mouth. "Jake had some money put away. He picked it up here and there, had it all stashed at his place. He said he was gonna open a surf shop with it, but I never saw him do anything like that. He just kept saying it and saying it, and then one day he told us his brother was coming and he was headed out of town for a while."

"Where?"

"I don't know. Maybe LA? I think he mentioned it once. His brother has some connections down that way. But I don't know what's going on with Derrick, okay? You really need to talk to him. He was besties with Jake. He'd know it all."

"All of *what*?" Camaro asked. "Selling drugs? Is that his thing?"

"You gotta talk to Derrick."

"Goddamn it, if you tell me that again..."

"I'm not on the inside, but Derrick is. I know where you can get all the answers: you can go right to Flickers. I'm supposed to meet Derrick and everybody there tonight."

"Where's Flickers exactly?"

"It's right on Lincoln. Hell, I'll draw you a map."

"I'll find it. And you listen to me, I will come back and kill you if you're lying to me," Camaro said. "I know where you live."

"I promise I'm not lying."

Camaro considered hitting him again. She saw the fear lit behind Loren's expression. She took one step toward him, and he shrank against the wall. He was taller than her by inches, but in that moment she was the larger of the two.

"Don't meet with Derrick tonight," she said. "And do yourself a favor and stay clear of Lukas if you see him. His world is about to get bloody."

"He's out of my life," Loren swore.

Camaro turned away and headed for the way out. Loren did not call after her.

CHAPTER FORTY-SIX

LUKAS LAY IN bed beside Vicki with the sheets pooled over his crotch. He smoked and used a water glass as an ashtray. She lay curled up, her back to him. Occasionally she shook, and the tremor passed through the mattress. He touched her idly. "That was good," he said. "You're real good."

"Please don't," she said. He heard her crying.

"Jake was too soft on you. Always a gentleman, right?"

For a while he thought she wouldn't answer, but finally her voice came. "Yes. He was always good to me."

"And now you're good to me. See how that works? It says in the Bible that if a man dies, his brother has to take his woman on. So I'm only doing what God says to do. You hear me? Open up your mouth and talk."

"I hear you," Vicki said, her voice faltering. "I'm really glad you're around."

Lukas smiled. "It's not so hard to be grateful. And I appreciate the help you gave Jake getting this deal together. Working capital is hard to come by for an entrepreneur like me. Can't get a loan from the bank, can't get investors without someone putting their nose in your business."

"If I give you more money, will you . . . will you go?"

"Why do you want me to go? Didn't I just say I was doing God's work here?"

"You can't stay here forever. They'll find you. People will wonder why Brendan isn't in school. That thousand dollars I have is all yours. And then you can do your business wherever you need to go."

Lukas took a long drag from his cigarette, then exhaled toward the ceiling. The swirling cloud was caught in the failing light from outside, murky and oddly alive in its way. "You ever been to Los Angeles?"

"No."

179

"Better than this goddamned place, that's for sure. Just sunshine and money and ladies all day long. I've been all over this country, but LA is the center of the world. New York City? It's bullshit. You want to make a name for yourself, you go to LA."

Vicki was completely silent.

An ugly thought crossed Lukas's mind. He frowned. "You don't have to wait too much longer," he said. "It's not like you don't got it going on, but a town like this is too small-time for a guy like me. I was happy to let Jake be the point man here, but he's gone. I got to make new plans."

"What kind of plans?"

"What's it to you?"

"It's nothing, Luke. I was only asking."

"Well, mind your own goddamned business. I tell you what I want to tell you. The rest of the time you keep your mouth shut. You hear me?"

Vicki didn't answer. After a while she slid away from him and got off the bed.

He looked after her. "Where you going now?"

"I want to take a shower."

"All right, you do that. And when you come back, I might want to dirty you up again."

"Okay, Luke."

"'Okay, Luke,'" he said mockingly. He considered throwing his cigarette at her. "You really are a dumb bitch. And your son's retarded. Get on out of my sight."

She fled, and Lukas chuckled to himself. He tipped ash into the glass. He thought of Camaro and the dead cop touring around town in the cop's car. He'd only seen Camaro from a distance, but he'd recognize her instantly when he saw her again. Some things never left his mind. Underneath the sheet he stirred thinking of her.

He heard the shower running. He dropped the cigarette into the glass and got up.

CHAPTER FORTY-SEVEN

THEY PARKED TWO blocks from Flickers because there was nowhere else to put the Hyundai and walked back, their collars turned up against a cold wind coming off the bay. The streets of Carmel were quiet, and most of the little boutique shops and galleries were closed for the night. It was possible to hear the party sounds from Flickers from a hundred feet away.

A crowd spilled out of the front door and onto the sidewalk. Cigarette smoke whipped away on the air, but a distinct haze was visible inside the entrance, lingering around neon lights and low-wattage bulbs.

Camaro tried to look past the thicket of bodies, but it was impossible to see more than a few feet inside the door. She shook her head. "We're going to have to go in."

"You want me to take point?" Yates asked.

"No. We don't know if he's inside. Watch the front. If he rolls up on the place, somebody has to be out here to catch him."

"Shout if you need me. That's if I can hear you."

She elbowed her way through the first layer of humanity and managed to get inside the door. The throng was like a living organism growing out of the bar on one side of the place, casting out thick feelers in every direction. Camaro was barely able to make out the man and woman tending bar. Voices were raised in a loud jumble, backed by music blaring from speakers placed here and there along the perimeter. Led Zeppelin's "Whole Lotta Love" rocked the house, Robert Plant's vocals cutting through everything like a clean, sharp blade. The walls were festooned with license plates and bumper stickers.

There was no clear place to start. Camaro set out perpendicular to the bar, skirting the edge of the space. Her path would bring her all the way to the far corner, then hook around to the other side and back up again. Tables were scattered all around the center, shadowy figures huddled over them in conversation. Some faces she could see easily and some not. She searched for Derrick's.

Clots of bar-goers fell into her path, and she struggled to get around them. It took a few minutes to make the back of the bar, and there she could better see the booths that were set up along two walls. Little electric tea lights glowed in each one, a touch of class in a place bereft of it. Only a few people looked up as Camaro sidled past. The men gave her a second glance, and the women frowned. None of them were Derrick.

She finally reached the farthest corner and turned back toward the front. Her eyes roved over everyone she passed, scanning left and right, catching glimpses between moving shadows. Up ahead there was a hallway that broke out through the wall opposite the street entrance. A lit sign declared RESTROOMS. Camaro used that as her progress marker, getting closer step-by-step.

She was coming to the end of the booths. Camaro reached another, where a man and woman sat opposite each other, yelling to be heard. The man glanced up, and in that instant they locked eyes. "Nic Thompson," Camaro said. She could barely make out her own voice above the din. The woman turned to look at her. It was Rosalinda.

Camaro was shoving her way toward the booth when movement near the restrooms caught her eye. She looked through the sea of bobbing heads and spotted Derrick emerging from the back hallway. He saw her in the same moment and spun away.

"Out of the way!" Camaro yelled as she bulled through the people ahead of her. Men and women tumbled over, yelling in surprise. She stepped over them and kept going, spearing her way between the last dozen of the crowd to reach the restrooms. The hallway was clear, the doors to the restrooms closed.

She hit the men's room first, slamming the door open. A man jumped at the urinal and sprayed himself in the leg. No feet showed under the wall of the single stall. Camaro rushed to the ladies' room next, kicking it open to find two women near the sinks, checking their makeup.

Camaro ran to the back of the hallway. There was a door marked OFFICE and another with the label FIRE EXIT—ALARM WILL SOUND. The latter hung slightly open. The alarm did not sound.

Cold air smacked her in the face as she burst out into the alley behind the bar. Her ears were ringing from the noise inside, but she still heard the slap of running feet. She looked left and saw Derrick at a dead run. Camaro sprinted after him.

He made it to the end of the alley long before she did and hung a right. Camaro's heart pumped as she dashed the final distance and skidded around the corner onto another quiet street. Derrick was twenty yards distant, running hard. She went on.

Derrick crossed a street at speed. Camaro closed the distance. She bounded off the uneven sidewalk onto the asphalt and was suddenly awash in the oncoming headlights of a car. Tires squealed as the car careened to a stop, only inches from Camaro. She was frozen in the glare, momentarily dazzled.

The man behind the wheel lunged out of the car. Camaro saw a gun, and then she saw his face. "Don't move! Hands where I can see them," Way commanded. "Piper, get after that guy!"

Camaro moved to run again, and Way stiffened behind the gun. She stopped. Hannon exploded out of the passenger seat and ran after Derrick, who was a block away and moving fast.

"He's gone," Camaro said. "Shit!"

"Put your goddamned hands where I can see them. Lean over the hood of the car. Interlace your fingers behind your neck."

She obeyed. Way approached her without lowering his weapon. He kicked her feet apart. "Who is that? It wasn't Lukas Collier, so who was it?"

"It's nobody," Camaro said.

"Don't give me that shit," Way said. He hit her on the back of the head, and her forehead bounced off the hood, leaving her momentarily dizzy. "Who was it?"

"Somebody who owes me money," Camaro said.

Way grabbed her by the elbow and wrenched her around until she fell back against the hood. He forced his leg between hers and pressed

183

the muzzle of his automatic into her cheekbone. "Was it Loren Masters? How about Nic Thompson? Derrick Perkins? Which one? You're onto Lukas, so tell me which one knows where he is."

Camaro stared at him. "I don't know what you're talking about."

Way leaned into her, pressing the gun harder for emphasis. "I could put a bullet into you right now. Resisting arrest. I should. You want to kill Lukas Collier as much as I do, except I do not get in line behind you."

"I'm on a public street. I'm not breaking any laws," Camaro said. She looked into Way's eyes. They were fevered.

"You're not breaking any laws? You're chasing a suspect. Do you think you're the law? Because you're not the law."

"I know I'm not the law," Camaro said.

Way scowled. "That's right. I am the law. Me. I'm the man. Who the hell do you think you are?"

"Keith?"

Way tensed. Camaro turned her eyes, but not her head. Hannon was there. Her face was stricken. "Keith, what are you doing?"

"This doesn't concern you," Way said. "Just walk in the other direction."

"I can't do that. Put your weapon away."

"I said *walk!*"

"Keith, I can't. I won't."

"She's interfering with our investigation," Way declared. "That's obstruction."

"Keith, put the gun away."

He was slow to respond. Camaro looked from him to Hannon and back again. Way took the pistol out of her face and holstered it under his coat. He backed away.

Camaro rose from the hood. She felt her cheek and the impression of the automatic's muzzle. She looked to Hannon again.

"Go," Hannon said.

"Piper, she's going to screw this all up."

"Go, now!"

Camaro turned from Way and moved. She expected a bullet in the back. It did not come. She ran to Yates, and neither marshal followed.

CHAPTER FORTY-EIGHT

"HE PULLED HIS weapon on you?" Yates said. "He put it in your face?"

"Yes."

Yates shook his head slowly. They sat in the parked Santa Fe on Lincoln Street, alone except for the occasional car slipping slowly past. Carmel went on as if nothing had happened. "This is a problem."

"You think?" Camaro asked.

"If they were down here looking for Jake's buddies, then they're on the same trail we are. It's only a matter of time before they talk to Loren Masters and find out you rousted him. Unless you think you put enough of the fear of God into him that he keeps his mouth shut."

"He doesn't want me coming back to him," Camaro said.

"Okay, then. So the big question is, who gets to Derrick first. If it's us, we have the advantage. If it's the marshals, then we lose everything. I'm not prepared to let all of this slip through my fingers. Not when we're so close."

Camaro pounded her fist on the armrest. "He's gonna disappear. Now that he knows the sharks are out, he's going to get in his car and drive until the heat is off. We'll never find him."

Yates was quiet awhile. "That's not necessarily so."

"What do you mean?"

"I've been at this a good long time, and the one thing I've learned is that people in general aren't that smart. They like familiar places and faces, and they don't like to stray far from the things that make them comfortable. Now if it were you or me, we'd be gone in a heartbeat. But Derrick, he's not a bright boy."

Camaro digested this. She turned over the conclusion in her mind. "He'll come around again."

185

"I won't say I guarantee it, but I'm leaning that way. We might not see him at that bar again, and he'll probably steer clear of his work, but that doesn't mean he won't pop up at home, even if it's to make sure he gets his toothbrush."

She looked at her watch. "I can't go at this all night. I need to see my sister. We can link up again in the morning. I'll come to where you are."

"I understand," Yates said. "I'll take you to the hospital now."

They drove out of Carmel. A waning moon broke through a temporary breach in the clouds, giving the cold woodlands a silvery mantle. Once Camaro saw a fox at the side of the road, its eyes glowing, before it broke for cover and vanished completely.

"How long have you been doing this?" Camaro asked.

"This? You mean skip tracing?"

"Yeah."

"Got to be forty years at least. Forty...three? Something like that. After the service I kind of bummed around awhile doing this and that. Worked construction, fixed cars, cooked food. Pretty much anything a man could do to earn a paycheck. Lot of lean years. Then I heard from a friend of a friend that a bail bondsman was looking for someone to track down some skips. His usual guy had appendicitis. I didn't know my ass from a hole in the ground, but I figured, how hard could it be?"

"Was it?"

"Sometimes. Like I said, most crooks are lazy as hell. You'd be surprised how many you can round up just by knocking on doors and asking politely. That's why I don't much like the term 'bounty hunter.' People get this idea in their head that it's all about kicking down doors and busting skulls when it's not like that at all. The damned TV shows don't help any.

"Anyway, I've been letting my son handle most things for a few years now. Got my own bail-bonding operation, so it's pretty much paperwork and phone calls every day. Long hours are the worst part, but my wife and I have been putting away a good amount for a while, and when the time comes I'm going to step away completely. Except..."

"Your son," Camaro said.

"My son," Yates replied, and they left it at that.

The Santa Fe wound its way up the drive to the hospital, and Yates let Camaro out with a good-bye and a promise to call. Camaro stayed long enough for him to pull away and then went inside. She knew which way to go, and she went on her own.

A sheriff's deputy was stationed outside Annabel's room, sitting on an uncomfortable-looking chair and reading a copy of *Entertainment Weekly*. He stood when she approached and put up a hand to halt her.

He asked for ID. Camaro did as he wanted. The deputy made a satisfied noise. He opened the door for her, and Camaro stepped into darkness.

The only illumination was the soft light from the window cast by that same moon. Camaro heard the whisper of Annabel's sleeping breath. She could just make out her sister's form beneath the covers, looking small and frail in the dimness. The second round of surgery was complete, and she was still alive.

She sat in the chair next to Annabel's bed and said nothing. For an hour she simply listened.

A soft rapping came at the door. Camaro straightened up. "Who is it?"

The door opened, and a man in a jacket and tie stepped through. He looked as though he was sliding into his sixties, his face lined but not unpleasant. He stopped respectfully just inside the threshold. "Do you mind if I come in?" he asked.

"Who are you?"

"My name is Lewis Brock. I'm a special agent with the Federal Bureau of Investigation."

"I have nothing to say."

"That's all right, I can do most of the talking."

He came in and closed the door behind him. He moved to the side of the bed and looked down at Annabel. "I happened to be here when you came in. I wanted to see how she was doing."

"She's making it," Camaro said.

"Have you talked to the doctor?"

"Not yet."

"You should. She has some good news for you. Internal damage wasn't as bad as they feared, and if your sister makes it through the next twenty-four hours or so, she's going to be all right. Or as all right as you can be after something like this."

Camaro put her hand on Annabel's hand. It was cold.

"I understand you've taken some hits yourself."

"You get that from Way?"

"We have our own resources. We don't have to go through the marshals. But the groundwork they did isn't going to waste."

"I'm glad it's working out for you."

Brock let the silence grow between them. Camaro didn't look at him. Annabel's face was obscured with tape and plastic and blanched almost completely pale. She was bloodless.

"It must be hard to keep the kind of secrets the two of you have kept," Brock said.

"You people don't have any idea. Not about either of us."

"Look, I've talked to Deputy Hannon. I know all about your past. I don't know where the two of you keep your stash, but I know you have it somewhere. That doesn't interest me. You can keep whatever you have. God knows if I got out of New Orleans one step ahead of some of the wrong people, I think I'd deserve some peace and quiet in a nice town like Carmel. Or on a boat in the Atlantic. But now people are dying in my neck of the woods, and I can't ignore that."

"So what do you want?"

"You killed Jacob Collier."

"I did."

"Lukas Collier tried to kill your sister."

Camaro remained silent.

"If it were me, and someone did that to my sister, I'd want payback. Don't you?"

Camaro looked at Annabel instead of Brock. "It wouldn't break my heart if Lukas Collier died tomorrow."

"I don't doubt it. And I'm pretty sure you'd like to pull the trigger on him yourself."

"So what?"

"So I'd rather you not do that."

"What difference does it make?"

"I think your sister's suffered enough. Jake Collier was a bad guy, and I don't need to have much imagination to know what that meant for her. She called on you to help, and you did. He's dead now. Maybe it wasn't the best way to resolve the situation, but he wasn't the kind of man who would let your sister just leave him. I understand how it works, I've seen it more times than I care to remember. Some folks would go after the both of you for what happened, maybe put you in prison. Maybe her, too."

Camaro turned her gaze on Brock. "My sister's innocent. If you want to take somebody, then you take me, but leave her alone."

"I will. Looking at her in this bed...she's paid a worse price than doing time."

Camaro regarded Brock carefully. "What do you want from me?"

"Walk away. You did what you came here to do."

"Lukas is still out there."

"And we'll get him. But you need to think about what's best for you, your sister, and your niece. If you go after this guy — if you kill him, or even if you try and miss the mark — I won't have any choice. You'll have to go down. What good is that for anyone?"

Camaro didn't answer. She turned to Annabel again and listened to the hiss of mechanical air feeding her sister's lungs. "You seem really interested in seeing us get through this."

"That's because I'm on the side of the good guys," Brock said. He headed for the door. "Think about it. But don't think too long."

CHAPTER FORTY-NINE

AFTER CAMARO ESPINOZA had gone, they sat in the car together for a long time without talking or going anywhere. The engine idled, and warm air blew from the vents.

Finally Hannon had to speak. "That can't happen again."

Way made a noise that sounded like the start of a protest, but it was quashed. Instead, he said, "I know."

"The deal was Lukas. That was all. Collateral damage is unacceptable."

"I said I know."

Hannon breathed out. "Derrick Perkins is in the wind. We need to change tactics if we're going to scoop him up."

"She rousted him," Way said bitterly. "If we'd gotten here ten minutes sooner…"

"It's done. We don't have to let it ruin everything. This whole area is tiny, and he only has so many places he can hide. We start with the most likely and work our way down the list."

"We need to split up."

Hannon looked at him sidelong. "Why?"

"We can't be welded together at the hip. If we work apart, we can cover more ground. Besides which, there's the FBI situation to deal with. That Brock asshole is going to pull the football out of the way before we have a chance to kick. I can't let that happen."

"So where do you want to go?"

"Salinas. Drop me off at the courthouse. I'm going to start with the Superior Court and work my way up from there. Whoever I have to get out of bed, I will. This is a twenty-four-hour-a-day job. Time people knew it."

Way put the car in gear, and they drove away. Hannon looked out the window, but she thought intensely. "While you're doing that, I'm going to follow up on Perkins," she said. "He's not out of this yet."

"Perkins is going to lead us right to the man," Way agreed. "These guys around here, they're just wannabes. They don't know how we operate. They think this is just like dealing with the local cops. What do you have in mind?"

"His place first. I know it's a long shot, but I have a feeling."

"You better hope Camaro Espinoza doesn't screw it up," Way said. He smacked the wheel with the heel of his hand. "She's a danger to herself and others."

"If I see her, I'll deal with her," Hannon said. "You don't have to worry about it."

"I do worry. We can't have someone running around, getting under our feet. The FBI is bad enough. If she doesn't watch it, she's gonna get herself killed."

"But not by you," Hannon said.

"What? Of course not."

"You had me concerned, Keith. I didn't know what to think."

"You don't have to think about it at all. I have a lid on it now."

"Okay," Hannon said, but she watched Way for any sign in his face. Only when there was none did she turn back to the night view slipping by the window.

They made good time back to Salinas and at last came to a stop in front of the Monterey County Superior Court. It was an Art Deco building with a bas-relief of a sword-wielding and sighted Justice above the main entrance. Carved faces looked out from beneath every second-floor window. Way put the car in park. "You take the car," he said. "I'll work out a ride."

Hannon got out of the car with Way. They exchanged sides. Way looked frazzled, and she wondered how she looked to him. "I'll be in touch," she told Way.

"I know. Be careful, okay? Lukas is out there."

"I won't try to take him alone."

"Good. Because he's mine. He's always going be mine." Way gave her a look filled with a contained darkness and then turned toward the steps.

Hannon got behind the wheel. She stayed until she saw Way go inside, and then she pulled away from the curb.

She drove with the image of Way and Camaro Espinoza at the forefront of her thoughts. She imagined a step further, a moment longer, a decision made, and then she imagined Camaro Espinoza dead on the ground. There had been no question in Hannon's mind that Way could have killed her, would have killed her if the circumstances were only slightly altered. Hannon did not like the road down which that ran.

Hannon felt Jerry Washington's loss. He was funny, he was dedicated, and he was the best friend a person could have when they needed one. He'd been there for Hannon when she needed someone. They never talked about it afterward.

Way and Jerry were bonded in a very real way, like men who'd shared the same foxhole during a terrible artillery barrage and come out unscathed.

The mood had been black when Lukas Collier killed Jerry. The commander handed her the case and instructed her to take on whichever partner would be best suited for the task of finding Lukas and putting him away. Way came to her then and told her what it meant to him to follow the trail. She let him in.

She'd known what she was doing. Way had never hidden his agenda from her. No one would say it out loud, but they all thought the same thing. Cuffs or a bullet. Cuffs led to a stainless steel table and the needle. A bullet was a more efficient way of reaching the same conclusion. She made an agreement with Way, and then they followed the trail. Norfolk had been close, so close, and now they were close again.

No police unit had been stationed in front of Derrick Perkins's home. A request to the locals had opened up an opportunity for Derrick to slip inside. They patrolled frequently, but he was invited into the gaps in the hope that he would expose himself going in or coming out.

Hannon slotted into place in front of an undistinguished-looking white house with blue trim a little way down from Derrick's duplex. She switched off the engine and let the hot metal slowly tick into coolness under the night sky.

She was tired. She made a note of all the cars and trucks on the street.

One light was on at Derrick's house, burning in the carport. The rest of the place was dark.

Two hours passed. Headlights turned in at the far end of the block, then winked out. Hannon yawned and went on watching. When she saw the shadowy figure moving along the sidewalk, she sat up and rubbed her eyes.

The man drew closer, but he was just a shape until he passed beneath the glow of a streetlight. Even at a distance she recognized Derrick Perkins. He moved past the houses, trying his best to stick to the darkness, before slipping across the lawn of his duplex and heading for the front door. Hannon saw the pale oval of his face as he looked around once before disappearing inside.

Hannon reached for her phone. She had it in her hand but then paused. She put it down. In the dark she waited for him to emerge again.

CHAPTER FIFTY

YATES WATCHED DERRICK'S place for hours, parked across the street and down two doors, where he had a full view of the duplex without being too obvious about it. He paid no attention to the cold, not running the engine even for warmth.

His body was hungry, but he did not allow that to distract him. Cars came and went. Yates waited with tension in his spine whenever a new vehicle appeared on the street, and remained coiled until he saw neither driver nor passenger was Derrick or Lukas.

It was false dawn when his phone rang. It was shrill and startling in the absolute quiet of the SUV's cabin, and Yates hastened to silence it. He checked the number and answered. "Hello, darlin'," he said.

"Jeremy," his wife said, "why haven't you called?"

"I didn't want to call until I had something for sure."

"And you don't?"

"I might. I don't want to get either of our hopes up."

"You sound tired."

"I'm fine."

Yates imagined her in their home. She was small and frail, four years older than he was but carrying the years differently. Some days she seemed younger and more vital, but other times he saw the age weighing on her, and it reminded him that fifty-three years was a long time and no marriage lasted forever. In the end there was no choice but to part.

"Are you there?"

"I'm here. Sorry. Maybe I am a little tired. A little."

"Are you eating?"

"Yes."

"You have to eat, Jeremy. Tell me you're eating."

"I'm eating," he lied. "I had a big chicken-fried steak for dinner last night with a baked potato. It was almost as good as one of yours."

"Are you staying safe? Are you letting the police do their job?"

"Yes. I'm only here to help. When it comes time to bring Lukas in, I'll step back and let them do all the heavy lifting. Then it's back on a plane and home again. I promise."

Trish was quiet awhile. "I dreamed about Stanley."

"Don't torture yourself, Trish."

"No, it was a good dream. He told me he made it to the other side and was with Grandma and Grandpa. He looked good, Jeremy. Healthy. And he didn't have that silly chin beard. You know how much I hated that thing."

"I know. I guess Saint Peter doesn't allow any chin beards through the pearly gates."

"Don't make fun of me."

"I'm not," Yates said. "I never would."

"He told me to tell you not to blame yourself. He made a mistake, he said, but it wasn't your fault."

"I think that's all I want to hear about this dream," Yates said.

"He said it, Jeremy. He wants you to know it's not your fault what happened. He knows you're taking it hard, and he wants to take that burden from you."

Yates looked at the dome light above his head and sighed. "I don't blame myself. I blame Lukas Collier and his gun. And Lukas is going to pay for everything he's done. In this life and the next. There's no heaven for him."

"I love you, Jeremy."

"I love you, too. I have to go."

"Call me soon."

"I will. Good-bye, darlin'." He ended the call and put his phone in the cup holder.

"Dreams," he said out loud. He heard the bitter sound in his voice and was angry at himself for it. He turned his mind to the scene on the street, the darkened duplex where Derrick kept his home. It was possible Derrick had beaten him there, but it was unlikely. The woman,

Rosalinda, was sleeping in her bed alone. Maybe she knew where Derrick was, maybe she did not. Sooner or later Yates would have to move, and that move would be toward her.

The hint of motion on the street caught the corner of his eye, and he peered into the shadows. Someone approached, and Yates knew without having to see more that it was Derrick. No honest man moved in this way, starting and stopping in the darkness and skittering past the light like a startled cockroach. Yates drew his gun and put his hand on the door handle.

Derrick came closer, then hightailed it across his lawn to the door before vanishing inside. Yates did not get out. He put his gun away and grabbed his phone. He dialed, and after one ring Camaro answered. "He's here," Yates said.

"I'm coming. Give me the address again. I'll take a cab."

Yates checked the rearview mirror as a car appeared at the end of the block and cruised closer. He waited until it passed and only then realized he'd been holding his breath. "Tell them to drop you at the corner," he said. "Come in quiet. You'll see me across the street. We'll visit him together."

"I'm going now."

"Good, because I don't know how long it'll be before he scoots again."

Camaro hung up without saying good-bye. Yates forced himself still and went on watching.

CHAPTER FIFTY-ONE

CAMARO DID AS Yates instructed and had the cab let her out a block away from Derrick's place. She approached on the far side of the street, looking out for Yates's SUV and spotting it from fifty yards away.

Yates unlocked the passenger door for her. She got in. It was no warmer inside than out. "You made good time."

"I got lucky. There was a cab making a drop-off in Carmel when I made the call."

"What about the cops? They see you on the way out?"

"They saw me go into my sister's place. They probably think I'm still in there."

"Then we have a little advantage. I've seen a couple of cops cruise the place while I've been waiting, but no one's settling in. They must not think Derrick's worth sitting on, or maybe they're playing a different game. The important thing is that we have a clear window to get this done."

"I have a problem," Camaro said.

"What is it?"

Camaro told him about Brock. She watched his face as she relayed the story. His face was stony, and he showed no reaction until she was done.

Yates sighed. "So I take it because you're here that you're not going to take this Special Agent Brock's advice?"

"That's right."

"I suppose it's your call to make. But I think you ought to consider what might come from this."

"I already thought about it." Camaro checked the house. It was dead. The sky was lightening. "He's still in there?"

"Unless he ducked out the back. He'll move before dawn, though. I can guarantee it."

"Then let's go."

She opened her door. Yates stopped her with a hand on her arm. "Hold on a second."

Camaro shrugged his hand away. "What's the problem?"

"Do we have a plan, or is this cowboy time again?"

"I can go in alone," Camaro said.

"I wouldn't advise it."

"This guy is a leech. He's not gonna hurt me."

"Thinking like that is what gets people hurt."

"Well, what's your suggestion, old man?"

"I'm only giving you the benefit of my experience. You go in there like a steamroller, you might get more than you bargained for."

Camaro eased the door shut again. The dome light went out. She reached for the small of her back beneath her jacket and drew Annabel's Glock. "I'm going in there with you or without you. I'd rather you came along. But if you don't, I have my backup right here."

Yates considered the gun. "You going to kill him, too?"

"If I have to."

"Just like that?"

Camaro looked at him.

He nodded. "Okay, then."

She put the gun away and got out of the Santa Fe. She waited long enough for Yates to join her, then jogged across the street toward Derrick's house. Yates was slower, and she heard him breathing as they came up on the dark side of the duplex, caught only by the light in the carport. "Front door or side?" she asked him.

"Front door. No light."

They went onto Derrick's porch and stood in the shadows. Camaro stepped up to the door and listened, but there was no sound. She drew the gun, stood with her back to the frame, and cocked a leg to kick. Yates waved for her to stop, and she froze. "What?"

Yates produced a small leather wallet. "There are quieter ways," he said, and then he knelt before the door.

Camaro waited the long seconds as Yates picked the lock. She checked her watch twice, but only a minute passed. As the sweep hand finished a full circuit, she heard the tinny click of tumblers falling into place. Yates tried the knob, and the door came open silently.

He drew his stainless steel .45 as Camaro passed through the door. They were in the front room where they'd questioned Derrick and Rosalinda before. No one was in sight, and the space was inky.

Yates pushed the door shut behind them, and they advanced in the dark. Camaro's vision adjusted to the dimness as she searched out ahead of her for sounds of life. A gentle snoring passed down the hall toward her.

They passed a bedroom on the right side. Camaro cleared it with the Glock, checking corners and the space behind the door. It was made up as a guest space, with a narrow bed. At the end of the hall past the room were two more, left and right. She heard sleeping breath on the left.

The door was half closed. Camaro reached ahead to gently press it out of the way. She saw into the darkened bedroom, noted the dresser and the window, the closet, and a chair piled with laundry. On the bed, Rosalinda slept beneath the covers, while Derrick sprawled atop the sheets, fully clothed, a half-packed bag at his feet.

Camaro entered. She motioned for Yates to swing around the far side of the bed, and he did so without a sound. For a moment they hovered over the sleeping bodies. Rosalinda sighed in her sleep. Derrick snored again.

She closed a hand over his mouth and pressed the muzzle of her pistol into his eye in the same motion. Derrick started awake, a shout muffled. Rosalinda was jarred awake, but before she screamed, Yates showed her his .45, and she stifled herself. "Shh," Camaro said.

Derrick's uncovered eye bulged. Camaro kept her hand clamped in place, and breath hissed through his nostrils. She felt an uncontrollable shiver pass through his entire body. Rosalinda made a small noise of abject terror.

"I'm going to take away my hand," Camaro told Derrick. "You don't speak until spoken to. You don't make any other sound."

Derrick agreed with a repeated nod. When Camaro drew her hand back, breath exploded from between his lips, and he sucked at the air as if he had been held underwater for a minute. "I'm not gonna—"

Camaro rapped him with the Glock. "I said *quiet*."

This time he didn't speak. He let one hand fall and sought out Rosalinda's. They clung together, shivering and silent. Rosalinda breathed in gasps.

"You were bullshitting us before," Camaro said. "You know exactly where Lukas is, don't you?"

"I swear I don't."

Camaro put the muzzle of the Glock against his forehead. "And I swear I will put a bullet in your skull right here, right now, if you don't start telling me the truth. And if you go, then your girl has to go, too. That's just how it works."

She felt Yates watching her. She silenced him with a gesture. He said nothing.

"You're running errands for Lukas. You sent something to LA for him. And now you're packing up for a trip. Was that money you sent ahead? What's Lukas doing with it?"

Derrick hesitated. "Can I talk?"

"Talk."

"Luke told me to get Jake's stash and send it to a friend."

"What friend?"

"Uh . . . Spencer. Konnor Spencer."

"Who is he?"

"I don't know."

"What does he want with Jake's money?"

She saw Derrick's eyelid flicker, and then she prodded him with her gun again. "I don't have all night, Derrick. He hurt my sister. He killed a cop who was only doing her job. This is the *end*. No more games."

"I'm not playing any games. Honest."

"Is he following the money to LA? Is he even in town anymore?"

"I really don't—"

"I'm going to count down from five," Camaro said. "Where is he?"

"I don't know."

"Five."

"You have to believe me, I don't know where he's hiding at."

"Four."

"Jesus Christ, I don't have any idea! I didn't know he was going to kill a cop. I would never go along with that."

"Three."

"Camaro," Yates said.

"Later. Two."

"Camaro!"

"One." Camaro put her finger on the trigger.

Derrick's bladder let go, and the smell of urine rose from the bed. He shook as though he were in the throes of a seizure, and he squeezed his eyes shut. "Oh, God," he said.

"He knows," Rosalinda said.

Camaro looked at her, but kept the gun on Derrick. "Talk."

"They've been on the phone a lot. Jake was putting together some kind of deal with his brother, and they were going to bring Derrick in on it. But they needed cash. That was Jake's job."

"What kind of deal?" Yates asked.

"He'll kill me," Derrick managed. His throat was tight, the cords showing beneath the skin.

"*I'll* kill you," Camaro said. "You are holding at one."

"Okay!" Derrick burst out. "It's all about bringing in grass, all right? Luke would get the stuff wholesale and then we'd retail it out all around Monterey Bay. It was easy green as long as Jake could come up with the seed money. We were all going to be in on it with him."

Camaro glanced at Yates. "Surf shop, my ass."

"Surfers smoke a lot of weed," Yates replied.

Camaro returned her attention to Derrick. "You were going to LA with Lukas?"

"Yeah. No more Jake, so he needed a local guy."

"He's got a lot of balls doing business, with everybody from the marshals to the FBI breathing down his neck," Yates said.

"Luke's crazy. But he said I'd be rich. I just want to make some money. I don't want anyone dying. That's not me. I'm not like that. But I couldn't say no to him once we got started. I'm in too deep."

"If you're still here, then he's still here," Camaro said. "Where?"

"He's staying with Vicki. Vicki Nelson. I can give you the address and everything you need."

"Talk," Camaro said.

Derrick reeled off an address that meant nothing to Camaro. Beside him, Rosalinda sobbed openly. Derrick still shivered and twitched. The room stank of piss now.

"This is where he's holed up?" Camaro asked.

"I only know he used to be there. Maybe he's moved on. He was going to call me when it was time to move."

Camaro spared a look toward Yates. He regarded her in the darkness, his eyes black. He put his .45 away. "We can find him now," Yates said.

Derrick spasmed violently when Camaro took the gun from his head. He reached for Rosalinda, and she gathered him to her. Camaro heard him crying now, too. She looked down on them entwined together. She put the Glock at the small of her back.

"We got what we needed," Yates said.

"Wait," Camaro said.

"He could be moving now. We have to go."

"If we leave here with them loose, Lukas will know before we're a mile away."

"Take their phones."

"Not good enough."

Derrick looked up at her. "You're gonna kill us anyway?"

"You got any rope? How about duct tape?"

"N-nothing."

"Then we tear up the sheets. You get her, and I'll take him," Camaro said.

They shredded the bedcovers and prized the two of them apart in a burst of tears and protest. Camaro bound Derrick hand and foot on the floor and gagged him with a washcloth from the bathroom. Yates mirrored her on the other side of the bed. Sunlight glittered through the bedroom window by the time they were done.

Camaro knelt beside Derrick and spoke directly into his ear. "Never let me see your face again," she said. "Ever. You're still holding at one."

Yates went behind her, and they came outside into the morning. "So that's how we're gonna run this from here on out?"

"You have a problem with that?" Camaro asked.

"Would it matter if I did?"

They crossed the street to the Santa Fe.

"Not really."

CHAPTER FIFTY-TWO

SHE WATCHED THEM go in, and she watched them come out. She knew Camaro Espinoza by sight, but not the old man. In the interim she heard no gunshots, and no one else emerged from the house during the time they were inside. She surprised herself at her own calmness, and her phone remained where it was.

The sun was brilliant behind her when they hurried to the SUV and drove away. Hannon started the car and slipped in some four car lengths distant, invisible to them in the glare. All around them Salinas was waking up.

Her phone rang. She answered. "Hannon."

"It's me," Way said. "What's the story?"

"I haven't seen anything," Hannon said. "I'm thinking this is a no-go. If you think it's worth a shot, maybe the locals can send a couple of unis to knock on the door and see who's home. I'm pretty sure somebody's there."

"I'll make the call."

"How are things on your end?" Hannon asked.

"Slow. The East Coast is up, so I've been on the line with New York and Washington for the last couple of hours. They're sending me up the totem pole to San Fran. I don't know if this means I'm getting somewhere or I'm getting set back. All I know is that no one's told me specifically to answer to Brock. As far as I'm concerned we're still independent."

"Do you need me for anything?"

"No, I'm good. Why don't you swing by the hotel and get some sleep? We can regroup around noon. I should have some answers by then."

"You could use some more sleep yourself."

"I'm doing fine as long as the coffee keeps coming."

"I'll be in touch," Hannon said.

"Yeah. We'll talk soon."

She ended the call. The SUV was still ahead, stopped at a light. Hannon slowed down, trying to time the red light out so they would not come bumper to bumper. She opened up the dialer to input 911.

"This is nine-one-one emergency. Do you require police, fire, or ambulance?"

"My name is Deputy U.S. Marshal Piper Hannon. I need to be put through to the local PD."

"What is your current location?"

"Salinas."

"Please hold while I make the connection."

There was a brief empty space where music would have gone, and then a man picked up the line. "Salinas Police Department, this is Sergeant Philbrick speaking. May I have your name again, please?"

"Piper Hannon. I'm a deputy U.S. marshal. You can confirm my identity with a Detective Wright in your department. I can hold if you have to make the call."

"That's not necessary. We were briefed on you. What can I do for you, Marshal?"

"I need a make on a license number for a black Hyundai Santa Fe. Are you ready for the number?"

"Shoot."

Hannon gave it to him and waited while he consulted his computer. The answer came back in seconds. "That's a rental vehicle registered to Enterprise here in Salinas."

"Can you give me a number for them, please?"

"Of course."

He looked it up for her, and Hannon made a mental note. She thanked him for his help and cleared the line for another call. An electronic switchboard at Enterprise forced her through a few choices before she was connected to a human. She introduced herself to the woman on the other end of the line and made her request. "You have a Hyundai

Santa Fe with that tag number out right now," Hannon said. "I need to know who the renter is."

"Don't you need a warrant for something like that?"

"Do I need to get one?" Hannon asked.

"No, it's just…well, that's supposed to be confidential."

"You can tell me. The information isn't going anywhere, and you'll be helping me out."

"Okay," the woman said. "It's rented to a Jeremy B. Yates."

"Do you have a home address? What city and state?"

"Norfolk, Virginia."

"Thank you for your help. That's all I needed."

"Can I get your number so my boss can call you if I get in trouble?"

Hannon killed the call. They were on the move out of Salinas, headed southwest on CA-1. Jeremy Yates, Stanley Yates's father, was behind the wheel of the SUV.

CHAPTER FIFTY-THREE

THE SUN HAD fully escaped the horizon by the time they reached the apartment building. The city livened as the morning developed, and theirs was just another of a few cars moving through the neighborhood. Camaro watched through the windshield as the street numbers ticked by. Lukas did not appear on the street, nor was there any hint of him.

Yates parked. "Looks like a pretty typical setup. One main entrance, probably another one out the back for garbage collection and whatnot. Got fire escapes on both sides. Those could be a problem. In a situation like this, I'd generally call for an assist from the local PD. They'd cover the exits and make sure things didn't get out of hand."

"No backup," Camaro said.

"I suppose not. We got to make sure we hit fast and don't give Lukas time to think. I think we both know what he's capable of. He'll kill both of us sure as anything."

"I'll drop him," Camaro said.

"You seem pretty confident in yourself."

Camaro didn't spare a glance his way. She watched the building. "I'll drop him," she said again.

"Then I guess there's no sense waiting around."

They got out of the SUV and crossed the street to the apartment building. It was four stories, and Vicki Nelson's was on the third floor. The building's front door was glass but protected by an ornate set of wrought-iron bars. Camaro spotted a speaker and a series of labeled buttons just to the right of the door. "We have to get buzzed in," she said.

"Look a little closer."

Camaro saw the narrow wedge of battered wood jammed in the bottom of the door. Up close she saw that it was barely enough to keep the lock from engaging. She pulled the handle, and the door opened freely.

"What did I tell you about people being lazy?" Yates said. "It's the same all over."

Inside it was warmer, but only just. Camaro passed the rows of metal mailboxes on the way to the stairs. She peered up them, hearing nothing and seeing nothing.

Yates went to the elevator at the back of the lobby and pressed the button. "We'll take the stairs, but we want the elevator on the ground floor when we hit the place. One less way out."

A door opened and closed somewhere overhead, and shortly afterward there were loud footsteps. Camaro caught a glimpse of a woman's hand on the rail two floors up. She did not know what Vicki Nelson looked like. "Coming down," she said.

The elevator whirred to a stop and the doors opened. "Is she alone?" Yates asked.

"I think so."

"Step in here and let her go by. She doesn't see anything, she won't say anything."

Camaro went into the elevator with Yates and let the door slide closed. It had a window in the center, the glass gridded with wires. They looked out through it together until they saw a black woman step up to the mailboxes. The woman rattled her key there for a moment, then headed out to the street alone. Camaro let a breath go.

"Let's hope that was her," Yates said.

The elevator door opened at a press of the button. Yates flipped the stop switch. There was no alarm.

Camaro went to the stairs. She took them two at a time, trailed by Yates, who moved more slowly. He made the second floor and coughed twice, breath coming harder. Camaro paid him no mind, mounting the steps to the landing, then finally to the third floor. A plain hallway with doors on either side presented itself, windows at both ends letting in the sun.

She waited long enough for Yates to catch his breath, then counted off the apartment numbers until she reached Vicki Nelson's. She stopped there, tuned to the sounds of the building. There was a morning energy, and somewhere music came to her quietly. Vicki's door conveyed no sound.

"Let me lead the way in," Yates said in a low voice.

"No way. You're behind me."

"Not this time. Age before beauty."

Camaro let a frown crease her face, then shook it away. "Fine. But don't get in my way."

"Don't shoot me in the back."

Yates drew his pistol, and Camaro did the same. He took a step back to aim his kick. Camaro stopped him with an upraised hand. "What about the quiet way?" she asked.

"This time we want the noise. Be ready."

Camaro placed her free hand just beneath her sternum and laid the Glock across it in Position Sul, oriented toward the ground. She steadied herself on both feet and focused on the door. "Do it," she said.

The door took two kicks to break wide, but it was only a matter of seconds to make the breach. Yates surged forward with his gun up and bellowed, "Bail enforcement! Everybody down on the ground!"

Camaro fell in behind him and saw the living area to the left and the dining nook to the right. A woman in a short robe emerged from the back of the apartment, her face drained of color. For an instant she looked at the two of them coming through the door, and then she screamed.

"Get down," Yates commanded. "Bail enforcement! Hands where I can see them!"

A door slammed farther back in the apartment, and there was a crashing sound. The woman was seized by the neck of her robe and jerked out of sight, still shrieking. Camaro's pulse leaped as she closed on the screaming woman.

"Hold up a second!" Yates commanded. Camaro went on.

The hallway ran side to side along the width of the apartment, punctuated left, right, and center by closed doors. Yates broke right, and Camaro took the middle door. Her door was partly broken, and it came apart into lightweight pieces when she kicked it in. "Bathroom," she announced. "Clear!"

"There's a boy in here!" Yates shouted out, and Camaro heard the terrified bawling of a child.

Camaro cut left and advanced down the hallway. She heard the muffled sound of the woman weeping. A boot to the door split it down the center, and one half tumbled to the floor while the other hung loosely from brass hinges. She was through it before thought, the Glock searching out ahead of her.

Lukas hit Camaro on the side of the head with his pistol in the moment before she saw him. She reeled, her balance unsettled, but she held on to her weapon. In the crazy tilt of her vision she saw Lukas with Vicki Nelson pulled to him. Her face was red and streaked with tears, and she pulled against his arm. Her struggling spoiled Lukas's aim, and he fired a round into the wall.

Camaro came at him hard, passing underneath his extended arm and catching him center mass. The three of them tumbled together, crashing into a dresser and spinning to the floor in a mass of limbs and flesh. Camaro lost the Glock then, the textured grip slipping free of her.

They rolled. Vicki fell loose. Camaro scrambled to mount Lukas, but he was already crabbing backward with the wall behind him, leveraging himself off the floor. His gun came around, and she grabbed his wrist. Lukas wound his free hand into her hair and wrenched her around. She twisted against him. His fingers found the side of her face and then her throat. The gun canted toward her.

Yates was inside the shattered doorway. "Let her go, Collier! You don't have a chance!"

Lukas's fingers closed around Camaro's windpipe. "Shoot him," she managed.

"Let her loose!"

"Fuck you," Lukas shouted. "Shoot me, and the bitch gets it!"

"Shoot him," Camaro hissed. Spots swirled in her vision.

"He won't shoot," Lukas said. "He doesn't want to hit you."

Yates sighted in Lukas. His aim was steady. "I'll drop you where you stand."

"I don't buy it. Throw the gun down or she's dead."

Camaro shook her head violently. She worked a foot backward

between Lukas's. He held the gun to her with his right hand and gripped her with his left. He didn't throttle her more tightly when she reached back behind his grappling arm. "Don't do it," she told Yates.

"I can't let him kill you," Yates said. "I won't have that on my conscience."

"That's right, old man. Drop it, and I let her go. It's that easy."

"Don't," Camaro forced out. She felt the blood trapped in her face. Her heartbeat was deafening in her ears. Vicki lay on the floor, sobbing. No one paid her any mind.

Yates kept his weapon leveled. "I'm not putting away my gun, son. That's not how this works."

"You dumb old bastard! Back out of the room."

"I'm sorry, Camaro," Yates said. He stepped backward through the door.

"And I'm sorry you have to go," Lukas said in Camaro's ear.

At the edge of unconsciousness, she moved. He was taller, and his center of gravity higher. She pulled with her arm and pressed back with her hips in the same movement, driving up through his body and turning herself into a fulcrum. Camaro heard him exclaim once as he went over, crashing hard to the floor on his back, his limbs tangled.

Air rushed back into her lungs, and everything sharpened. Lukas rolled onto his knees and brought his pistol up. Camaro blocked it aside, and another shot went wild. She cocked a fist in the moment he speared her, exploding off the floor and driving his shoulder into her gut.

She hit something, and it gave way in a clamor of breaking glass. Air fell away behind her, and then she landed on metal, something stabbing her leg. Lukas was above her, his face twisted. Camaro got a knee between them and thrust him back. He hit the shattered frame of the broken window.

A gun thundered once and then a second and third time. Lukas launched himself down the skeletal steps of the fire escape they were on, trailing glass fragments as he went. Camaro's lungs bellowed, still pumping oxygen into her system. She struggled to get to her feet. When she sat up, she found herself on the broken windowsill.

She saw Yates entering the room with his gun up, and on the floor

Vicki with Camaro's weapon clasped in both hands. She fired again, though Lukas was gone, and Camaro felt the heat of the bullet. Yates covered her with his body then, forcing the weapon down. Vicki let go, and the Glock tumbled free.

Camaro lunged for the fallen gun, fire in her leg. She made it to her feet. "I'll get him, take care of her!"

"Camaro—"

"I don't have time to argue with you! Take care of her!"

She climbed through the window onto the fire escape. Without looking back, she descended quickly, jumping steps to each landing. Lukas was not in sight. Camaro slid down the ladder to the asphalt alley bordering the apartment building and spun in place, searching for a sign. She chose and moved.

The space at the back of the building was open, with two Dumpsters filled with trash. Alleys split off in three directions. Camaro dashed down the nearest one until she emerged onto the next street. Lukas wasn't there.

She backtracked and headed for the front of the building. Sirens were in the air. The sidewalk came into view, and she bulleted toward it. She reached it at the same moment a car screeched to a halt a dozen feet shy of the curb. The driver looked at her through the windshield. Camaro recognized Hannon.

Hannon opened her door. Camaro spun on her heel and ran back the way she came. No bullet chased after her, and no one cried for her to stop. The sirens were louder than ever, and when she made it to the next block she put her gun away and slowed to a fast walk.

CHAPTER FIFTY-FOUR

WAY GOT A ride to Pacific Grove with a Salinas police officer. He tapped his thumb insistently on the armrest as they plodded along in morning traffic. They passed through the streets almost lazily. Way simmered. By the time they reached the apartment building the simmer had grown to a rolling boil, and he bailed out of the unit before it had a chance to completely stop in front of Vicki Nelson's building.

A trio of Pacific Grove Police Department vehicles was parked out front with an ambulance, and a police line had been set up, manned by two officers. Way showed his badge and ID to them as he approached. "Deputy U.S. Marshal Way. Who's in charge of the scene?"

"The FBI just got here."

Way ground his teeth. "Okay. I'm coming in."

He ducked under the tape and entered the lobby. From upstairs came the clamor of voices in conversation, and he mounted the steps one by one, feeling a rod of tension in the back of his neck that hooked into the base of his skull and held on like a claw. Blackness hovered over him. The cops were congregated on the third floor, and they stopped talking when they saw his look.

Way showed his ID again. "U.S. Marshals. Is Special Agent Brock here?"

"Inside," one of the policemen said.

Way noted that the front door was broken open and there were black boot prints just below the knob. A man's foot. In the living room was another officer and two men in coats, their backs to Way. When Way cleared his throat, they turned. Brock smiled. "Glad you could make it," he said.

"Where's Lukas Collier?" Way asked. He kept his voice modulated.

"We don't know, but there's a BOLO."

"There was a BOLO before. What are we doing now?"

"We're getting ready to take the witnesses out."

"What witnesses?"

"We have the woman Lukas was shacking up with in custody in the back, plus her son. They're both in shock, so we have a medic with them. We're also holding a man who says he knows you."

"Who?"

"Jeremy Yates."

Mixed anger and surprise stabbed at the back of Way's eyes. He blinked the pain away. "Jeremy Yates the bail bondsman. From Virginia."

"Seems like it."

"Where's Hannon?"

"She's with Yates."

Way turned toward the back of the apartment, but Brock put up a hand.

"What?" Way asked.

"You look a little on edge. Maybe you want to let us handle things for a while. We're taking the whole thing back out of here as soon as the county's crime-scene people have a chance to go over the place."

"I'm fine. I want to see my partner."

Brock looked at him and then shrugged. "Okay."

Past Brock and the rest, Way looked into one of the bedrooms, its door shattered, and saw a woman with blankets wrapped around her, face and eyes puffy from tears, talking quietly to a female paramedic. She clung tightly to a small boy, whose face was likewise distorted from crying. Way made a note of the broken window, the glass scattered inside and out.

He found Hannon and Yates in the second bedroom. It was perfect for a child, with a neat IKEA bed and posters on the walls. A small table was set up for coloring and crafts. Yates sat in an adult-sized chair in the corner, and Hannon had a spot on the bed beside him. They were discussing something when Way entered but stopped as soon as he stepped through the door. Yates regarded him from across the room. Hannon opened her mouth to speak, but Way raised a finger to her. "Not a word," he said. "Out."

Hannon stayed silent and left the room with only one look back toward Yates. Way closed the door behind her and rested his forehead against the thin wood. Seconds turned into a minute until finally he turned toward Yates. He said nothing.

Yates broke the impasse. "Nice to meet you face-to-face," he said. "If you're Way."

"I am."

"Looks like you're a step behind again, Deputy. You missed my son's murder, and now you missed Lukas Collier. You're going to give the Marshals Service a bad reputation."

"How long have you been in California?"

"Long enough to know you folks don't really know what you're doing."

"And you do?"

"I've got boots that are older than you, Deputy Way. Finding people was my business a long time before you got into it."

"So how does it work?" Way asked. "You kick down the door, you come in guns blazing, but you miss the target?"

"I told the whole story to Deputy Hannon. She's an agreeable woman. You're lucky to have her on your team."

"I don't want to talk to Hannon. I want you to tell me how it is that you're here and Lukas is not. And I want you to make it clear to me why I shouldn't have your ass dragged off to jail for interfering with the apprehension of a fugitive."

Yates stuck his booted feet out in front of him and relaxed into his chair, his hands folded over his stomach. "You ever heard about something called *Taylor v. Taintor*? A little case from 1873. They probably covered it at marshal school."

"*Taylor v. Taintor* covers your ass if you're licensed to operate as a bail fugitive recovery agent in the state where you are. You're from Virginia, and this is California. You're a long way from home."

"California allows out-of-state bail enforcement for anyone with a bench warrant establishing cause," Yates said. "All I have to do is deliver my skip to state authorities within forty-eight hours of picking him up. It's all in the law books."

Way's voice shook. "You have one of those warrants, Mr. Yates?"

"As a matter of fact, I do."

Way took a long step toward Yates. "Then where the hell is Lukas Collier? If you're so goddamned smart, why don't you enlighten me on that subject? Since you like dealing with people who are agreeable."

Yates's eyes grew dark. "You better watch how you talk to me."

"I'll talk to you however I want," Way said. He rounded the bed to stand over Yates. "I'll put you in cuffs and bury you under paperwork until you don't even remember what year it is, let alone what your rights are. You think just because the FBI is here that I can't put you down? Because I can and I will. Everyone here seems to think they can skirt the law. It. Stops. Now. You tell me what you know, or I swear to God I'll drag you out of this room in cuffs."

"You telling me you can't run your own circus?" Yates asked.

"Don't you push me, old man."

Yates was still. "Send Deputy Hannon back in. She and I get along."

CHAPTER FIFTY-FIVE

CAMARO KEPT ON until she could barely hear the police sirens. She made it out of Pacific Grove in the back of a taxi she called from the phone at the front desk of a Howard Johnson Inn. She had the driver drop her off at the same church she'd used as her way station beginning with her first rendezvous with Yates and followed the path through the woods to Annabel's house.

She scrambled over the back fence and ran in a crouch to the rear door. Empty flower beds were laid in on both sides of the steps, ringed with black rocks. Camaro found the plastic rock with the house key inside and let herself in.

Several times she tried to call Yates, but he didn't answer his phone. At first it rang, but after a while it went straight to voice mail. The silence gave her pause.

In the quiet of the house she took her boots off in the guest bedroom and set her gun on the nightstand before lying down in her clothes. She closed her eyes and practiced breathing, in through the nose and out through the mouth, until her body felt heavy. She let darkness overtake her, and she fell completely away.

When she woke again it was not from any sound. The house was as still as before. She sat up and tried Yates again. No answer. She dialed the hospital instead and asked to speak to her sister's doctor. They had her on hold for a while. Finally a woman answered. "This is Dr. Fort. Who am I speaking to?"

"My name's Camaro Espinoza."

"Michelle Amado's sister."

"That's right. I wanted to ask about her condition."

"Are you available to come in, Ms. Espinoza?"

Camaro stood up sharply. "What's wrong? What's happened to her?"

"Don't be alarmed. Your sister is out of the intensive care unit. I would consider her condition serious but stable. There's always the chance of complications, but she's improved so much in the past twenty-four hours that I'm feeling confident. I thought you might want to see her."

"Is she awake?"

"From time to time."

"Can she speak?"

"She's off the respirator. The rest is up to her."

"I'll be there," Camaro said.

She ended the call and dropped the phone on the bed while she changed clothes. Something stung at the back of her leg when she took off her jeans, and she noticed the gash on her thigh for the first time. There was blood down her leg and a slash cut in the denim. The bedspread was stained red. Camaro felt for glass in the wound, but there was nothing.

She went to the bathroom and found a bottle of alcohol under the sink and a white washcloth. She twisted to see the back of her leg in the mirror and poured alcohol over the wound. The stinging was sudden and intense, but she made no sound. Afterward she soaked the washcloth in steaming-hot water and dabbed away the blood before exploring the laceration more carefully.

It was wide enough and deep enough for stitches, and it was still bleeding. Camaro rummaged in a cabinet. A square hand mirror with a fake tortoiseshell frame was stuffed underneath a pile of towels. She left the bathroom and passed through the house on bare feet, bringing the mirror, the alcohol, and the washcloth with her. In the kitchen she went to the beading case in the corner and lifted it onto the table.

The case folded open in sections to reveal compartments full of colorful beads, large and small. Camaro searched through the bottom of the case until she found some loops of fine wire, which she set aside. She looked further and found a spool of lightweight fishing line with a four-pound test. Another quick search turned up a needle. She took these.

She turned on one of the stove burners and let the flames rise, blue tipped with orange. Afterward she ran the sink until the water steamed. She measured out a length of fishing line and clipped it with a pair of kitchen shears. The line she scrubbed under the water, and then she doused it in alcohol in a cereal bowl.

The needle was not fine, but it fit the line. Camaro held it over the burner, just letting the flames touch it, until the metal was almost too hot to hold. She lifted the dripping fishing line out of the alcohol and fed it through the eye of the needle.

She set the mirror on a chair and held the needle behind her back. When the hot tip touched her flesh, she groaned through gritted teeth. As the metal penetrated, she made herself breathe normally. She drew the edges of the wound together with a continuous locking stitch, then tied off the end and cut it close with the kitchen shears. She tossed the bloody needle into the bowl of alcohol and sighed.

Back in the guest room she changed into a different set of jeans and put on her boots. She raised her phone to call Yates again, then stopped. She opened her call log and saw the recently dialed numbers there. A press brought up received calls. She looked at the numbers listed.

Camaro found her bag, put it on the bed, and packed quickly. Afterward she ensured that a round was in the Glock's chamber and slipped the gun in the back of her waistband. She took the bag with her when she left.

CHAPTER FIFTY-SIX

WAY CLOSED THE door on her, and Hannon found herself in the apartment's hallway alone. She heard Brock and the other special agent talking to each other in low voices. She went to the other room and peeked in. The woman, Vicki Nelson, was whispering something to the paramedic, whose name Hannon didn't know. Her son was rigid and silent, looking as though he might erupt into a scream at any moment. Hannon knocked quietly on the door frame, and their conversation stopped. "May I come in?" Hannon asked.

"Sure," the paramedic said.

Hannon entered. Pieces of door were all around her on the floor. A stiff, cold breeze blew through the broken window, lowering the temperature into the forties. Vicki had been barely dressed when Hannon arrived on the scene. Now she was in sweatpants and a sweatshirt, thick socks on her feet, a quilted blanket draped over her like a cloak.

The paramedic had latex gloves on, and her jump kit was open on the floor. She stood up as Hannon stepped over the threshold and came close. She spoke to Hannon quietly. "You can't keep her here. She's going to need a full examination at the hospital, including a rape kit. She's riding right on the edge. I gave her some Klonopin, and that's enough to keep her from getting hysterical again, but this is not a good situation for her. The kid's in bad shape, too. He needs a counselor from Social Services."

"I'll take care of it," Hannon said. "I'll talk to her for a few minutes, and then we'll see about getting them both out of here, all right?"

"I'll clean up my gear."

Hannon stilled her with a hand on her arm. "Leave it for now. Wait out front with the officers and tell them what you told me. When I'm done, I'll let you know."

The paramedic seemed reluctant to go, but Hannon patted her and gave her a smile. Hannon went to the corner and grabbed the chair there. She dragged it around so she could sit almost face-to-face with Vicki. The woman stared into the middle distance and shivered as if she were nearly frozen.

"Do you remember me?" Hannon asked Vicki. "I'm the deputy U.S. marshal who found you and Mr. Yates."

Vicki was silent, staring, and Hannon thought perhaps she was lost to any further conversation. Then slowly Vicki's eyes turned toward her, and she nodded slightly. "Yes," she said.

"Great. Then you know I'm one of the good guys."

"He made me," Vicki said.

"Who did? Lukas Collier?"

"Yes. He made me do it all."

"What's your son's name?"

"Brendan."

Hannon addressed the boy. "Did he do anything to you, Brendan?"

The child shook his head slowly, his eyes brilliant and wide. Vicki stifled a sob and pulled him closer to her. "He said he'd kill my boy if I didn't…"

"I understand. He's a real bad man."

Vicki said nothing. She shivered again.

"How badly did he hurt you?" Hannon asked. "If you don't want to talk in front of your son, you don't have to."

Fresh tears welled up, and Vicki shook violently. "No. I'll tell you. He came in and he told me to take care of him like I took care of Jake. I knew he'd kill Brendan and he'd kill me if I didn't do what he told me to do. Even when he…when he took me to bed and I had to—"

"Shh," Hannon said. She reached out to touch Vicki, but the woman flinched away. Hannon dropped her hand. "I don't think Brendan needs to hear that. They'll do a rape kit on you at the hospital. Whatever he did to you, they'll make sure it's all recorded. But he's not going to hurt you anymore. That's done. He's never coming back here again."

"He hurt me," Vicki said.

"Yes, I know. Do you understand you're under protection now? There's going to be a police officer with both of you every step of the way until Collier is in custody. You are safe."

"Okay," Vicki whispered. It was barely audible.

"Do you have any idea where he might have run to? Any people he talked about? Any places? Did he mention what he planned to do with the police looking for him?"

She didn't answer.

"Vicki, listen," Hannon said, "I can't help you if you don't help me. Anything he told you, anything at all, you need to tell me now."

"He talked about that woman," Vicki said.

"What woman?"

"The woman he wanted to kill."

"Did he mention the name Camaro Espinoza?" Hannon asked.

"Yes. Camaro. It's a funny name. He said he was going to get her to come to him and then he was going to hurt her bad. And then he was gonna kill her. But she came for him. She came with that old man, but I don't know where she went. Out the window after Lukas. Gone. Both of them gone."

"To where? Try to remember. To where? Did Lukas ever say?"

Vicki continued, her voice gaining strength. "He was talking a lot about Los Angeles. How he had friends there and he was going to make a whole lot of money. I didn't want him to tell me anything. I thought he was going to kill us so we couldn't say anything about him. I thought he was going to kill us!"

"It's okay, calm down," Hannon said.

"You have to believe me, there was nothing I could do. If I tried to tell the cops anything, he would have gone crazy. He would have killed us both. I couldn't let that happen."

"I understand. No one's judging you. But, listen, I need you to do something for me, okay? Can you do something for me?"

"Anything you want."

"When someone asks you who came into the apartment, you tell them—"

A man's voice cut in. "Deputy Hannon?"

Hannon looked behind her. Special Agent Brock stood in the doorway. "Yes, Agent Brock?" she asked.

"When you're done questioning Ms. Nelson, I understand she needs to be seen at a hospital. We'll take over from there. Tell Deputy Way when he's finished talking to Mr. Yates that I'd like to see him outside."

"I'll do that," Hannon said.

Brock smiled thinly. "Much appreciated."

CHAPTER FIFTY-SEVEN

WAY CLAMPED HIS jaw shut and listened to everything Brock had to say. He endured the passive-aggressive scolding and the smarmy declarations of interagency cooperation, and then he walked away. He found Hannon waiting by the car, and a new wave of ire passed over him. "You and I need to have a serious conversation."

"Let's have it," Hannon replied.

"Not in front of them. Let's go."

They got into the car. Hannon turned the engine over and let the car idle. Way stared straight out through the windshield, watching Brock confer with the county crime-scene examiners. His thumbs hands ached from clenching them.

"I guess what I want to know is how you ended up here without me," Way said after he saw Brock and the other FBI agent walk toward their dark blue Lincoln Navigator. "Because that seems kind of odd to me. Seeing as how we're supposed to be on the same page."

"There wasn't time to wait for you. I had to follow."

"I could have been on the scene with a police unit. I could have been right there! But you follow Yates all the way here without so much as a phone call letting me know what's up. So when I finally hear, it's all over with. The lady and her kid are saved, and the old bastard's in custody."

"I didn't even know who he was," Hannon said. "I've never seen the man."

"But you followed him anyway. Why? Because you had some kind of divine inspiration? A random old man wanders down Derrick Perkins's street, and you make the connection between him and Lukas? Is that how it works? Tell me how it works, because I'm not sure I'm completely up to speed."

224

He glared at her. "I made a spur-of-the-moment decision to follow up. I didn't know he was going to lead me directly to Lukas. I had no idea if he was involved at all. It was a guess, and it paid off. Until the shooting started, I could have been following anyone."

Way thought of Yates and scowled. "I told them to charge him with reckless endangerment. And he's not allowed to kick down a door in the state of California. I checked that. He thinks he has his ass covered, but it is hanging out there. Man, it is *hanging*."

"Did they let him go?"

"Yes," Way spat. "Free as a bird. They told him not to leave the area, but you know that's going to do no good. The first chance he gets, he's going to fly out of here and never come back. And if you think these idiots are going to go through the bother of trying to reel him in again, you're crazy. No, he's totally clear of all this. Walked in and screwed up the whole goddamned thing for the rest of us, and now he's out with no consequences. They're even letting him keep his gun."

"I'm sorry."

"Yeah, to hell with that. Everybody's sorry for something. What I want to know is where he got his intel and if he has a line into Lukas we don't know about. Because if he's set to make another run at Lukas somewhere else, I want to be there."

Brock's Lincoln drove away. Way resisted giving him the finger as he went.

"Unless you want to tail him everywhere he goes, we can't know where Yates will be," Hannon said. "And that's assuming he doesn't give up and leave like you said he will."

"He's not gonna give up. Lukas killed his son. He flew three thousand miles just for the chance to put a hole in the man. He'll do what he has to do, and then he'll run like hell. But first he has to find Lukas, and there's no way Lukas stays around here after this. No way."

Hannon offered nothing. She turned on the heater, and a warm flow of air passed over Way's feet. He was sweating in his coat already, but he didn't object. Other thoughts turned over and over in his mind. They slowly coalesced around Yates, settling into detail. His gaze drifted across the GPS screen in the center console.

"What's Yates driving?" Way asked.

"A Hyundai Santa Fe."

"Rental, right?"

"Sure."

"You think a vehicle like that has a built-in GPS?"

Hannon turned to him. "It might."

"Get the rental company on the horn and find out where their offices are. We'll go straight from here to there."

"Keith—"

"Just do it," Way said.

He listened while she made the necessary calls. It took five minutes to get what they needed. Hannon put the car in gear and rolled.

"They're going to talk to the woman some more at the hospital," Way said. "She's gonna be useless. What's her deal? She his girlfriend or something?"

"Or something. She was his hostage. He used her like a piece of meat. If Yates hadn't come in there when he did, he might have killed her and her kid."

"What else did she tell you?"

Hannon was slow to answer. "Keith, maybe this isn't worth it. We're too exposed. There's no way Lukas is going to let himself be taken alive, so no matter who finally nails him, it's going to be done."

Way felt darkness pool in his stomach. "What are you saying?"

"I'm saying maybe it's time to let it go."

Way ground his teeth until they ached and made no reply at all.

CHAPTER FIFTY-EIGHT

CAMARO ASKED FOR Dr. Fort at the front desk and was directed to an office near the emergency room. She waited ten minutes until the woman arrived. She was black and slim, with a serious face. She seemed very young. "Ms. Espinoza?" she said when she offered her hand. "I'm glad to meet you."

"Is my sister awake?"

"I think she might be."

They went to Annabel's room together while the doctor reeled off the damage done by Lukas Collier's bullets. Cracked scapula. Punctured lung. Bullet fragments in the liver. A kidney too damaged to function. Camaro heard with half an ear, her attention focused ahead of them, step-by-step, all the way. At the door, Dr. Fort held it open, and Camaro went through.

A soft light over Annabel's bed glowed white, painting a pale shroud over her. At first Camaro thought she was asleep, but at the sound of her footsteps, Annabel stirred. Her eyes opened. They were wet and dark.

"So she is awake," Dr. Fort said. "Michelle, I'm going to have a look in your eyes for just a moment. Be ready for a bright light."

Camaro watched Annabel submit to the doctor's examination. She flinched when the penlight shone in each eye.

"We were worried about a concussion when she was first brought in," Dr. Fort told Camaro, "but she's looking good. Everything's great. Your sister is tough."

"Yeah," Camaro said.

"I'll leave the two of you alone."

Dr. Fort stepped out and closed the door behind her. Camaro stayed where she was. She looked at Annabel, and Annabel looked at her. Neither said anything as a minute turned into two. Finally Annabel sighed, and her hand twitched like a fallen bird. She lifted it from the covers and held it up shakily.

Camaro came close and took her hand. There was more heat in it than there had been before, but it was still cool.

"I'm still here," Camaro said.

Annabel nodded. Her lips were badly chapped. She breathed raggedly, but it was real breath. "Becca?" she asked. Her voice creaked.

"They tell me she's okay. I'm not sure where she is."

"He tried to kill her."

"I know."

"That policewoman is dead."

"Yes."

A tear formed in the corner of Annabel's eye and rolled heavily down her cheek. Her lower lip trembled. "I'm so scared."

"The doctor says you're going to make it. Everything looks good. But it'll take time. It all takes time. You can't rush it."

"Where is that man?"

Camaro frowned. "He's out there. Somewhere."

"Are you going to find him?"

"I'm going to try."

Annabel inclined her head very slightly in the merest of nods. "Good."

"Annabel," Camaro said.

She saw Annabel's eyes quicken at the sound of her full name. Her rough breathing hitched in her chest. Camaro heard the thick wetness deep in her lungs. Annabel said nothing.

"You're going to have to do the rest of this without me. With Jake's brother gone, I have to follow. So whatever happens next, you're going to be alone."

Annabel's hand twitched. She felt around her until Camaro closed her hand over hers. "You can't let him kill you," Annabel said.

"I won't. But listen to me, I need you to understand something. Even if I get him, I have to stay away for a while. Maybe for a long time.

There's too much heat here, and there are too many questions. It's better if we don't see each other until all of that goes away."

"You're leaving me?"

"Not forever. And I promise you one day it'll be different. You said you wanted to be a family. I can do that. I think I can, anyway. But for now it's too complicated."

"I don't want to go on being apart," Annabel said, and she clung to Camaro's hand with sudden strength. "It's what killed Dad. As soon as we stopped being together, it went bad. First Mom, and then you. We can't lose everything."

Camaro touched Annabel's hair and tried a smile that died on her lips. "It was always more complicated than that."

"Promise me you're telling the truth. Promise me you'll come back to me someday."

"Someday," Camaro said.

"Promise."

Camaro felt the corners of her mouth turn down. She felt a weight on her that she hadn't been conscious of before. Annabel still squeezed her hand. "I promise."

"Then go kill him. Kill him and get it over with."

"I will," Camaro said, and she bent over Annabel to kiss her sister lightly on the forehead. Annabel's skin was cool.

"I love you, Camaro. Always."

"Always."

She left before the doctor could return. No one called her back.

CHAPTER FIFTY-NINE

CAMARO SAT IN the coffeehouse where she had spent a quiet half hour with Carly Russo a lifetime before. She had a turkey sandwich with Swiss cheese and a hearty mustard and drank a large cup of hot tea that was redolent of cinnamon and other, unidentifiable spices. Her bag was stuffed under the table, and she kept her back to the rear wall so she could watch the street.

The coffeehouse burbled with sound, the other tables busy with customers taking lunch or tapping away on laptops with earbuds plugged into their skulls. A pair of servers worked their way around the room, delivering food and fresh drinks, while still more customers lined up for take-out service and that important noontime burst of caffeine.

She had the ringer turned down on her phone, but it vibrated on the table. She checked the number and answered. "Where have you been?"

"Police custody," Yates said. "I missed you there."

"I got out. I'm in Carmel now. It's a place called the Roastery, on Ocean Avenue. Do you think you can find it?"

"Yeah, I think I can find it. The question is, what do we plan to do once we meet there? Lukas is long gone. He's in the wind."

"What if I told you there was a way to find him?" Camaro asked.

"I'd say I'm interested to hear it."

"Come meet me. I'm not going anywhere."

She waited twenty minutes and then saw Yates's Santa Fe cruise past the front of the coffeehouse. Another five minutes passed, and then he was there, stepping out of the cold into the warm, scented air. He spotted her and wove his way through the tables to hers. He sat down opposite her.

"You're looking run-down," Camaro told him.

230

"I always look this way."

"Order something to eat. We have time."

Yates flagged down a server, and she brought him a menu. Camaro waited until he made a selection, and they stared at each other.

"How's your sister?" Yates asked.

"She's going to make it."

"How does she feel about you haring off after the man who shot her?"

"She's okay with it."

"Runs in the family, I guess."

"She knows I can't let it go."

"I suppose that's something you and Lukas Collier have in common."

"I don't have anything in common with him."

Yates made a gesture of surrender. "Forgive me."

"Forget it."

"You said you had a way to find Lukas," Yates said. "I'm all ears."

"He's gonna run. You said yourself he'll run."

"That's true. Lukas may be a nasty son of a bitch, but he's not completely stupid. He had a pretty good shot at getting you for a little while there, but as soon as we rolled up on him in that apartment, he had to know the game was up. Whatever he planned on doing, that's totally shot. His best bet now is to run and keep running until he leaves the heat behind. They'll never stop looking for him, though. Not after he killed a cop. There's not a corner in this country where they won't search."

"Could he lose himself in a big enough city?"

"Sure, for a while. People have been known to stay lost for years. But here's the thing: sooner or later they slip up. And you have to remember it's the Feds and the Marshals Service after him. Doesn't matter if it's one year or ten years, they won't forget about him. They even got Whitey Bulger."

"Who?"

"Never mind."

"My point is that everything says Lukas will run to LA," Camaro said. "He sent money ahead, and he's got some kind of plan. So maybe he's only going to run a little way before he turns and fights."

"It would be foolish of him."

"We have an address where he sent the money. We have a name: Konnor Spencer. Those have to be good for something. And there's something else, too."

Yates's order came, and Camaro sat back while he ate his soup with a piece of crusty bread to sop up the last drops. He slurped his coffee when he drank it, and the corners of his mustache got wet. Camaro said nothing.

After a while Yates colored slightly and wiped his mouth. "Quit staring, will you? I'm a little bashful when I eat."

"I wouldn't waste your time if all I had were a couple of clues and nothing else to go on. What I have can put us right on top of him, and he won't even know it's happening."

"Well, don't keep me in suspense. What do you got?"

"We need to get to LA. Like right now. If we get there fast enough, we have a real chance."

CHAPTER SIXTY

THEY GOT ON the road. Camaro gave Yates an address in Los Angeles. They would be on the road for hours, and for a while they simply listened to the satellite radio and drove on US-101, skirting Los Padres National Forest and skipping through farmland carved out of the space between high-riding hills and low mountains. They were two hours out when Camaro's phone rang. She checked the number and answered.

"I understand you left today," Special Agent Brock said.

"That's right."

"It's good you took my advice. There's nothing left for you here."

"I won't be back," Camaro said. "Not for a long time."

"I didn't think you would be. Thank you for that. It makes my life a lot less complicated."

"I had to kill Jake, you know. I didn't have a choice."

"I know. I never questioned it. And it turns out he was putting the screws to his other woman as well. She gave him six thousand dollars over the last twelve months, all in cash. Don't know where it went or what it was for, but he wasn't exactly living the high life. Who knows? Maybe he was going to get into his brother's business."

"What is his brother's business?"

"Whatever he can buy, sell, or trade. If it's illegal, Lukas Collier wants a piece of it. Before he set out for California he was neck deep in a trafficking scheme, bringing guns up from places like Virginia and selling them in New York and New Jersey. That got him on ATF's radar and eventually the Marshals Service's. We have a hand in that, too."

"So who goes after him? All of you people want him."

"We're working on that. I'm finding Deputy Marshal Hannon very easy to work with."

"The other one's a prick," Camaro said.

"He is. But you don't have to worry about it. Good-bye, Camaro. Enjoy Miami."

Camaro ended the call without saying anything else. Her heartbeat was up, and it made her stitches throb. The fishing line was holding. She toyed with the phone for a few moments before stuffing it back into her pocket. Yates glanced over at her, but she directed her attention away from him, out into the winter fields that dragged by beyond her window.

"So which one was it?" Yates asked.

"Who?"

"On the phone."

"The FBI."

"He doesn't seem like a bad kind."

"I wouldn't know."

"Why don't I believe you?"

Camaro shot Yates a look. "Believe what you want. I'm here for my sister."

Yates made an affirmative sound. "You're the one she always came to? Big sister? Always there?"

"Something like that."

"That's a good thing. I had a younger sister who died when she was about your age. Stomach cancer. Ate her up from the inside. I was there every step of the way, and before that I was the one who ran off the bad boys who'd come sniffing around her skirt. I made sure she got together with a good man. I always wished she'd had sons and daughters of her own so we could see how things turned out for them."

Camaro didn't speak for a while. She watched the lane line slip by on the highway ahead. "When my sister was fourteen she was seeing this guy in secret. He was nineteen. One day she tells me she thinks she's pregnant and she doesn't know what to do. The guy won't talk to her anymore. She can't tell our dad or he'll go crazy."

Yates listened.

"So I went to the guy's apartment and I knocked on the door. When he opened up, I kicked his ass. I kicked it hard. He had a girl with him, and she was so scared she locked herself in a closet and called the police."

"What happened then?"

"I left. The cops came, and he wouldn't identify me. A few days later he drops an envelope full of cash in our mailbox with Bel's name on it. So she could take care of things. Then he moved, and neither one of us ever saw him again.

"My sister doesn't make good choices," Camaro said. "Whatever helps a person steer clear of trouble, she doesn't have it. And that's definitely true when it comes to men."

Yates spared a look in her direction. "How about you? What are your men like?"

Camaro's mouth turned down. "I don't have that problem."

"Don't like men, or don't pick the wrong ones?"

"I don't keep them around at all," she said. "That's the easiest way to do it."

"Loneliest, too."

"I'm not lonely."

The miles passed with no more conversation between them. Yates fiddled with the dial and found a station playing classic country from Willie Nelson, Waylon Jennings, and others who fit the mold. Camaro listened with her face pressed into a frown. When the radio played "Okie from Muskogee," she reached over and turned it off completely.

"Not a Merle Haggard fan?" Yates asked.

"I'd rather listen to nothing."

"That's classic music from my youth. Ol' Merle wrote that to support the troops over in Vietnam. I was back by then, but I appreciated the sentiment. Only got a few folks these days who'd write a song like that."

"I still don't want to hear it."

"Fair enough. What's your song?"

"My song?" Camaro asked.

"Sure. Everybody's got a song. My wife and I, we like 'Unforgettable.' They sang that at our wedding reception for the first dance. I have an old record I bought back in 1961 with all of Nat King Cole's hits on it. We play it on our anniversaries and dance right there in the living room. I won't say it makes me feel young again, but it does make me feel a little less old."

"I don't have anything like that," Camaro said.

"That's too bad. It's hard going through life without a song."

"I'll take your word for it."

Yates eased back in his seat and was quiet for a while. Finally he said, "I know it's none of my business, but the old man in me makes me want to impart some wisdom."

"Like what?"

"I looked at you, and first thing I knew you were tough. You went ahead and proved it, too. But the thing is, it's not enough to be hard. You have to let the softer side show through now and again, or you lose it, sometimes for good."

"I don't have time for that right now."

"Do you ever?"

"Hey, you don't even *know* me," Camaro said.

"Not in particular, but I know your type in general. Got a fight in you the whole world is welcome to. Some deserve it, most don't. All I'm saying is, don't let somebody like Lukas Collier turn off the lights in there."

Camaro turned away from Yates and looked at the hint of her reflection in the window. "Lukas isn't taking anything from me. Not anymore."

"That's good to hear, because you seem like someone worth knowing, Camaro Espinoza. I'd hate for you to turn away from that."

She looked back toward Yates. "You going to tell me to save my soul?"

"Souls are God's lookout, not mine."

"I just want to see him die."

"I hope your wish comes true. I surely do."

They said nothing else. After a while Camaro heard him humming the Merle Haggard song to himself. She did not stop him.

CHAPTER SIXTY-ONE

IT WAS IN the upper sixties under clear, bright skies when Lukas passed Santa Clarita and drove into the sprawl of LA. He put the windows down and let his left hand play in the air streaming past the car. He angled down into the Hollywood Hills on the way downtown. Almost at random he took the Alvarado Street exit and ended up on Sunset Boulevard.

He saw no stars, but there were out-of-season tourists on the sidewalks and filthy vagrants who hadn't yet been driven off by LA's finest. He spotted a Super 8 motel, painted canary yellow and wedged into a corner lot. For a moment he considered passing by, but instead he slowed and turned into the parking lot, taking the spot farthest from the street.

The manager behind the counter was a short, round Filipino man in a crisp white shirt. Lukas filled out the registration form with a lot of nonsense and passed it over.

"May I see your ID, please?" the man asked.

"I'm paying cash."

"We still need to see an ID."

Lukas scowled. He put a hundred dollars on the counter, then laid another hundred next to it. "One's for the room, and the other one's for you. I just want a place to lay my head until tomorrow, and I like my privacy. You got your form."

The manager examined the form doubtfully, then swept the bills off the counter. He made a card key for Lukas and handed it over. "It's on the second floor. I'll mark a map for you."

"Thanks, friend," Lukas said.

He had nothing to take with him except the clothes on his back, and he ascended the outdoor staircase to the second floor. The ice machine and a couple of vending machines were at the far end of the building, well away from his door, which meant peace and quiet for the time he'd be a resident.

Inside, the room was small and plain, without even a piece of generic art to adorn the off-white walls. Lukas locked the door and set the bar guard before heading to the sink. He washed his face with cold water, then scratched his scalp vigorously. He made a decision and took a towel from the wall rack, letting himself into the small room with the tub and toilet. He locked this door, too, before stripping out of his clothes.

The Colt went on top of the toilet tank. Lukas washed himself all over, twice, aware of tiny stinging cuts on his arms and neck that he hadn't noticed before. After he dried off, he examined his clothes for glass fragments and found a few in his shirt and clinging to his jeans. He dressed and went out into the room.

For a while he allowed himself to vegetate in front of the television, surfing channels, but eventually he realized he was only delaying the inevitable. He drew his phone out of his pocket and dialed.

It didn't take long for Konnor to answer. "My brother! I was starting to worry about you. No calls, and I got your package."

"Everything in there like it should be?"

"Close to ten thousand. Your brother came through."

"Is that going to be enough to make the buy?" Lukas asked.

"Plenty. We won't be able to tip, but who cares? I have people coming to make delivery at the toy store tomorrow, so all we need now is for you to make the connection."

"It'll be done. I got to make a call."

"Maybe you, me, and Jake can go out and grab some drinks tonight. See about picking up some ladies. Make a party out of it. What do you think?"

Lukas didn't speak for a long moment. "Jake's dead."

"What? When the hell did this happen?"

"A couple days ago. He got himself shot dead in his old lady's place."

"The same old lady you were talking about before?"

"It doesn't matter. We still have a connection in Salinas. One of

Jake's asshole friends. Guy doesn't know much about anything, but that doesn't mean he can't learn. But I can't head up there while he figures it out. I've got more heat coming down on me. I might have to keep my head down for a little while."

"Whatever you need, man. Semper fi."

"Semper fi," Lukas said without enthusiasm. "We make this first deal, I can afford to take a vacation for a while. Catch some waves. Maybe I'll shack up with one of those beach bunnies down by the boardwalk. Work out my grief."

"Well, you know I'm here for you. Anytime, anywhere."

"I'm gonna hold you to that. Talk to you later."

Lukas ended the call. He muted the TV and sat up in bed, then dialed a second number. This one took longer to go through. In the background he heard the thump and rhythm of hip-hop playing. "Yo, who's this?" asked the man on the other end.

"Otilio, it's Lukas."

"Lukas? Hey, Lukas! I was starting to wonder if I was gonna hear from you again, cuz. You keep me waiting too long, I make deals with someone else, you feel me?"

"Yeah, I feel you. I had some things to take care of, but it's all better now. My people tell me we can have the goods ready for you in forty-eight hours. We meet, we settle up, and everybody goes away happy until the next time."

"Are we still talking about the same amount of merchandise?"

"No change. You get everything you ask for, so long as I get everything I'm asking for."

"Have I ever cheated you before?"

"Never. That's why I like you."

Otilio laughed. "White-boy love! Okay, listen, I can get you exactly what we agreed on and deliver it anywhere at any time."

"You'll deliver when we deliver. Even exchange."

"You don't trust me?"

"Just doing business. I'll give you an address twelve hours in advance," Lukas said. "I don't want to see a huge crew."

"No *problema*. Talk to you soon, Lukas."

When the phone beeped and the call was over, Lukas took a deep breath and held it for a count of three before letting it ease out of his lungs. He wanted a cigarette, and he wanted something to drink with it. There had to be a liquor store nearby. But first he had to talk to Derrick. The deal was incomplete without someone to haul the load.

He called and called again. He left two messages. Derrick didn't answer. Lukas's mood grew dark. He left the room and lit a cigarette down in the parking lot, and then he went in search of beer.

CHAPTER SIXTY-TWO

THEY WERE IN Los Angeles with some time to spare before sundown. Traffic was dense and unforgiving. Camaro projected herself past all the slow-moving cars, trying to ignore the spring that coiled up steadily inside her, waiting for release.

"Take the exit onto the 10," Camaro said after a while.

"What next?" Yates asked.

"Watch for the 710 exit. Go south toward Long Beach."

"Will do. You think this is going to pay off?"

"As long as he still has the same phone."

"He might have ditched it. He might be over the border already."

Camaro glared at him. "You got any better ideas?"

Yates shook his head. "No, ma'am. I'm just being the voice of reason."

"You said crooks are stupid. They do dumb things and slip up."

"I did say that."

"So this is my play."

"I'm pulling for you. I really am."

"Watch for that exit. It comes up fast."

They were east of downtown, and if they kept on they would end up in Monterey Park, but the exit would carry them farther south. When the signs for I-710 south appeared, Yates followed them, and from there Camaro directed him off the freeway and onto the surface streets. They hadn't gone far when she called for a stop.

The street was narrow and ran along the length of the Long Beach Freeway, closed off on that side by a concrete wall. Houses had barred windows and sturdy fences built into low ramparts. Camaro pointed out a stretch of empty curb, and Yates parked. He killed the engine. "Where are we?" he asked.

"This is the house where I grew up," Camaro said.

She saw his eyes drift past her to the little white house with flowering vines overgrowing the fence in spots and a single tree on the lawn. When Camaro looked at it she saw through time, and in the driveway was parked a '74 Plymouth Barracuda with the cover pulled off and the hood up. A shiny V-Max motorcycle stood just inside the mouth of the open garage door, sharing space with a well-loved FXST Softail bought off the line in 1984.

"This is where it happens?" Yates asked.

"No, but it gets us there. Wait here."

She climbed out of the SUV without waiting for an answer and stepped off onto the dead grass adjoining the sidewalk. Two more steps brought her to the fence. A gust of wind caught her as she put her hands on the white-painted metal. She stood for a long while looking at the house. She had not seen it for a lifetime.

A glance back showed her Yates was still in the SUV. She nodded to him and set off along the street, heading two doors down to a house sided in red brick. The gate was unlocked, and there was an old Ram 1500 with scratched and dull black paint in the driveway. Camaro let herself into the yard and went to the front door. She rang the bell.

The curtains in the front window rustled, but she did not see the person looking out. A few moments later the door opened with the safety chain still in place. A gray-haired woman peered out. "Who are you? What do you want?"

"Mrs. Trujillo? It's me. Camaro Espinoza? I lived up the street from you. My father's name was Hector."

The woman looked at her, thoughts ticking. "Espinoza?"

"Yes. You remember us? My father died in 2007."

The moment was a long time in coming, but Camaro saw the light dawn. Mrs. Trujillo's face brightened. "Oh, yes! *You* are Camaro? You're so much older now!"

Camaro smiled. "Yes."

"One moment."

The door closed. Camaro heard Mrs. Trujillo unfastening the chain. The door opened again, wide this time, and Camaro saw the roundness of the old woman in her housedress. She stepped out and took Camaro by both shoulders before moving to kiss her cheek. Camaro had to stoop to allow it. Mrs. Trujillo was small.

"Come inside. Come in and see me. I haven't seen you in a long, long time. How is your sister?"

"She's good. She has a daughter now."

"Incredible! You must have a husband and a family, too."

"Not yet," Camaro said.

Mrs. Trujillo tsked. "You are a beautiful woman. Don't let it go to waste. Find a husband and then come back to the neighborhood. We miss Hector so much. He was a gentleman and a good friend to Roberto."

"I was hoping to see your husband."

"He's here. He's having a nap before dinner. Come sit down in the kitchen, and I'll wake him up."

The kitchen was not large, because none of the houses in this neighborhood were large. Camaro had a vague recollection of the Trujillos' house being like theirs, with three undersized bedrooms. It was difficult to raise any family of size in a home like this one, but it was done and had been for time out of mind.

Mrs. Trujillo stationed Camaro at the kitchen table and went to fetch her husband. She was back in a few minutes and bustled around the space, making fresh coffee and putting out cookies. After a short while Roberto Trujillo appeared.

Mr. Trujillo was the same age as Camaro's father would have been, and he was fleshy and well fed, like his wife. He wore a red plaid work shirt open over a white T, and his hair was mussed from sleep. When he saw Camaro he smiled, and she rose to let him hug her and touch her cheek. "Camaro, Camaro," he said. "Where have you been all this time?"

"She was in the army, remember?" Mrs. Trujillo said.

"Of course I remember. How is your sister, Camaro?"

"She's great."

"That's good to hear. We hoped she'd keep the house when your father died, but I guess she didn't see the point in staying. It would have been nice if she had, though. The new family is not the same. It's been ten years, but it's not the same."

"You'll stay to eat?" Mrs. Trujillo asked.

"I can't, actually," Camaro said. "I have someone waiting."

"Outside? Tell them to come in."

"We don't want to be any trouble."

"It's no trouble."

"Don't worry about it. He's fine out there. Really."

Mrs. Trujillo sighed. "If you say."

Roberto Trujillo reached across the table to take Camaro's hand, and she let him. "You have to tell us everything," he said. "It's been forever since we saw you last."

"Okay," Camaro said. "But I have a question for you."

CHAPTER SIXTY-THREE

YATES SAT IN the SUV for an hour waiting for Camaro. He almost didn't see her when she left the house down the street. She approached quickly and got in. "West Third Street," she said. "A place called iFix."

Yates set off. Camaro stared out the windshield at the road, saying nothing and doing nothing. She could be utterly still.

"How did it go back there?"

"Fine."

"How long has it been since you saw this place?"

Camaro shot a look in his direction. "I was here when my father died."

"How long before that?"

Camaro was quiet, until Yates thought she wouldn't answer.

"Six years," she said.

"Long time."

"It's complicated."

"I imagine."

"I don't want to talk about it."

"Then we don't talk about it," Yates said. "Everybody has secrets."

They drove awhile. Yates considered turning on the radio again for the first time in two hundred miles.

Camaro said, "It's not a secret."

"No?"

"When I joined the service after 9/11, my father wasn't happy. I guess he thought I was better off doing something else."

"Like what?"

Camaro shrugged. "Meeting a guy. Getting married. Like any guy would want to marry a girl who breaks down bikes for fun and can kick his ass."

"Father teach you all that?"

"Yeah. I put my hands on an engine when I was seven. He had me in Jeet Kune Do after that, showed me boxing at home. I got on the wrestling team in high school. After that . . . I didn't have anywhere to go. He didn't have any good ideas."

"What did your mother say?"

"She was gone a long time by then."

"I'm sorry to hear that."

"It happens."

"At least you were honest with him. Honesty's always the best way. In fifty-three years I've always told the truth to my wife but once, and I regret that every day of my life. I taught my son to be the same way. Have it out on the table. Get down to the truth of things."

"Sometimes people don't want to hear the truth."

"Doesn't mean lying is better. Your father probably appreciated you talking straight."

"I don't know. He just thought it would all work out. So I came home after Basic and we had it out, and then we didn't talk at all. He had a stroke that messed him up pretty bad, and then he had another one that killed him. I got home in time for the funeral."

Yates nodded slowly. "It's tough not getting a chance to say good-bye."

"Yeah."

"My son and I got along better than it sounds like you and your old man did, but we had our disagreements. It would have been nice to hash those out in our own time. But now that's not gonna happen."

Camaro kept her silence.

They were close to their destination. Yates took the La Brea exit. "You want to tell me what we're walking into?"

"There's a guy who used to live in our neighborhood who worked on electronics. He could do all kinds of crazy stuff, like wire the lights in your house to turn on and off by radio. Things like that. I know he does computers and phones, too."

"How long has it been since you've seen him?"

"The same."

The directions on Yates's phone led them in a tight combination of lefts and rights until Yates saw the sign among a string of others on both sides of the street. There was a nail place on one side, and a psychic reader had a storefront two doors down. There was just enough room to squeeze in across the street and not overlap into the red zone. He turned off the engine. "So you really think he can do this?" he asked.

"If anybody can find that phone, Mr. Cabrera can."

"It's illegal. He up for that? You haven't seen the man in an age."

"You got some extra cash?"

"I'm doing all right so far."

"Then let's find out."

CHAPTER SIXTY-FOUR

THEY SWITCHED SEATS halfway through the drive to Los Angeles, and now Way was behind the wheel. He had a direct connection with a woman named Marjorie Banner at Hyundai's Blue Link service, and he'd left strict instructions with her to contact him whenever new addresses were entered into the Santa Fe's navigation system, but there had been only one additional call between the time they left the Monterey area and when they finally reached LA.

It was easy for Way to spot the rented SUV once they were on the right street. He breathed deeply, but his pulse was up and he was getting a headache. He'd already swallowed six ibuprofen. The pain was tenacious. He was aware of Hannon next to him, seeing what he saw, thinking whatever it was she thought.

They couldn't park close, but Way found a spot fifty yards past the address and slotted the car into place. He left the engine running.

"I think we should talk," Hannon said. It was the first time they'd spoken in nearly three hours.

Way adjusted the side mirror to better see the entrance of iFix. He rubbed his temple with his thumb. "We already had a talk."

"I need to know what we're going to do here."

"We're going to look and listen." Hannon said nothing. He felt her watching him. He glared at her. "What?"

"I don't like the way we left things before," Hannon said.

"We're on the road six hours and you finally have something to say about it?"

"Keith—" Hannon began.

"Let me cut you off right there. I'm not having a replay of our last conversation. You have objections, and I understand that. But you knew going in how I felt about this, and you said you were clear on what we were going to do."

"I knew," Hannon said.

"Okay. You know Jerry and I came up together. We joined the marshals together, we worked together. He was like a brother to me. He *was* my brother. Anybody, and I mean anybody, who stands between me and taking out Lukas Collier is going to pay the price. So I'm sorry if you're having second thoughts, but I'm not. I'm doing this."

"I need to know if you're going to do something to Yates and Espinoza."

"I'll do whatever I need to do. If they're smart, they'll stay out of my way. If they're not, I'm not going to take responsibility for them."

"That concerns me, Keith. These people aren't the bad guys."

"They are interfering with my duties," Way said sharply. "I don't give a flying fuck about Yates's rights as a bail bondsman. That means shit to me. And what the hell is Camaro Espinoza even doing with him? Her sister's in Carmel; her niece is there, too. They need someone looking out for them. She should be back there playing house and keeping her business to herself. But, no, she's decided to make Lukas Collier her problem."

"He came after her family," Hannon said. "She has cause to worry if he'll come around again."

"He's never coming around again. He's not going to come around anywhere again."

Hannon didn't reply. She turned around in her seat to see iFix. "What do you think they're doing in there?"

"I have no idea, but I don't think they're trying to get their computer repaired."

"We know where they are now. We should get on Lukas."

"We are on Lukas. These two are going to take us right to him."

"How do you know that, Keith? How do you know?"

"It's the vibe I get off Yates, and it's definitely because of the sneaky shit going on with Camaro Espinoza. Yates is harder to fit into the picture, but Espinoza—she has dirt all over her. We didn't have to dig down an inch before we found everything she's been mixed up with."

Hannon turned away. She brought out her phone and fiddled with it. Way kept one eye on her and the other on the shop. She did not stop looking at her phone. Way shifted in his seat. "Man, I wish I had some sound in there. Some video, too."

"We have what we have."

"And that's dick."

"Can you at least tell me you'll try to keep them clear of whatever happens?"

Way wanted to grit his teeth, but he knew that would only make his headache worse. "Do you want out?" he asked.

"You're making it hard for me. I'm only—"

"It's a real simple question. I'll handle it on my own. You sign off as the lead on the case, but I'll do what has to get done."

Hannon fell silent. Way watched her, and she turned her face away from him so he could not see her expression. "I don't think I'm asking a lot," she said.

"You're asking me to take the chance that I won't get Lukas. That is unacceptable. I will not allow that to happen."

She looked at him. "What if it's me between you and Lukas? Would you kill me, Keith? Because that's what I'm thinking might happen."

Way stared back at her. "Don't get between us, and you'll never have to find out," he said flatly.

Hannon shook her head and looked away. Way went back to watching the shop. No one went in or came out. His headache boiled.

CHAPTER SIXTY-FIVE

JUAN CABRERA WROTE an address on the top sheet of a pad of yellow paper and tore it off. "Who wants it?" he asked.

"I'll take it," Camaro said. She looked at Cabrera's scratches. "Sunset Boulevard."

"Where exactly?" Yates asked.

"I don't know the place, but I know the area. It's about twenty minutes east of here if traffic's all right."

Yates laid five hundred-dollar bills in Cabrera's outstretched hand. "Thanks for your help, *amigo*. And if we need an update?"

Cabrera folded up the money and put it in his pocket. He was a very thin man with a few strands of hair pulled across a bald pate. His shoulders were spindly in his yellow iFix golf shirt. "You only have to call. Anything I can do to help old friends."

"Let's go," Camaro said.

Camaro jaywalked in a hurry and waited for Yates to get the SUV open. She got into her seat and buckled up. As soon as the engine turned over, she called up the GPS and entered the new address. It lit up on the map of Los Angeles, tracing a route north to the location of Lukas's phone. The blue line pulsed in time with her heartbeat. As they drove, Camaro checked her weapon.

"We get there, let's make sure we get the lay of the land first," Yates said. "I don't want to rush into anything."

"Okay," Camaro said.

"I want him, too."

They drove until they reached Sunset Boulevard, and then Camaro's eyes searched ahead. She saw the Super 8 and pointed. "There," she said. "That has to be it."

"You have reached your destination," the GPS said.

"I'm going to put us on the street," Yates said. "If he gets past us, I want to be able to pull out fast."

He found a place along the curb and parked. Camaro steadied her breath.

"Let's go."

The breeze plucked at them on the street. It was cooling rapidly toward dark. Camaro forced herself to walk alongside Yates and not ahead of him. They reached the entrance to the motel's parking lot together. She peered around the corner and scanned the lot. Any car could have been Lukas's.

"I'll take the manager's office. You watch the rooms," Yates said. He had his bail-enforcement badge out.

"Don't take too long," Camaro said.

He vanished inside the office, and Camaro stood half hidden by a pillar on the ground floor. The visible rooms all faced the parking lot, the stairwells exposed so no one could ascend or descend without being seen. There were security cameras at the front and rear of the lot.

Yates returned. "Second floor. Room Two-one-three."

"Where is that?"

"Right above us. The manager marked up a map."

Camaro consulted it. A red ink arrow followed halfway down one side of the lot and ascended. Another arrow directed them to Lukas's door. She nodded and pushed the map away. "I got it."

She went, and he followed. She slipped the Glock into her hand as she reached the stairs. She held the gun in both hands against her body in the compressed ready position. With Yates at her back, she approached the corner and peeked around it. Lukas was not there.

They advanced past still rooms with drawn curtains until they reached 213, then fell in on opposite sides of the frame. Camaro touched the door. It was metal, and the frame was also metal. She shook her head at Yates. He put his gun away and reached for his picks.

The sound of an ice machine dumping a load of cubes carried to them from the far end of the walkway. Camaro looked up as Lukas came around the corner.

A pause lengthened between them in which time seemed to suspend. Lukas stood with a bucket of fresh ice in his hand, his shirt unbuttoned to expose the pistol tucked in the front of his waistband. He froze, his mouth dropped open.

Camaro pressed the Glock out and up, aiming past Yates, squeezing the trigger, and feeling the gun recoil in her grip. Her bullet struck the wall ten feet behind Lukas. The sound spurred him into motion. The ice bucket tumbled from his hand, spilling chunks of frozen water across the concrete in a silvery fan. He twisted and drew his .45 from his jeans.

Yates stepped in front of Camaro as Lukas's gun went off. Blood spattered the wall, and the old man groaned. He sagged against Camaro, and she lowered him to the ground. "Go," he said through gritted teeth. "Get him."

Camaro moved. Lukas had vanished around a corner. Camaro dashed quickly past the remaining rooms, rounding the same corner to find a through hallway that punched out onto the far side of the building, where more rooms lay. She charged down it and turned the next corner. She had only an instant to see the butt of Lukas's gun coming at her face. Then she saw lights.

Her knees folded, and she crumpled. She saw Lukas swinging his weapon around again, the gaping blackness of the muzzle coming into line with her face. She'd lost her gun somewhere. Her hands went up instinctively, closing over Lukas's pistol. She felt his hand flex, and the hammer fell on her finger, a sharp metal bite.

She wrenched the gun one way and then another. Lukas cursed, his finger caught in the guard. Camaro twisted until she felt something give and Lukas cried out. The gun came loose between them and clattered to the concrete.

He kicked her in the side, and pain shot through her ribs. He kicked her a second time as she rolled, clipping her as she made it to her feet. She raised her guard too slowly, and Lukas punched her squarely in the jaw. Her head snapped around, and she saw lights again.

Camaro staggered and drove out a leg. Her heel glanced off his thigh, and then he was on her, swinging her around by arm and neck to crash headfirst into the wall. Blood was in her mouth. She pivoted and ducked, but a rising left snapped her teeth together and sent her reeling.

They exchanged a rapid flurry of blows. Camaro managed to get inside and bloody Lukas's nose. He hit her with an elbow in the temple that nearly took her off her feet.

She drove into him with her shoulder, but he outweighed her by thirty pounds and flung her back. She barely deflected a swinging right that would have closed her eye, but caught a sudden left in the stomach.

They clashed together. She hooked his ankle and sent him down to one knee. He charged back to his feet and rocked her. Camaro had something hot and sticky in her hair, and the only thing she could smell was more blood. A sharp strike directly to the point of her chin sparked stars. The ground came up, and she fell completely.

"Federal marshals! Don't move!"

Way's voice boomed out behind her. Camaro saw Lukas take up his gun and run. She scrambled for her own, a persistent spinning in her skull tilting her balance askew.

"I said stop!"

Her hand closed on the Glock. Camaro raised the gun to fire. Lukas was nearly at the far end of the building.

"Stop where you are, Collier!"

Lukas turned at the moment Way stumbled over Camaro. Camaro was flattened again, the Glock skittering out of her grasp as she and Way became entangled. A burst of exhalation exploded in her ear, almost as loud as the ringing pair of shots from Lukas's gun. Camaro heard a woman cry out.

Way flailed on top of her, cursing as they unraveled the knot of their limbs. He fired his weapon twice, the report profoundly deafening at such close range. Then he was up on his feet, running after Lukas.

Camaro tried to make it upright. She saw Hannon on the ground, clutching her chest. Her gun was loose beside her. Camaro ignored it and went to Hannon instead. There were two distinct entry marks in the front of her dark jacket, but no blood.

"I . . ." Hannon said breathlessly. She grabbed Camaro by the arm.

"Don't move," Camaro told her. Her brain struggled to put together the next steps, the right words. She kept seeing spots. "Just lie still. Breathe."

Camaro opened Hannon's jacket and saw where the bullets had passed through the material of the marshal's blouse as well. There was still no blood. Her searching fingers felt the stiffness of a layer of Kevlar underneath.

"Way," Hannon said.

Camaro sagged to the ground beside Hannon. She could only place a hand on Hannon's vest. She sucked air, and little by little it cleared her head. "I said lie still," she managed to say. "You could have...cracked ribs."

Multiple gunshots sounded nearby, the reports of at least two different weapons. Camaro distantly heard Way shouting, and Yates, too. She forced herself back onto her knees and leaned over Hannon. She tore open her blouse to expose the body armor the marshal wore underneath her clothes. Two slugs were embedded in the white material.

Hannon shuddered. Camaro felt her hands, and they were cold. "You're going into shock."

"You're hurt," Hannon said. "You're bleeding."

Camaro shook her head. "I'm fine. Breathe like I told you. You're going to be all right."

Camaro didn't hear the footsteps falling behind her, but the sudden blow behind her ear sent fresh sparks into her vision. She wobbled, one hand still on Hannon, the other on the unyielding concrete walk.

She turned enough to see Way standing over her, his gun in his hand. Blood stained his left arm. He hit her with the butt of his weapon again, and something hot dripped into Camaro's vision. She fell on her back and put a hand up. Way hit her again. He panted, knelt over her, and stuck the barrel of his pistol in her face. "Don't you move. Not one muscle."

CHAPTER SIXTY-SIX

LUKAS WAS GONE. Yates surrendered himself into custody, and Way kept them both under the gun until the local police and EMTs arrived. Hannon was taken away on a gurney, and Camaro didn't see her anymore. Yates went, too. Way said nothing to any of them and spoke only to the LAPD officers who bundled Camaro into a unit. The car drove northwest to Van Nuys, where the LA County lockup was.

The processing was the easy part. A female officer was assigned to Camaro and took her photograph and her fingerprints. She was asked a series of questions about her drug and alcohol history. They wanted to know if she was suicidal. She told them she wasn't.

"You're banged up. We'll have a medic check you over."

"I saw one already."

"We'll have them check you again."

She was escorted to a large area filled with rows of chairs locked together. It looked like a DMV, and there were televisions bolted to the ceiling in two corners so the men and women waiting in the chairs could occupy themselves. The deputy informed her that she had free access to the phones on the far wall so long as no one else was waiting to make a call. For the rest of the time she was obliged to sit in a seat and wait.

Camaro took a spot in an empty row. The television was tuned to a basic cable channel, and the show was *Cops*. She sat and willed stillness into herself. Her body ached profoundly, but it did not hurt in the place where she went. There was a constant murmur of noise from the bank of phones as detainees made calls for lawyers, for bail bondsmen, for loved ones. She didn't hear them.

She looked at the holding area. A pair of deputies sat behind an island of counters to one side of the room, working at computers and only occasionally glancing up to scan the assembled men and women. Now and again another two or three officers would pass through the area, either to talk or to escort a new body to one of the holding cells that dotted one long wall. Some of the cells were small enough for a single occupant, but most were large, with broad windows impregnated with wire, through which Camaro saw idle men and women deemed too uncontrollable for the plastic chairs and the reruns of *Cops*.

On the far side of the counter island was the processing area. Through there a direct exit to the outside opened into the loading zone where Camaro had been brought in. There were other hallways leading out, but those were certain to be secured by locks Camaro had no means to bypass.

No one carried guns inside the jail, but the officers were armed with Tasers and collapsible batons. On the way in Camaro had watched her escort check her weapon into a locker outside the detention area, so even the police who passed from the outside into processing were unarmed. Traffic was slow. There were never more than two or three cops present at any given time.

She shook her head. There would be no jailbreak.

A nurse came as they promised, and Camaro was taken to a side room and asked to strip. She had her wounds cleaned for the second time, and the nurse clucked her tongue at the bruises on Camaro's face. When she saw the gash on the back of her leg, she made a disgusted noise. "Who sewed this up? Is that *fishing line?*"

"It's all I had."

"Well, it's torn now. I'm going to put a real suture in, but you need to get looked at by a doctor."

"I'll be all right."

It was done, and she was returned to the chairs. After three hours a deputy came for her. "Up," she said.

Camaro stood. "What's going on?"

"Walk ahead of me along that row of doors."

Camaro did as she was told, and the two of them walked past the cells to another hallway, also lined with cells. They went four doors down, and the deputy instructed her to stand with her nose against the

257

wall and her hands behind her back. The deputy opened a cell then and took her arm to guide her in.

The door was closed. Camaro looked around the space. The cell was empty. There were no chairs, only benches molded from concrete. A short wall at the back sheltered a toilet. There was no sink.

She sat down, but it was only a minute before she heard the deputy's key in the door again. The door swung wide, and Way entered. Camaro didn't move.

They were shut in together. Way stood over her, watching her, and said nothing. Camaro glanced away from him and stared at the opposite wall instead. She heard him breathing. A tense vibration emanated from him, tangible in the still air of the cell.

A minute passed before Way broke the silence. "You look bad," he said.

"Thanks."

"I thought you should know that you're going to go in front of a judge in a few hours. You're being charged with unlawful possession of a firearm, assault with a deadly weapon, and a few other things you probably don't give a shit about. But the fun part comes when the U.S. Attorney's office gets involved, because we're going to step in on the federal level and run your ass all the way to prison."

Camaro remained silent.

Way waved his hand in front of her face. "This registering with you? Because now is the time to help yourself. Felony interference with a federal agent isn't a joke. Your friend Yates, he might make out okay with the right lawyer, but you have no leg to stand on. You're a straight-up criminal, and you got my partner shot."

She looked at him for the first time. "How is she?"

"She'll be fine."

"And Yates?"

"He's a lucky old man. The bullet hit him at an angle and glanced off his shoulder blade. He's going to be stiff, but he's gonna live."

"That's good."

"You're damned right it's good," Way said. "If either one of them had died, I'd look to put you away forever. And I mean forever."

Camaro looked away again. "It doesn't matter."

"Why not?"

"Because Lukas is gone. You screwed up the whole thing. You'll never catch him."

"I screwed up? I am the only one with the authority to pursue Lukas Collier. I don't give two shits about whatever bond he skipped out on. I'm pursuing the wanted felon who killed a federal marshal and a cop. And that's before we even bring kidnapping and every other person he's killed into it. I am the big dog. I told you that back in Carmel, but you wouldn't listen. And now what do you have? Nothing."

"I'm tired of talking to you," Camaro said.

Way stalked the small cell. "I don't think you realize the barrel I have you over. We are talking about prison time. Hard time in a federal penitentiary where you get one hour outside your cell every day. I have the power to put you there and keep you there until your tits fall and your hair turns gray. You get me?"

She saw him grinding his teeth and smiled inside.

"You know, I've been thinking about it," he said. "Identity fraud is a federal crime. You want your sister to be in the same pen with you? Of course, your niece would have to go into the system, seeing as how her father is dead and you have no immediate relatives. Rebecca's coming up on five years old, right? The maximum sentence for identity fraud is fifteen years. So she'll be almost old enough to take her mommy out for a drink when she gets out. What do you think about that?"

Camaro didn't speak.

"So I guess that's what we're going to do. Innocent people are going to be hurt because you won't come clean. I'm glad I'm not in your family."

"What do you want from me?"

"I want you to tell me everything you know about where Lukas is going and what he's going to do when he gets there."

"How the hell would I know that?"

"You knew he was headed south. How?"

Camaro pressed her lips together and didn't answer. Out of the corner of her eye she saw Way smile.

"You had Lukas's personal cell phone number and used it to track him to that motel. Yeah, yeah, we talked to that stupid bastard who traced the signal for you. We know all about it. I want to know when you talked to Lukas, what you talked about, and everything you learned. And if you do that, I'll see about getting you a spot in minimum security instead. That's not so bad."

"I can't help you," Camaro said.

"Don't screw around with me," Way said.

"I want a lawyer, and I don't want to see your face again."

Way said nothing. He stood staring at her, and she felt his eyes boring into her flesh. She didn't look his way and didn't move. She sat and waited and took each breath as it came until finally he moved to the door. He rapped on the thick glass. "Open up."

The deputy unlocked the door.

"Hey, Deputy Way," Camaro said.

Way paused in the doorway. "What?"

"There's one more thing I want to say."

"Spit it out."

"Better luck next time."

Way stepped out. The door was closed again, and the lock engaged automatically.

Camaro rested the back of her head against the wall and let the corners of her mouth turn up just a little as she heard him walk away.

CHAPTER SIXTY-SEVEN

FOR THE SECOND time in a day, Lukas fled the sound of sirens. He saw a bus stopping for passengers up ahead in the failing light of sunset, its interior brightly lit. The doors were already closed when he got there, but he thumped his fist on the glass and the driver let him on. "Hey, man," Lukas said, "is there a Greyhound station on this line?"

"Not on this line, but you can transfer at Long Beach and Hill."

"Great." Lukas fed some bills into the fare taker and went to sit down. The marshal had clipped him with a shot. His leg was bleeding, and he had no way to stop it. Droplets fell on the floor of the bus. No one seemed to notice or care.

He watched the stops light up on an LED sign just above the driver, and fifteen minutes later he was off waiting for his transfer, a slip of paper in his hand. He threw his phone away in a trash can mounted on the side of a lamppost.

The Number 60 bus picked him up and drove east until it reached his stop. The driver instructed him to keep walking another half a mile to reach the Greyhound bus station. He did as he was told and made it to the station without spotting a single police cruiser along the way. He stopped once to pull up the leg of his jeans and examine his wound. It was only oozing now, though it hurt to put his full weight on that leg.

There was a bank of disused public phones tucked away in a neglected corner of the station. Lukas scrounged in his pocket for change and fed one of the phones. He called Konnor and waited through an interminable series of rings until Konnor picked up. "I've got trouble," Lukas told him.

"What's happening?"

"I got jumped at the motel. Couple of bounty hunters and some U.S. marshals. I got away okay, but I'm hit in the leg and I'm bleeding. I need you to pick me up and get me somewhere I can get patched up."

"How bad's the leg?"

"It doesn't have to come off, but it needs stitching."

"I can handle that, so long as there's no bullet in there. Where are you?"

"Greyhound station off Seventh."

"I know it. Give me half an hour."

"Don't be late."

"Just sit tight."

Lukas left the phones and found a spot on a scratched wooden bench. It wasn't busy in the station, but there were eyes enough that he felt uncomfortable being out in the open. Without thinking he tried to cross his legs, and pain shot through his bullet wound. Lukas gasped and saw an old woman glance his way. He forced a smile and nodded, and she looked in the other direction.

The time on his watch ticked away until thirty minutes had passed. Lukas didn't see Konnor, and another ten minutes went by without the man appearing. He started to count out change again when he heard his name spoken across the room. "Hey," Konnor said. "I'm here."

Lukas got up. His leg throbbed. "About time."

"Traffic. What are you gonna do?"

"Let's get out of here."

They went out to the parking lot, and Konnor directed Lukas to a white Chevy pickup with a Harley-Davidson decal spread across the entire rear window. Lukas managed to climb in and stuck his wounded leg out from his body as far as he could.

He saw Konnor look at his bloodied pant leg. "Hurting?"

"What do you think?"

"We'll get it taken care of. I've got a stash of Vicodin that'll take the edge off."

"Still living with the beaners?"

"Yeah, the neighborhood's got plenty. But you know how it is."

"Sure."

Konnor drove. For a while they didn't talk. It was Konnor who broke the silence. "How close are these people to you? The bounty hunters and the marshals?"

"Too close. I have a pretty good idea how they found me before. I dumped my phone, so I need a new one. I thought that shit was illegal, but I guess not. They homed right in on me."

"Is it gonna be a problem? You know, for the deal?"

"We can still make the swap. I talked to Otilio, and he's ready to make delivery so long as we hold up our end."

"It's all arranged. We're on for tomorrow. Pay the cash, get the goods. Then we make the exchange on Sunday. The candy store is closed that day, so we'll have it all to ourselves. How's your pickup man doing?"

Lukas cursed. "I can't get ahold of him. If he's running scared, we might be stuck holding the load for a while until we can arrange for someone else to take it. If Jake hadn't gone and gotten himself killed, this wouldn't be a problem, but Jake's still causing me trouble. Him and his goddamned friends."

"Amateurs."

"That's the size of it."

Konnor let the silence grow between them. "You want to talk about it?"

"Talk about what?"

"Jake."

"What's there to talk about? He was stupid. He was always stupid. As soon as he told me he could sell weed all around the bay, I should have known it was gonna be trouble. He couldn't be counted on to wipe his own ass."

"But he was still your brother."

Lukas shot Konnor a look. "What are you, my mother? Yeah, he was my brother, and I don't take it lying down when someone messes with my blood. But business is business, and I have to go on. One day I'll nail that bitch when she doesn't expect it."

"Who is she?"

"I don't know. She's got skills, that much I can tell you. She's no

Marine, but she could really get into somebody's ass if they aren't careful."

"You look a little banged up. Her?"

"Yeah, it was her. What of it? I put her down when it came to it. She was mine."

Konnor shook his head slowly. "It's a shame. Even if Jake was a screwup, he was all right sometimes."

"He never would have made it in the Sandbox. You and me, we came out the other side. He would have bought it there. He wasn't strong enough. He was never strong enough. But that's what happens. I did my best with him."

"We'll pour one out for him."

"Yeah, we'll do that. Then we get down to making money. I might have a long vacation after this."

CHAPTER SIXTY-EIGHT

HANNON ENTERED THE jail through a secure passageway bookended by heavy doors set with glass inches thick. Whenever she breathed, she felt a painful pressure in the center of her chest. At the hospital they had stripped off her body armor, jacket, and blouse to reveal the blackened cluster of a bruise directly over her sternum. The bruise had twin centers, one for each of the slugs that crashed into her vest.

She stopped by an island staffed by Sheriff's Department deputies and showed her identification for the sixth time. "Deputy U.S. Marshal Hannon," she said. "I'm looking for my partner, Deputy Way."

"I think he's in that office over there," the deputy told her.

Hannon thanked him and followed his pointing finger to a small office set at the end of a line of cells. One wall was half reinforced glass. The door was shut. She saw Way sitting at the desk, his cell phone pressed to his ear, speaking intently. He glanced up, saw her, and beckoned her in.

The office was unlocked. Hannon stepped through the door and let it close behind her. Way continued his call. "So we can have the indictments put together by morning," he said. "Yes, I understand. I'll check into it. Sure. You can reach me at this number. I'll be up all night. Thanks."

He hung up and put his phone away. They looked at each other across the desk.

"Was that the U.S. Attorney's office?" Hannon asked.

"Yes. What are you doing here? You should be resting."

"I'm bruised up, I'm not dead. I want to stay on top of things."

"I have it under control."

"What's happening?"

Way paused, as if considering not answering her. Then he said, "Espinoza's been processed into holding. The old man's out of the hospital, and he's going through the system right now. We're set to see the local judge tonight. We're still going to let them file charges, but we have the priority. They'll be transported to federal court in the morning, and at that point our people take over completely. The locals can get them when we're finished with them."

"Have you talked to either of them yet?"

"I talked to Espinoza."

"What did she say?"

"What do you expect? Nothing. She thinks she's bulletproof. But I have her dead to rights. We're going to run right over her."

Hannon sat down in the chair opposite the desk. "What about Yates? Have you questioned him?"

"Not yet, but I will."

"I'd like to be there."

"You're recovering."

"The vest took the slugs, Keith. I'm fine to work."

"You just got shot. Give it some goddamned time. You could have died."

Hannon heard his voice falter at the last. "I didn't die. I'm not dying."

"Well, I'm not losing anybody else."

"I want to talk to Espinoza," Hannon said.

"Why?"

"She stopped for me, Keith. She could have gone after Lukas, but she stopped for me. I don't know about you, but that means something to me."

"Camaro Espinoza is a stone killer," Way said. "You think she stopped for you? She was probably just trying to get hold of your weapon."

"That's not what happened, and you know it."

"Yeah, well, the FBI will want another crack at her once I get a chance to talk with someone in charge over there. I'm convinced she was on the scene when Yates took down Vicki Nelson's apartment. She's a liability with a gun, and she's not telling everything she knows."

"What do you think she knows, Keith? What do you really think she's going to tell us?"

Way's eyes shone. "She was in contact with Lukas. She had his number. They talked. I've subpoenaed her phone records, and I'm willing to lay odds that when I get them, it's going to show at least one phone conversation between the two of them. She's hip deep in this somehow, and I'm going to use her to find Lukas."

"Lukas is gone," Hannon said. "It's over."

"No! He's in the city somewhere. He has ties here going way back. We punch up his KAs from when he was last in California and we start running them down, one by one. Somebody's gonna give, and then we'll have his ass."

Hannon shook her head. "This has to stop."

Way's mouth flattened. "I'm not having that conversation again. This is happening. We're about two steps ahead of the Bureau right now, and I want to keep it that way. By the time they figure out what we're doing, he'll be taken care of and we walk away clean."

She waited, and she thought. Way stared. "I want to work together with you on this, Keith. I want to be a part of it. I won't let you go on alone."

"Then you'd better get on board with what's happening, because we are going full ahead on Espinoza and Yates."

"When will you talk to Yates?"

"Soon. Everybody who's anybody is off tonight, so I have to roust some people out of bed to get things moving. He can sit and stew for a while. Maybe if he gets enough time to think about what's at stake, he'll be more cooperative than Espinoza was. And I'm not letting any of that *Taylor v. Taintor* bullshit knock me off his ass this time. He's stepped over the line, and he knows it. The minute he pulled Espinoza in on his fugitive recovery, he broke the law. The only thing that's going to get him out of this mess is if we step in and put pressure on the right people, and that's not gonna happen."

Way stood and Hannon did, too. Hannon felt the air between

them, thick and uneasy. "Do you mind if I talk to them before you do?"

"Yes, I mind."

He went for the door, and Hannon stepped aside. She let him leave. He walked away, visible through the window until he passed down an adjoining hallway. The weight of his absence remained.

CHAPTER SIXTY-NINE

AFTER WAY LEFT, Camaro sat in the stillness of the cell, listening to the burble of voices passing through the vents in the door. She stayed quiet and stared at the blank face of the wall for a long time until she heard keys in the lock.

"Stand up," said a deputy with a crew cut. "Face the rear of the cell."

She did as she was told. She was cuffed again and taken out through a side door. The deputy escorted her with a hand loosely on her elbow, guiding her through nondescript hallways and out through a secure exit into another building. She expected to find a courtroom at the other end, but she was brought to a darkened office. The deputy turned on the light to reveal a reception area with a small couch and chairs. Camaro was directed onto the couch. She sat facing a tiny coffee table strewn with magazines she could not pick up and read. The officer went outside.

The office had a clock on the wall. It was just past midnight. Camaro heard the click of hard soles on the tile floor outside, and the door opened. Yates entered first, handcuffed as she was. They put him in a chair. Hannon followed. "Thank you," she told the deputies with him, and then they were left alone with the door closed.

Camaro looked at Yates. He nodded to her silently. She turned her attention to Hannon. "I thought I was due in court."

"You both are. You're supposed to be there now."

"Then what's happening?"

"What did you intend to do when you found Lukas Collier in that motel room?"

"Don't you know?"

"Say it."

"We were going to kill him."

"Even though your sister's going to make it and your niece is all right?"

Camaro indicated Yates with her head. "His son is still dead. And I can't have him come back at Annabel again."

Hannon took one of the chairs and dragged it around to face them. Camaro saw her wince at the effort and touch her chest. When she sat, she was slightly pale. "If I take the two of you to that courtroom, it's going to be over. You'll both be remanded into custody pending a date in front of a federal judge."

Camaro watched her carefully, Yates doing the same.

"Keith—my partner—is playing phone tag with all the people we need to have you charged by the U.S. Attorney's office. I figure we have an hour, maybe a little bit more. Two if we're lucky."

"So what does that have to do with us?" Camaro asked. "You have us. We're not going anywhere."

"The District Attorney's office is ready to file the paperwork that lets you walk on local charges. It doesn't get a federal prosecutor off your backs, but it buys you some more time on the street."

"Why would you do that?" Yates asked.

"I have my reasons. The question is, can you find Lukas again?"

Camaro glanced at Yates. He inclined his head just slightly. "Maybe not where he's hiding, but where he's going to be."

"How do you mean?"

Yates spoke up. "Lukas's brother put together a pot of money for a drug deal. Lukas had that money sent on to LA before he left Carmel. We have the address."

"Let me have it."

"Not until we get some assurances," Camaro said.

Hannon shook her head. "I don't think the two of you get it. You will go to *prison* if I don't help you out of this jam. If you know something, you need to share it, because I already have one person in my life who's shutting me out."

"Right now that address is the only thing we have to go on," Yates said. "You can keep us out of jail, but what can you do to help finish this?"

Hannon pursed her lips in thought, then spoke. "I have some room to maneuver. But whatever you do, do it fast. Because this won't last. Once Keith knows you're back on the street, he's going to lose his shit, and I mean that."

"What the hell is his problem, anyway?" Camaro asked.

"He lost a good friend. He hasn't been the same since. Anyone he thinks will get between him and Lukas Collier, he'll take apart. He doesn't care anymore."

"You care?" Camaro asked.

"I do. I understand the world's a better place without Lukas in it, but there's a line between good guys and bad guys. You don't hurt good guys to stop the bad guys."

"How do you know we're good?"

"I don't. Not for sure. But when you picked me over Lukas, I got a pretty solid idea."

"If your partner's going to go as crazy as you say, we're going to have a whole new set of problems besides Lukas Collier," Yates said. "Can you put a muzzle on your boy?"

"I wish. He got me turned around pretty badly. He got me thinking we were doing the right thing by putting Lukas in front of a gun. But that's not going to bring Keith back from the edge. He needs somebody to save him from himself, otherwise he's going to go somewhere he can't get back from."

"So it's okay if we do it," Camaro said, "just so long as he doesn't."

"I don't expect you to get it."

"Oh, I get it."

"I'm not going to argue about whose honor is worth more," Hannon said. "All I know is Keith can't think straight, and he's never going to think straight as long as Lukas is out there. I'm barely hanging on to him now. If he gets a whiff of Lukas again, I can't control what happens next."

"We'll do it," Yates said. "You don't have to be a party to it."

Hannon stood and went to the door. She cracked the door slightly and peered out, then pushed it shut again. She sat down with a sigh of pain and looked at them for a long time in silence. "All right," she said finally. "Let's do it."

CHAPTER SEVENTY

THEY CALLED A cab and quickly walked a few blocks away from the Los Angeles County Superior Court to wait for it. Yates made a series of phone calls while they waited. Camaro didn't listen to his side of the conversation. Instead, she watched the empty street for any sign of Deputy Marshal Way. He did not appear.

The cab arrived, and they slipped into the back. "Santa Monica and Fairfax," Yates told the driver.

"West Hollywood?" Camaro asked.

Yates looked at Camaro. "There's an all-night coffee place there. My man will link up with us. He's bringing us some wheels. No rental cars, no paperwork, nothing the marshals can use to track us. Which reminds me, it was nice of the deputy to give them back, but we need to get rid of our phones as soon as we can."

"We can pick up a couple anywhere," Camaro said. "They're cheap. Hardware is going to be a bigger problem."

"That's been on my mind," Yates said. "I'm still working on that part. I'm gonna miss that Hardballer. My wife gave it to me as a present."

They rode. The driver seemed uninterested in making conversation. He glanced into his mirror occasionally and Camaro saw him looking at her, but he said nothing. There would be a record of their trip from the courthouse. It would not be difficult for Way to find it.

"What do you think?" Yates said when there had been enough quiet. "About what?"

"This lady marshal. Do you think she meant a thing she said?"

"I do."

"That partner of hers is going to eat her alive."

"He'll try."

"The way I figure it, if we don't get Lukas within the next twenty-four hours, we're gonna be out of options. Way? He'll have everybody but the National Guard out looking for us. Looking for you in particular. From what you tell me, he has the hots for you in a big way."

The streets were washed in clean, white light. Los Angeles had done away with the old sodium-vapor streetlights years ago in favor of LEDs. The look of the city by night was wholly different from the city Camaro remembered from her youth.

"He's not the first one to come gunning for me. He won't be the last."

"You run right up to a dangerous edge," Yates said.

"I don't have a choice."

"Don't you?"

Camaro shot him a look. "I don't go looking for it."

"That's good, because if you did, then that would mean you have a problem. The kind of problem only dying seems to fix."

"Lukas is the one who's gonna die."

"So you figure we still have a shot at him?"

"You don't think so?"

"Let's just say I want to believe," Yates said. "In my time I've gone out on some shaky limbs, but I can't recall a situation where the limb was quite so shaky as this one. We got two tries, and he slipped us both times. Are we third-time lucky? I can't say for sure."

"I'll follow him alone. You don't have to come," Camaro said.

"You think I'm saying all of this because I want to cut you loose?"

"Aren't you?"

"We've got too much invested to walk away now. I only want to make sure we keep our feet on the ground, that's all. Too easy to get blown away otherwise."

Camaro caught the driver looking at her again. She glared into his mirror until his eyes flicked away. "I'm sorry about your son," she said. "I don't think I ever told you that."

"You didn't have to. You never knew him."

"I'm still sorry. My sister, she's still alive. Your son...he's never coming back. No matter what we do, he's never coming back."

Yates turned his gaze toward the window. "No, he isn't."

They let silence grow between them until they were off the freeway and into the streets of West Hollywood, weaving past the Dolby Theatre and finally at their destination, a coffeehouse planted directly on the corner of Fairfax and Santa Monica Boulevard. Yates moved to pay, but Camaro brushed his hand away and gave some bills to the driver. "Stay safe," the driver told them.

The coffeehouse was surprisingly busy for the hour, mostly with young folks taking their caffeine in the middle of the night so they could talk until the break of dawn. Camaro scanned the tables and booths until she spotted the man they were looking for. She didn't know him by sight, but he was the only person in the place over forty, and he was seated alone. Yates waved to him, and the man waved back to confirm it.

"Camaro Espinoza, this is Ronnie Curtis," Yates said when they reached the man's table. "Ronnie, this is Camaro."

"Great name," Ronnie said. "You two sit down for a minute. I have a slice of pie coming."

Camaro sat angled toward the door. Yates settled in beside her. The table was small and round, designed to bring groups of people together in an intimate circle. Ronnie had a newspaper he set on an empty chair.

"You got a ride for us?" Yates asked.

"Right up the street. Red Mustang. You like ragtops?"

"In the winter?" Camaro asked.

"Hey, what do you want? It's short notice, and it's what I could spare. Picked it up at a police auction a couple of years ago. It runs okay, and it'll get you where you need to go in a hurry if that's what you're after."

"How much do I owe you?" Yates asked. He reached for his wallet.

Ronnie waved it away. "Nothing. As soon as Anita called and told me what was up...It's a goddamned tragedy. When one of us gets shot, it's like we lost a brother. Take that car and do whatever you need to do with it. And if you can't return it, no sweat. Small price to pay."

"I'm much obliged to you," Yates said.

"It's the least I can do."

"There's just one more thing."

Ronnie nodded. "Sure, I know. Check the trunk. Two pieces, like you asked. They're clean, so don't worry about anything blowing back on me."

"You're a real godsend, Ronnie."

"Just make sure you get the son of a bitch, Yates. That's all I'm asking."

CHAPTER SEVENTY-ONE

WAY WAS VERY quiet for a very long time. When he finally spoke, his voice barely rose. He did not look at Hannon. "So what you're telling me is that without my knowledge or consent, you filed the paperwork necessary for two known felons to walk out of custody and disappear without a trace into one of the biggest cities in the country?"

They had stepped into a conference area designed for attorneys and their clients outside the courtroom. The door was shut, and no sound entered from the hallway, where a steady stream fed into and out of night court in a ceaseless dance. Way sat. Hannon stood.

"Is that what you're telling me?" Way asked.

"That's one way to interpret the situation."

His eyes flickered toward her. They were dark and sharp, but there was too much white around them. "Okay. Tell me another way to interpret it."

"They're trying to resolve the situation, Keith."

Way brought his fist down on the scratched surface of the conference table. "They're trying to resolve the situation? What in the hell does that mean?"

"We don't have any idea where Lukas is," Hannon said. "He could be in LA, he could be in Mexico, or he could be in Las Vegas by now. Who knows? Those two have a line on him, and with them on the street we have a chance to finish this the way you said you wanted to."

"I wanted to do this myself. I'm not farming it out to some ancient skip tracer and a war hero who's probably so screwed up from PTSD she doesn't even know what country she's in. You know what I found out when I was making some calls? She cage-fights. She fights in a god-damned cage like an animal. And this is who you decide you're going to trust? Her? Not me, but her?"

276

Hannon took a deep breath. She put her hands on the back of a wooden chair and held on. "Yes."

Way's face reddened. His expression screwed up, and he spat out his next words. "Of all the stupid goddamned—"

"Stop right there!"

Way went silent and fell back in his chair, a startled look passing over his features.

"I have been with you every step of the way through all of this," Hannon said. "I was there for every crazy thing you did or said from coast to coast. I have taken your shit and listened to your ranting, and now I am *done*. You clear it with me when we decide what we do next."

"You don't have the authority," Way said.

"Yeah, I *do* have the authority. You are only in on this because I convinced them you could handle it. But you can't handle it, Keith. You've tried to walk over me from the start. It's over. I can get on the phone right now with the commander and tell him that you are out of your goddamned mind. You are unstable, you are reckless, and you are unprofessional in a way I have never seen in my life. You loved Jerry? We *all* loved Jerry. And when he died, we *all* took it hard. Why do you think I didn't bat an eye when you told me you didn't want to bring Lukas in alive? Why do you think I stuck with you through everything that went down until we ended up at that motel and I got shot? I am on your side, but you are so out of your mind you can't even see that. I'm just another problem to you. Well, I'm not the problem here, Keith. You are the problem."

A dense silence fell between them. Hannon still clung to the chair, her nails dug into the wood. The back of one leg trembled. She felt the chemical surge of adrenaline rising up through her spine, exploding into her brain, and making the lights overhead brighter, the colors of the room sharper.

"Is that all?"

"You need to hear this. You are way too close to this, and you are coming apart. I've tried to hold you together, but I can't do it alone. You have to do your part."

Way put his hands on the table and blew a breath. He looked down at his knuckles and stayed that way for a time, unmoving. Hannon waited.

"Maybe I've been unfair," Way said after a long while had passed.

"There's no maybe about it."

"I have my reasons."

"I know all about it."

"You don't know! You weren't there. It wasn't your gun that killed Jerry. Now we have one shot to make this right."

"Keith, what are you going to do?"

"I'm going to coordinate with LAPD and throw a net over this city so tight a mosquito couldn't get through. Then I'm going to hunt down Lukas, and I'm going to do what I said I was going to do from the beginning. On my own."

"I'll be there, too," Hannon said.

"Maybe it's better if you're not. You have your doubts, and I can't guarantee it won't get ugly. You don't want to go down with me? That's fine. I can do this on my own."

"There's no need for that, Keith. I just need you to take it down a notch. It's the best thing."

"Sure," Way said. "Whatever you say. Let's go."

"I'll be just a minute. I have to make a quick call."

"It's the middle of the night."

"You're not the only one with things going on. I'll be right there."

Way cast a doubtful look toward her, then shook his head. He left the room and closed the door behind him. Hannon brought out her phone and opened text messaging. She keyed in a number from memory. *He's on the move,* she typed. *I'll tell you more when I get the chance. Watch your back and be careful. Steer clear of local PD.*

She sent the text, and no reply came. Hannon tucked her phone away, stood, and straightened her clothes. She let herself out and hastened to follow Way down the hall.

CHAPTER SEVENTY-TWO

THE HEADQUARTERS OF the Los Angeles Police Department was on the 100 block of West First Street. It was aggressively modern, composed of sharp concrete shapes and a patchwork of illuminated glass hallways. There was no street parking, and it took nearly ten minutes for Way and Hannon to get their vehicle squared away and make it to the entrance to the lobby. The doors were unlocked, and two uniformed policemen guarded the space.

One moved to intercept them. "Sir, ma'am, is there something you need?"

Way brandished his ID. "Deputy U.S. Marshal Way. This is my partner. We're here to see a Captain Cobb."

"It's four in the morning."

"Captain Cobb has made herself available. So if you could just show us where to go, we'll be on our way."

The policeman looked at them both, then shook his head. "Okay. Elevators are over there. Room Ten-thirty-nine. Office of Operations."

"Thank you," Way said, and he turned away from the man without another word. Hannon hurried behind him. She slipped her phone from inside her jacket and opened up a text window. *Downtown with LAPD,* she wrote. *Where are you?*

The phone was silenced, so the reply only vibrated in Hannon's hands. *Close.*

Will keep you informed, Hannon texted as they reached the elevators. *Stand by.*

"What are you doing?" Way asked her.

"Nothing." Hannon put her phone away. "A friend of mine's going through a breakup."

279

"It's seven o'clock on the East Coast," Way said. "Tell her to go have a coffee."

They took the elevator to the tenth floor and emerged in a corridor that was only half lit. Way ticked off the offices as he went. Hannon sensed the vibrations emanating from him. He snapped his fingers when he saw Room 1039. He went in. Hannon followed, her hand on the phone in her pocket.

There were multiple offices inside the space, and all but one was dark. A woman emerged from it. "Are you Deputy Marshal Way?" she asked.

"Yes. And this is Deputy Marshal Hannon."

The woman came close with her hand extended. "Priscilla Cobb. I'm glad to see you got in all right."

"Do you have some coffee?" Way asked.

"There's a machine. I'll put on a fresh pot. In the meantime you can wait in my office."

Priscilla Cobb's office was large and comfortable, with a table for meetings and a broad desk. American and California flags stood in miniature on both sides of her nameplate, and she had a plastic Slinky and a container of Play-Doh next to her blotter. Photographs of children were on display.

"Did you get those files I e-mailed?" Way asked when Cobb returned.

"Jeremy Yates and Camaro Espinoza? These are your fugitives?" Cobb asked.

"Sort of," Hannon said. "They—"

"They're two of them," Way interjected. "Our primary target is Lukas Collier. You're working from his biometric data."

Cobb nodded. "That's all been processed and sent through."

"I'm sorry," Hannon said. "Biometric data?"

"That's right. We have CCTV cameras all around the city and county, and all that information comes back to one of our operations centers for analysis. We can take any booking photo, any snapshot, even images from another camera, and create a three-D model of the subject's face that can be matched across the board almost instantaneously. I just sent the photos for Yates and Espinoza on. They should be in the system in an hour or two. We can sweep for faces individually or cross-index them with others in the search group, so if they gather in one area, they're more likely to be identified. So far we haven't had any hits. Are you sure Collier's in the city?"

"It's—" Hannon said.

"That's the theory we're working from. These other two are involved with him somehow. We expect them to turn up where we find him, or close to it. They have pending federal charges against them."

"I should tell you that we received an inquiry from the FBI last night regarding your fugitive."

"Local field office?"

"Yes, and a Special Agent Brock from up north. He said some things I don't really understand. This *is* a fully authorized fugitive pursuit, isn't it?"

"Yes. Special Agent Brock's interest is parallel to ours, but we don't fall under his authority."

"All right, then. Our capabilities are at your disposal. Everything our people see, you'll be able to see. When we're done here, I'll make you comfortable in our briefing room, and you'll get real-time updates."

"Thank you. And we'll need you to move when the time is right. Do you have the manpower to handle that?"

Cobb smiled. "Deputy Way, we have enough manpower in Los Angeles to fill a football stadium. We're ready to mobilize twenty-four hours a day, every day. We wouldn't be doing our jobs if we weren't ready for anything."

"Okay," Way said. "I think we're on the same page."

CHAPTER SEVENTY-THREE

Konnor took Lukas to his place in Alhambra and spent the better part of an hour tending to his leg wound. Lukas knew Konnor had been an EMT for a while after Iraq, but things went a different way for him when he got hooked on painkillers and couldn't get off. Konnor was still taking, but it was the kind of thing he could keep under control now, and he had suppliers better able to maintain his needs than he could ever get from his jump bag.

"Where's your old lady?" Lukas asked.

"Out of town for the weekend, visiting her folks in San Diego."

"Good."

He gave Lukas three pills from his stash and told Lukas to chew them. Lukas washed the bitter taste away with beer. In an hour he was floating away, dimly aware of the recliner underneath him and the vague discomfort of his wounded leg. He might have slept, or maybe he was in a halfway dream.

It was early morning, before dawn, when he returned to his senses. He limped around Konnor's small house, digging some bacon and a couple of eggs out of the refrigerator before frying all of them in a skillet. He was sitting at the kitchen table, finishing them off, when Konnor came in. The man scratched the back of his neck and then stood in front of the open fridge for a long while as if mesmerized.

They sat together as Konnor chewed cold cereal. The two of them looked out through the window blinds at the quiet, dawning street. Lukas was the first one to say anything. "This is not how I figured it to go."

"Shit happens."

Lukas shook his head. "I've been sloppy. Lately I've been wondering if I'm losing my edge. Gone soft."

"I don't think you have. You're still one tough son of a bitch. They don't make soft Marines."

"Oorah," Lukas said without enthusiasm.

"You thinking about that woman? She gave you a pretty good shiner."

He resisted touching his face. He could feel the bruise. "That's what I'm talking about. No way would I ever let some chick get the best of me."

"She didn't get the best of you. You said you put her down."

"She's still alive, ain't she?" Lukas returned. "She should be *dead*. I should be toasting over her body."

"One day."

"One day. Listen, I'm gonna call up Jake's boy and see if he's on his way. When do we pick up our toys?"

"Eleven o'clock."

"Whereabouts?"

"Skate park about half an hour from here."

"Real public."

Konnor shrugged and then drank the milk from his bowl. He wiped the corners of his mouth with his thumb and forefinger. "It's a real smooth transaction. They bring a rental truck with the goods in the back. We check it out, if it's all good we give them the cash and they leave us the keys. We just drive on out. Nobody knows anything about what went down. Trust me, I've done it before."

"I'll take your word for it."

Lukas went in the other room and used the new phone he'd bought from a convenience store a mile away. He listened to Derrick's line ring and then got voice mail again. He killed the call without saying anything. His leg was hurting again.

Konnor appeared with a pair of jeans. "Hey, I got some pants you can try on. Get out of those bloody ones. I got some shirts, too, but they'll probably be big on you. If you don't mind that, at least you'll be clean."

"Thanks. Got to look my best."

He was left alone with the jeans. Slowly he stripped out of the ones he wore, and he took another look at the bullet wound. It was sewn together tightly now, but it had lain open like a mouth before. He'd been running full tilt when the marshal shot him. He'd seen enough to know the man's face. They'd been five feet apart in Newark and one trigger pull away from ending it for good. "Asshole," Lukas said aloud to no one.

The pants fit well enough when cinched tightly with Lukas's belt. Konnor brought more clothes, clean socks and an undershirt and a checkered blue button-down that hung on his body. Konnor was broader than him, and thicker than him, and wearing Konnor's clothes made Lukas feel like he was dressing up in a big brother's hand-me-downs.

For the next few hours he tried Derrick off and on, but it was always the same. Every time he heard the beep of Derrick's voice mail, his tension notched a little higher. Even taking another one of Konnor's Vicodin was not enough to quell it. Konnor stayed clear. He knew when to talk and when to be silent.

They were forty minutes out from the deal when Konnor entered the living room, tapping his watch. Lukas called Derrick one last time and got nothing. He wanted a cigarette, but he hadn't carried enough cash to buy a pack at the store. He chewed the inside of his cheek instead.

Konnor waited until they were on the road to talk again. The bag of money was between them. Lukas kept his hand on it. "You good to drive?" Konnor asked.

"Yeah. Why?"

"Somebody's got to bring the truck back to the candy store. I figure we split up. You bring my truck home, and I take the goods. It's probably a good idea to keep you off the streets as much as possible."

"Don't try to shut me out of the deal."

"What? No way! We're together on this. But there's no reason for you to show your face at the candy store until it's time."

Lukas didn't reply. He watched the city slip by. Weekend traffic wasn't as dense as it got during the workweek. LA freeways were parking lots from Monday through Friday. The only way to take a breath was on a day like today.

Eventually they found their way into a residential neighborhood, and Konnor kept to the speed limit. The skate park was tucked in among the houses, hemmed with a gray cinder-block wall painted blue along the crest. It had a modest parking lot with only a few cars sitting under the bright late-morning sun. The yellow Penske rental truck was parked in the corner. Konnor pulled up alongside.

Two men got out of the rental truck. Unconsciously, Lukas touched the .45 in the back of his borrowed pants, and then he dragged the bag of money out. The men were middle-aged and white, their military-style haircuts heavily gray. One of them had an American flag pin on his breast.

Konnor shook hands with both men. Lukas stood out of arm's reach. The men studied him, and he did the same. "This the guy you were talking about?" asked one of them.

"Yeah, he's my boy. We were both in Anbar Province."

"He see any action?"

"You can talk to me directly," Lukas said.

The man turned another appraising look on him. "You kill some of them hajjis?"

"I killed enough."

"Then you're all right with me. Bunch of savages. Let's have a look at what we got for you."

The rental truck had its rear door pointed toward the wall, and the four of them stepped into the narrow space that was left so the men could undo a heavy steel lock. They rolled the door up. Inside it was dark, but Lukas's eyes adjusted. On the floor were dark green crates, each locked. From nearby came the *click-clack* of skateboard wheels on concrete and the shouts of teenagers.

Konnor glanced down at Lukas's leg. "I'll climb up."

The men got in the truck with Konnor. The man who'd quizzed Lukas took a second set of keys and began undoing the locked crates one by one. His partner laid them open. Even from where Lukas stood, he could see the guns.

"We got a half-dozen carbines, like you asked," said the man with the keys. "All brand-new with magazines. Tactical rails so you can customize to order. Thirty automatic handguns, mixed calibers, guaranteed never fired."

"Or my money back?" Konnor asked.

The men laughed. Lukas did not.

"Let's see your green."

Lukas tossed the bag of money into the truck. He wanted to get his weight off his bad leg, but there was nowhere to rest. "It's all there."

The man with the flag pin knelt down and unzipped the bag. He looked over the banded stacks of cash, riffling each one before putting it back. When he was done, he nodded to his partner.

"Gentlemen, a pleasure as always," Konnor said.

"Likewise. Keys are in the ignition."

"Keys to the locks," Lukas said.

"You can have those, too."

Lukas stepped back to let the men climb down. He jerked his head toward Konnor. "We'll wait until you drive away. Everybody's friends."

"Good hunting."

The two walked to a waiting Chevy across the lot and got in. Lukas watched them drive off. He returned to Konnor as he finished relocking the crates. They conferred at the rear bumper. "That's it," Konnor said. "I'll take these to the candy store, and you can call your people again. What do you think?"

Lukas clapped Konnor on the shoulder and smiled for the first time in a long time. "I'm feeling better already."

CHAPTER SEVENTY-FOUR

THEY PARKED ON the street because there was nowhere else to park. On one hand was the back side of the Seventh Street Produce Market, a long structure without rear-facing doors and with high windows it was impossible to reach from the ground. Farther down the block was a spice and garlic company with a warehouse open to the public. It advertised nuts, grains, and fruits and had a bright red jalapeño painted on the white wall.

The sun rose slowly, fat and lazy, spreading over the city and casting long shadows onto the Mustang. Yates sat behind the wheel, utterly quiet, watching the same thing as Camaro: a blue-and-white building festooned with candy signs and the block letters WHOLESALE CANDY & TOYS over the shuttered front doors. The side door was also sealed behind steel.

No one came or went. Camaro began to get sore in her seat. She shifted uncomfortably. There had been no word from Hannon.

"Want to get out and walk around?" Yates asked Camaro after the silence had gone on for hours.

"I don't want to move in case he comes."

"You think he's gonna have a taste for some Tootsie Rolls at dawn?"

Camaro sighed. She felt fatigue on her like a smothering blanket, but she knew she couldn't sleep. "He's not coming here," she said.

"You sure of that?"

"It's a goddamned candy store. What's he going to do here?"

"He sent that money on for a reason."

"Do you think it's in there?"

"Couldn't say. Can't rule it out."

She brought out her phone and texted Hannon. *Still waiting. Status?*

The answer came instantly. *No sign of L. Cameras have your faces. Keep your heads down.*

287

Your partner?

I'll run interference here. Good luck.

Thx.

"What does she say?" Yates asked.

"She says it's handled."

"You think that's true?"

"I don't know."

"That fellow Way is like you; he's not going to sit still for very long."

"She says they have our faces. Cameras."

"I figured as much. Wave of the future. You know they have satellites that can read a license plate from orbit? Pretty soon they'll be able to find anyone, anywhere, just by punching a few buttons."

"Then you'll be out of a job."

"Somebody's still got to knock on the door."

Camaro turned in her seat and looked down the long block. "I don't see any cameras around here."

"There's gonna be dead zones wherever you go. We stray out of this pocket, Way will come down on us hard."

Camaro rolled her head and listened to her neck crackle. "Hannon just has to keep him off us for a little while. Long enough for us to finish what we started. After that he can have whatever's left. I don't care."

Time passed, emptiness looking for something to fill it. Hunger gnawed at Camaro. Her belly made a noise, but Yates didn't comment on it. The sun rose higher, and the shadows began to shrink.

A car turned the corner well ahead of them and crept down the street. The breath caught in Camaro's throat. She felt Yates tense beside her.

"It's not him," Yates said.

The car passed them, then right-handed into the parking lot. It went to the far corner and stopped. The taillights flashed once, and then the driver got out. It was a woman in a pink collared pullover. She slung a backpack over her shoulder and went to the side entrance. Camaro watched her unlock the shutter and slide it open. She let herself in.

"Opening time," Camaro said.

"You want to go in and check it out?"

"In a minute."

After a short while the shutter over the front doors was unlocked from the inside and rolled up. The same woman in pink checked the doors, then vanished inside.

Two more cars arrived in short order. The people who climbed out of them were all employees, marked by the same pink shirts the color of bubble gum. Once they vanished into the warehouse-sized store, the street grew still once again.

"I'm going in," Camaro said.

"Get me a ring pop."

She got out of the Mustang and crossed the street. She used the side entrance facing the parking lot. When the door opened, the smell of sugar came rushing at her. An electronic chime sounded a tone.

Inside it was cavernous, broad aisles marked out by heavy metal shelving fully loaded with brightly colored merchandise. Jolly children's music played on the PA. Camaro passed pallets loaded with plastic party favors, boxes and boxes of candy bars, and then a gumball dispenser taller than she was. She heard voices ringing out here and there, the employees talking over the music. Dozens of brilliant piñatas dangled overhead.

The front of the store was given over to massive displays stacked high with more sugary delights. The center was jammed with shelving, which reached all the way to the high ceiling. Rolling yellow stepladders stood in each row, allowing access to the highest stacks.

Camaro went deeper until she reached the working heart of the store. Here the candy had yet to be unboxed and was held in titanic blocks of brown cardboard stamped with brand names and bound together with bands of heavy-duty plastic. Some blocks were wholly shrink-wrapped. A couple of forklifts stood idle near a loading dock.

"Help you?"

She turned at the man's voice. She saw him, heavyset in his pink shirt, his face young, broad, and friendly. If he noticed the marks from her fight with Lukas, he didn't react to them. "I was just looking," Camaro said.

"Anything in particular? We have a *lot* of stuff in here, and it can get really overwhelming."

"You just sell candy and stuff?"

"Like it says on the sign. Candy, toys, party favors, decorations, kids' games—anything you want. Having a party soon?"

"No," Camaro replied, and she felt suddenly sluggish, as if the candied air were fuzzing her brain. "I'm only... Hey, do you know a guy named Lukas Collier?"

The man thought. "I don't think so. Did he use to work here?"

"I don't know. I thought maybe you might know his name."

"Doesn't ring any bells, sorry. I'm Randy, by the way."

"Randy, do you remember anybody getting a special package here in the last couple of days?"

"You mean not candy-related?"

"Right. Something unusual."

"Well, we got a guy who does loading and unloading for us who gets packages here sometimes. I think one came in. He doesn't like having stuff go to his place, because he's here so much. People steal things off his doorstep, I think."

Camaro took a step toward Randy. "What's this guy's name? Konnor Spencer?"

"Yeah, that's right. Do you know him?"

"I've heard his name around. How about you? How well do you know him?"

Randy's brows knitted. "I, uh, don't really know much about him at all. He's older than me, kind of looks like a biker. I think he is a biker, actually. He has a Harley."

"When does he work next?"

"Later today, I think. Only a couple of hours. Hey, is there something I should know about? Is he in some kind of trouble? Because I try to mind my own business."

"No trouble," Camaro said. "Don't worry about it."

"Okay, but—"

Camaro walked past him without another word. She stalked out from among the stacks of candy and out into the light. Yates sat behind the wheel of the Mustang, still as ever. Camaro ran to the car and got in.

"You get my ring pop?"

"Konnor Spencer definitely works here." Camaro brought out her phone.

"Who is he to Lukas?"

"I don't know, but it's something."

"Hannon?"

"Working on it."

He fell quiet again, and Camaro's thumbs worked as a new car pulled into the candy-store lot.

CHAPTER SEVENTY-FIVE

WE NEED TO know more about Konnor Spencer.

Hannon looked at her phone. *What do you have?* she texted back.

He's real. He has the money. Works at the candy store. What can you find out?

I'll check.

Let me know.

She watched Way through the glass door into the briefing room. The room was dominated by a long conference table, but at one end of the room was a massive bank of monitors feeding out real-time information from across the city. It was a nerve center where the LAPD brass could see and hear everything as it happened. Data was processed and spat out in columns of text or captured images, still or moving, the influx unceasing. Priscilla Cobb had put Way in the path of this deluge, and he hadn't moved from that spot.

Around eight o'clock in the morning, members of the Office of Operations had begun to filter in, just a few on a Saturday, meandering to their offices without much interest in Hannon or Way. A man in shirtsleeves and a tie who looked like he might have been an accountant joined Way in the briefing room. They talked quietly. She could not hear them through the door.

Cobb stopped by the door and looked in at Way. "He's a dog with a bone," she remarked to Hannon.

"That's one way to put it."

"When will he take a rest?"

"Never."

"What about you?"

"I could use some information if you're willing. I could go through our people, but it might be faster if I lean on the LAPD."

"What can I do?"

"A man named Konnor Spencer. Konnor with a *K*. Any record he might have, home and work addresses, registered vehicles. The works."

"I can do that. I'll put the request in right now. Meanwhile, do you want to lie down in one of the empty offices? There's one with a couch."

"I don't think I can."

"Take an hour. If something comes up, you'll be the first to know. I'll have a full jacket on this Spencer."

Hannon took a deep breath, which turned into a yawn. She acceded reluctantly. "An hour," she said.

"I'll show you where it is."

The office was easily twice as large as Cobb's and had its own meeting area, complete with a small conference table, comfortable chairs, and the promised couch. The walls were hung with plaques citing decoration after decoration. "Whose is this?" Hannon asked.

"The assistant chief's. But don't worry, he's not in today."

Hannon took off her jacket and lay down on the couch. "Don't let me sleep too long. And if Keith moves, I have to know. Don't let him leave here alone."

"You don't trust him, do you?"

"It's not that."

Cobb tilted her head slightly. "It's not?"

"Okay, maybe a little. He has some issues with perspective."

"And you keep him on track."

"I try to."

"I won't let him slip away."

"Thank you."

Cobb closed the door. Hannon pulled her jacket over her and shut her eyes. She was asleep in seconds.

There were unformed dreams, cold and dark and full of icy rain. Way's face floated to the surface more than once. And Jerry Washington's. She caught a glimpse of Camaro Espinoza. The old man was more indistinct, but he was there, too.

Someone shook her. She woke. It seemed like she'd lain down only a few minutes before. Cobb stood over her with a sheaf of papers in her hand. "Deputy Hannon?"

Hannon sat up slowly, her thoughts sluggish. Her eyes felt gritty. She rubbed them and yawned. "How long was that?"

"About two hours."

She felt a stab of adrenaline. "Is Way still here?"

"He is, just like I promised. He's coordinating with Herman, one of our data guys. They're sifting a lot of faces. It could be a while. As it was, it took me a little longer than it should have to get Konnor Spencer's information."

"Let me see."

It was dim in the empty office, but Hannon saw enough. They had Spencer's driver's-license photo and a list of minor infractions mostly related to traffic. He had never been in jail, and he had no convictions for anything serious. They had a work address for him Hannon recognized and a home address on Danzig Place, right in Los Angeles.

"Everything you were hoping for?"

"How far away is this? His house."

"Not far. You could get there pretty easily. Mind if I ask how he ties in to your fugitive?"

Hannon got up from the couch. "I'm still working on that. Could you e-mail this information to me?"

"Sure, just give me a couple of minutes."

Cobb left the office. Hannon shrugged on her jacket. She sorted through the pages again. Very little. A truck and motorcycle registered to his name, something they could feed to the maw of LAPD's software. But that meant Way would know. She folded the papers and slipped them into an inside pocket.

She texted. *Have a line on Spencer.*

What is it?

Home address. Vehicles. I'm going to forward an e-mail to you. Not much longer.

She walked over to the briefing room. She pushed her way through the glass door. Way did not look in her direction. He stood watching the monitors with the man Cobb had called Herman. "What do you want?" he asked.

"Anything?"

"Not so far."

"Then maybe it's time to shut it down."

"No. They're here. It's just a matter of time."

"You've been at this for hours. You haven't slept, you haven't eaten. If you blinked, you could have missed them."

"I didn't blink. These cameras don't blink. Right, Herman?"

"That's right. Just because they haven't passed in full view of a camera yet doesn't mean they won't. Coverage isn't total, but it's good."

"It's over, Keith."

Way turned on her. "It's not over. I made some calls. Those KAs we talked about? LAPD started knocking on doors an hour ago. We can cover the whole list by the afternoon."

"You can't call for that kind of thing yourself. You don't have the authority. The commander—"

"The commander can hear about it when it's done! I'm not going back to him with my hat in my hand, begging for a chance to follow up. They'll hand it off to the marshals in the Southern District and we'll be out. That's not happening."

Hannon exhaled. "You aren't listening to me again. You're not listening!"

"Maybe I should step outside," Herman said.

"Yeah, do that," Way replied. "But don't go far. This won't take long."

They waited until Herman left the room. Hannon spoke first. "I agreed to keep working with you if you got a handle on yourself, but you are cutting too many corners. There are procedures to follow, and if that means someone else takes over from here, then that's the way it's going to go. You have to be prepared to fail."

Hannon's e-mail tone chimed. She didn't look down at her phone.

Way raised a shaking finger. His face was dark. "I am not going through this again with you."

"Fine. Then I'm calling it. My detail, my prerogative."

Hannon turned on her heel and left the room. She grabbed her phone and texted *Trouble on this end.*

Cobb was in her office. Hannon saw the recognition on the woman's face when she entered. "Something's wrong?" Cobb asked.

"We have a difference of opinion."

"Is there anything I can do?"

"Brace yourself."

Hannon's phone vibrated. *How bad?*

LAPD mobilized in force. Keith on the warpath.

How much time do we have?

Not long. Spencer's jacket is coming your way. Do what you have to do and get out.

"What are you doing?"

Hannon looked up sharply. Way was in the door. He grabbed at her phone. She clung to it, but he twisted her wrist and the phone came free. He looked at the screen. His face darkened. "Who is this you're texting? And don't say it's your friend."

"It doesn't matter."

"If you are undermining this operation..."

"What, Keith? What are you going to do? What *can* you do?"

Way held up the phone. "Is this Espinoza? Is that who it is?"

"What difference does it make anymore?"

"You're communicating with her?"

"I've been in contact with Camaro. She's keeping me advised."

"'Do what you have to do and get out,'" Way read aloud. "What does that mean? What have you done? Who's Spencer?"

Hannon was acutely aware of Cobb watching them. She considered her words. "They can help us. They can get to Lukas. We can use them."

"They're using *you*," Way said. He threw the phone at Hannon. She caught it. "Goddamn it, who is Spencer?"

"Konnor Spencer," Cobb interjected. "Deputy Hannon asked me to look into him."

She saw the interplay of emotions on his face, none of them good. "She did? And nobody told me? That changes right now. I want his information, I want to know what his connection is to Lukas Collier, and I want to know *right now*."

"I don't like your tone, Deputy Way."

"I don't give a shit whether you like my tone! Are all of you people stupid? I am in pursuit of a federal fugitive! That supersedes any kind of territorial claims you have on this city and gives authority to me. Me! You're going to tell me everything. Where they are, where they're going. Everything."

"We're not doing it," Hannon said. "You're finished."

Way stepped toward her. "Don't play games with me!"

"You're done, Keith. I'm making the call. We're out."

"You get out. I'm staying in. You have screwed me for the last time," Way said. He wheeled on Cobb. "The information on Konnor Spencer. On my phone in fifteen minutes, or I'm going to make sure your life turns upside down."

He left the office. Hannon glanced at Cobb. The woman sat frozen in her chair, her mouth slightly open. "I don't know what to make of that," Cobb said finally.

"If you don't send it to him, he'll find out another way," Hannon said. "Do it. Let him hang himself."

She went after Way and found him back in the briefing room, gathering his coat. He was shouting at Herman, and the man wilted under the onslaught. "If they're walking, I want to know what sidewalk. If they're on a bus or a train, I want you to tell me every stop they make. If they're driving, I want make, model, and license plate number. Don't wait, don't think, just do it. Do you understand?"

"Yes, sir, I understand."

Way stopped when he saw Hannon. "Out of my way," he said.

"Keith, don't do this. I did what I did to protect you from yourself. You gave it your best shot. It's not too late to step back."

"You know I can't do that. I have to play this all the way to the end."

"If you kill one of them, I'll tell them everything. The whole story. You won't get out from under it. They'll take your badge. You'll go to prison. Is that what you want?"

"We'd burn together. You think I wouldn't tell them how you let it happen?"

"Just try, Keith. They'll never believe you."

"I guess we'll find out. In the meantime, I want to see Lukas Collier

297

dead. And if those two stop that from happening in any way, I'll see them dead, too. Get out of my way."

Hannon stepped aside. Way pushed through the door. She watched him go.

CHAPTER SEVENTY-SIX

KONNOR SPENCER'S INFORMATION came. Camaro shared his photograph with Yates. She paged through the document. "His home address is here. We should check it out."

"One of us should."

"Where are you going to be?"

Yates surveyed the candy store from where they sat in the Mustang. "A long time ago I learned to trust my feelings when it comes to this kind of thing. You said Spencer's supposed to come here today?"

"For a couple of hours."

"What time do they close up?"

"Four. What are you thinking?"

"I'm thinking this is a pretty good place to do a deal. If Spencer has access to the inside, he can make his buy off the street and in private. Nobody looks twice at a candy store. It's got loading and unloading in the back, so depending on the size of his load he's good to go."

Camaro thought. She looked at the parking lot. It was half filled with cars. People had been going in and out steadily as the morning wore on, coming out laden with bags and packages. Some pulled around back with pickup trucks or vans and came away with heavy stacks of shrink-wrapped blocks of candy. "We could be waiting awhile."

"Lukas has to be feeling the heat right about now. He knows they're on him up north, and the marshals already put two and two together. The only thing he has is this deal. That'll buy him some time somewhere the cops aren't watching every corner."

"We still have to check the house."

"You should. I'll stay here."

"Where?"

"Missy, I've been watching places incognito since before you were born. I think I can manage for a couple of hours on my own."

"And if Lukas shows up while I'm gone?"

"I'll be sure to give him your regards."

Yates reached to the small of his back and drew the weapon he had hidden there. It was a Springfield Armory 1911, the finish Parkerized, the walnut grips lustrous. He dropped the magazine, then pressed it back into place before working the slide. He eased the hammer down. They exchanged gazes for a moment, and then Yates stepped out of the car. The gun had already vanished.

Camaro got behind the wheel. "Don't get yourself killed," she said.

"Not today."

She drove away. Yates shrank in the rearview mirror. When she reached the corner, she saw him walking into the parking lot of the candy store. She turned. He was gone.

The 101 wasn't a nightmare on most weekends. Camaro put the radio on but listened for only a few minutes before snapping it off again. She got off on the 10 to cut across the city eastward. She felt tense in the pit of her stomach, the muscles drawn tight.

Off the highway it was harder to find her way around. She used the GPS on her phone to make it through the neighborhood streets. The houses here were not palatial by any standard, but the roadways were clean, and there were even a few white picket fences. Kids felt safe enough to play outside, though the windows everywhere were solidly barred. Los Angeles was a city of bars, of sheer concrete walls and restricted access. The rich kept the best for themselves, while everyone else had to grab some small part of the endless sprawl.

She passed dead lawn after dead lawn, deprived of moisture for so long, the only thing that remained to mow were patches of hardy desert grass that couldn't cover the bald earth. Finally she found it: a blue house with white trim and the same, inevitable bars, perched on the corner of his street.

Camaro passed the mouth of the street and parked well out of sight. She checked the gun that had been given to her, an anodized black P220 with eight rounds in the magazine and one in the chamber.

It had no hammer, no safety. Every trigger pull was double-action. She put it away.

The sun glared almost directly overhead as she made her way back to the house. It had a separate garage on the side and a low chain-link fence cordoning off a barren backyard. Three houses down there was a group of kids shooting baskets on a hoop at the curb. They didn't look her way.

Konnor Spencer owned a truck. It was nowhere in sight. The motorcycle might have been inside the garage, but Camaro saw no windows to peer in. She felt exposed on the street and went quickly to the fence. She hopped it like she was meant to be there and passed into the rear yard.

All the rear-facing windows had blinds, and they were completely shut. Camaro made her way to the back door. Its blinds were half open, and she could see through the gaps into a darkened kitchen. A hallway opened up on one side, also dark. She could not see past the corner on the opposite end.

She examined the door. It was barred like the rest, the window broken up into nine identical panes, but it was possible to reach between the bars and touch the glass. Camaro thought a moment, then stopped to remove her boot. She stripped off her sock and wound it around the knuckles of her fist.

She chose the lower left pane. She put her knuckles against the glass and punched once, hard, in the space she had. The pane cracked. She punched again and a third time, until the pane was riddled with spidery, broken veins. Then she stopped and looked and listened and heard nothing.

It took three more short punches to break the glass. Camaro picked at the broken edges. She pushed back the sleeve of her Henley, then snaked her arm through the opening. Tiny teeth bit her skin. The fit was tight. She pressed in elbow deep, aware of blood running from fresh cuts. She felt around for the doorknob, then above it to where the dead bolt locked. The angle was bad, and the tendons in her wrist ached as she turned it with her fingertips. The lock clicked.

Camaro pulled her arm back out. The cuts would heal. The door opened easily now.

The utter stillness of the house told her no one was there. In the kitchen she found evidence of breakfast for two, a greasy skillet in the sink, an inch of water inside, suspending globs of congealing fat.

There were two bedrooms, the smaller of which was used for storage, boxes piled high. In the other the bed was unmade, but Camaro didn't know whether one person had slept there or two.

In the bathroom she found a pair of dirty socks in the wastebasket, one bloody. When she checked the trash in the kitchen, she discovered a pair of jeans with a blood-soaked lower leg, along with the remains of treatment: red-stained gauze and cotton balls, discarded packets of alcohol-infused wipes. She followed through to the living room and saw the medical kit. There were traces of blood on the leg rest of a nearby recliner.

"Camaro Espinoza?"

The voice carried from the kitchen, and Camaro froze.

"Camaro Espinoza, it's Deputy Marshal Way. I know you're in there. Come out where I can see you and keep your hands up."

CHAPTER SEVENTY-SEVEN

CAMARO HEARD THE back door open. She looked left and right. The front door was ten feet away, but anyone coming through from the kitchen on that side could see straight through to the front of the house.

Way's footsteps were on the linoleum in the kitchen. Camaro moved away from the front door, deeper into the house. There was a closet to her right, the bathroom on her left. She eased open the closet's bifold door and checked inside. It was full, but with room for her to just squeeze in. Camaro slipped inside and tugged the door silently shut behind her.

Light filtered in through slots in the closet door. She heard Way moving around. His footfalls were muffled. He was on carpet now. "I don't know where you are in here, but I know you can't get out. I put in a call to the local PD when I saw you'd broken out the glass back there. They should be on the scene in ten or fifteen minutes. You won't get away."

It was dusty inside the closet. Camaro breathed shallowly. Her nose itched.

"Was he here? Did you just miss him?"

She kept her silence. She knew he was in the living room.

"I don't have to tell you what I'm gonna do to you when I find you. All those promises I made? They're going to come true. I will put you away forever. I'll put that old son of a bitch Yates away forever. I read you're from LA originally. Maybe it's good that everything ends here. Poetic justice. What do you think?"

He advanced down the hall. Camaro heard him breathing now, a raspy sound roughened by adrenaline and fatigue. A shadow fell across the opposite wall as he came closer. She held her breath as his weapon came into sight, followed by the rest of him.

303

Way stopped directly in front of the closet. "I don't want to play any games with you. If you make me, I'll have to shoot you, and you don't want that. So how about you just come out and give yourself up and we talk like a couple of adults? You tell me where Lukas is, or where he's going to be, and I'll make sure they send you somewhere that's not half bad. What do you say?"

Specks danced in Camaro's vision. She held on until Way moved forward. He looked into the bathroom, and she heard him rattle the shower curtain. He made a noise. She knew he'd found the socks. She let her breath go slowly.

"So Lukas was here," Way called out. "I knew I hit him. Not bad enough, but I hit him. You know, his friend Konnor has medical training. Got it in the Marines. Put Konnor and Lukas together in one person and they're you, you know that? There's not any difference between you and Lukas at all. He thinks the law doesn't apply to him and does whatever the hell he wants. Kill anybody, hurt anybody. Lie, cheat, steal.

"It's my job to put people like you behind bars. You don't belong with good folks, with *decent* folks. You think that Silver Star of yours buys you any sympathy from me? I don't care what you did in the ass end of the world. You and Lukas both. He got a medal fighting in Iraq. Doesn't mean a thing."

He was out of the bathroom now and moving deeper into the house. Camaro couldn't see anything except the space directly in front of the closet door. She pressed the hinge delicately, and the door folded open on quiet tracks. One glance showed the hallway was clear.

She stole out of the closet and shut it behind her. Way had said nothing else. She wasn't sure exactly where he was. She turned toward the living room.

Way's shoes thumped on the carpet. Camaro darted into the bathroom. She left the door open and slipped the patterned shower curtain aside. Plastic rings clicked against one another on the rod. Her tread was light inside the tub. She closed the curtain and pressed herself into the corner.

She heard him jerk the hall closet open. "Goddamn it," he said. "Just come out! Come out!"

Camaro willed stillness into every part of herself.

"I'm talking to myself," Way said. "I'm standing here talking to myself."

He was in the hallway. He was in the living room. The locks on the front door shot, and it opened. Camaro heard his fading voice as he made a call on his phone.

It was time to move. She stepped out of the tub and rushed down the hallway. On her left she saw the living room and the front door hanging open, daylight spilling into the dim interior. Way's voice was more distinct now. On her right was the kitchen. She went right.

In the backyard she jogged to the fence and vaulted it again. She forced herself not to run on the street, only walking fast back to the Mustang. As she started the engine, the first black-and-white LAPD unit passed her, turning onto Spencer's street. She eased off the curb and drove without looking toward the house and Way, who was sure to be on the front lawn.

She dialed her phone and left it sitting on the passenger seat as she drove. She counted the rings until Yates answered. "He's not here," she told him.

"Lukas?"

"Neither one."

"I can explain part of that. Spencer's here."

"At the candy store?"

"He rolled in a few minutes ago, driving a rental truck. Parked it out back and unloaded something into the store. I told you I had old man's intuition."

"Then tell me where Lukas is."

"I couldn't venture a guess, but now we know he won't be far."

Camaro didn't tell Yates about Way. "I'm headed back."

"I'll keep it warm for you."

She drove on.

CHAPTER SEVENTY-EIGHT

LUKAS SAW THE police cruisers as soon as he turned onto the last street before Konnor's house. He didn't slam on the brakes or touch the accelerator but kept on going as if the sight made no difference to him. He glanced toward the house as he passed it and saw two uniformed officers in conversation with a man he recognized from the motel. His leg twinged at the sight of him.

He drove out of the neighborhood in no direction in particular. He called Konnor. "Don't go home," he said when Konnor answered.

"Why? What happened?"

"Cops are at the house. If I'd been there fifteen minutes earlier, they would have had me. We got to figure they've been inside and they know everything."

"Shit, do I need to get out of here? They have to know where I work."

"They'll jerk each other off for hours before they get down to you. First they'll want to take your place apart for fibers or some shit, and then they'll start using their heads. But this means we have to step up the timetable. How long till the candy store closes?"

"A few hours."

"I'm going to call Otilio and tell them we're moving up the exchange. We get it done today, then you and me will head up the coast."

"Salinas?"

"Nah, Salinas is screwed. Carmel, Pacific Grove—that whole place. We're gonna need to take it farther north. I don't have the same connections up that way, but when you've got ten keys of weed to unload, you can make friends in a hurry."

"I don't like it."

"So what? Since when has this been a democracy? This is my deal, and I run it my way! You want to take your chances with the Feds, be my guest, or you can pull up stakes and start making some serious bank up north. I just wish those assholes in Oregon hadn't legalized it. Screws up the whole deal for the rest of us."

"Okay, we'll play it your way."

"That's what I thought. Talk to you soon."

"You're coming here now? People are here."

"No, I'm gonna find someplace to stay cool until it's time to move. We're better off if we're not seen together. Not yet."

"Tell me it'll be all right, Luke."

"It'll be all right. Don't get your panties in a bunch."

He stabbed the phone with his thumb, ending the call. He was headed farther east. He knew a mall in City of Industry that would be busy on a Saturday afternoon. Konnor's truck would be lost in the parking lot, and Lukas would be another face in the crowd.

The decision made, he made a second call. Otilio answered. "Hey, my man," he said. "What's happening?"

"The deal is happening. Today. Four o'clock."

"Hey, what happened to giving me twelve hours' notice?"

"My timetable's changed. I need to unload my shipment and get the green in the next few hours or it's off. This is a limited-time offer, so if you can't deliver, I'll take my business elsewhere."

Otilio spoke in Spanish to someone away from the phone, his voice muffled; then he came back on the line. "I might be able to get you what you want. But it's gonna cost you."

"Same deal as before. I deliver the guns, you give me the weed. No bullshit and no renegotiation."

"You're stressing me out, cuz. This was supposed to be smooth and quiet. I don't like all this rushing around. You got heat on you?"

"It doesn't matter. What matters is I got what you want, and you got what I want. So let's do it."

"Fine. But if this goes the wrong way on me, some people are going to be very upset about it."

"I'm shaking," Lukas said, and he cut Otilio off.

He glanced into the rearview mirror and saw a cop a few cars back and one lane over. Immediately he checked his speed. He was going no faster or slower than anyone else on the road. The touch of a knob tilted the side mirror so he could have a better look at the cop without lifting his eyes. The cop behind the wheel didn't look his way.

Lukas kept steady. When an exit presented itself, he put his signal on and gently changed lanes, careful to monitor the cop's progress relative to him as he made the maneuver. He started to lose speed for the ramp. The cop didn't slow down. A moment later they were abreast, two lanes apart. The cop didn't even turn his head, his eyes fixed on the road ahead.

Lukas let out a breath as he descended on the ramp. A gas station was just ahead. He slotted in next to one of the pumps and got out. His hands trembled slightly. He made fists until it stopped.

Traffic passed. People filled their tanks. Lukas opened the gas cap and put the pump nozzle in, but he didn't pay for any gas. He stayed where he was for ten minutes, and when the time had elapsed, he took the nozzle out as though he had finished up like everyone else and then got back in the truck.

His hands were rock-steady now. As he pulled out on the road, he had an image locked in his mind of flat packages bound with tape and shrink-wrap. Break the seal with the point of a knife, and the air was filled with the rich, unmistakable odor of resin. It was the smell of money.

CHAPTER SEVENTY-NINE

Where is he?

At Spencer's house. Where are you?

Candy store.

He'll come there.

I know.

Camaro stood near Yates behind a wholesale produce business that seemed closed for the day. There was an alley that traversed the length of the entire block, branches letting out between buildings. There were Dumpsters filled to the brim with rotting vegetables and fruit, others snarled with plastic packaging and cardboard. Where they found shelter, the shadow of a Dumpster fell over them, and they had a clear view of the candy store's loading dock.

"How's our friend?" Yates asked.

"Worried. She's right. It's just a matter of time until Way comes here. He was ten minutes behind me at Spencer's house."

"Let's hope we have more lead time than that here. If Lukas comes now, there are innocent people inside that store. And we've already seen what happens when innocent people get in the line of fire when Lukas is around. I won't have that on my conscience."

Camaro watched a couple emerge from the side entrance of the candy store with a gigantic piñata between them, their wrists laden with plastic bags. She made a note of the yellow rental truck. "The place will close soon," she said. "After that, they have the whole store to themselves. Lukas has to show then. We see him, we move on him."

"That's the general idea."

"Is your shoulder all right?"

"I can move it, if that's what you mean."

"If we have to do this the hard way, do I have to worry about you?"

Yates turned from the candy store to look at Camaro. He squinted in the late afternoon sun, and his mouth was almost hidden by the brush of his mustache. "You worried about me, Ms. Espinoza?"

"Yeah. I am."

"Maybe you're not as cold as you like to think you are."

"I'm not Lukas," Camaro said.

"No, you're not. I can see that now. I trust you to watch my back. Lukas? I wouldn't trust him to watch my clothes at the laundromat."

"I'll still kill him."

"That I don't doubt for a second."

Together they waited. Not far away, a police siren called out among the concrete walls of the city and was ultimately smothered. Time passed. People came and went, but never Konnor Spencer, and never Lukas Collier.

Camaro sweated, a thin band of perspiration on her spine. Every time a car passed on the quiet street, she tensed anew. The parking lot thinned out. She checked her watch. "Almost time," she said.

"Keep your eye out. He's coming. I can feel it."

The last of the customers departed. The employees at the candy store stayed inside another ten minutes, and then they filed out in their pink shirts. Randy was among them. They closed the shutter behind them.

"Spencer's still inside," Camaro said.

"Waitin' for Lukas."

The employees drove away. Randy's little Toyota was the last out of sight.

"Truck," Camaro said.

A black pickup appeared on the street. The windows were tinted, but Camaro knew the profile. She took a step forward. Yates put out his hand to stop her. "Hold up. There's more coming."

"Where—?"

As she spoke, three other vehicles cruised into the parking lot from the opposite direction. One was a van painted white, dirty and badly abused. The others were immaculate, a red '67 Impala that sat low on its wheels and a Ford Shelby GT500 painted blue with a twin stripe splashed from nose to tail.

The van circled around to the rear while the cars parked in the center of the small lot. Camaro saw movement on the loading dock. Konnor Spencer was there.

"Update our lady friend," Yates said.

Lukas was out of the truck and shaking hands with a lean, muscular Latino, the sides of his head shaved and his arms heavily inked. There were four others with the leader. They scattered around, casting looks here and there but not seeing Camaro and Yates where they hid.

It's happening, Camaro texted.

I've lost W.

When?

An hour ago. Not on Spencer scene.

We need time.

Calling him. No good. Not answering.

"Damn it," Camaro said out loud.

You are exposed.

L could leave. Got to move.

I'm coming.

Careful.

"I suspect the news is not good," Yates said quietly.

"Way's loose. Hannon's coming."

"How far out is she?"

"Minutes. If we want this, it happens now."

Lukas and the Latinos climbed the steps to the loading dock and vanished inside. Camaro's heart raced. Her mouth was dry.

"I'm going to let you call it," Yates said. "Last chance to step back and let the good guys take him."

"Do you think he'll let that happen?"

"Can't say. But it's a crowd in there. It's not going to be one-on-one anymore. The question is whether you still want him, and how bad."

Camaro watched the store. She tried deep breathing to slow her pulse. "I have to look him the eyes," she said.

"Even if you can't take him out?"

She flexed her hands. The muscles in her back were locked. She was frozen in place with competing visions in her head. Lukas dead. Lukas taken away. She licked her lips. "If it comes to it, Hannon can have him."

"But you want him to know it was you."

"Yes. And you."

"Then I guess the decision's made. Let's go."

Camaro emerged from cover with Yates a step behind. They skirted the low wall that offset the parking lot from the alley, steel bars preventing ingress, then made their way in from the street. She fell in along the wall of the candy store and moved forward.

She heard voices ahead, slipping easily from English to Spanish. Camaro understood enough to know they were only shooting the breeze. The business hadn't started yet.

They reached the corner of the building. Yates touched her on the arm. She bent close to let him speak into her ear. "Step in like you got a hundred men behind you. Don't let 'em see you sweat."

Camaro acknowledged him with a pat on the shoulder. She drew the pistol from her waistband. Yates's was already out. They advanced on the concrete steps leading to the loading dock. She held the P220 low ready, against her belly. She took the steps one at a time.

More than half the lights were off in the candy store. Camaro had the sun at her back when she stepped into the open. She brought the gun up smoothly as all seven men came into view. Lukas was framed in the center, three men on each side of him, standing over an open case with a trio of black carbines inside. The hollows of the store were murky behind him, filled with deep shadows. The place had no windows.

"Hey," Camaro said quietly.

The men reacted at once. They reached for guns under the loose tails of shirts or at their bellies. Lukas simply stood, and when Camaro's eyes met his, he smiled.

Yates ghosted in behind her. "Guns down!" he commanded. "First man who moves gets shot."

Lukas still smiled. "Relax, *amigos*," he said. "It's old friends."

"What the hell?" asked one of the Latinos. The bottom of his Lakers jersey was pulled up and hooked on the butt of a Glock at his hip. His hand hovered over the weapon. "Is this a rip-off? Goddamn it, Luke, you son of a bitch!"

"No rip-off," Camaro said. Her gaze held Lukas's. "I'm here for Lukas."

"Gonna shoot me now? Is that how it goes down?"

Camaro's finger rested lightly on the trigger. "Is that how you want it?"

"Cops," said the man in the Lakers jersey.

"No, they ain't cops," Lukas said. "They're concerned citizens."

"Why don't you gentlemen put down your weapons?" Yates asked. "Nice and slow. Nobody gives us trouble, nobody has to get hurt. Like the lady says, it's Lukas we want. The rest of you can go on about your business."

"You can't shoot all of us," said Konnor. He stood two from Lukas, his hand behind his back. Camaro knew his fingers were on his weapon. She heard it in his voice.

"Who wants to volunteer to be first?" Yates asked.

Camaro's vision narrowed. She closed out Konnor, she closed out the man in the Lakers jersey and all the men he'd brought with him. She saw Lukas's face, Lukas's eyes. He didn't blink. Her finger tightened just a little. "You lose, Lukas," she said.

"Boys," Lukas said, "I think it's time to finish our deal."

He blinked. Immediately the collection of men snapped into Camaro's focus. Konnor whipped a pistol from its hiding place and squeezed the trigger in the same motion. She felt a slashing pain in her arm just as Yates's .45 boomed.

The men scattered and left Konnor kneeling on the floor, blood soaking his pink shirt. Camaro moved right and Yates left. She put a bullet into the leg of a fleeing man and saw him go down on his face.

Return fire began to explode from inside the store, sounding like cannon. The gunmen melted into the shadows, and only the sharp flashes of their muzzles revealed them, like burning fireflies.

"You hit?" Yates asked her.

Camaro glanced at her arm. It throbbed, the fabric ripped and fresh blood underneath. Flexing the muscle was painful. "It grazed me," she said. "I'll be all right."

"I'll go high, you go low."

"Let's do it."

They entered the store as one. Camaro picked out a shape in the half-darkness and squeezed the trigger. A short yelp was followed by silence. All the shooting had stopped. Her stunned ears could barely make out the voices sounding farther inside the cavern of the store.

Together they skirted the cases on the floor and moved through the loading area. Camaro used a pallet of candy boxes nearly as high as herself for cover. Yates knelt behind a forklift. She pointed to herself, then gestured with her head. Yates gave her an okay.

She stepped out from behind the candy and dashed for the nearest aisle. Yates triggered his pistol twice into the dark, and the vaulted metal ceiling slammed the report down onto them like an open hand.

A peek around the edge of the shelving revealed a dark, open aisle shadowed at the far end. Camaro saw no one. She emerged from cover, crouching low and moving quickly, weapon up. Her arm was wet with blood and burned more and more by the minute.

A shape loomed out of the dark, and Camaro zeroed in on it. The contours of the giant gumball machine solidified. She took shelter in its shadow just as its plastic globe exploded.

Gumballs showered Camaro and sprayed out across the concrete floor. She sighted on another vague shape in the dark and fired. She saw the shape sink to the ground and lie still.

She slipped on the gumballs as she crossed open space to reach the man she'd killed. Up close she could see it was the man in the Lakers jersey. An automatic lay inches from his hand. Camaro left it and advanced.

More shooting erupted behind her. She dropped to the floor and scrambled toward a display of plastic party favors, their colors dulled by the poor lighting. A man screamed. Another gunshot silenced him. Camaro listened. "Yates?" she called out. "Yates!"

His voice carried over the stacks from somewhere: "Still alive. You see him?"

"Working on it."

The deeper into the store she went, the spottier the light became. It shone in pools ahead of her where the registers and the office were and in spots and splashes. Camaro spotted the end of an aisle and made for it, her boots scuffing as she moved forward.

She reached cover and stopped. She breathed hard, and her vision limned with silver. She exposed herself to peer around the corner.

Lukas seized her by the gun arm and whirled her around, jerking her halfway off her feet. She squeezed the trigger, and her pistol went off between them, a sudden flashbulb of muzzle flare that lit Lukas's face. He hammered her wrist, and her grip on her weapon loosened. His hand closed over hers, and her fingers strained as he twisted the gun from her grip. The gun clattered on the floor.

He backhanded her across the face, and she felt the healing stitches on her brow open up. She came at him low, driving her elbow deep into his ribs. The wind rushed out of him as he fell back. She kicked him hard, and he went off his feet entirely.

Gunfire detonated close by, and a bullet skimmed off the floor between them. Camaro scrambled for her gun. Her hand closed over it, and she fired instinctively.

Lukas threw himself on her. Two hundred pounds, and his breath was in her face. He had a hand on her gun arm, and he slammed her weapon against the concrete. Camaro brought her knee up hard. Lukas cried out.

They rolled. Camaro tried to bring her gun to bear, but Lukas's grip was unbreakable. He closed his other hand around her throat. She gouged him in the eyes.

He torqued her wrist, and she felt something give. Her hold on her weapon slackened. She fired into the floor by Lukas's head, and they both screamed at the close-range report. Dark blood oozed from his ear.

Lukas got a leg between them and pushed her up and off. Camaro went over, striking her head on the floor as she tumbled onto her back. She still had the gun in her hand, but her grip was weak.

Shooting sounded all inside the confines of the store, echoing and reechoing. Someone called for his mother in Spanish. Yates was yelling for Camaro, but she was breathless and hurting.

She saw Lukas make it to his feet. A string of gunshots sounded as rapidly as crackling fireworks. Camaro was misted with blood, and Lukas reeled. She couldn't raise her right hand to fire as he retreated into the dark. She grabbed for her gun with her left, opened fire at his retreating back as it merged with the shadows.

Yates was there. "Are you down? Are you hit?"

"I can't move my arm. I think I tore something. Help me up."

Men shouted to one another in the dark. Yates looked around. "I don't know how many more we got to deal with."

"Get me on my feet."

He helped her rise. She opened her mouth to speak in the same moment a shrill alarm sounded. A red light flashed two rows down, and then there was the sudden burst of white light from outside. "Fire exit," Camaro said.

"I'll go," Yates said.

Camaro shook her head. "No. Hold them off for me."

"You're hurt."

"He's hurt."

"It should be me."

Camaro looked at Yates in the dark. "It has to be me."

"What about Hannon?"

"She's too late."

CHAPTER EIGHTY

CAMARO BURST OUT of the store into the space between it and the chili wholesaler next door. She heard renewed gunfire inside, but there was no time to think more of it. Alley access was fifty feet away. Lukas was already out of sight, but there were scattered red droplets on the dirty ground.

High up in the air, the sound of skirling police sirens carried. Camaro ran to the alley, skirting a Dumpster filled with discarded packaging. Her lungs bellowed.

Her arm was hurting more and more. Blood ran down her hand in a steady stream. She knew she'd feel foggy soon, and after that she'd feel nothing. Her fingers were numb. She dashed ahead, heedless of her own booming pulse. She made the main alleyway just in time to see Lukas vanish thirty yards distant, limping hard.

Camaro ran on, the gun in her left hand, her right arm hanging. She tripped on a loose chunk of concrete and stumbled to one knee, splitting open her jeans. Bracing herself with her weapon, she found her feet again.

She reached the alleyway Lukas had ducked through and saw it reached the street. Heedless of the flecks in her vision, she sprinted after him until she was on the open thoroughfare. Lukas was across the street and pulling away. Camaro fired after him, but her aim was faulty. She saw him pitch forward and then struggle onward, dodging between another pair of buildings.

The racing of a car engine made it to her good ear, but she did not look back. She made it to the break between buildings and skidded around the corner into a barrage of bullets. They crashed into the brick wall on one side and cut the air so closely she felt the heat of them. She spun away behind cover, chased by rounds that chipped at the building she sheltered behind.

Camaro dared a look. Lukas was framed by the space, a chain-link fence behind him blocking the way completely. The slide on his .45 was locked back. He dropped it and ran to the fence, catching it with both hands and digging in with his toes. He began to climb.

Camaro followed. Lukas was halfway to the top when she shot him twice in the back. ·

He plummeted six feet and crashed to the asphalt. He squirmed there, bleeding. Camaro approached him. Her left hand shook. Her body felt cold. Her limp right hand was covered in blood. "Don't move," she said.

She did not expect him to smile. He did. "You don't look too good," he said.

Camaro stood over him. His arm looked broken. He had blood on his teeth. One of Yates's bullets had gotten deep into his side. "Neither do you."

"Seems like every time I see you, I can't seal the deal," Lukas said. He coughed. "Why is that?"

"I'm lucky, I guess."

The police sirens were much closer.

"You gonna let them take me?" Lukas asked.

"Should I?"

Lukas didn't answer but coughed violently until a gobbet of bloody sputum spattered his face. He shivered from blood loss. Camaro knew it would only get worse. "It doesn't matter anymore."

"Then I guess this is it."

"My brother said you were a soldier."

Camaro only nodded.

"Let me go out like a Marine. One to the head."

"I don't think so," Camaro said. She raised her boot and stomped down on his throat. She put her weight on him as he began to struggle. Lukas scrabbled at her leg with weakening fingers, his eyes turning bloodshot and his face gone purple.

She kept on until finally he was still.

Camaro put her pistol away and turned from the body. She walked back the way she came, aware she was swaying slightly. Out on the street, she looked back the way she'd come. The first bullet struck her low, just above the belt line. Another crashed into her shoulder, and she lost her equilibrium, collapsing backward.

Camaro saw only sky. Consciousness wavered. She tried to focus on the things around her.

Way approached her with his weapon up. Camaro struggled to lift her hips to reach the pistol at her back, but the blazing pain immobilized her. She scraped her heels against the dirty sidewalk and managed to push herself a few inches. Way closed the space.

Camaro was breathing too fast, too shallowly. She could not bring her pulse rate down. Blood on the ground soaked her back. She gasped out loud.

The marshal stood over her with his gun at his side. His eyes were hollow from lack of sleep, and dark. "Where's Lukas?"

Camaro could not draw a breath deep enough to make words.

He looked toward the space between the buildings. Camaro saw the moment he recognized Lukas's body.

"You killed him," Way said. His face turned into a rictus. "That was for *me! I* was the one who was supposed to kill him!"

She tried for her pistol again, but he stepped on her wrist.

"Do you have any idea how long I was after him? Do you know what I sacrificed? Everything. Everything. I called in every favor anyone ever owed me, and I burned bridges. But people knew how much I wanted it. They knew."

When he talked he gestured with his gun, the mouth of the barrel passing over her dangerously. His finger was on the trigger. Camaro felt the bones of her wrist straining under his foot. She would have two ruined hands, and then it would be over.

"And then you. You and that goddamned old man. My own partner turned on me because of you. I've got nobody. All I had was this."

He knelt and laid his full weight on her wrist. He pushed the muzzle of the pistol against the raw wound in her shoulder until Camaro cried out. She thought she tasted blood. The smell of it was thick in her nostrils, even stronger than the odor of spent gunpowder. The fingernails

319

of her trapped hand scraped the dusty ground, but she was not strong enough to pull clear. Her vision narrowed.

Way stood and leveled the gun on her head. "I'm going to kill you now," he said. "We're all done."

Camaro heard the shot, but there was no blackness. She felt no fresh pain. Way stood above her, and his expression melted away into confusion and then slack nothingness. He collapsed sideways, and his gun clattered on the ground.

Hannon appeared. She holstered her weapon and knelt over Camaro. She touched Camaro's wounds lightly, but even that was enough to bring pain. Camaro grunted. "Can you walk?" Hannon asked.

Camaro managed a nod. Her throat rebelled against words. She forced them out. "I think so," she said.

No part of Camaro was free of pain. Hannon muscled her into a sitting position, and Camaro put her good arm around Hannon's neck. Her right was immobile. Every movement jarred her and brought new agony.

Camaro got to her feet and half walked. Then Yates was there. He rushed forward to take her from Hannon. Hannon ran from them, and for a long moment Camaro thought she wouldn't return. An engine rumbled, and a black Charger with LAPD markings surged up the street toward them. Hannon got out to open the rear door. Together she and Yates slid Camaro in the backseat.

Doors slammed, and the police sirens were everywhere. Hannon gave the Charger gas, and the V8 engine pushed Camaro into the cushions. They made two sharp turns, wheels screeching, and then picked up speed. Camaro's head whirled.

Yates twisted around in his seat. He offered a bloody hand, and she took it. He squeezed her fingers. "You're gonna be okay," he said.

Camaro let her eyes slip closed. In her mind she heard the thunder of approaching rotors and the sting of grit kicked up by the wash. All she felt was the heat of coursing blood and the pain that went with it. And the grip of Yates's hand in hers.

"Don't go, Camaro," Camaro's father said.

She faded into darkness.

CHAPTER EIGHTY-ONE

THE POCKET BEACH was barren of people, ten minutes north of Malibu and hidden among the rocks and along a rugged trail that usually dissuaded the casual visitor. Seagulls rose and dipped in the offshore breeze. The sun was low on the horizon, coloring everything orange and bloody red, the sun itself a stained disc.

She sat with her shoes off, letting her bare feet sink into the sand. The pain in her side when she held herself seated was tolerable, held back by a pair of pills taken every four hours. Her right arm was in a cast to the elbow. The bullet wound in her shoulder barely hurt at all.

Camaro heard Yates coming. She looked back and saw him aglow in the colors of the western sun. He held a large paper grocery bag with loops for a handle. "Is anyone sitting here?" he asked.

"Not right now," Camaro said.

Yates lowered himself onto the blanket and put the bag between them. He brought out food wrapped in wax paper and a pack of six beer bottles. "I got cookies, too," he said.

"Open one of those for me?" Camaro asked.

Yates did as she asked and passed it over. Camaro drank deeply. He watched her. "How do you feel?"

"Alive."

"Better than the alternative."

Camaro nudged the wax-paper packages. "What are these?"

"Fish tacos. You like fish tacos?"

"I'm a local girl. What do you think?"

"Then I'm glad I guessed right."

She dug a hole for the beer bottle and set it beside her before going

321

after the tacos. They were good and clean-tasting, like the sea. She said nothing to Yates while they ate.

"No deputy," Yates observed. He wadded up his wax paper and stowed it in the bag.

"She's late."

"She has work to do. Can't be easy explaining how two people you deputized ended up in a gunfight in a candy store with a stack of dead bodies to show for it. Especially when you didn't file the paperwork. It's always the paperwork that gets you."

"She'll come."

Yates nodded. "I never did thank you."

"For what?"

"For Lukas."

Camaro didn't answer. She ate her last taco.

"You know, my wife wants to meet you."

"Why?"

"I expect she'd like to see the woman I've been spending so much time with. She's the jealous type, the missus is. I think it probably won't help much when she gets a look at you."

"Maybe one day I'll get to Norfolk," Camaro said.

"Maybe."

They watched the Pacific for a while. The ocean lapped at the wet expanse of sand. "I need to see my sister," Camaro said.

"Get your niece to sign your cast. Kids like that."

"You want to sign my cast?"

"I'm not a kid anymore. But thanks for offering."

Camaro picked up her beer. She drank until it was empty and reached for another. Yates opened it without being asked. It hissed quietly, the sound almost lost in the murmur of the sea.

"Camaro?"

"Yeah?"

"I've been meaning to ask you something."

"So ask."

"Do you get too much charter business in the winter months?"

"Sometimes. Depends. It's the slow season."

"I was wondering," Yates said. "Just wondering."

Camaro waited for him to finish. The sun grew lower still, fattening as it touched the water and turning the long shadows of the rocks into pools of darkness. There were no lights on the beach. The beer was good. The quiet was good. The city teemed with life, but here it was only the two of them.

"I find myself in a situation," Yates continued. "And I could use some help."

"With what?"

"Have you ever considered a career in bail enforcement?"

ACKNOWLEDGMENTS

I'd like to thank first and foremost my wife, Mariann, for once again keeping me on course when it comes to my work. I could not function at the keyboard without her. I'd also like to thank Elizabeth A. White for her guiding hand during the pre-editing phase, as she was a breeze to work with and made critical recommendations that made the book better. In addition, I would be remiss if I didn't thank my editors at Mulholland Books and Mulholland UK, Wes Miller and Ruth Tross, for making bang-up suggestions that transformed *Walk Away* into a lean, mean thrilling machine.

Finally, it would be inexcusable if I didn't thank my agent, Oliver Munson, for all his help getting me to this point and for the services he continues to provide in terms of insight into my writing and making it possible for people to read me at all. I am greatly indebted to him.

ABOUT THE AUTHOR

Sam Hawken is author of the Camaro Espinoza series, which begins with *The Night Charter,* as well as the Crime Writers' Association Dagger–nominated Borderlands trilogy. He was born in Texas and currently lives outside Baltimore with his wife and son.